triscelle publishing

presents

Dark Alliance
Morrigan's Brood Book III

By

heather poinsett Dunbar

and

christopher Dunbar

map of story locations

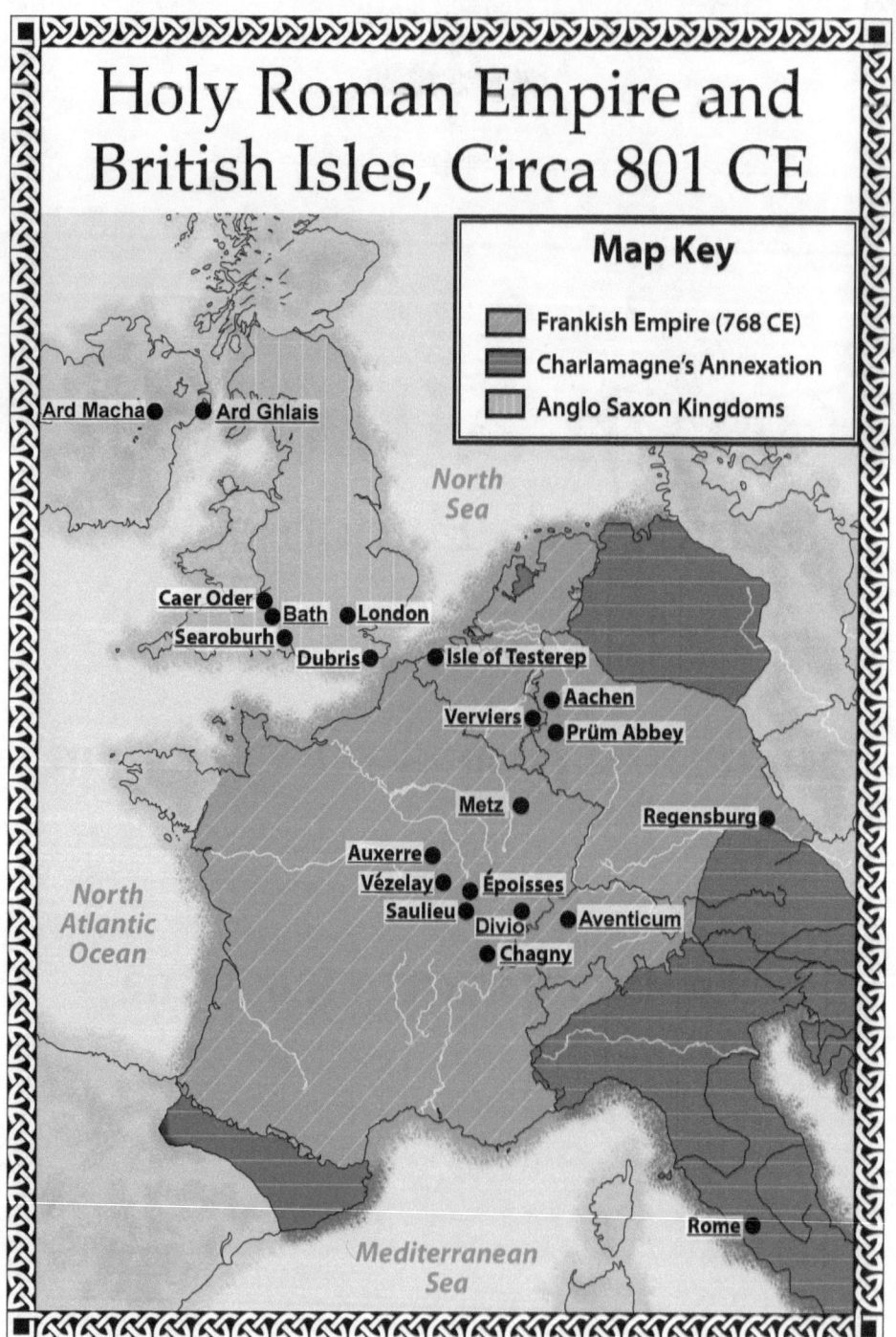

Holy Roman Empire and British Isles, Circa 801 CE

Map Key

- Frankish Empire (768 CE)
- Charlamagne's Annexation
- Anglo Saxon Kingdoms

North Sea

North Atlantic Ocean

Mediterranean Sea

Ard Macha
Ard Ghlais
Caer Oder
Bath
London
Searoburh
Dubris
Isle of Testerep
Aachen
Verviers
Prüm Abbey
Metz
Regensburg
Auxerre
Vézelay
Époisses
Saulieu
Divio
Aventicum
Chagny
Rome

Map details are on the next page

map guide

Holy Roman Empire and British Isles, Circa 801 CE		
Period Name	**Modern Name**	**Modern Country**
Frankish Empire / Carolingian Empire / Holy Roman Empire		
Isle of Testerep	Oostende, Westende, and Middelkerke	West Flanders, Belgium
Verviers	Verviers	Liège, Belgium
Aachen	Aachen or Aix-la-Chapelle	North Rhine-Westphalia, Germany
Prüm Abbey	Prüm/Lorraine	Rhineland-Palatinate, Germany
Regensburg	Regensburg	Bavaria, Germany
Aventicum	Avenches	Vaud, Switzerland
Auxerre	Auxerre	Burgundy, France
Vézelay	Vézelay	Burgundy, France
Époisses	Époisses	Burgundy, France
Saulieu	Saulieu	Burgundy, France
Divio	Dijon	Burgundy, France
Chagny	Chagny	Burgundy, France
Metz	Metz	Lorraine, France
Rome, Papal States	Rome	Rome, Italy
Eire		
Ard Macha	Armagh	Northern Ireland, United Kingdom
Ard Ghlais	Ardglass	Northern Ireland, United Kingdom
Anglo-Saxon Kingdoms		
Caer Oder, Kingdom of Mercia	Bristol	England, United Kingdom
Bath, Kingdom of Mercia	Bath, Somerset	England, United Kingdom
Searoburh, Kingdom of Wessex	Salisbury (formerly Old Sarum)	England, United Kingdom
London, Kingdom of Mercia	London	England, United Kingdom
Dubris, Kingdom of Kent	Dover, Kent	England, United Kingdom

Dedication and Copyright page

Dedicated to Khanada Taylor

September 2011

Dark Alliance

Morrigan's Brood Book III

ISBN-10: 1-937341-20-8

ISBN-13: 978-1-937341-20-6

by Heather Poinsett Dunbar

and Christopher Dunbar

Published by Triscelle Publishing

Edited by Sarah E. Aalderink

Cover art, map, and website by Khanada Taylor

Proofread by Jillian Rosenburg

Triscelle Publishing Logo by Dayna Hartley

Printed by permission in the United States of America, the United Kingdom, or Australia. See back page for printing information. For any issues with print or binding quality, please contact the company through which the purchase was made and give the code number on this book.

Visit our website and find us on WordPress, Goodreads, Shelfari, Facebook, the Library Thing, LinkedIn, Twitter, and many other places on the Net.

www.triscellepublishing.com

triscellepublishing.wordpress.com

Also available in several eBook formats

acknowledgments

Heather's Acknowledgments

I would love to first thank the readers who have enjoyed our stories and have offered much encouragement. I would also like to thank our editor, Sarah (Sally), who isn't afraid to edit our stories with honesty; Khanada, whose artwork whether it be a cover, map, or website still renders me speechless and wondering how she did it; and Jillian who does a superb job on proofreading with little time. Also, much love and thanks to our growing circle of friends who tell me periodically to get my butt in the chair and write, especially Heidi, Tracy Angelina, and Kara whose work inspires me. I must also thank both of our parents for being here for us, and last but never least, I thank The Hubby, who is a talented storyteller and supports me no matter how crazy my ideas are.

Christopher's Acknowledgments

I would like to first thank our readers, fans, and friends for all of your moral support and for buying our stories. I would like to thank Khanada Taylor, Sarah Aalderink, Jillian Rosenburg, and Dayna Hartley for all of your contributions to the series thus far. I would also like to thank my parents and my wife's parents for being there for us. I would especially like to thank my wife for being there with me, through thick and thin (mostly thin) during this extended career adjustment phase, which appears to have reached a new Spring.

gods and goddesses of the series

Irish Pantheon – Tuatha dé Danann (People of Dana)	
Aine (*An-ya*)	*Goddess of love and fertility*
Aongas Og (*An-gus Og*)	*God of love and youth*
Brigid (*Bri-jid*)	*Goddess of healing, writing, water, and cats*
Dagda (*Dah-dah*)	*The 'good' God of many skills*
Dana (*Day-na*)	*The mother Goddess*
Lugh (*Loo*)	*Multi-skilled God of battle, light, writing, and the harvest*
Medb (*May-v*)	*Goddess of sovereignty*
Manannán Mac Lir (*Mannan-awan Mac Lir*)	*Guide to the Otherworld and God of the wind, travels, sea, and sailing*
Morrigan (*Mor-ee-gan*)	*Goddess of death, battle, blood, and rebirth*
Nuada (*Nu-a-da*)	*God of healing and weaponry*
British Pantheon	
Cernunnos	*God of animals, wilderness, fertility, and the Wild Hunt*
Greek / Roman Pantheon	
Aphrodite (*af-rǝ-dy-tee*) / Venus ('wɛnʊs)	*Goddess of love, beauty, and sexuality / Goddess of love, beauty, and fertility*
Ares (árɛːs) / Mars (*Mārs*)	*God of War and Manly Virtues / God of War; part of the Archaic Triad*
Hera (*Hēra*) / Juno ('juːnoː)	*Queen of the Gods and Goddess of marriage, women and birth / Patron Goddess of Rome and Goddess of women; part of the Capitoline Triad*
Zeus (*Zews*) / Jupiter	*King of the Gods and God of the sky, thunder, lightning, law, order, and justice / King of the Gods and God of the sky and thunder; part of the Capitoline Triad; Patron Deity of Rome*
Arabic (Zoroastrian) Pantheon	
Verethragna	*God of war and sexual potency*
Assyrian Pantheon	
Zaltu	*God of Strife*
Hindu Pantheon	
Kali (*Kālī*)	*Goddess of Time and Change; "She who destroys"; "Redeemer of the Universe"*

Lines of Blood-Drinkers

Algul – An Arabic blood-drinker, created by their God of war, Verethragna. Their known abilities include the power to create visual hallucinations in both mortals and other immortals. However, their vulnerability lies in strong smells. Their numbers are small, due to a genocidal war between themselves and the remnants of the Ekimmu.

Deargh Du – An ancient line of blood-drinkers from Eire (Ireland) that trace their ancestry to the Goddess, Morrigan. Their true talents lie in their magical skills and their fae-like beauty, known as glamoury. They can fly, create glowing light, heal mortals as well as other immortals, and draw down darkness and shadow. Their major weakness is the metal gold. After the creation of the Ekimmu Cruitne, the Deargh Du withdrew back to their native land and ceased interacting with other blood-drinking races.

Ekimmu – A group of blood-drinkers originating in Assyria from Zaltu, the deity of strife. They grew in strength and power, eventually dominating the Middle East. However, other races, such as their enemies the Algul and the Lamia, began to hunt them down, decimating their population.

Ekimmu Cruitne – The Ekimmu, fleeing a genocidal war, removed themselves to the northern regions of Alba (Scotland). After meeting some of the Deargh Du, who traveled with the Scoti tribe, an Ekimmu and a Deargh Du conspired to tip the balance by creating a new being. Morrigan, in her rage, sought to confine them to their lands. Ekimmu Cruitne are struck by illness whenever they try to cross the ocean. Their greatest talent is their olfactory sense, making them excellent trackers. They can also heal others, fly, read minds, and enjoy manipulating games of chance. In addition, they can create the sensation of pleasure as well as harm in themselves and their victims.

Lamia - According to legend, Lamia was a Queen of Libya who seduced Zeus. In retribution, Hera killed all of her children. Heartbroken, Lamia began feeding on the people of Greece, and before long, she had many new immortal children. The Lamia infiltrated Roman society, and soon Rome became their seat of power. The Lamia's skills lie in mind-bending, or manipulation. They even have an ability to enter dreams and manipulate the dreamer.

Ouphe – An ancient Saxon line of blood-drinkers that moved into Briton during the Saxon conquest. Their strength is in their monstrous lycanthropic nature; many blood-drinking races can die from the wounds given by an Ouphe. Yet, the Ouphe are severely affected by silver. Their origin is a mystery.

**Strigoi** – A line of blood-drinkers that began from a cursed Greek beauty named Iris. Aphrodite's curse did not grant Iris and her victim's immortality until later. Yet, they only survive fifty years after their transformation. The Strigoi are telepathic and unleash uncontrollable madness upon mortals and immortals alike. Affected mortals tear at their eyes and puncture their eardrums to escape the onslaught of sights and sounds. Despite their talents, Strigoi are physically weak, stunted, and are the ugliest of the blood-drinkers.

**Sugnwr Gwaed** – A British group of blood-drinkers created by Cernunnos, the horned God of animals, wilderness, and the wild hunt. Their strengths include enhanced communication with animals and their talent for vocal persuasion. They can convince their victims of almost anything. They also fly, like the other Celtic lines, and have an aptitude for healing others.

Other lines will be revealed in future works.

character guide

Marcus Galerius Primus Helvetticus	Marcus
Formerly a general and Praetor of Gaul under Gaius Julius Caesar, Marcus became a Deargh Du, and eventually led their armies against the invading Lamia. With the war over, he finds himself exiled from Eire with Máire.	
Mandubratius	Awvarwy (*a-war-wee*)
As the co-Consul of the Lamia, the former self-proclaimed Chieftain of the Trinovantes failed to acquire the prize, but now, he must face an enemy of terrifying ferocity, and he knows that alone, the Lamia will fall.	
Maél Muire Ní Conghal Uí Máine	Maél Muire (*mal mure*) or Máire (*moya*)
Formerly Chieftain of the Uí Máine of Beal Atha an Fheada, Máire, a Deargh Du, finds herself exiled from Eire, and she must put up with her Bath house mates, who send her on adventures all over the world, just for wagers.	
Claudius Metrius Sertorius	Claudius
Originally a lieutenant under general Marcus Galerius Primus Helvetticus, Claudius later became a Sugnwr Gwaed and then moved in with Marcus, and their mutual friend Mac Alpin, who live in Bath.	
Arwin Mac Alpin	Mac Alpin
Once the scourge of the Romans, Arwin Mac Alpin, an Ekimmu Cruitne, now shares a large house in Bath with his Roman friends Marcus, a Deargh Du, and Claudius, a Sugnwr Gwaed. Of course, Máire and Edward also live there.	
Tertia Amata Antonia	Amata
Once the third daughter of a wealthy Roman merchant and then a prostitute, following her husband's death, Amata reached tremendous heights when she became Co-Consul of the Lamia. Now, she watches Mandubratius' back.	
Téa Uí Cennedi Uí Máine	Talia de Burgundy
Few knew her true identity as being granddaughter to King Godomer of Burgundy, who was killed by the Franks. However, this Lamia has not forgotten, and she plans to use her gifts to take back her birthright.	
Patroclus Statilius Messalinus	The Legate
Once a legate under Emperor Trajan, Patroclus now serves the Lamia Co-Consuls as their advisor, bodyguard, and problem solver. However, his loyalty is first to the Lamia. Should either Co-Consul stray, he would fix the situation.	
Edward	Edward, Edwina, Edgar, Edna
Despite being called a variety of names by his father-in-darkness, Edward manages to focus on his alchemy work, making explosives of various kinds, after gaining such knowledge from the Greeks, the Chinese, and others.	

Sáerlaith Ní Adhamdh	Sáerlaith (saer-la)

Now leader of the Deargh Du Council of Five, Sáerlaith must keep the Deargh Du united in their cause of maintaining the balance, yet her actions over two hundred years ago have left fractures in their foundation, and they are growing.

Caoimhín	Caoimhín (kev-een)

Caoimhín has lost many friends in the war against the Lamia, but he manages to flourish as Sáerlaith's right-hand man. Still, it is difficult to live the happy life of a blood-drinker when others threaten his mistress and she won't listen.

Ruarí Mac Flan	Ruarí (ro-ree)

Nearly as old as Sáerlaith, as well as her closest friend, Ruarí spends his time teaching the forbidden practices of the Druids to mortal and blood-drinker alike. When he is not teaching, he can be found seeking out lost knowledge.

Emperor Charles / Charlemagne	Karl der Große, Carolus Magnus

This son of King Pepin the Short and Bertrada of Laon became King of the Franks in 742 CE and then was crowned Imperator Augustus in the Christmas of 800 CE. Despite his power, he just wants wine, women, and song … lots of it.

Pope Leo III	His Holiness

After becoming Pope in 795 CE and fleeing those who wished to gouge out his eyes because he was of common stock, Leo sought and gained King Charles' favor by crowning him Emperor, but the blighter won't do what Leo says…

Julien de Divio	Julien

What a wonderful life it is to be the third son in a noble family. You don't need to serve in the military or join the clergy, but then no one pays you any regard. Still, Julien has found success serving in the gendarme.

Heloise de Divio	Heloise

As the matriarch of a noble family, Heloise must deal with loss, such as the losses of her husband and her second son. Still, she takes great pride that her daughter shares her heretical beliefs and that she has a beautiful granddaughter, Clotilda.

Reginald de Divio	Reginald

After his father died, Reginald assumed his father's mantle and served the Kingdom with distinction. He later married Flor, Julien's childhood friend, and produced three children of his own… Clotilda, Jakelin, and baby Ledger.

Horatio di Reate	Horatio

A child of Lombards, Horatio only knew Frankish rule as he grew up within the Papal States. When he was of age, he joined the Papal Army, and then with his father's wealth and influence, he became a member of the elite cavalry.

prologue

Rome, 801 C.E.

he warm rains pelted his body as mists danced over the moonlit woods. The muggy scents and heat grew as Mandubratius moved closer to his next meal. The rain dripped from the cowl of his cloak, joining the small drops that muddied the sylvan paths. Green warred with the nighttime skies. Clouds shifted, separating the stars and moon from the landscape. A chill breeze swept through the leaves. The foliage started moving together, creating a beautiful sound that seemed to spread across the forested glen from one tree to its surrounding neighbors.

He sensed his prey shift its movements, darting around branches as if teasing him. A strange scent of honeyed sweetness greeted his nose, and with a start, Mandubratius realized that Rome had disappeared over the horizon and that he stood in the wild lands of Briton or Eire.

His senses reeled as he noticed movement towards him.

A soft tap on his shoulder sent a shiver through his frame. Mandubratius turned around and scrutinized a pair of glowing, green eyes. A Deargh Du studied him from a distance. Mandubratius tried to discern its features, but darkness shrouded all but its eyes.

Damn their tricks.

The Deargh Du stared at him, as if trying to ascertain his motives. Mandubratius did not move. He considered reaching for his sword, but he could see no malice in those strange and radiant eyes.

Before Mandubratius could debate his choice, he extended his right arm and open hand to the other blood-drinker. This could be his last movement. A slender yet strong hand clasped his. He exhaled, relieved that no sharp blade greeted his limbs.

A scream shattered his thoughts, causing him to jump, as he released the Deargh Du's hand. Mandubratius landed and then spun to face the Deargh Du, only to observe the other blood-drinker fall to its knees as it covered its ears. The Deargh Du uttered a soft cry, as if pain overwhelmed it. An unnamed dread curdled Mandubratius' confidence. He tried to spot the source of the scream from his crouch, but the growing horror of nameless childhood fears began to overwhelm him.

The featureless Deargh Du grew silent. It stared at something over Mandubratius' right shoulder, revealing an apparent confusion and growing fear. Mandubratius turned his head, staring into the darkness. He could discern nothing at first.

Then the dull remembrances of his childhood horrors became crystal clear, as the monstrous shadows roared. Fearing for his life, Mandubratius drew his blade. A nondescript black form took shape before moving forth from the darkness. Soon its *features coalesced, revealing a familiar face that he wished to forget.*

"Your strength fails you now, Awvarwy," the beast taunted him, calling Mandubratius by his true name. It knocked the sword from his shuddering hands. He heard an unseen woman begin screaming, as the monster turned away from him and loped to an altar in the distance. The terrified shrieking grew louder as the beast landed on the mortal woman. The beast howled with glee and pleasure as it began to tear the mortal to shreds on the altar. The woman cried in agony and fear. Her heartbeat became a furious drumbeat. Mandubratius considered running away into the looming forest, as he had in every nightmare as a mortal child, but he resisted the urge to flee.

One glance back at the Deargh Du revealed that it still remained immobile. How could the other blood-drinker continue staring blankly into nothing?

Mandubratius inhaled to calm his nerves. He felt a strange compulsion to study the monster and its victim, so he turned his head to face them. As always, the two beings faded into a shrouded and mist-filled darkness. Yet, even as the figures faded, howls of fury, pain, and pleasure seared his ears.

After a few seconds of focusing his vision, while trying his best to ignore the nightmarish screaming and growling that still echoed in the woods, Mandubratius glimpsed a third figure lurking in the darkness. A grinning and repulsive skeletal face leered at him from behind the shadows. Its eyes revealed madness and a joy of tormenting others by manipulating fears.

"Strigoi?" Mandubratius murmured. His whisper seemed louder than the moans of pain and shrieks of pleasure.

The Strigoi's orange eyes glowed as it examined him. These blood-drinkers from the East lived to draw out horror in mortals and other blood-drinkers.

The Strigoi's insane laughter nearly drowned out the dying screams of the poor victim. Mandubratius looked away from the Strigoi to see the monster and what remained of that poor woman, but as soon as his eyes returned to the monster, it looked up from its dead prey and lumbered towards him. It pulled out a bloody scythe. The Druidic tool fused with the beast's dirty hand and became a claw.

Mandubratius remained still and closed his eyes. This was just a mandrake-influenced fantasy.

Then a shrill banshee scream made him cover his face in fright, as his deep-rooted fears from the battlefield in Eire resurfaced. Pain tore at his very being, and Mandubratius felt himself begin to scream in terror.

"Shhhh. You were screaming, my love." Soft and gentle hands caressed his shoulders. "What happened?"

Mandubratius stared at Amata. The mandrake started to fade away like fraying fuzz from silk in his brain.

"I was hunting a mortal," he began, retelling the dream as he watched her pull away to write down notes. "A Deargh Du joined me, and then I experienced an old nightmare from my mortal childhood. It melded with a newer fear," he admitted. Amata stopped writing and ran her fingers through his hair.

"That fear is not here. We are safe in the Temple with our patrons." Amata leaned in and kissed his brow.

Mandubratius closed his mouth, wanting to give no more away. These fears once threatened his leadership in the Lamia.

He stared at Amata. "No more mandrake, ever," he said.

"But it gives us insight," she answered.

"It gives you insight, and it only gives me fear and harm," Mandubratius whispered, before sitting up.

"However, it may give us clues as to what has befallen so many of our number," Amata said. Her hand caressed his bearded cheek, and she turned him to face her. "You are not the only one who has experienced this fear. However, you have fortitude, Mandubratius. You had the strength and will to overcome your concerns and terror after our time in Hibernia." She kissed him again, this time on the lips, and then released him. She then pulled away, pushing her long dark hair behind her ears.

Objects in the shrine of the temple grew clear and focused. He could see the statues of Mars and Venus staring at him, Mars' eyes, bold and demanding, and Venus' coy and playful. The smell of incense now seemed too strong. The constant smoke and scent seemed to stifle him. One could scarcely draw a clean breath within the temple. It would always be home, but it felt suffocating at present.

Mandubratius sensed a desire to run outside of the temple and into the warm and welcoming night. He also experienced an odd and ever-increasing longing to sail to his ancient home in Trinovantum. Yet, the prevalent forests of his mortal residence disappeared with each invasion. First Rome arrived and cleared the forests. Then, the swell of Saxons, Angles, and whatever else those barbarians called themselves, took over the place.

His descendants had moved to the marshes in the west. It seemed such a shame. Then again, the true Britons remained in their new home, and the Saxons became the rulers of the various kingdoms throughout the former Briton.

The presence of a nearing Lamia kept him seated in place on the gilded cushion next to the luminous Amata.

He heard the door open. Amata called to the visitor.

A messenger stared at them. "Dominus and Domina, the holdings in the North and East are overrun! Lamia have been lost! Our legions are decimated."

"What do you mean?" he asked the messenger, trying to regain his senses. Damn that incense. Perhaps it was time to make the underlings clean everything out and open the doors one night. Then again, the city itself stank of dung during the late winter and burgeoning spring.

He wondered what would smell worse, dung or incessant incense?

Mandubratius returned his attention to the messenger.

"They were attacked, Dominus. A few survived, but they suffer from a lingering madness. Each night brings some improvement, yet they are still not themselves."

Mandubratius looked over to Amata. Her blue eyes settled on his.

"Strigoi," he whispered.

"Messenger, go wait for further orders outside," Amata directed the other Lamia. After the door closed, she turned herself to face him. Her long, graceful arms rested against her knees.

"Did you see one in your visions?" she asked. Amata's voice grew querulous. He could see growing fear in her eyes.

"Yes," he whispered, grasping her arm.

"What about this Deargh Du?" she asked, stroking his brow with cool fingers. She prompted him to rest his head in her lap. His worries kept his mouth shut on matters regarding her pleasure. He looked up at Amata and remembered her question.

"I think it was him, Marcus, I mean. At least that is my suspicion. Against this threat, it seems we need the Deargh Du as allies," he whispered, "or we will face something... I am not sure whether it is annihilation or an opportunity. It may give us a chance to rejoin our brothers in Constantinople, but I cannot see that future clearly. After all, we have lost so many Lamia, we have to move past old quarrels and commence our strategies. It is time for our friends to do what needs to be done, Amata. I will think more clearly when this dream fades into oblivion." He met her clear, blue eyes, feeling a calmness radiate from her being. Gods, he loved feeling her soft hands caress his hair.

Amata smiled at him with supreme gentleness, looking much like a radiant Venus. "After all we have done to each other, dear brother, do you think the Deargh Du and their friends would accept us as allies? Do you not remember what happened in those times after we returned? Of all we have been through in the last few decades?"

Mandubratius shuddered. "Do we have a choice, or do they, for that matter?" he whispered, leaning into her shoulder, seeking comfort. "I am almost certain that the Deargh Du will see it as their divine duty to Morrigan. The Strigoi would disrupt their precious balance, after all. Now it is time to entertain the idea of visiting someone who will not welcome us with open arms... rather, you. Marcus would receive you with much courtesy, I feel. Do watch out for her, though. Maél Muire may not be as welcoming to you or to

Patroclus."

"Patroclus?" Amata asked. "He was with our northern legion. He may not be... alive," she whispered.

"Patroclus wouldn't die on us. Besides, the Legate and Marcus respect one another, or so I believe." Mandubratius closed his eyes for a moment. "Patroclus is devoted to you and to me. He believes in the solemnity and dignity that we give to the Lamia, Amata. He will protect you from the Deargh Du. Patroclus will not fall to the glamoury of that beautiful Maél Muire." He opened his eyes and studied Amata's entrancing eyes. "Part of me would love to see Maél Muire again so that I can continue my games with her, but I must have the upper hand at our next meeting."

Amata chuckled. "I know very well you look forward to a game of cat and mouse with her, sweetheart, but I wonder which of you will be the cat."

"That will be what makes the game fun," Mandubratius purred. "Yet, it is not a game worth risking you in. That is why Patroclus will join you. He is honorable and not into games and mind-bending, as are most Lamia."

"You still think Patroclus will keep me safe?" Amata's blue eyes reflected the gold of the shrine. The fortunes of the Lamia returned now, thanks to Holy Mother Church.

Mandubratius closed his eyes. "I do not always care for Patroclus, but he will protect you, Amata. You are my co-consul. We have weathered the storms of the past together. I need you at my side to meet the Strigoi."

chapter one

Bath

The sound of music echoed through the halls, dissipating as it flowed out into the garden. A light misting rain dusted over the land. Bath still shone in its radiant beauty. Out of all of the ancient Roman homes that once stood in the town, only one survived. Now, Saxon houses and farms dominated the landscape.

The town bordered on two Saxon kingdoms. It took many years to get used to a new language, new customs, and new people. Most of the Britons moved to Wales after the Saxon invasion in the distant past. Then the Saxons and other tribes melded with the lands and those Britons who remained.

The new flavors in the vitae of the mortals suited him as well as the others of Briton… or the Saxon kingdoms, quite well.

His home remained the same, at least as much as he could keep it. He kept his guests out of the lower levels, because he feared that it would be nearly impossible to replace anything they might break. Yet, willing craftsmen would create furnishings in older styles for the right coin.

His guests considered him odd, but hospitable, the last of an ancient Romano-British family. The village had no idea what to make of Máire, Edward, Claudius, and Arwin, not that the thoughts of his guests really mattered. If Marcus kept the village entertained with drink, food, and merriment, they never seemed to give his family's or friends' oddities a second thought.

"Excellent feast, neighbor," Alfred remarked as he raised a cup to him, revealing his wrinkled face. "Have you heard the latest continental news?" Marcus' neighbor then leaned in closer. "They say the Basileus Irene from Constantinople seeks to form a marriage alliance with Emperor Charles. Can you imagine such a joining of forces?" Alfred chuckled and shook his head. "One must wonder whether they will plan on coming here next."

"Sounds like mere speculation, Alfred. Mercia, Northumberland, Wessex, and the rest of the kingdoms here are not rich enough for their interest, and we are too far from the center of Emperor Charles' realm. Our worries should center on those hordes of Norsemen. Now, I must see to the mead and ale. My servants lack refined tastes, sometimes. Please excuse me," Marcus said, backing towards the music and the mortal women. He could see several young women watching him with eager eyes.

Whom to enjoy tonight?

The men ignored them, speaking only of the hunt. Oh well, he supposed this would be their husbands' and fathers' losses and his gain. Marcus smiled at the gathered ladies and allowed a little of his glamoury to escape.

He witnessed their eyes gleam over for a moment.

"Well, lieutenant," he called over to Claudius. "What do you think of the lovely selection tonight?"

"I'm thinking that, by the Gods, it must horrendous to be a woman today. That, and their men are fools," Claudius answered. He turned to study the women. "The blonde on the left is lovely. What is her name? We were introduced, but I have forgotten it."

"Do you mean the one that is nearly falling down or the sober one?" Marcus asked, finding a great deal of amusement in the wealthy class of Bath. "The sober one is Isobel and the other is Althea, I think. However, I did catch up on gossip, even the gossip that involves us. At least I think so. My sources are notoriously unreliable. Our neighbors have changed their opinions on you, Edward, Arwin, and Máire again."

"Really?" Claudius grinned. His dark eyes lit with a growing amusement. "So, I'm not your bastard son, Edward isn't your lover, Máire isn't a defrocked nun, and Mac Alpin isn't on the run from a gruesome wife who beat him?"

Marcus laughed. "I thought Arwin and I were lovers, and you, Edward, and Máire were our flock of bastards."

"You are so out of touch with the town," Claudius laughed. "So what is this other gossip?"

"Did you hear the news about the Basileus Irene?"

Marcus noticed Arwin carrying over his mug of bloodmead and then looking over the daughters and wives.

"I heard that the high and mighty ancient empress wishes to take an old barbarian to bed," Mac Alpin guffawed, running a hand over his messy hair. The blood-drinker had yet to find a decent barber. "Very amusing," he added.

"Amusing, but doubtful," Edward said. "I heard that rumor on the way here. Yet, I heard the wily emperor's court grows ever more debauched." He chuckled, his blue eyes brimming with glee. "I should like to visit this court."

"Edward," Arwin commented with a smirk, "we all know that despite the emperor's attempts to defend Christianity, he is as much of a heathen as us, what with all of his wives and concubines. Concubines… what a grand idea! Leave it to a Frank to come up with such a great scheme. He gets to be the most powerful leader in Christendom, enjoys the patronage of that foolish Pope Leo III, and sleeps with whatever woman he wants."

"Yes, for being barely literate, Emperor Charles must be quite brilliant," Edward added.

"I remember some of the Frankish women as being breathtaking," Claudius added. "Once you get them out of those horrible dresses and veils, that is."

Marcus watched himself smile in a reflecting bronze mirror that brightened the room. "I hear tell that the emperor's cousin, Gundrada, is the most beautiful flower of the court, and yet she manages to keep her legs closed. It would be quite the feat to bed her. We should forgo this rambling chatter and consider for our next wager which one of us can couple with Gundrada first?"

Marcus fell silent as the front door slammed open, and he could hear stomping feet. A lingering pull told him the identity of the late arrival. The trace of primed sweetness gave him pause to think of the long, red curls and ire-filled, green eyes that would turn around the corner at any moment. He could almost smell the boiling fury within her body. Ranting echoed against the marbled walls, and the statues shook as her voice thundered through the party. The musicians continued to play despite the racket caused by Máire and her boots.

Marcus turned, took the jade tiger from its place on the table, and held it behind his back. He smiled just in time as his rampaging, soaked, daughter-in-darkness walked into the great room. The guests stared at her in gape-mouthed surprise, or possible horror.

"Well, I went to find that tiger you told me about!" she yelled.

"Hello, Banbh Ceanúil," he purred in Gaelic. She both loved and hated being called 'endearing piglet'.

"Do not interrupt me, Marcus. I searched all over that palace, and it could not be found! I know someone took it." Máire paced, ignoring the mortals, who watched her with much interest. She pushed back the hood of her cape, revealing her damp hair, which gleamed in the candlelight.

He pulled the tiger from behind his back and presented it to her.

"How did... where did..." Máire stammered.

Marcus watched Máire's eyes focus on him. Her predatory gaze turned accusatory.

"You tricked me, again!" she raged.

Marcus, who could not help himself, felt a slight grin form at the corners of his mouth.

"Who was it this time?" Máire demanded. "Who went against me in this race?"

He noticed his guests grow silent.

Máire stared at their friends.

"Arwin, did you take part in this?" He heard Máire's words echo through his home.

The elder Ekimmu Cruitne backed away.

"Maél Muire, it was not me," Mac Alpin stated.

He watched her turn away. Máire then raised a supercilious brow in

Claudius' direction.

Marcus watched Edward take a slow step back. He knew that Edward hated these games, but only because he detested the subversion and trickery involved. After all, Lamia used subversion and trickery, not the Celtic lines.

"Máire, I did not go to Persia to find the jade tiger," Claudius said, saying little else regarding his involvement in the bet. He batted his dark eyes at her and smiled.

Máire rolled her eyes at Claudius.

"Edward!" Máire appeared to notice Mac Alpin's newest child-in-darkness edging toward the gathered mortals.

Marcus watched Máire grab his wrist. Any other strength might reveal their nature to the gathered mortals.

Edward winced at the undeniable pain.

"You did this?" she accused.

"But, but-" he began, before Máire cut him off.

"Yes?" Her eyes began to glow like bright emeralds.

"Marcus and Claudius put me up to it," he admitted, ignoring the horrified stares of the mortal men, who considered Máire to be something of a frightening figure.

Máire closed her eyes and gently released his bruised wrist. "Thank you for your honesty, Edward. Unlike our associates, I know you speak the truth."

Arwin and Claudius lowered their heads. Marcus heard soft chuckles emanate from their direction.

Máire turned on her heel and walked past the other blood-drinkers to move in closer to him. On her way, she elbowed the chortling Claudius in the stomach.

"So, what did you win from your lieutenant?" she asked in Gaelic, keeping her words private from the mortals.

"Whatever do you mean, my dear love?" Marcus grinned and put down the small statue. Máire did not seem to realize how much fun it was to bring her to anger. It was the only opportunity to see her passionate about anything.

The revelers moved towards the musicians, trying to avoid what looked like a most odd domestic dispute.

"It is obvious," she huffed. "You bet Claudius that Edward would beat me in this contest to find some ridiculous trinket you dropped in Persia. I want to know what you won." Máire's flashing eyes demanded the truth.

Marcus pulled a pouch from his belt and shook it, allowing her to hear the jingle of coin.

"Twenty pieces of silver," he told her.

"My hard work, time, and effort are only worth twenty pieces of silver to you?" she inquired, incredulity evident in her voice.

"Not exactly," he replied, meeting her eyes, searching for some miniscule amount of amusement.

"Not exactly?" she asked as she blinking her eyes.

"In a way, you and Edward were a team. You both brought back the tiger. Therefore, your adventure was a resounding success. You had fun, admit it, Banbh Ceanúil." He gave her a ready grin, hoping she would find charm and wit in his answers.

He watched her face grow red as if she were about to explode in the manner of a raging volcano. He pondered for a moment on the appropriateness of referring to her as 'Vesuvius'.

In the midst of their conversation, Marcus saw Máire turn to regard his guests, who stared at her. Then, her strong fingers encircled his wrist with a fierce, burning pain, and dragged him toward a private chamber.

"Stop smiling," she hissed as she slammed the door shut. She pushed him against the wall and then slapped him.

The slap stung, and Marcus felt his face turn away from her hand. The numbing pain surprised him.

She growled in annoyed frustration and then forced his arms to his sides as she kissed him furiously, thrusting her tongue into his mouth.

Before Marcus could think of what to do, she flung him onto a bed. Máire threw off her cloak and then straddled him. He could feel water seep through their clothing. Together, they started tearing at each other's clothing with wild abandon.

"Goddess, I have missed you," he whispered as their fierce coupling began in earnest.

She bit into his throat and began drinking his blood. Marcus closed his eyes, rapt with the delicious sensation of her feeding from him.

Her body twined with his, and he rolled her over. In his excitement, he ended up falling out of the bed, pulling Máire with him. Their discarded clothing cushioned his landing. He could not help but laugh as he landed.

She chuckled breathless as she sheathed him.

Marcus wrapped a hand around her throat, desiring to taste her again. It had been too long, and his memory of Máire's flavor had weakened and withered in her absence.

The sweet essence of spiced honey melded with flowers and apples. He slid a finger over her, hoping she would stop over-thinking the act and feel pleasure, for a change.

He felt some disappointment as she uttered a sound of false pleasure.

Máire made it impossible at times for him to tell the difference between what made her shudder in true gratification and what simply annoyed her.

Then again, this did not exist as an issue only between them. It dwelled between herself and every other man since that bitter mother Seosaimhín cursed Máire. Love, or any emotion or passion, dissolved into nothing more than an act, most of the time.

Marcus pulled his hand away from her as her writhing continued. He pushed away tendrils of her wet hair and then stared into her eyes, but instead of looking back at him, Máire squinted her eyes shut, as if in concentration, perhaps willing herself to enjoy their coupling.

Máire rested against Marcus' chest, daring now to meet those silvery, blue eyes that could inflame her with such a rage at times. Yet, now was not the time to study them and become lost.

"Marcus," she began. "It is getting to the point where I do not trust you anymore." She ran her fingers through his dark hair. Sometimes it seemed to be almost the color of ink. However, when she studied it closely, it appeared to be a very dark brown. A few silvered hairs revealed that he was older than her, but he still managed to act like an irritating child at times. Then again, all of his friends acted the same way. Máire wondered sometimes whether her experience with Marcus compared with women who grew up with several brothers.

"Why is that?" he asked, twisting a bit to allow her greater access to play with his hair. He smiled at her caresses.

She playfully slapped Marcus on his chest. "You know exactly what I mean, General. You have done this many times, because you find some perverse amusement in sending me to find antiquities. Remember the fairy wand? The supposed Spear of Destiny? I think you tell tall tales just to see my reaction." She pulled away from him and lay down at his side on top of her damp cloak.

"This must stop," she said. "I may be your child-in-darkness, but I am not a toy to amuse you and your friends." She almost began to cry tears of frustration. Her voice broke a bit as she continued. "I feel that you respected me more when I was a mortal, chroí. Frankly, I am tired of the jokes that you and your comrades find endlessly amusing. I honestly wonder whether you, Claudius and Arwin spend your nights asking, 'what should we get Máire to do next?'"

Marcus turned to face her, took her hand, and brought it to his lips. "I am sorry. We just wish to give you amusement and pleasure, Máire. You seem to find joy in puzzles and quests. I've seen your face light up when discovering new facts, and we take satisfaction in seeing you in such a blissful and cheerful mood. What better test for this new knowledge of yours than providing you with an insurmountable task?"

He stared into her eyes, and watched as the reflection of her glowing eyes faded. He smiled at her, and her heart warmed at seeing his smile.

"It is very difficult to find new quests for you at times. Claudius, Arwin, and I have nearly run out of legendary artifacts." His words grew soft. "The jade tiger isn't even a legend. Arwin made up the story. Claudius bought the tiger and took it to the palace on that journey he made for the Sugnwr Gwaed earlier this year. We just wanted to make you happy."

She watched his face turn up in a grin again.

"Will you forgive us?" His eyes became serious and the trickster faded.

The question, delivered in a soft lilt, melted away her icy fury.

"Please," he purred.

"Of course," she answered, before sitting up. Máire leaned in for another kiss. "I cannot deny that you bring me joy, though with a measure of annoyance."

Her lips pressed against his. His arms moved around her body, and then he rolled her onto her back.

The sounds of the party drifted through the closed door. However, the noises became easier to ignore, as he stroked a finger over her.

Máire slid her legs around his waist and wondered whether he could bring her pleasure now, if not satisfaction.

Rome

"Benedicat vos omnipotens Deus Pater, et Filius, et Spiritus Sanctus. Amen," Pope Leo III droned to the gathered congregation of the gathered faithful, effectively closing the cathedral mass. His mind wandered away from the genuflecting leaders of Rome to the news from the eastern realms of the holy empire. He stepped off the dais and walked past the poor, who pleaded for alms, leaving his priests to tend to their needs.

Weightier matters sucked away his contentment, making the papal crown grow heavy. Leo pushed aside the doors to the secretarium and strode into the room, fending off his assistants as he contemplated these tales of horror from the east. Soldiers and knights of the realm, who must have been used to blood and battle, tore out their eyes and deafened themselves with sticks. The few lone survivors told harrowing tales of frightening devils who walked the earth, reveling in a fight between their victims.

"Such dire portents," he murmured to the growing shadows within the palace.

"Your Holiness?" Bernard, his faithful clerk, queried after walking into the secretarium and bowing. "May I assist you in some way?"

"Yes," Leo acknowledge before holding out his arms to receive help removing his vestments. "We are troubled over this latest news from the East," he said. "We must send a faithful follower to the emperor's court, Bernard."

"Is it wise, Holy Father, to have an ear in Charles' court?" Bernard asked with soft words.

Leo opened his eyes wide and stared at the cleric, waiting for an answer.

Bernard lowered his head. He exuded the foolishness of youth. Perhaps one day, he would outgrow it.

"Forgive me, Holy Father," Bernard murmured.

"You are forgiven," Leo acknowledged with a nod and a small smile. "Thank you for giving me this important news, earlier."

"Of course," Bernard said as he returned the nod. "However, there is one more matter which requires His Holiness' attention."

"Yes, yes, what it is?" Pope Leo felt his patience drain.

Why does God have to teach us the value of patience?

"A guest waits for you in the hall, Your Holiness," Bernard answered.

"Well, does this guest have a name, Bernard?"

"I do not..." his assistant stammered. "I do not know his name. He just informed me that this matter is one of utmost urgency and that he must see you."

"Tell him to go away. I will not speak with people who do not have the decency to provide their name, or at least their title."

The sound of creaking iron hinges made Leo pause. The door swung open, revealing a tall and dark figure with green eyes. The man smiled, revealing white teeth. The stranger then bowed with grace and dignity in his movements.

"Michael?" The pope smiled as he beheld his old friend, the very one who protected him the night he nearly lost his eyesight and his tongue to Paschalis' men. His predecessor's family never got over losing their control of the Papacy. Gaining favor would always be a challenge with them.

"Michael Tolomei, stop bowing and join me. It's been so long." Leo stood and welcomed his guest, embracing him. "Sit, sit," the pope bade, while gesturing to a chair. "Bernard, bring us my best wine."

With Michael's arrival, Leo's problems seemed to fade into the mists.

Michael took a seat near the table. His green eyes gleamed with pleasure. "How does the Holy Father feel tonight?" Michael asked.

A pleasing numbness overwhelmed Leo. This man always seemed to make him feel at ease. His problems disappeared, causing Leo to feel invincible. Soon he gained his thoughts and started to speak.

"Michael, there are horrible stories from Emperor Charles' realm… stories of devils possessing men and making them do unspeakable things. The God-fearing people of our lands will turn on us both if such horrors do not disappear, old friend. It will undermine their faith in Jesus and in us." Leo sat down as Bernard arrived with wine and sustenance.

Leo poured goblets of wine for them both. "I have need of your strength again, noble knight." He scrutinized Michael's face for a moment before continuing. "It is strange. I asked our Lord and Savior for assistance, and here you are, much like your namesake, the Archangel Michael."

Michael smiled at him. "Anything you wish for, Holy Father, I will do. You are God's representative here, and I am yours to command."

Leo closed his eyes for a moment. He found himself so grateful that Jesus had sent someone to ensure the survival of the His Church. After this warrior's initial assistance, Leo had graced him with the title of 'Benedicto Novi Militus'. The establishment of Michael as a spiritual knight of the Church filled Leo with hope and confidence.

"After our meal, you will go to the support staff and receive a contingent of soldiers, attendants, and advisors, Michael. Next, go to Aachen and assist His Imperial Majesty with the search. You must investigate this threat for me. Let us both pray that this is but the wild, fevered imagination of a few soldiers and not devils striding the earth."

"As I said earlier," Michael responded as he took a sip from his goblet, "I will assist you in whatever steps need to be taken. I am greatly pleased to help you, and you inspire my own faith. However, I was thinking… many in the emperor's court may doubt my word that I represent you."

The pope nodded his head. "Yes, I understand." Leo rose from his seat and walked over to a gilded shelf. He then picked up a jewel-encrusted box, and displayed it for his guest. Leo extended it towards Michael, who smiled before leaning forward.

"Wear this with pride and know that I will pray for our success against these demons. You are my emissary," Leo bade, before opening the box.

The soldier reached into the box and withdrew a papal signet ring.

"Thank you, Your Holiness," said the warrior. Michael's green eyes settled on him, causing Leo's heart to race for a moment. "I know that this ring will gain their attention and grant us both the respect we deserve."

Mandubratius exited the cathedral and walked towards the Lateran palace with the requisitions in hand. Sometimes it became too easy to manipulate mortals. His gambit of intervening in the church paid off again, as they believed that he and his 'family' were gifts from God, Jesus, whatever names they chose to use for the Jewish God.

He walked around the pilgrims, priests, beggars, students, and assorted rabble, trying to keep from smiling too much, hoping to resemble a dour and devoted knight of Christianity. The buildings of the church shone as the one remaining beacon of beauty within Rome. The rest of the buildings remained a dark and stench-filled, indicative of splendor long dead. The current dominant religion of Rome reflected the city's own physical contradiction, as the ancient beliefs withered, as did the buildings. It seemed a bit strange to combine a so-called peaceful religion with war, but then again, that had always been the case in Rome during the days when Olympian, Etruscan, and various other Gods and Goddesses roamed the streets, temples, and homes of Rome.

So, Pope Leo wished to hand over a troop of soldiers to him with little more than a mental nudge. Mandubratius headed towards the quartermaster's building. Upon arrival, he handed the letter bearing the papal seal to the squat, little soldier within the front foyer.

While this duty required sobriety and dignity, Mandubratius hoped for an opportunity for fun. Christians could be so grim and severe sometimes.

He considered the idea of playing both sides of the coin. He could point out the Church's foibles and later extol their virtues. Otherwise, it would be nothing more than a long and dull journey across the Western Empire. Then again, he had helped the Christians build this church. He could not just tear it down completely.

Aachen

The series of reports and scrolls lay sprawled on Julien's desk. He snuck a glance at them, wishing the trivialities of the drunk and disorderly people from last night would disappear during his mid-afternoon break. Then again, after the past few months of traveling to dispense justice on a band of murderous cutpurses, a return to court, and his home here, seemed a welcome respite.

Julien returned to studying the papers, describing the healing properties of plants. His mother presented the scrolls to him upon his decision to leave home and join the Gendarmes. Plants seemed a far worthier subject in his mind, or at least more interesting than dealing with the local troublemakers. His other private collection here included a small book on Pythagorean philosophy, as well as a translation of the emerald tablet. His private reading collection remained hidden under a sea of old scrolls and documents, detailing his duties, criminal activities, and the works of his underlings and predecessor, in a large, wooden trunk.

Julien chuckled. Very few in Aachen knew how to read or write, with the exception of the students of the palace school. His somewhat questionable reading list would be safe. Besides that, his official office bordered the palace, and few came to the palace to look for dubious scrolls.

Upon reflection, the men of the Church might have a different view of his collection. Their world still rested on Augustine's beliefs that anything involving investigation and inquisitiveness bordered on dancing with the devil, and at the very least might be found heretical.

A knock at his closet interrupted Julien's thoughts, and he put away his scroll.

"Come in," Julien called, picking up official court proceedings regarding the latest trial of a poor thief in order to give the impression that his work kept him very busy today.

A court messenger walked through his door and then bowed. "His Imperial Majesty wishes his head gendarme to come to court as soon as possible on a matter of the greatest importance to him and his subjects."

"Send word to His Imperial Majesty that I shall be there."

The messenger bowed again before leaving Julien alone in his office.

Julien stared at his clothing after the messenger left, wishing this summons did not require his changing into his 'official' attire.

Julien walked through the halls of the Imperial Castle, shivering a bit. Loud talk and laughter echoed through the halls, and he could hear Emperor Charles' voice. Spring promised to arrive soon, but the loud roars of the great fireplaces seemed to come from only a few feet away.

The ornate décor almost appeared to draw strength away from visitors and make them feel lost within the boundaries of the Imperial palace. No home or residence within the empire could compete with this beauty. The palace reflected the lost days of Roman opulence and the emperor's wishes to recreate that era.

When Julien had first arrived here as a gendarme, he almost felt as though the ancient Caesars of Rome peeked around the huge columns and watched over this exquisite home with a mixture of pride and protection. Yet, perhaps older forces than the imperial family of Rome guarded this dwelling.

Julien shook away his thoughts, considering that such blathering could endanger him and others.

As he neared the throne room, Julien nodded to the guards, who seemed to recognize him.

Soon, Julien overheard a loud conversation between peers.

"I sent a message about this to the Holy Father," he heard, as the emperor's voice grow louder. "I am the emperor, and he is the chosen successor of Peter. He is supposed to pray for us and say mass, while we are in control of the secular matters of the empire. Leo wished me to take this imperial crown when he needed my protection, and now he appears to want it for himself. Do we yet have time to leave Aachen?" The emperor uttered a loud burst of laughter that made the guards ease a bit. Their increased number seemed strange at this peaceful time.

Then Julien observed that the secretary Ercanbald had taken notice of him. The secretary raised his right hand to Julien before walking over to the emperor. The secretary stood waiting for the emperor to cease talking before announcing Julien.

From his position near the guards, Julien spied the emperor, before realizing that the emperor had met his gaze.

"Clear the court," Emperor Charles said to the secretary. "Only those I designate may remain."

The room began to clear of other courtiers, including the ladies and their children.

Emperor Charles beckoned Julien with a finger. Julien acknowledged his emperor with a nod before walking towards him. As soon as he stood before Emperor Charles, Julien bowed.

"Thank you, Julien, for coming so quickly to the palace. Please dispense with your bows," the emperor began, with a dismissive wave of his right hand. "We have little time for niceties. I have a matter of extreme importance to discuss with my best gendarme." A small smile graced the emperor's face as he gestured to a large table covered in parchments.

"I am most honored to have been placed in such high esteem, Imperial Majesty," Julien acknowledged.

"You have earned such respect with your record in enforcing our laws in our empire, and of course dispatching my potential assassins," Charles explained. "I do not forget those who serve me well." Emperor Charles leaned over the table and pointed to a map of Burgundy, Franche-Comte, Alsace, and Savoie. Several red X's marked certain areas.

"I am certain you have heard the rumors about our missing cavalry patrol near Strasbourg, Julien, and how they were attacked by a horde of lost Avars." The emperor pointed to Strasbourg. "That story is only partly true. Two weeks ago, they encountered something that slaughtered them in a most strange and vicious manner. Only one survived the attack, and he has lost much of his senses. He says that he saw the devil that night. I would normally believe such babbling to be a case of infirmity, yet the stories of these strange sightings continue across these regions. We need you to find the source of these sightings, Julien. Does the devil walk the earth, or does some other sinister being that hides in a frightening form kill our people?"

"Imperial Majesty," Julien began, a little afraid of touching on the topic that had brought forth such anger in Emperor Charles earlier. "May I ask what Pope Leo has to say about these sightings?"

The emperor's posture changed. He furrowed his brow, and his eyes grew dark. "I sent a message to the Holy Father, and I expected a long delay on a reply, but I just received his response. He sends forth a papal emissary, with an entourage, to assist with the investigation."

Julien studied the emperor. All knew that despite the fronting of friendship against the emperor and his protégé, Pope Leo, the two expressed different views on their varied duties.

The secretary started wringing his hands. "Imperial Majesty, what do you wish to do when the emissary and his entourage arrives?" he asked.

"Provide them with the best hospitality of the court, Ercanbald!" shouted the emperor, revealing disbelief at the question. "Do you think I would declare war upon my Christian brethren while the heathen Avars and the Caliph of Spain encroach on our territories? We are surrounded by pagan hordes." The emperor sighed and paused for a moment. "Despite my private rumblings about the separation of the religious and secular rule, this emperor and his court hold His Holiness in the highest regard, Julien. We support his spiritual reign. You are to lead the investigation into these strange deaths and confirmed devil sightings. You have my leave to report to me personally on this matter."

The emperor stopped speaking. An uneasy quiet settled.

Unsure whether the emperor waited for a reply, Julien interjected, "And what of this papal emissary and his entourage?"

"Patience. My answer is forthcoming," Charles replied. He grew silent yet again for a protracted moment before continuing. "It is not clear whether these deaths are secular or spiritual in nature. You will have to work with the papal emissary, yet, he will confine his quest to the spiritual realm, and you will investigate the secular side of these matters. If you feel the emissary is crossing the line, I wish to know immediately."

"Yes, Imperial Majesty," Julien replied.

"You will have full use of the court's facilities, and you will receive your usual transport and lodging. I will increase your compensation to reflect your new title, Inspector General, and give you new credentials."

Julien felt a grin light his features. "Thank you, Imperial Majesty."

"You are dismissed. We will call for you when the emissary arrives."

Julien bowed before turning and walking towards the hall.

When the pope's emissary discovers that this is not a spiritual matter, he will not leave.

Julien's own personal, heretical beliefs would not allow for a spiritual answer to this question. He did not believe in a devil, though he knew evil everywhere in the world. At this point in his life, he questioned God's own existence, even the Gods and Goddesses his mother espoused. How could any deity allow such atrocities to happen in this world?

chapter two

Bath

The early evening turned the sky to a soft purple. Edward tried to remember what he wanted to acquire tonight at this particular shop. The shops in Bath offered much to buyers that ventured through the dangerous roads at night. Most merchants, weary of business, would offer great prices after nightfall.

One such weary trader from Antioch waxed impatient as Edward looked over minerals, while trying to avoid watching Máire.

She picked up a quartz crystal and played with it in the candlelight for a moment before placing it back on the table. Máire refused to dress according to the fashion of the era and locale, and so she left her hair uncovered, strands of it streaming like glossy and fiery ribbons down her back and shoulders. Her dress revealed too much of her grace. Women today hid beauty under shapeless clothing and veils that covered their hair and neck.

What a waste.

Why did he feel like a foolish, young boy staring wistfully at a toy he could not possess? Then again, many blood-drinkers considered the idea of possessing a single lover an absurdity and unnatural. After all, they shared the blood of fae and Gods. Monogamous love seemed a peculiar notion. Certainly, love existed between partners, but to limit oneself to just one lover would not be considered normal. Those who did often regretted their actions.

Arwin, Claudius, and Marcus would talk of stories of married blood-drinker couples who drove each other crazy after twenty or more years. Arwin himself had attempted faithfulness once, yet now, his ex-wife would barely speak with him.

Edward wished for a bit more of a connection with a woman, even if the relationship involved others. Máire could not deal with emotions at this point, so she remained a poor choice for his affections.

Marcus never appeared unhappy with his situation, and his bond with Máire seemed strained at times. That may have been why the invitations to join them had arrived over two hundred and fifty years ago, appearing just in the nick of time, as Edward had accidentally burned down Arwin's house a week earlier.

Their visit to Bath became a shared living situation. Máire and Marcus seemed content to stay in Bath as representatives for the Deargh Du and the Cothromaigh.

Claudius' arrival in Bath that same month came as no surprise, as he had become exhausted with the politics of the Sugnwr Gwaed. Claudius had resigned his leadership, annoyed with the constant bickering between the elder Britons and Romans and the newly transformed Angles, Jutes, and Saxons. Then, for a time, the Sugnwr Gwaed gave up on their internal squabbles in order to gather together with many Ekimmu Cruitne and pushed the remaining Ouphe out of the English kingdoms and Scotland. After the battle, Claudius had returned to London to work with the Sugnwr Gwaed council, but he left for Bath a scant week later, saying that he missed the hot baths too much.

Perhaps this was just an excuse to stay with family, at that point. Then again, the selection process for Sugnwr Gwaed leaders confused Edward. It involved tests of some sort upon which Claudius refused to elaborate.

Máire glanced back at the crystal. Edward found himself staring at her hair again while she looked away.

There would be no option for emotional closeness with Máire, but at least they shared friendship. Edward smiled in her direction. She must have noticed him staring at her through her peripheral vision, because she grinned back at him, before starting to walk through the shop.

The merchant cleared his throat in an impatient manner and addressed Edward. "Are you here for the brimstone again, my friend?"

"Oh yes," he replied, distracted by the dark blue swirl of Máire's gown as she paced.

The merchant nodded and then stated a price to begin the haggling. Edward's unfocused mind ignored the merchant's words.

"Oh all right," he said, not in the mood for the game, "just make it a pound." Edward ordered a relatively small amount, because both Marcus and Arwin worried about his experiments blowing up.

The merchant handed over the stinky substance in a woven bag.

"Anything else?" the merchant roared, as one would yell to the deaf.

"I do not think so," Edward replied in a calm voice.

The merchant rested his hand on Edward's arm and confided, "If I were you, I would not let my wife parade about Bath in such a fashion."

Edward sighed. "It would be wonderful if she were my wife," he replied. "If only that were so." He then realized Máire could hear his every word, as would any blood-drinker.

Máire burst out laughing. "Oh, Edward, I'd make you miserable," she stated. "Everyone knows I can't love. Seosaimhín made it so." She walked back to Edward from the back of the shop and patted his arm.

"I believe you would make any man pleased and content, if you were his wife," Edward replied before kissing her cheek. "Now, do you see anything you like?" he asked, wondering whether she would accept a gift.

Máire barked another unladylike laugh. She sometimes sounded a great deal like her father-in-darkness. "I must say your odor has been improving, that is until this moment." She smiled as she pulled away from him, her lips a gentle tease of movement. Why did the Deargh Du make themselves so… lovely?

"Do you think so?" he babbled. "I started wearing sandalwood oil to mask the scent of the materials I use in my experiments. I did not think you would notice. Should I try something different?"

"No, I meant what did you buy, Edward? It stinks!" she teased.

He stared at her, confused and a little hurt.

"Oh Edward, I just like to tease you and the others sometimes," she said. "Nothing here interests me, as I don't wish to reek of incendiary devices. Are you done with your shopping?"

"Yes," Edward answered.

"Alright, let's visit the scroll shop. I need some new reading materials, and Marcus' winnings threaten to burn a hole in his purse."

"Do you need help with that? I do not want my scrolls reeking, Edward." Máire glanced at him over her shoulder as she paced the scroll shop. She waved the empty coin purse with obvious glee, spinning it in a circle overhead as one might use a sling.

"No, I insist that I will carry back your scrolls," he offered with a smile, feeling rather foolish again. Edward hoped she would not hit any scrolls. Máire looked too happy, having emptied Marcus' purse.

"Edward, I have spent a mere drop in an ocean of wealth. He will not even notice. If he does notice, however, I hope this experience will make my point, that I am not to be fooled." Máire beamed at him. The radiance of her smile grew dazzling.

Just then, Máire seemed to lose her concentration, and her grip on the purse. Edward ducked as the coin purse flew over his head before hitting a series of handwritten tomes above the trader. The purse then fell harmlessly to the floor. Edward heard laughter before hearing the door close. Máire no longer stood in the store.

"Nice girl," commented the trader. "A bit odd, but she seems friendly and patient. You are a lucky man to have a wife like that."

Edward mumbled under his breath before paying the trader and gathering their scrolls.

"Are you sure you do not need help with those?" the Greek seller recommended as Edward started to stack them. A few scrolls obstructed his direct line of sight.

"If you could just open the door," Edward suggested. He soon heard bells ring in a cheerful manner. Assuming the trader held open the door, Edward turned and walked to the door and into another customer, who himself held a large number of scrolls. Following the collision, their papers lay strewn about the floor, a collage of white and beige.

"Oh, I am so sorry," a voice slurred in uncertain Latin.

The stranger picked up several scrolls from the floor and handed them to him. Edward muttered his thanks, before sorting through the papers, making sure that these were the scrolls he and Máire purchased.

"Edward, hurry up!" Máire called from outside.

Edward gave up checking the scrolls and hurried into the darkness with his burden. Hunger swelled in the pit of his stomach.

Máire curled up in the chair at her desk in the stronghold. She watched as Edward deposited her purchases and walked off, muttering something about alchemical elements of nature. She lit candles to make it easier to read. While her Deargh Du gifts enabled her to see well in the dark, she needed light to reflect their contents.

The first scroll she removed from the pile seemed new and fresh. She carefully unbound the scroll, unrolled it, and began reading in earnest.

The Greek writing seemed odd, in fact, she could not remember buying a single Greek scroll.

Máire read a few sentences and then sat down. She let the scroll drop from her fingers. In haste, she retrieved the vellum from the floor before heading towards Edward's quarters.

"Edward!" Máire shouted as she banged on the door.

The door opened, revealing Edward's head. He shushed her before whispering, "I'm working on something... something that requires my concentration."

"Edward, are some of your scrolls missing?" she asked, trying to remain calm.

"Yes," he answered, "one of mine. I bumped into another customer at the shop, and we must have swapped scrolls."

"Praise the Gods for clumsiness! Your ungainliness has brought forth new knowledge," she rallied, feeling great excitement. Máire turned back to the hallway in order to return to her room.

"What is this new knowledge?" he asked, stopping her.

Sometimes Edward found new wisdom as exciting as she did.

She regarded Edward once more. "It's a myth detailing the creation of the Strigoi in Greek. I know next to nothing about that line of blood-drinkers. It is most interesting."

She studied Edward for a moment before continuing. "So, you swear on Sulis, the ancient Patroness of Bath that you did not deceive me with these scrolls. This is not another joke, right?" Máire met Edward's pale, blue eyes.

"I swear," he answered.

She nodded her head. Marcus must know about these scrolls. "I owe you many thanks," she began. She spun on her heel and strode back to her room to gather the mysterious scroll.

"Marcus! Marcus!" Máire called as she ran to the downstairs baths, paying little attention to their resplendence. She finally saw his naked form floating on his back in the water. His eyes remained shut as if he slept. He appeared to be at peace.

Her joy at learning about the true origins of the Strigoi gave her a strange and fevered excitement. She could not understand why this news seemed so important, but it did. Máire placed the scroll on a table, safe from the large cooling pool, and leaned over the edge of the water.

The cool, wavy surface of the pool reflected the frescos on the walls, revealing mythical figures dressed in tones of blue and silver. She raised her eyes to look directly at the walls and noticed that the drawings concentrated on the Tuaths and the Twylyth Teg, rather than the legendary tales in the lives of Greek and Roman Deities. A few Roman figures remained in the drawings, but their space on the walls seemed small, although Roman forms dominated the statues guarding the pools.

Máire crouched next to the pool, cupped her hand into the cool water, and then splashed Marcus. She tried to keep from laughing as she disrupted his meditation.

Marcus sputtered and spat out water, before shifting his body so he treaded water. "There are less intrusive and irritating ways of gaining my attention, you realize. Next time, why not try jumping in?"

As Marcus swam towards her, Máire pulled away, remembering the times he would pull her off balance into the pool.

"This is important," Máire insisted, trying not to laugh as he reached out and clutched her arm. She yanked it away before grabbing the scroll. "We must discuss this. It's important... very important."

She noticed his eyes turn quicksilver gray, which indicated irritation. Perhaps she had spoiled his fun. Sometimes he could be so cranky.

Marcus rested his arms on the edge of the pool and stared at her. "Máire, there is more to life than what resides within scrolls! Do you think I care about the information contained in this particular scroll when I have not been able to relax since the feast? I wish to finish my bath. I do hope you enjoyed spending my winnings. I had planned to purchase a lovely gift for you, but now you'll have to settle for that scroll."

She watched his lips turn up in a bemused half-smile. With the apparent dissolution of his annoyance, Marcus pushed away from the edge and began swimming again.

"Marcus," she pleaded, "this is no joke! Please listen. It is very interesting, and I think it is something that may aid us in our future duties for the Cothromaigh."

At that moment, Leander walked into the bath chamber, cleared his throat, and said, "Sir, there are two people waiting for you upstairs."

"Really, Leander?" Marcus asked as he swam over to the edge of the pool again. Máire could see him watching Leanders' approach. "Do these visitors have names?"

"They would not say, my lord. The woman says she is a cortigiana and that you and she met long ago. I did not understand her meaning, and asked for a name, but I..." Leander trailed off before rubbing his forehead. "She said it was not necessary. It was a most strange conversation. Indira allowed them in first and seemed greatly affected by their presence. My own wife barely seemed to recognize me."

Máire looked down at Marcus, who looked concerned.

"That does not seem like Indira," Marcus murmured.

Leander nodded his head. "My apologies for not handling this matter, sir." Leandros Galerius' descendent then lowered his head.

"Leander, I believe this is no fault of yours or Indira's. I think I know why you and she are not yourselves. Bring our guests to the baths," Marcus instructed. Leander nodded and then started to leave the room.

Marcus motioned for Máire to toss him a sheet. "We will try to not keep you and the rest of the mortals awake for much longer," he called as Leander exited the baths. Marcus swore he heard, "Yes, Dominus."

Máire grabbed the scroll before finding a clean, folded sheet on a side table. She then tossed the sheet near him, happy to see him have to leap in order to catch it before it could drop into the water. With the moment concluded, Máire returned to contemplating the identities of their guests.

"Who could it be? I've never seen Leander so pale, and Indira is as stubborn and stalwart as her ancestor, Berti." Máire stated, before regarding Marcus. "What is 'cortigiana'? I mean, I understand what it means, but is it a code?"

"Other than its' normal meanings, 'lover' or 'highly-paid prostitute', I have no idea whether it's a code or something else." Marcus started to wipe his face, but he remained in the pool.

She turned away from him, smelling an odd fragrance, and then she sensed them. "Lamia," she whispered. Máire used her gifts to race to the first candelabra she could wield as a weapon. "Two," she confirmed as she sensed the second Lamia. Three sets of footsteps echoed from the stairs.

Marcus caught her attention and motioned her to stand down.

She obeyed and set down the candelabra, but she felt disappointed.

Leander opened the door for the two blood-drinkers, who walked into the chamber. Máire studied them intently. The first, a female Lamia, turned a curious, crystal-blue stare in her direction. The woman brushed off a wet strand of ink-colored tresses from her shoulder.

A Lamia soldier stood behind her, or Máire believed him to be a soldier or some sort of bodyguard. She could tell nothing more about him at the moment. Máire returned her attention to Marcus.

He smiled at his guests for a moment, peering at them from within the pool, displaying only calm resolution, much in line with his normal disposition. Máire contemplated his temperament as a mortal soldier.

"Domina Amata, what an interesting surprise," Marcus commented. "Are you two at the head of an invading army that desires my surrender," Marcus drawled as he walked to the steps of the pool, climbed out, and began patting himself dry, "or do you wish to supplicate yourselves and surrender to me?"

She watched Marcus wrap the sheet around his waist facing them.

"Neither, I am afraid," the female Lamia, Amata, replied.

Máire wondered whether Marcus would introduce her or leave her as nameless as Amata's guard.

Amata smiled at Marcus. Her ivory-colored face beamed like a marble statue in candlelight, which seemed odd for the face of a Lamia.

"I do remember great pleasure when last I supplicated to you. I miss those times together," she added. "Sadly, we are here to discuss other matters, Marcus."

"What other matters would the Lamia wish to discuss with us?" Máire asked, interrupting them. She found herself tired of being ignored.

"Calm yourself, Máire," Marcus replied, giving her a small grin. He motioned Leander to gather his clothing with a mere inclination of his head. He took the proffered tunic, breeches, and belt, and started to dress. "Máire, show our guests to the gathering room. We can discuss these other matters there, Amata. Leander, please ask the others to prepare proper refreshments for our guests. Thank you."

Máire sighed, realizing she had been dismissed. She headed for the staircase, motioning for the Lamia to follow her.

"Recline and rest," Marcus said, while motioning to the strange couches.

Máire took a seat in one of the lounges, finding it most uncomfortable, as always. The red material felt silky and luxuriant, yet still alien to her skin. Máire studied Amata as the Lamia curled up on another lounge opposite from Marcus. The soldier stood at attention, meeting Máire's eyes for a moment. His blue eyes reminded her of the sapphire-colored sea from her days as a mortal. They seemed a stark contrast to his straw-colored hair and pale skin.

"Máire, will you not join us in the spirit of the occasion? Relax, as you see Domina Amata doing. After all, it is not every day that actual Romans get to appreciate my customs and accoutrements."

She noticed both Lamia look about as if somewhat impressed.

"This is quite elegant, Marcus. Would you not agree, Legate?" Amata's crystalline blue eyes moved to gaze upon her escort.

"Domina, this reminds me of Trajan's imperial home. However, it is somewhat strange to see a fourth lounge," he told her. Máire watched the soldier smile, revealing his teeth.

Amata looked over her surroundings again. "Yes, but I suppose, Marcus entertains more than nine people at a time. This is a lovely home, Marcus, yet it is missing slaves. It is so nice to have people to do things. One man to pluck grapes from a bushel and pop them in my mouth, one to fan me, and of course one to drench my face with the pearly cream of the Gods." Máire thought of her own servants from her time as a mortal.

Máire tried not to groan as Amata shared a most musical laugh.

Amata's smile faded. "I am pleased with such gracious hospitality, Marcus. Truly I am. Thank you." She lowered her eyes, revealing some embarrassment.

"I imagine that only a dire situation would have brought the two of you alone, all this way to Bath," Marcus stated.

Amata glanced at the Legate and then regarded Máire and Marcus again.

The Legate bowed his head. "We humbly request an alliance with the Deargh Du to deal with a common enemy," he bade.

Marcus stared at Amata as her face lowered. Máire wondered why he did not acknowledge the Legate. However, she still fumed at the lack of formal introductions. Máire demanded recognition and respect.

"I can contain myself no longer," Máire began, rising from her lounge. "Why do you not look at this fellow Roman? Why do you not acknowledge he stands there? Why have I not been announced?"

She walked to Amata with long strides.

"I am Máire Ní Conghal Uí Maine, former chieftain of my clan. Who are you, Amata?" Máire drawled, hearing sarcasm lace her words.

The other woman rose from her lounge and met Máire's stare with glowing, red eyes. Máire could sense an ensuing battle, yet the other blood-drinker closed her eyes in apparent restraint.

"Forgive me, Máire Ní Conghal Uí Maine. I am Tertia Amata Antonia, Co-Consul of the Lamia," Amata offered, bowing her head.

Máire nodded back at the other woman. "Thank you for the honor of learning your name though you have many," she mumbled in Gaelic.

"In answer to your question, this is the Legate, Patroclus Statilius Messalinus," Amata added. "The reason Marcus has not acknowledged him in this formal visit is because I have not given the Legate leave yet to be conversational. He is, after all, a soldier, and I am his commander." She turned on her heel to face the Legate. "However, I feel we should dispense with the formal bearing. I suppose we should learn the cultural differences between the Hibernians, Britons, Scots, Saxons, and we Romans so we will not insult one another were my actions considered rude?" Amata asked as she turned to regard Marcus.

"In the Hibernian and Briton way of thinking," Marcus began, "yes, Domina."

Máire watched Amata smirk at her.

"Marcus is socially my better, and yet he calls me 'lady'," Amata chuckled. "He is without a doubt the most polite of blood-drinkers. Please stop referring to me as Domina, Marcus. It is unseemly. You are Deargh Du, not my underling. As I was saying, let us dispense with the formal bearing and make our meeting smooth. Patroclus, join us. Take a glass of... what is this?" she asked, indicating the goblet before her.

"It is bloodmead," Marcus replied. "As you already know, blood keeps better when mixed with fermented drinks. Mead is–"

"Made from honey. I am not an utter fool on regional beverages," Amata chuckled, taking a sip of her drink. "It is very sweet and most pleasant," Amata offered before gesturing to the Legate. "Patroclus, sit."

"Very well." Patroclus walked to the lounge next to Máire's and took one of the goblets.

Máire watched Amata and Patroclus relax on the lounges and attempted to do the same. She caught Marcus watching her with bemused eyes, entertained by her improper posture and discomfort.

"So," Marcus began, "please tell me about this enemy we share."

"Have you ever heard of the Strigoi?" Amata asked.

"Yes," Marcus replied.

"They are attacking and killing Lamia and mortals, though mostly mortals are their victims," Amata explained. "Their control expands to Central and Northern Europe."

"I have heard of these beings," Máire said, wondering whether she needed to make mention of her scroll. She shifted around, trying to find a comfortable position. "Though I will admit to the fact that I have never seen one. Even with readings about them, I do not have a clear image of how they look and of what they are capable." She watched the Legate close his eyes.

"Once you see a Strigoi, you will never forget. They are as ugly as the Deargh Du are radiant." Patroclus' blue eyes opened and settled on her for a moment. "I hear the mortals call them 'Satan incarnate'. They believe these creatures to be demons. One cannot help but think of such stories as folklore and mythology run amok. However," he added as he looked over at Amata and Marcus. They both leaned forward, towards Patroclus. "The mortals' description of devils is not far off."

"They are monstrous, yet weak. While their bodies are frail and they die within fifty years of their transformation, they have a significant and lethal weapon at their disposal," Patroclus warned. "Madness."

The Legate leaned forward before continuing. "We are not too sure about their creation, but their curse does not only extend to deformity of the body… it seems to affect their brains as well."

"The curse of Venus," Máire mumbled, recalling her recent research.

She saw the three other blood-drinkers turn to study her.

"I found a scroll detailing their creation. By coincidence, I decided to bring it to Marcus' attention." She picked it up from a table and tossed it over to Marcus. "The tale says that an Athenian named Iris, whose beauty matched that of Helen of Troy, feared someone might be believed to be lovelier than her. A female stranger came to Athens, whom Iris feared was more beautiful, and so Iris became enraged and scarred her visitor. I am certain you three know who had taken the guise of this woman." Blank stares greeted her.

Máire took a sip of bloodmead and continued. "Venus, or Aphrodite, cursed Iris. She took all her beauty, and the loss of self-image was too much for Iris, and so she went insane and became the first of all Strigoi."

Amata sighed. "I could care less about the mythical story of Iris. I just wish to understand how to destroy the Strigoi. Patroclus, continue with your knowledge of them."

Máire stared at her feet, disgusted that her research seemed to matter little. She looked up as Patroclus continued, and his eyes settled on her.

"As I said before, their weapon is madness," Patroclus began anew. "The very derangement that infects their minds can be projected into others. Horrors from victims' memories become reality. For immortals, this causes paralysis, which gives Strigoi the chance to kill blood-drinkers without the risk of retaliation.

"However, a mortal is not so fortunate," Patroclus continued. "While the Strigoi feed as do other blood-drinkers, the victims of their feeding are struck with incurable insanity for the remainder of their miserable lives. What is even worse, the Strigoi can maim and kill mortals with their madness."

"How do you mean?" Máire asked, in a half-whisper.

"I suppose they can manipulate internal pressures within their victims, my la– Máire," the legate answered. He had grown paler within the last few moments. Patroclus took a long draught on the bloodmead before continuing. "In the thrall of a Strigoi, the mortals begin to bleed from the nose, mouth, eyes, ears, and even from their pores. They scream, and then they try to scratch their eyes and deafen themselves. I have witnessed mortals banging their heads against the walls, trying to silence their own screams or fears."

Máire gulped down the rest of her bloodmead.

"What of the Lamia armies and the other blood-drinkers on the continent?" Marcus asked.

"We have been pushed back at every encounter," the legate replied. "Those of us who are not under the spell of their madness have just moments to pull the paralyzed out of the fray. The other lines have moved into hiding. We've had no contact with them."

"For all we know," Amata added. "Those lines may have been annihilated, as we have heard little from them. What few messages have we received recommended hiding ourselves within our temple."

Marcus smiled for a moment. Máire could tell he wished to say something about the Lamia tending to hide during the last few centuries.

"Returning to Patroclus' statements, I find it incredible to believe the Lamia were pushed back," Marcus began. "I remember the fighting style of the Lamia and how they reminded one of the golden days of Rome. These Strigoi must be quite effective, especially to send all of the other lines into hiding."

"It seems as though the Strigoi can hide in plain sight, even with their dreadful and repulsive appearance," Patroclus stated. "They seem to travel individually or within small bands. If you encounter one, more follow quickly, yet I have never heard them call to each other. They just seem to know…" His words trailed off, as he seemed to take a moment to consider his next sentence.

"They attack from all sides, with mere utterances of evil that can pierce through one's heart. Their numbers seem to quadruple in an instant. There are voices, so many, many voices, overlapping, speaking in different tongues."

Patroclus began to rub his forehead, and his voice began to break, revealing fear. "Then the images came, colors, changing before my eyes like the rush of a strange rainbow. The colors then became solid and appeared to come from the ground, threatening to engulf me. Forces seemed to pull me from so many different directions, and darkness closed in." Patroclus stopped for a moment.

"Even in the darkness, the voices grew louder. If you were lucky, your comrades would drag you away, and hopefully you would wake, thinking it was all some strange nightmare." His voice choked.

Amata arose from her couch and walked over to the Legate, placing her hands on his shoulders. She rubbed him with what looked to be gentle touches.

"Patroclus lost half of his men in a battle with forty Strigoi. His lieutenant managed to carry him out," Amata said.

Marcus rocked back and forth, rubbing his hands together in earnest agitation. His newly green eyes glowed, revealing tension. He then clapped his hands. "Leander!" he called out as his words echoed in the house. "Go find the others and bid them join us." Marcus then marched to his writing desk and began to scribble onto a piece of parchment.

Máire looked over to Amata and Patroclus before clearing her throat. "Would my blood assist him?" she offered.

The Legate looked up at her with eyes that belied a strange mixture of confusion and fear.

"That is a very kind offer," Amata replied with what looked like a true smile.

Máire moved closer to Patroclus. "You seem very troubled at having to retell such horrors," she said. "Our blood can give relief to other blood-drinkers. At the very least, it will give you a moment of peace. Allow me to be a proper hostess." She sat down next to the Legate and extended her arm.

"You are most kind," Patroclus praised as his eyes focused on hers for a moment. He turned his face to her wrist. Máire watched as he extended his fangs, bit her arm, and began to drink.

Her initial pain faded into a dull throb. Máire chuckled, hoping she could calm him. She could now smell a cold sweat from the Legate.

"Be tranquil now," Máire suggested. "I have been frightened of many things as a mortal and as Deargh Du. It would be wrong for me not to try to balance your fear, if that makes sense. Besides, it is considered rude in Eire, as well as here, to not meet the needs of guests."

"Even if they are former enemies?" Amata asked with a raised brow.

"Even if they are current enemies," Marcus replied while he continued writing. "Hospitality is very important amongst the villages here. It is the height of rudeness to not give what your guests require."

"This sharing and welcome can make friends of enemies," Máire added, feeling a bit foolish at this point. Romans, with the exception of a few, would probably not understand the motives behind hospitality.

Máire patted the Legate's back with her left hand, signaling an end to his feeding. Patroclus released her wrist and then leaned back. Soon the sound of footsteps echoed from upstairs, and then all grew silent. The Legate smiled, as if in a mild daze.

"That was delicious," Patroclus whispered.

She could sense that the other blood-drinkers stood near, yet they remained still. Then she heard the sound of blades being drawn.

"Marcus, Máire are you well?" Claudius called out.

"We smell Lamia and blood," Edward added. Then she heard the sound of what she believed to be Mac Alpin muffling Edward.

"Calm yourselves, for we have guests," Marcus called back.

"You can smell us?" Amata asked.

"May I point out to you three that you just revealed a secret to our guests?" Marcus yelled from his writing table. "Now please come in and join us. Sheath your swords. I promised our guests that they would not be harmed."

The three Celtic blood-drinkers walked into the room. Edward and Mac Alpin appeared stunned. Claudius glared at the Lamia with a mixture of disgust and confusion.

Marcus turned to regard the Lamia. "These are friends of ours... Arwin Mac Alpin, Edward, and Claudius Metrius Sertorius. I believe you have met Arwin and Claudius on the field of battle." The three Celtic blood-drinkers remained still and silent.

"This is Tertia Amata Antonia and Legate Patroclus Statilius Messalinus," Marcus added.

"Yes, I remember them," Claudius said. "I remember that fateful night when a hundred good soldiers, men and women, Deargh Du and other races, died. Soldiers that Arwin, Marcus, and I had trained. All dead." His words ended in a terse hiss.

"They died for a fool's errand," Mac Alpin spat. "And here, poor Máire has to suffer their feeding to be a good hostess."

"Please, you two. They are here, seeking an alliance," Marcus explained.

"What!?" Claudius roared.

Máire looked over at Mac Alpin, who raised a brow at Claudius' unusual outburst.

"Is this true?" Mac Alpin asked while glancing at Marcus.

Marcus finished his letter and then handed it to Claudius. "I do not have time to repeat what has transpired this evening, old friend." Mac Alpin and Edward leaned over Claudius' shoulder to read the message.

"Suffice it to say, the Lamia have encountered a vile enemy that also threatens mortals and immortals here and in Eire," Marcus continued. "They have requested our assistance. I need to send the message you hold to the Deargh Du council to prepare them for our arrival."

"You are taking them to Eire to meet the council?" Edward asked. Mac Alpin and Claudius continued reading the message.

"Claudius, if you do not doubt my decision, seal that note and make haste for Ard Macha. If you believe my decision is a poor one, you have my leave to ignore this request and return to your routine with my apologies," Marcus said, before addressing the Lamia. "You two may read this note as well."

Edward finished the note and then backed off. His countenance became dark and fraught with concern.

Mac Alpin and Claudius' eyes skimmed over the note many times, and their expressions changed from anger to horror and shock.

"I will deliver this in all haste," Claudius stated before clasping arms with Marcus.

"Travel with Her blessing," Marcus offered in Gaelic.

Claudius raced out of the room.

Máire noticed Marcus follow Claudius' departure before regarding Mac Alpin and Edward. "Would you two like to take a boat ride with us to Ulster? We must depart for Caer Oder and then sail to Ulster. I know of your fondness for ocean water."

"A little seawater will not kill us, eh?" Arwin bellowed as he elbowed Edward.

Edward coughed before covering his mouth. His face turned green, causing Máire to wonder whether he had almost vomited.

"So, Deargh Du cannot cross oceans? I know you've traveled over water before," Amata stated. "I assumed you would fly there and leave us to find passage."

"Forgive me, Amata, but I forgot to tell you that Edward and Arwin are Ekimmu Cruitne, and yes, their line grows ill crossing bodies of salt water. Generally, they are not fond of it," Marcus replied. "We Deargh Du, however, have no such geis. We would be happy to sail with you across the sea. Claudius will fly ahead of us to Ulster in order to give them advanced notice of our arrival." Marcus grinned at them.

"And Claudius is Deargh Du?" Amata incorrectly ascertained.

"No, he is Sugnwr Gwaed. However, the three Celtic lines have most of the same abilities," Marcus replied.

"Yet, Máire is definitely Deargh Du," the Legate observed after a long silence, his wits apparently returned. "There is no question on that."

"Yes, she is my daughter-in-darkness. That is the term we use, as opposed to sponsor, patron, initiate, acolyte, or other words or phrases I have forgotten, which all mean the same. We have a connection by blood."

Marcus pulled Máire up off the couch and announced, "Now let us commence packing. We have a long voyage ahead."

chapter three

Caer Oder

The sound of the rain against the ship seemed peaceful and soothing to Máire, despite the storms, which surged over them. The Lamia, however, grumbled about the weather. Amata had seemed to be in a foul mood ever since they reached the ancient port town of Caer Oder, almost as if she, and perhaps other Lamia, despised the rain and cold of the north. Upon boarding the ship, Amata promptly secured the captain's quarters for herself and for Patroclus, Mac Alpin and Edward took spots in the storage, and Máire and Marcus took two of the crew's hammocks.

"I suppose that we are indeed lucky that the Verys had spots for us," she commented. With a groan, Máire sank down to sit on the floor. The hammocks smelled rank, and she did not wish to spend more time in them than necessary.

"Arthur is always accommodating," Marcus commented. "I think he was a little surprised, though, that I wished to book passage for people instead of supplies."

Máire nodded her head. "How do you think our reception will be?"

Marcus smiled before sitting across from her. "Poor, I fear, excepting for those few Deargh Du, living in the stronghold, who like the Roman and his whore. Those few will be most happy to see us, I think. Of course we are both exiles, banned from returning on pain of death, unless circumstances warrant our trespass."

"I should say these circumstances warrant our return, don't you?" Máire asked.

"Indeed," replied Marcus.

Máire smiled. "I miss Eire, but not always the Deargh Du."

"Yes, I feel the same. However, sometimes I sense a calling to come back to Eire." Marcus rubbed at the day's growth of beard on his chin. "Now, come sit beside me and tell me more about the Strigoi. Knowing their origin could serve us well."

Máire grinned as she scooted next to Marcus. A squeak signaled the arrival of a rat, and Marcus' swift movement brought him a snack.

He looked into Máire's eyes. She assumed he intended to share.

"Not unless I'm starving," she countered, chuckling.

"Mmmmm, I remember a time when I would have celebrated finding a rat." Marcus sniffed it and said. "It's diseased. Best I kill it before any mortals fall ill." He turned it over and then bit into the rat's side.

"It smells vile," Máire gasped.

"It tastes just as bad," Marcus commented. "Tell me more about the Strigoi, and then we could play Fidchell, if you want. I brought my set." He grinned. Marcus never tired of games.

"We'll play Fidchell after we get to Ard Macha. I'm exhausted," Máire replied.

The boat rocked for a moment as the captain called for the crew to cast off from the docks.

"Well, Iris was not the only person who Aphrodite cursed," Máire added. "Aphrodite apparently went on a rampage, before realizing what a strange effect Her curse had on mortals. According to the story, She tried a number of cures, some of which worked. However, use of such cures disappeared when the worship of the Olympians faded away."

Máire paused in order to glance at Marcus. "Anyway," she continued, "the first cursed ones still had some characteristics of being mortal. They bred with each other, giving birth to children, yet their brood hated the light as we do. Then the Strigoi found a taste for blood and stopped giving birth to little Strigoi. They became blood-drinkers, somehow. The scroll does not speculate why. The last comments within the writings indicate the Strigoi prefer caves and travel in small groups."

"Amata may find little use in knowledge about these beings, but I am grateful my coin went to an excellent cause," he reasoned aloud.

Marcus rose to his feet, stepped over to one of the hammocks, and sat down on its edge. He then rolled into the hammock and turned onto his side, exaggerating each movement as a seductive stretch. He patted the hammock next to his and gestured for Máire to sit down.

She tossed a blanked over the dirty hammock and climbed in.

"Let us sleep on this new knowledge. Things always appear clearer after sleep. Sleep well, Banbh Ceanúil," Marcus murmured, using her nickname in Gaelic. He blew her a kiss before leaning over to extinguish the lamp.

"Rest well, General," Máire purred as she settled into the hammock. "Just do not let Amata and her soldier know that you call me Banbh Ceanúil. I don't mind you, Claudius, Edward, or Mac Alpin calling me that name, but I would prefer that Amata and Mandubratius did not."

"Your nickname will remain our secret," Marcus promised. "At least, they will not know about it from me."

Máire extended her hand towards him and smiled as his fingers wound about hers.

Kalikata, India

The years of walking through the shadows seemed to pass like soft, radiant moments, drifting across moonbeams that could charm the coldest of hearts. Seosaimhín lost track of time since leaving Eire. The east beckoned with an extended finger, and she grasped that finger like an eager child. Here, the people accepted the world of death with little fear, permitting her studies to continue while surrounded by silks and strange-smelling spices. The rest of reality seemed but a blur.

"No more makeup of white for us," she said to the walls of their room within the temple. Here, the people gathered for insight. They worshipped her and the others as an avatar of some strange Goddess of theirs named Kali. Yet, for now, no one transgressed this sanctuary.

Sometimes, they forgot their names, forgot their mortality, and forgot that they were not Kali, but were something else. Seosaimhín closed her eyes, but the sound of beating wings and thousands of voices, though with one demanding dominion over the others, woke her.

"Do you hear those voices?" Nagirrom asked. His voice eclipsed the growing din of confusing sounds. She opened her, eyes and the room faded away, replaced with the green trees and grass of the lands to the west. Then the green merged with dancing colors that swarmed around. The white crow landed on a nearby tree, remaining static and pure white, like an avian snowflake, a strong beacon of light.

"Do you hear those voices again, my child?" Nagirrom queried.

Seosaimhín looked around the growing field and sylvan landscape. "We hear a cacophony of sounds. It is like standing amidst a throng of gossiping matrons."

Nagirrom laughed, apparently finding amusement in her words. "These are the words of the Strigoi. Have you heard of them?"

"My mind delves into the pools of knowledge, yet none of us have found the bottom," Seosaimhín answered.

"The Strigoi are a race cursed by Venus. They are not my children, yet they can serve my ends, with your leadership."

"Yes, great Nagirrom," Seosaimhín whispered. "What do you need from these sheep in your service?"

"Go and adopt them as your children," He suggested. "Teach them focus and clarity, for they are powerful, but they are scattered. Try to bring them together. You can harness their power, Seosaimhín. Then, unleash them upon the mortals and blood-drinkers of this plane."

"It shall be as you desire," Seosaimhín assured the white crow.

Nagirrom cawed before taking off in flight. The bird flew in a circle over her head and then banked, diving straight toward Seosaimhín.

Seosaimhín opened her eyes at the moment of impact, but no bird had struck. She rubbed her eyes, seeing only the ornate interior of the temple. "It shall be as you desire," she repeated.

Aachen

The messenger banged on the door and then walked in, giving Julien a moment's notice to finish his entry regarding the day's events. The sun had faded away, and the night drew close.

"Inspector General, the papal emissary and his entourage will arrive at the palace in an hour at most," the messenger began. "Emperor Charles requests your presence at his arrival."

Julien gathered his cloak. "Give me a few minutes to change." He wished the emissary would have given them all more time to prepare.

Julien rushed into the palace, ignoring the rain and mud. He moved around the edge of the courtiers to get a look at the papal emissary. A cloak hid the emissary's features, until the emissary pushed back his hood. Julien could hear soft murmurs of approval from the emperor's daughters and granddaughters. He felt a bit of annoyance at that. What could possibly be so wonderful about an Italian stranger? Julien figured that the papal emissary would be quite hairy, emaciated from spending time fasting and at prayers, nearsighted, and probably suffered from a huge beak of a Roman nose.

He felt some disappointment in noticing that ugliness had no influence on the pope's emissary. In fact, Julien could now understand why the emperor's female family members seemed taken with their visitor. Still, the papal emissary would probably be of little use in the field, as he and his party seemed too well dressed for any serious traveling.

The emissary bowed to the emperor with a gentle grace and presented the papal documents, fastened with Pope Leo's seal.

"Michael Tolomei," the emperor addressed with a nod. "All your requests have been met. Welcome to our humble home. Is this the first time you have been to Aachen?"

Julien recognized the name of one of the leading families in Rome, but a nudge and giggling from a neighbor distracted him from the emissary's reply and the ensuing conversation. Gundrada, the emperor's cousin, smiled, pointing out his muddy shoes with a waggling a finger.

He felt his cheeks bloom and heat as she and several other women started adjusting his clothing and wiping off smudges of dirt. Julien felt like a very young boy being cleaned up for important guests as the emperor's daughters, nieces, and cousins spat into their fingers, and on pieces of cloth, and began swabbing at the flecks of mud on his face and neck.

"Inspector General, it is nice of you to join us," shouted the emperor before laughing. The rest of the court joined in the merriment at Julien's expense. At least his clothes were dry

Julien looked on as the emperor glanced at his guest. "Despite his sullied appearance, Julien de Divio has a talent for taking care of troublemakers in these lands. He also saved me from several assassins, and he managed to find them shortly thereafter."

The emperor returned his blue-eyed stare to Julien. "Now, if you do not mind us continuing with the business at hand..." The emperor smiled at the ladies and then motioned for their dispersal with his hands. Soon, the room became bereft of women. "Julien, I wish to introduce you to His Holiness' Emissary, Michael Tolomei."

Julien watched the dark-haired stranger walk toward him and extend his right hand. A ring, bearing the seal of the pope, encircled his middle finger.

Julien hesitated for a moment and then bowed and kissed the ring. He looked up and witnessed a pair of green eyes studying him, amusement pooling within them. He rose and turned back to the emperor.

"Inspector General, as we have discussed, you are in charge of the secular half of this investigation." The emperor's gaze shifted to the emissary. "I felt it may be necessary for you to have assistance if this is indeed a secular matter."

"I would have it no other way, your Imperial Majesty," Michael answered. "Yet, I believe the devil does stalk these lands."

"Well my... lord?" Julien began, uncertain how to refer to the emissary. "I endeavor to offer you the tools of the trade that I feel we need to unearth this culprit, whether he is the devil or a demented man."

"Excellent, then we will start on our search tomorrow night," Michael replied. "These demons attack at night, and I do not want to waste the hours with sleep."

Julien tried to guess the emissary's place of birth by his accent, yet he could not find success.

"I will leave you to work out these details," Emperor Charles stated, as he touched Julien's left shoulder with his right hand.

"Walk with me, if you will, Inspector General," the emissary requested before heading out of the court chamber.

Julien followed him through the corridors and down the steps. The emissary remained silent during his walk, leaving him to ponder the necessity of leaving the court. In the distance, Julien could hear the sound of the hot springs splashing over rocks. A hot bath could offer the relaxation he needed.

Perhaps the emperor would invite him for a swim with the rest of the court after Julien completed his duties. Then again, perhaps this journey would allow him time to visit Divio and see his brother's family. The children seemed taller every time he called on Reginald and Flor.

Julien's distraction ceased as Michael stopped walking and turned to face him. The emissary's green eyes blazed with a strange intensity, and then a somewhat worrisome smile gleamed over Michael's visage.

"You paused before you knelt to kiss my ring. Why?"

Julien began to reply, but the emissary interrupted him.

"Are you a heretic or non-believer?" Michael demanded.

Julien waited to make sure he would not be interrupted before saying, "I am a humble servant of Christ. I am in awe of being in the presence of an emissary of His Holiness and his ring."

"Prove to me that you are a servant of Jesus," Michael ordered.

"How do you wish for me to prove this?" Julien asked.

"During Christ's temptation, quote for me how he rebuked Satan after the forty days and nights of fasting," Michael challenged.

Julien closed his eyes for a moment, trying to remember the scriptures that the abbot had insisted he learn.

"'Get thee behind me, Satan: for it is written, you shall worship the Lord your God, and Him only shall you serve'," he quoted, wondering whether his memorization of the words would suffice, but he began to second-guess his memory.

"Very well done, but simple recall of the material does not make you a true soldier of Christ. I will be watching you, and so will God, Julien de Divio."

"I welcome the scrutiny, for I have nothing to be ashamed of," Julien answered, hoping he sounded convincing. He knew he had sinned in the eyes of God, but his own morals did not match with the Christian morals taught by the monks and abbots.

"God will be the judge of your sins," Michael Tolomei replied, before turning on his heel and marching back into the emperor's home.

Ard Macha

Claudius gazed upon the new Ard Macha, much larger than he remembered, and observed traders who hocked their wares in the torch-lit roads. They spoke in both Latin and Gaelic, now. Soon, their calls to potential customers grew quiet, as the stars and crescent moon became bright in the night sky. A few merchants began closing up their carts and settling in for the night.

Claudius walked over to the gate in a wall that surrounded what appeared to be a somewhat modest house. A sweet, telltale scent overwhelmed him as he moved towards the gate. As modest as the home appeared to be, the ornate and well-crafted stone wall surrounding it gave too much away, in his opinion.

He saw a few faces at the rear of the yard turn towards him in recognition. Their owners nodded, before moving towards the gate. Before they got too close, their captain pushed them away and then walked over to the gate to speak with Claudius.

"What do you want, you pizzle-drinking blood-drinker?" The strange Deargh Du captain yelled at him in old British. Claudius felt some unexpected pleasure at the recognition of his line, but he had to wonder why a Deargh Du would shout so that the entire village and the surrounding farms to hear.

"I have a message for Sáerlaith," he replied in Gaelic, in a much quieter voice. "My name is Claudius Metrius Sertorius." The Deargh Du who seemed to recognize him began to open the gate.

"Halt and close the gates," the Captain shouted as he cuffed one of his soldiers. "Give me the message," the captain retorted.

"But sir," someone began, "I fought with Claudius at Bonniconlon." A chorus of other recognizable and memorable male and female voices began to agree. No one moved to close the gate.

"Quiet!" the captain yelled, causing the guards fall silent.

Claudius walked through the partly open gate.

"I fought the Lamia with the Deargh Du," Claudius explained. "I even trained many of those I see here tonight in the arts of Roman warfare. I am also a member of the Sugnwr Gwaed Assembly." He nodded to the few familiar faces who whispered proper greetings.

The captain blocked his path and leaned in. "I don't care who you are. All I know is that you're nothing more than one of The Hunt, and I abhor your line almost as much as Morrigan's bastards," the captain whispered, though it seemed to be more of a growl.

Claudius chuckled, impatient for this oaf to let him in. "The Hunter and I have little time for this. My words are for Sáerlaith alone. Now, either let me pass, or I will rip your tongue out of your mouth."

The Deargh Du unsheathed his sword.

Claudius lifted the guard's sword arm and stabbed him in the stomach with the concealed dagger in his left hand. He then grabbed the sword, tossed it away, and seized the guard by his throat with his left hand. Claudius wiped the blood from his dagger on the Deargh Du's tunic before sheathing it. He glanced at the other Deargh Du, who were watching him as he pried the guard captain's jaw open, gripped his tongue with his fingers, and ripped it out. Blood drenched Claudius' arm.

"I am a man of my word," he said to the gathered Deargh Du, "though

I am sure most of you remember that." He tossed the tongue away before wiping his bloody arm on a clean spot on the captain's tunic.

The captain stared up at him with his bloody maw gaped open. He appeared to be more in shock than in pain.

"It will grow back," Claudius said with a shrug.

He heard chuckles and laughter. The friendlier Deargh Du began to chatter at him and ask about his journey.

"Did you come across any Vikings?" Maon asked.

"We hear that more are coming our way," Fianait added.

"Later, later," Claudius placated with a grin. "Bring me bloodmead after sunset tomorrow night, and we can talk about those vile barbarians. The sun rises soon, and after I speak with Sáerlaith, I plan on sleeping."

Sáerlaith paced around her quarters before sitting down to re-read the latest reports from Deargh Du agents in the other parts of the world. She sighed as she came to a report from her agent in Bath. Marcus had commented that many blood-drinkers he encountered saw most Deargh Du in unflattering colors… bigoted, egotistical, and snobbish, among other choice adjectives. She glanced up at the triscelle painted on the wall and thought of the many Deargh Du she knew who embodied those words.

Many Deargh Du wished to distance themselves from their fellow Celtic blood-drinkers, but Sáerlaith believed that the Deargh Du needed to maintain a strong alliance with the two other Celtic lines. They had extended friendship to the Deargh Du, through Marcus, yet the Deargh Du had not helped the other Celtic lines to the extent that they assisted the Deargh Du.

Hardly a relationship of balance.

Now Vikings impinged upon the shores of Briton, rather the various kingdoms of England and Scotland. Soon, Sáerlaith believed, the assistance of the Deargh Du would be required, and she hoped that when their allies called for assistance, the Deargh Du would answer.

Her stomach grumbled as her hunger rose.

A soft knock at the oak door interrupted her thoughts.

"Come in," Sáerlaith called. Her seneschal, Seamus walked in.

"Forgive me, my lady, but there is a man here to see you."

"Indeed? What is his name, Seamus?"

"He's a Sugnwr Gwaed, his name is Claudius Metrius Sertorius."

"Well, quit dawdling," she sputtered at Seamus. "Let him in! He is an old friend. Go secure bloodmead for us. No wait, a moment."

Sáerlaith checked her nails and examined her face in a mirror. It would not do to be unkempt in front of a friend. She then sat down and motioned for Seamus to retrieve Claudius.

She closed her eyes. As Claudius and Seamus neared, their scents grew stronger. Soon, she heard the door open.

Sáerlaith opened her eyes and smiled. "Claudius," she called to her friend as he walked through her door. She arose, feeling foolish for sitting, and then embraced and kissed him. "Are you in need of refreshment?" He looked pale and felt cold to her touch.

"Yes," he admitted, sounding weary. "I flew here directly from Bath."

"Seamus, do you wish to offer your life blood?" she asked her seneschal.

"I am most humble to feed any guest," he replied, before folding his léine and offering his arm.

She watched Claudius feed, pleased to see him regain his color.

"Thank you," he said to Seamus.

"Please bring us bloodmead, Seamus," Sáerlaith stated. "I hunger as well." Seamus nodded before departing the room.

"My duties keep me busy at times, but not too busy to entertain my dear friends," Sáerlaith explained as she patted Claudius' arm. "Please rest after your journey." She then motioned for Claudius to sit. Claudius sat in the proffered seat. She too sat in an adjoining chair.

"I must say that I was a little surprised at my reception," Claudius explained. "While I found myself welcomed by many, several strangers looked at me as if I were an enemy. You will have to apologize for me to your captain of the guards. I seem to have removed his tongue."

Sáerlaith inhaled, in shock at the insult paid to one of her dearest friends, but considering the discontent following Máire's aborted assignation of Aisling, one of the isolationists' strongest voices, Sáerlaith felt little surprise. "Well, I apologize for the treatment you received. We owe you, your brethren, and our mutual friends a great deal, Claudius. The line of the Deargh Du is fraying. I know you can understand this, after all of the problems your line has faced, what with the Saxons, Angles, Jutes, and now the dreaded Northmen. Many of the Deargh Du wish to return to the old ways of holing ourselves in our home and forgetting the outside world. However, I, and a majority of the council, feel that this would be a grievous mistake."

She watched him smile. Claudius' eyes became the color of gold.

"It would indeed be a mistake," he said. "We are allowing ourselves to become too involved in the politics and wars of the mortals. In fact, I am here because of some problems on the continent, but it has nothing to do with the Norse, although, I know we will soon all have to deal with that issue."

"Now what brings you here from Bath?" she queried.

Claudius passed a letter to her. "Marcus asked me to give this to you."

Seamus returned to the room, bringing forth the bloodmead. He poured one cup and passed it to Claudius. Seamus poured a second cup, but Sáerlaith motioned the mortal away as she broke the seal and began to read.

After reading the first few lines, Sáerlaith found it difficult to maintain her composure. The very idea of becoming allies with those treacherous Lamia almost made her consider ripping the letter in half. She continued reading and then closed her eyes after finishing the missive. She rose and paced about the room for a moment, holding onto Marcus' communication.

"I... I..." she stammered, and then she yelled, "Seamus!" as she found her voice. "Send forth messages to all the Deargh Du who can join us. We will have a council meeting the night after tomorrow. We are sending troops to Francia after we join forces with our former enemy. We will need mortal escorts as well. We will leave in two weeks. Altogether, that should be a little over five hundred warriors. I know it's a small number, but it's what we have available."

She uttered a nervous chuckle as she watched her servant run to relay her orders. Sáerlaith sat down again and stretched her hand out to Claudius. He took it and gently squeezed.

"So, will the Ekimmu Cruitne and Sugnwr Gwaed join us?"

"I have not sent word to the Assembly, but I am certain that my line will join the fray," he answered. "As much as I dislike the Lamia, we will not allow invaders who make the Ouphe look like friendly puppy dogs into our home. The Ekimmu Cruitne will not be happy about suffering through a boat ride to Francia, but somehow I doubt they will take this news of potential Strigoi attacks well. Besides, they have such fond memories of battles with the Ouphe that they have been looking for someone to fight for many years." He chuckled. "Arwin still grumbles about missing out on fighting the Lamia during the battle at Bonniconlon. He is held in high esteem in his line, even though their council finds him a bit too headstrong. Mac Alpin's word will draw many to do battle."

Sáerlaith grinned. "I hope you are right." She inhaled and sensed the rising of the sun. "Well, we can go find quarters for you, or..." Her voice trailed off as she considered whether he would take an invitation to her quarters as more than friendship. "You can stay with me if you wish. I share my quarters with students, so I have extra beds."

She watched him smile. "That is kind of you to offer," he replied.

"The truth is, I have been cursed with bad dreams for the last few months. Perhaps they were warnings about the Strigoi and our futures," she admitted. "I feel safer when I hear someone nearby. Please tell no one."

"You have my word," Claudius answered. "Shall we retire?"

Aisling sat at one of their chairs in Conlan's temporary office, busying herself with cleaning her fingernails as Conlan read a scroll. She then heard a squeak from outside the office, and by Conlan's raised head, he noticed the noise as well. Aisling could sense a Deargh Du outside, yet no one knocked on the door.

With a look, Conlan urged her to investigate, and so Aisling got up, walked to the door, and opened it, only to see Érémon fiddling with his bloodied mouth and tunic.

"Tell Érémon to get in here," she heard Conlan whisper.

Aisling grabbed the guard captain by his collar and yanked him into the room. She then shut the door behind her.

"Have you sufficiently recovered?" Conlan asked.

"I just... you knew about that? Claudius..." Aisling could see Conlan glare at the captain. "...of course you knew. Yes, I have nearly recovered," Érémon stammered.

Conlan shook his head. "I am ashamed you did not fight back. So, Claudius is here. You've done your job... now go."

Aisling watched as Érémon moved his mouth as though he wished to speak, but he said nothing and then left the room.

After a few moments, Conlan whispered, "Idiot. Anyway, Morrigan is displeased with Her children. We are a clean race, Aisling. We are not to associate with the unclean, cursed blood-drinkers and bastards, yet Sáerlaith insists that Roman 'outcast' Marcus should rule our warriors, and of course you have your history with that daughter-in-darkness of his."

"How I hope to see her soon," Aisling admitted, "so I can watch her suffer by my hands and then take her life."

"In time, we will excise them and these other abominations from our midst, my daughter, and soon that time will come. These reports I am reading reveal strange tidings... Did you know that we may be allying with the Romans?"

"The Lamia?" Aisling asked. "That is unlikely. Even the Roman outcast hates the Lamia."

"Does he?" Conlan countered with a raised brow. His brown eyes turned dark, and he scratched at his reddish beard. "The Roman and his slut were friends with the Lamia once." Conlan began to pace his room. "Do not worry, Aisling. Tides are turning, my daughter-in-darkness. Our race will be free of these outcasts and their friends very soon."

Aisling nodded. Part of her wondered why anyone would consider allying with the Lamia. Perhaps the Norsemen inspired such fear, or perhaps it was something worse.

Regensburg

Omid woke up hearing the nightingales' song. His body felt heavy with the strain of the aftereffect of the herbal medicines, along with his own hunger. He picked up the bottle of blood mixed with the bitter wine and managed to swallow it before the taste nearly made him ill. He ignored the urge to vomit, holding his desires in check. The blood soothed him, and the inclination to purge passed.

He started mixing the herbs again, reminding himself of why this had to be done. He could still recall the strange Latin symbol on the soldiers' shields. The missionaries and the soldiers had arrived in Persia over four hundred years ago, seeking converts for their Gods. He remembered hiding from them, fearful of their martial and religious fervor. Did their God act in such a manner, demanding such obedience from all? He could hear his father and mother asking patient and slow questions with the hesitation that came from a lack of understanding Latin or Greek. He recalled hearing anger from the soldiers at his parents' misunderstanding. Omid's mother began screaming, and then a sinister silence had weighed over their simple home.

Omid's hands shook with rage at the thought of their death. Did their peaceful God demand such bloody sacrifices?

Omid had crept out of his home a fearful child, though he had managed to find his way into the shop of an herbalist. The herbalist, Hassan, suffered from a painful illness that kept him out of the sun. Omid trained under him for fifteen years, running the shop for Hassan, and learning Zarathustra's teachings about Ahura Mazda.

One day the master had told him of the secrets of Immortality and of the Ekimmu. Hassan had grown up in Assyria and apprenticed many worthies in the old ways in order to protect the knowledge and skills of Assyria and Persia when the Romans sought to take all. Hassan had offered the gift of immortality as a way to pass down the knowledge. Omid had eagerly accepted, yet for reasons that had little to do with the ancient teachings of Mithras and more to do with revenge.

The master had told his student that the gifts of the Ekimmu line could not be used for retribution. Revenge offered nothing to its adherents, other than a hollow shell of a life.

Omid had left Hassan a year later, tired of the same rants about tolerance. He watched the mortals of the world wage wars in the name of Gods who probably wanted little to do with their bloodlust. He understood now what these Christians really wanted… lands, money, and riches, just like so many others who conquered territory, using the excuse of bringing wisdom to those who did not comprehend.

Omid could not help but wish to send retribution to those who killed indiscriminately. He would feed, yet he would not kill. Then, one night he had met one of the cursed Strigoi and watched the horrible power it could wield over mortals.

A mortal had begged for mercy and pleaded with Jesus to save him from the devil. Omid had tried to save him, but the Christian monsters from childhood returned in his mind with their bloody swords and horrific trophies. A few hours later, the visions had disappeared.

Omid had reasoned that perhaps these Strigoi could be used for his retribution, since mortals feared the devil, and they considered anything that they could not understand to be demonic. The religious leaders would lose power if their followers lost their trust in their abilities to protect the people from Satan. After all, the political structures used their followers' lack of education to their advantage.

The next night, Omid had mixed together a powder of herbs and plants, hoping in vain it would work. It did, yet it took a few more times exposing himself to the Strigoi's madness to perfect it. The Strigoi whispered words of Aphrodite's curse, though he probably understood the words as much as they did. He had studied the legend, dressed as Aries, Aphrodite's lover, and then he managed to control them by using his powders to bring on insanity from within. The powder mixture counteracted their mental attacks.

Omid actually believed himself to be Aries when he took the powders. Even the Strigoi had fully accepted him as a God. After all, who but a God would be able to ignore their attacks?

This night, Omid poured the vile potion into the bottle, leaving it to settle until tomorrow night. In the beginning, he had spent a few days simply imbibing the elixir. That practice allowed an immunity to build up, strengthening his resolve. Despite the long-lasting effects of the potion, Omid still took a course of it every evening after waking.

After he finished pouring potion into the bottle, Omid exited the cave and called to one of the Strigoi near him. The beast ignored him as it stared at his reflection in a stream. Omid then noticed that the body of a victim lay nearby. The dead mortal's flayed skin lay on the ground. Omid had seen the Strigoi do worse to their prey. In fact, the time drew near to allow them to do worse.

"Call for your brothers and sisters," he ordered, gaining the brainless dolt's attention. The Strigoi then lumbered into the darkness.

When the rest arrived, he would tell them to multiply.

Only one matter still nagged at his conscience… the truly innocent victims, but then again, his parents had been innocent as well.

---

chapter four

Verviers

"This is the last place we have on record with reports of devil sightings, my lord," Julien said as he nudged his horse towards the torch-lit town. He watched fearful faces peer at them from the candlelit windows. A cautious watchman bearing a torch approached.

"Let me speak," the emissary demanded as he pulled his horse to a stop and dismounted. "Watchman, I am the papal emissary, the traveling arm of His Holiness, Michael Tolomei."

Julien watched Michael extend his hand and tried not to roll his eyes.

"Oh, bless you for coming to us, my lord. We have been so frightened of the beasts that walk the night. We could not go to church last Sunday," the watchman said. "We all smelt brimstone, as if hell had descended in God's house. There is also an unholy buzzing within. We could not find our priest. Satan stole him and some others away. I will speak no more of such horrible happenings." He then crossed himself. "I am not even the true night watch. He disappeared with our priest."

"You pray for us and keep watch on our horses. We will go to the church and search for the fiend," Michael told the watchman as he glanced in the direction of the stone hewn church.

Julien dismounted, grabbed his supply kit, and watched the six members of the entourage join him in checking their weapons. They then started for the church.

"Stand behind me, my lord Emissary," Julien said as he passed Michael and the others in the party.

"As much as I appreciate the gesture, Inspector General, if we are truly facing Satan, it is I who shall protect you," Michael replied.

Foul odors exuded from the doorway as Julien inhaled and exhaled. He could hear a strong buzzing within, now. He looked at the two doors before trying to push in the door to his right with his left shoulder, but it would not open.

He heard the emissary clear his throat. Julien backed away and looked on as Michael seized something from within the vines to the right of the doors. Julien then heard a click.

"That may help you," Michael said with a superior smirk that Julien tried to ignore. "I believe I have released the locking latch."

"Thank you," Julien said as he opened the door. The pungent smell of rotting flesh made him turn away and cough. The retinue of guards and Michael backed off.

Julien reached into his pouch. "I have oil of peppermint. It is somewhat overwhelming, but it may help us." He doled out two drops onto his right index finger and then rubbed the oil onto his upper lip. After applying it to his face, Julien passed the bottle to Michael. The papal emissary made a strange face at the scent, but he used it anyway.

"The burning of the oil is much better than the alternative of smelling that abomination," commented Michael.

After passing around the oil, the entourage grabbed torches and lit them.

"I will lead the way," Michael insisted, as he moved ahead without the assistance of a guard or a torch.

Julien followed him, along with a young, shaky guard at his side, who whispered the Lord's Prayer, as they entered the church. Once inside, the walls appeared to move. Black flies swarmed around the torches, though some exited to the outdoors with the doors now open.

Bodies hung from the ceiling, many with their entrails hanging out, and several severed body parts lay strewn about the floor. Julien tried not to gag at the sight of such gore. He grew so shocked to see the body parts that he tripped over a rotting leg and nearly fell. The walls teemed with dried blood and skins covered the windows. The stone altar rested on its side, and intestines lay scattered across the floor.

"Let us walk the wall," he said to the young guard, who shook with apparent trepidation. "Do not fear, God will protect us," he said, hoping that his hollow words would soothe the guard. God did not exist in this place.

Michael stood frozen in place, staring at the northern wall of the church.

Julien began to count the bodies and body parts strewn about the church. The bodies appeared to be blindly wrenched apart as if in an act of rage. He stepped over to peer at a lifeless torso that still had a head attached. It lay face down in dried blood and other indistinguishable substances. Julien stooped to his knees and rolled the body over. A woman's face stared back at him in steadfast horror, her mouth open in a silent scream, her skin a sickly shade of gray and blue.

He felt like vomiting, but he forced his revulsion to pass. "I am so sorry," he whispered to the lifeless corpse, hoping no one would hear. The sounds of further buzzing made the rest of the torch-wielders jump.

Ignoring the distraction, Julien lowered his torch closer to the women in order to ascertain how she died. A series of strange markings on her throat caught Julien's eyes, and he turned her with his free hand to the side to determine what he beheld. After closer inspection, Julien saw two strange holes, a few inches apart, bore into the victim's neck. He ran a finger over them. They were puncture marks. He wondered what would cause such markings. The wounds looked older, as if they had started to heal before the woman's untimely end.

"Inspector General, have you found something?" the papal emissary queried.

"No, my lord," Julien lied. Michael would no doubt claim that such wounds would be the torturous work of Satan and his minions. Julien would have to take notes on this later. He measured the distance between the two holes with his fingers.

He noticed Michael looking over another body. "Have you found anything?" Julien asked.

The pope's emissary shook his head.

"Gather up all the body parts," Julien suggested, "and get someone to lower the bodies from the ceiling. We can weigh them with the scales from a shop owner or miller and estimate how many people were slain."

He walked to the altar and then stopped, when he noticed a message written in blood, at least it looked like dried blood. Gods only knew what substance it could be.

"Here festers the body of Christ," Julien whispered.

"Hello?" a muffled voice called from outside of the church. "Hello, is anyone in here?"

Julien walked to the door and saw a man standing outside, his face sweaty. The five men of the emissary's entourage kept the man back, but Julien gestured for them to let the man approach him.

"I am Julien de Divio, Inspector General of the Gendarme," he said, giving the stranger a thorough once over. He wore no weapons, but Julien wondered whether this man might be one of the responsible parties. The way the man's eyes darted about during when he spoke made him suspicious, yet it could just be overwhelming fear. "Who are you?" Julien inquired.

"I am the deacon of this church. My name is Buiron," the man replied.

"What are you doing here at this time of night, Buiron?" Julien asked. "This is not the time for God-fearing men to be awake, with the exception of the village night watch."

"The people told me that men of authority were at the church, and I wished to meet with them," Buiron replied.

"Buiron, what has transpired here?" Julien inquired, passing over his bottle of peppermint oil. The deacon twitched a bit, making a face at the smell that dispersed from within the church.

"Thank you, my lord," Buiron acknowledged as he took the bottle, but he seemed confused as to its purpose.

"It's oil of peppermint, and it has a strong smell. Rub a few drops on your upper lip, and it will keep the noxious odors at bay."

The deacon followed his advice and dabbed peppermint oil on his lib. "This is excellent. How did you know of this?"

"My mother spends a great deal of time in her garden," Julien answered with a shrug. "Her favorite plant is peppermint." His mother had brought large quantities of the plant to another village to have them create the oil.

The deacon raised his brows. "I see...," he replied. "Well, ten nights ago, two men and a woman disappeared. One of the men was our night watchman. Throughout the night, others vanished. We tried in vain to find our priest, Father Tyeis, but we never did find him." The deacon's voice grew weak. "The church was barred from within," he added. "We knocked, but no one answered."

"We found the means of unlatching the doors," Julien explained as he pointed to the vines concealing the doors' release. "It was rather easy to open, once the emissary discovered it."

The deacon nodded before chancing a look into the church. He covered his mouth and gagged. When he recovered, he met Julien's eyes. "We had to cancel our mass. We were so afraid that we sent word to our diocese. I presume they sent for you."

Julien nodded his head a bit and said, "Not for me exactly."

"For me."

Julien heard the papal emissary's voice over his left shoulder and turned, wondering for the briefest of moments how Michael managed to walk about without making a sound.

"I am Michael Tolomei, Emissary of Pope Leo III."

The deacon's face grew blissful, and he bowed before kissing the ring on Michael's extended hand.

"Oh, bless you for coming, my lord," the deacon groveled.

"Bless you my son," Michael said.

Julien tried to keep from revealing surprise at that statement, granted it had been a long time since he had done anything but drift off in thought or sleep during mass. However, it seemed a little strange to hear a layman of the church give blessings as if he were a man of the cloth.

"We are here about the reports of Lucifer stalking the night," Michael explained.

The deacon crossed himself. "I was about to tell the inspector general that I have seen him myself. I witnessed him taking Irmine, the smithy's wife. When Satan looked in my direction, I fell to the ground, and his eyes moved past me.

I prayed to have a quick death, but thanks to God, the demon disappeared. I got to my feet, and then I saw that the Prince of the Underworld was gone."

"What of Irmine's family? Are they here?" Julien asked.

"No, Inspector General," Buiron replied.

"Did Satan take them as well?" Michael asked.

"Not exactly, my lord. We feared that the husband and children were in league with Satan, since he took the wife. We tried them, and we found them to be heretics, so we burned them."

The papal emissary placed a hand on Buiron's head. "You did what any good Christian would do. You have the pope's and Christ's blessing, my child."

Julien closed his eyes and bit his tongue.

Stupid, pious fools! How could anyone condone burning the victims?

Julien tried to keep from contradicting the words of the emissary and instead stared into the darkness, concentrating on the silent, cold moon.

"Thank you, Emissary," the deacon blathered as he got onto his knees. "Thank you and bless you."

"You have done well. Continue your diligence. If you find out anything, send your missive to Rome and to the Imperial Palace at Aachen. Go home and find peace with your family," Michael advised.

Julien watched the deacon walk away. He tried to ignore his growing rage, but he found it difficult. "Did you see the writing on the altar?" he asked Michael in a half-growl, which he could not control.

"Yes indeed," Michael replied. "'Here festers the body of Christ'."

Julien nodded before taking a deep breath. He then fixed his gaze on the silent figures in the sky. "I am not privy to any information regarding these attacks in the churches. Have there been any defilements such as these in other holy places?"

Michael turned to face him. His green eyes gleamed. "Yes, Inspector General. In each instance, similar messages were left behind. Each time, the priest was not amongst the dead."

"There appears to be nothing left to do here," Julien commented. "Other than leaving the doors open and hoping the stench may dissipate. Perhaps the townspeople can reclaim it and bury the dead. There is nothing else we can learn here." Julien got to his feet and started back for the horses, when a hand clamped on his right shoulder. The strength in the grip overwhelmed him. Julien turned back to Michael.

"Inspector General, please remember to refer to me as 'my lord' or 'Lord Emissary'. It is only proper," Michael stated before releasing Julien's shoulder.

"Yes, Lord Emissary," Julien replied, ignoring the pain in his shoulder.

"My apologies. The extent of destruction within the church has affected my sensibilities. It will not happen again."

"See that it does not," the emissary replied before walking towards the horses.

"It could not get any worse than this," Julien whispered, as he watched the rest of the entourage catch up with Michael.

The Irish Sea

"Three! Your luck runs bad tonight," Marcus cheered with a chuckle. He took the dice and cup from Máire after finishing his meal of bloodmead from a flask.

They sat in the ship's hold with Amata and Patroclus, trying to ignore the sounds of retching emanating from the other hold. Máire studied her nails as Marcus continued his war story. Amata appeared uninterested in the story, but Patroclus seemed to hang on every word.

"What happened next?" Patroclus demanded. "I mean, I know the story, but hearing a first-hand account is much better."

"As I was saying, the Belgae chose to cross the river at that point. Caesar's luck held, and we killed many of those who crossed. After that horrendous defeat, they left their camp to return to their tribes, yet they did so without any attempts to silence their retreat. We routed those men. After that battle, I moved up in rank from Legate to General, and then Praetor." He grinned as he emptied the dice, but the numbers did not favor him. Marcus pouted a bit. "Your turn," he said as he passed over the cup to Amata. He looked across the table and studied Patroclus.

"Did you fight in the Battle of Sarmizegetusa?" Marcus asked. "I'd love to hear about that battle."

The Legate grinned as Amata's roll of the dice continued her unlucky streak. "Yes, I did. Decebalus was a most worthy and wily foe. We destroyed the fortress and the Dacians as a whole. Their treasure was overwhelming. I had never seen so much gold and silver."

Patroclus took the cup and dice from Amata and rolled. "Eleven," he yelled before gathering the pot and rolling again.

"Neither of you can tell a decent war story," commented Amata. "I could put more excitement into a description of the last time I trimmed my nails than you have both mustered in your pitiful war stories."

Máire took the cup and dice from Patroclus and tried to keep from laughing. After all, she heard about almost every battle that Marcus and Claudius had participated in, though Arwin preferred to tell stories about his disastrous marriage.

"Alright, Amata, tell me of what trials you faced," Marcus said as Máire shook the dice in the cup and rolled.

"How about I tell of how I became Lamia?" Amata answered.

Máire gave Marcus the dice and cup after her failed roll.

"Alright. I think I should enjoy this tale," Marcus agreed as he grinned back at the other woman.

"My family was of ancient Etruscan royalty, so I married well, but my dear husband died while fornicating with a slave and left me nothing except his debts. Therefore, I became a cortigiana with a well-connected and wealthy boss. He owned the finest brothel in Rome." She took her turn and grumbled as she placed more money into the pot than before.

"The brothel had been the home of a wealthy family fallen on hard times and unlucky politics. It had baths, marble, tiles, and rooms decorated with the most beautiful furnishings. It was a dream. Sometimes, I would pretend it was my old home."

Amata's blue eyes sparkled for a moment before staring at Máire with a ready smile.

"I had a client who came back every night for almost two months. I could not remember much about those nights, but I had a wonderful time, and I slept well afterward. His name was Felician. One night, when I waited upon his arrival, my boss sent me to another customer's home, someone I had never met before."

Máire noticed Amata's smile fade. "That… bastard raped me and beat me. All he was interested in was controlling a woman. Apparently, he gained a taste for it on the battlefield. Roman soldiers always had a chance after victory to take anything they wanted from the conquered people, including women." Her voice grew harsh. "I am sure you and Patroclus did that yourselves, but I digress." Her voice lost its harsh quality and became a throaty purr once again.

"That… customer threw me into the street. There I lay in a ditch, dirty and bruised with broken bones. I thought I would die. I even prayed to Venus for the peaceful release of death," Amata said.

Marcus held the dice, apparently waiting for Amata to complete her tale before rolling them.

"I passed out, yet when I woke up, I found myself in a well-appointed bedroom in the most comfortable of beds. I still have yet to find a bed that wonderful," Amata purred.

"I found myself bandaged, and I could smell herbal medicines. I finally noticed Felician watching me from a corner of the room. He fed me broth and talked to me about my night."

"Felician asked me whether I wanted to kill the customer who raped and beat me. He said he would give me the strength if I wished it. Well, I wished for vengeance, and he therefore gave me that strength. I healed, and the next night, I returned to that bastard, a victim no more.

"You have not rolled," Amata said to Marcus.

Máire noticed the cup in Marcus' hand. She elbowed him, and he tossed the dice.

"I wasn't ready," Marcus complained, but he still passed the cup and dice to Amata after his failed role. "Well, that was certainly a poignant tale of suffering and transformation, Amata. However, it's not a war story," he pointed out.

"I would say that was a war story. Your turn," Máire challenged.

"Tell us about your transformation, Máire," Amata smirked as she took the dice from Marcus. "Mandubratius told me about how you pulled someone's heart from his chest, squeezed it, and then drank from it. What on earth possessed you to do such a thing?" the Lamia asked with a smile while she shook the dice in the cup.

"Transformation for a Deargh Du causes severe physical and mental changes. Through the mental changes, I was largely insane. Well, my insanity was mixed with my desire for retribution, following the discovery of my husband-to-be's involvement in the death of my love. I guess I just decided it was the best way to get even. I hated him for raping me, fooling me, and for allying with the Lamia... no offense, so I channeled my rage, and my body did the rest."

"None taken. How do you feel about us now?" Amata asked as she rolled the dice. "Nice!" she cheered before pulling in her winnings.

Máire stared at Amata for moment, trying to keep various emotions in control. "I suppose time heals all wounds," she answered. "However, I have not yet forgiven Mandubratius for his part in his plans, or rather his amusements."

"What do you plan to do when you see him again?" Patroclus asked as he took the dice and cup from Amata.

"It depends on him," Máire replied. "I probably will not kill him, but he may be in pain for awhile." She chuckled, seeing the Lamia trying to hide their smiles. "So Amata, what do you believe he would do when he sees me?"

Amata's eyes grew coy as she twirled an inky strand of hair around her right index finger. "I am not sure," she admitted with a smile. "He believed you had betrayed him once, but that was two centuries ago, and time always cools his rage. Now, rumor has it, he is quite enamored with you. I imagine he would attempt to give you quite the reception when you and he meet again."

Máire watched Patroclus roll the dice, though the results proved unfavorable. "I see," she grumbled. "So Marcus," she said as she turned towards him in hopes of changing the subject. "What will you do when you meet with him after so many centuries?"

"I have not decided what to do," he answered, meeting her eyes. His eyes started to gray.

"You have not decided what to do?" Amata asked as she raised an eyebrow at him.

"Um, let me correct myself… I have decided what to do, though I have yet to decide whether I will use one gladius or two."

"From what he has told me, you two have a history. I can understand why you do not have an affinity for one another," Amata interjected. "However, given the situation, can you not put aside your differences and work together?"

Marcus clucked his tongue and pouted a bit. "Oh must I?" he purred. Marcus managed to look quite mischievous.

"Yes, you do," Amata demanded with a giggle.

"Oh, I suppose," Marcus replied.

Máire felt his hand slide over hers.

"So, where is Mandubratius?" Máire asked, taking the dice and cup from Patroclus. "Why is he not here?"

Amata grinned. "He is doing an investigation of the Strigoi on his own. We will meet with him in Aachen."

"I am certain we all look forward to that night," Marcus stated. Máire could hear a soft hint of sarcasm lace his words.

Auxerre

Mandubratius nudged his horse to a faster trot, wondering why he continued with the charade. He found himself mildly impressed that the emperor sent him someone who had a brain between his ears. While most of these superstitious, ignorant peasants believed in what they were told without question, Julien sought proof. The Lamia could always use another soldier who did not jump to conclusions, like so many of the poor and uneducated seemed to do.

Mandubratius slowed his mount and allowed the gendarme to catch up. He studied the Frank for a moment, thinking over what kind of Lamia this mortal might make. Mandubratius decided it might be best to first test Julien's skills.

"Inspector General, I would like to try something different this time," Mandubratius began.

The gendarme looked over at him with some amount of curiosity in his blue eyes. "And what would you like me to do, my lord?"

My, he did manage to hide that rage very well. I can almost smell the wrath emanating from Julien de Divio.

"I would like to see how you would investigate these matters if it were strictly a secular matter. In fact, when we arrive, pretend I am not there."

"But you are the pope's emissary," Julien replied. The mortal smiled a little. "Do you not feel that the people will gain comfort from your presence?"

"I feel that they may leave out important points to our search for the truth regarding these attacks if they know who I am too soon."

"Very well, I will do so." The inspector general nudged his mount towards the center of the small village, and Mandubratius followed.

The smell of rot poured forth on the breeze, wafting between the small farmhouses of the vassals, the sturdy homes of the merchants in the village, and the large expanse of farm and forested land near the home of the nobility. The village looked very much like most of the others in Francia and the Western Empire. Nervous and gaunt candlelit faces examined them from the small openings in the lord and lady's house as they approached. Their whispers drifted with the stench on the winds.

Several torches moved towards them. The night watch had arrived.

Julien waved to one of the watchmen of the town, "Walaric?"

"You know the watchmen?" Mandubratius asked in a whisper.

"My sister and her husband used to live here. I know a few of the townspeople," the gendarme answered.

The watchman trotted over. "My lords," Walaric called out as he engaged the gathered party.

"We have heard about the nighttime attacks, Walaric. Are you and yours well?" Julien asked after he dismounted. "These are associates and friends of his Imperial Majesty who have joined me to find answers."

"Yes, my family is well. Thank you, my lord. We only lost a few to that thing," the watchman replied.

"Are Arno and Theoderada well? I do not see their guards out," Julien asked.

"The Lord and his Lady ran off to Aachen," Walaric replied in a stony voice. "No offense to Lady Lirienne's former in-laws, but they cared little for us and left us behind."

Mandubratius dismounted and watched Julien's eyes grow dark.

"They left you, and took their guards with them?"

"Yes, my lord, they did just that. I believe they said something about people on foot slowing them down," Walaric sneered a bit, but then he seemed to realize his rudeness. "I beg your pardon."

"No, I beg yours," the inspector general muttered under his breath. He looked over at Mandubratius for a moment. "I never cared for my brother-in-law's family. They always seemed to be a cowardly lot. I'm not sure why my brother allowed our sister to be married to such…" The inspector general stopped speaking in Latin and said something in their native tongue and then grinned at Walaric and the others.

The watchmen all guffawed at whatever the joke had been. Walaric smiled and shook his head before uttering a reply in what Mandubratius assumed to be the Frankish vernacular.

"And the rest of you, are you safe and sound?" Julien asked Walaric in Latin.

"Quite so," Walaric replied, "except for poor Baldewyn's family and Father Hervisse. Whatever attacked Baldewyn and the good father destroyed the inside of our church. We are still cleaning it. After Baldewyn disappeared, his wife and children ran off for fear of what we might do to them. Serena is not well. She was there when it took Baldewyn. She believed that we would burn her and her children as heretics. We have heard news of this happening in other villages and towns."

"What happened to the Church?" Julien asked.

Walaric shook his head. "I have never seen such… blood everywhere, my lord. Even on the battlefield, it was not like this. Body parts…" The watchman grew silent. "Words cannot describe it," he said to the men, looking at them all.

"We have seen such defilements in other towns," Mandubratius added.

Walaric nodded his head. "I last saw Serena hiding near the western edge of the stream. I left some food for her children," he said with a shrug. "I fear for them. She seems… ill."

"Let us find them first. Perhaps she can tell us more," Julien suggested as he climbed back onto his horse.

"Be careful," Walaric advised him. "Serena has a dagger, perhaps more weaponry. Her children are named Ameline and Rabel."

"We will return to look over the church later, Walaric."

"My family would not forgive me if we did not offer you and yours a place to stay," Walaric proposed.

Mandubratius watched a smile light up the inspector general's face. "That is most kind, Walaric. Thank you."

Julien heard someone gag. He turned and witnessed several members of the papal emissary coughing. He then noticed a pair of slight figures watching them.

"Brimstone?" Michael asked as he made a face. "Why does she burn it? Pass me some of that oil of yours please."

Julien tried to think of a reason as he handed over the peppermint oil.

"Protection," he said. "Many believe evil is repelled by bad smells. This is old folk wisdom handed down through the ages since the time before Christendom."

He wondered what kind of comment the emissary would make to such blasphemous talk, yet Michael remained silent.

Julien gave the two children a wave. "Try to smile. They are frightened." He dismounted and then moved in closer towards them. Julien sat down a few feet away, pulled out his bag, and held out a small loaf of bread. The two children came closer and cautiously reached for the bread.

"Walaric sent me to speak to you and your mother," Julien said in as congenial a voice he could muster. "My name is Julien de Divio."

The older of the two took the bread and divided it with shaking hands, handing half to her younger brother.

"Ameline?" Julien inquired. The girl looked to be about ten years old, and her brother appeared to be about seven or eight.

"Yes," she said as she turned and looked at him. "Are you here to burn us?"

Julien shook his head. "I would never do that," he answered, hoping she would believe him.

"You might not. They look like they would," Ameline whispered, glancing over at the papal emissary and the rest of their emissary.

"Mama always says some of the worst people hide behind the cross," Rabel, the boy, whispered. He had finished off the bread in a few moments. His sister ate with the same gusto.

Julien grinned before reaching back into his bag to pull out more food for the children. "I promise I will not let anyone harm you or your mother. If you like, we can leave them behind, although I need to make a report on what your mother tells me. Let me find someone to scribe notes."

The brother and sister stared at each other and then nodded.

"Walaric protects us," Rabel stated softly. His tone belied his maturity. Perhaps he had grown up a great deal in the last few days.

Julien stood and looked over his shoulder at them. "Stay there, I shall return soon."

He walked over to Michael and his entourage. "My Lord Emissary, do any of your men write?"

"Not that I know of," Michael answered.

"My Lord, I can write," the youngest of the guard replied in an unsteady voice. "I schooled at a monastery, but I can only transcribe in Latin."

"Reynard, can you transcribe as someone talks?" Michael asked. "That is what you wish him to do, correct?" he queried Julien.

Julien nodded his head.

"I believe I can do that, my lord," Reynard answered.

Julien grabbed a bag attached to his saddle and passed it to Reynard. "I have a writing surface, quills, and ink… everything you will need." He turned back to Rabel and Ameline and approached them, hoping Reynard would not frighten the children. "We are ready."

"Salt, salt, for salt is protection, protection…," he heard a woman say frantically. "I need… we need. Yes, yes. Jesus, Jesus, please protect us." As Julien drew near to the babbling, he watched as a woman paced around a circle tossing salt about. Splotches of white mottled her dark hair, however her face revealed her youth. Serena, if he remembered her name correctly, could not have reached her third decade of life.

"Mama?" Ameline called out.

The woman turned her face to her children and the strangers. Her eyes stared at them, reflecting a great confusion and grief. She held a small dagger in her right hand.

"You have brought the enemies to the gate?" she cried, looking directly at the children.

"We just wish to help you, Serena," Julien said. "I only want to speak to you about Baldewyn's death. This is Reynard, and I am Julien de Divio. The emperor sent me to try to find who took your husband. May we join you?"

"You," Serena whispered, pointing at Julien. "You may come inside the circle. The scribbler stays outside. He smells of ungodliness wrapped in a cross."

Julien motioned for Reynard to sit. "Take down our words. Try as best as you can to keep up. I'll attempt to keep her speaking in Latin." He walked towards the woman and crossed the boundary ring of salt. Serena motioned for her son and daughter to come to her. She smiled a little as they curled up next to her, and then her eyes cleared.

Serena dropped the dagger, allowing it to fall away from her. "What do you need to know?" she asked.

"Describe what happened, Serena. Please do so in Latin. I'm afraid Reynard doesn't understand Frankish," he said.

Serena bobbed her head. "Baldewyn and I like to walk together, my lord." Julien watched her smile. "When we were courting before marriage, he and I would meet under the stars and moon to talk of our secret plans. Then his father died, and being the eldest, he had to take care of his family. We have not been able to take many walks together, but now, there is free time before the planting starts." Serena began stroking her son's golden hair.

"That must be beautiful. I am most jealous, as I have very little free time these nights," Julien murmured. He wished for some female companionship, yet at court it was always about what one owned. Third sons in general owned nothing. If he could choose any of the available women in Aachen, Gundrada would certainly be his choice, although she had never brought forth any feelings of love from him. The only woman who had ever captured his heart was Flor of the thousand graces. She resided in Divio, but they could never be together for more than for a few precious nights at a time.

Flordelis, or Flor, and he once played together as children in the sun-filled past when their mothers came to meet in the groves. That all changed when her family promised her to his eldest brother, Reginald. Then Julien's work in Aachen became too consuming. He tried in vain to forget Flor, yet thoughts of her consumed him. She had busied herself with the rearing of his niece, Clotilda, and his nephews, Jakelin and baby Ledger. He felt he could make no claims on her and so he had pulled away from Divio. The only woman who could even compare to Flor would be Gundrada, yet many desired Gundrada, and she treated Julien as if he were a beloved brother or relation, not a potential suitor.

The radiant Gundrada remained in Aachen, promised as a bride to foreign royalty. She looked after her chastity like a vigilant guard. If he wanted a good time, the emperor had daughters and granddaughters who would be willing and able to join in. The emperor preferred to keep his daughters and grandchildren nearby and allowed them a great leniency in choosing lovers. Several bore bastard children who were treated with the same love and respect as the legitimate ones. Unfortunately, he never had time for such frivolity.

"Then you should experience the nights here in Auxerre, my lord, for the stars and moon are breathtaking," Serena said. "I will miss those peaceful walks." He heard her voice crack. She wiped away her tears with a sleeve and continued. "Baldewyn and I spoke about the planting and the possibility of buying land from Lord Arno. The Lord wants to move closer to Aachen, so he is selling property. Amazing is it not? So seldom can people of my husband's and my class own property. Then something… something… came upon us. Spiders, spiders, all around. Spiders screaming, my mother screams. Fires do not die, and the holy men come to burn us all. You know of what I mean. You fear it too," Serena covered her eyes. "Make it stop, Jesus, make it stop!" Her shrill voice turned from pleading to ordering.

"Who took him?" Julien asked.

"Monster stole him. Blood trails on his body and down, down, down, towards the river. I tried to follow, but spiders and fire hunted me," Serena said. "It took another. Colors hunt me too," she sobbed. "Only the brimstone and salt protect… my mama said so."

"Monster? Was it a demon?" he asked.

"Words in my mind say yes and no," Serena stated. "Yet words play tricks. So many words and they never stop."

Had the woman's mind disappeared after the attack or before? Perhaps this was the only way to answer for the tragedy that had overwhelmed her.

"Some do, Serena. Please concentrate. There are no spiders here, and I promise to keep you and your children safe. It is the duty of my family to do so."

Serena appeared to calm down.

Julien waited for her to meet his eyes again. "Now, please tell me, Serena, where did this being take Baldewyn?"

"Here, here, here!" Serena repeated, each time, her voice grew in volume. "We stood here and here we waited! I could not see where it took him. Some say it crossed holy ground. Some say it took the priest for taking money from His Holiness in Rome. Is this the wrath of the divine trinity?"

The woman raved now. She grabbed the knife and yelled, "The colors grow. Do you see them? Do you see the monster on his horse to the west? They all hide, waiting to feed when the sun descends. Skin burns quickly, it does." She pushed her children away and rose, holding her head in her hands, resting the knife along the right side of her face. She clenched the dagger in her fist. "I do not want to see what they see and say anymore. Forgive me, son and daughter."

Julien jumped up and tried to grab her before she pushed the blade of the dagger into her heart, but his efforts failed. He wound up with the dying woman in his arms. The children screamed and then rushed out of the circle toward Reynard, forgetting their earlier fears.

Serena pulled him in close. "Watch for those who hide behind Jesus, for–" Her eyes rolled up, and she said nothing more.

Julien closed her eyes and looked at Reynard. "Take them to Walaric." Reynard just stared. "Go!" he ordered.

Reynard dropped his supplies and then picked up the two children and ran towards the village.

"The church is nearly clean, but it still smells horrible," the emissary reported to Julien, as several villagers carried Serena's body towards one of the small huts.

Walaric pulled the children into his home. Julien could hear the sounds of Walaric's wife, Rixende, cooing over them.

"This is terrible," Michael muttered, while rubbing his forehead. "Did you learn anything before she..." His eyes almost appeared to glow.

"She witnessed something horrible drag her husband away from her. I

Heather Poinsett Dunbar & Christopher Dunbar

do not know what other conclusions to make at this time. I feel I am missing important pieces," Julien replied.

He heard a huff, and then an arm grabbed Julien's wrist. "You get inside right now," Rixende said. "You two look as pale as unearthly spirits. Already there is enough pain and death here. Dawn approaches, and I will wager that none of your party has eaten tonight."

"I agree, there is more to learn," the emissary replied. "Yes, madam, we are all ravenous and are in need of rest."

Julien noticed the emissary study Rixende and smile. He looked over at the pope's representative, surprised at the evident leer on the man's face. Then, Michael's face revealed purity of thought again.

Julien wondered whether his imagination played tricks on him. Perhaps it could be lack of sleep and hunger.

Rixende pulled him inside.

Mandubratius awoke to the sound of footsteps outside the luxurious accommodations that the lord and lady of Auxerre had abandoned. He covered his face with the soft bedclothes, yet he continued to listen to the members of his emissary and the gendarme, rather the inspector general, discuss the possibilities of traveling to Metz and Épinal before returning to Aachen to gather more supplies. The travels at night weighed heavy on the mortals. In fact, Mandubratius found their travels to be just as wearisome as they did. Sitting on a horse for hours on end made him anxious to be on his feet. Mandubratius sat up in bed, musing over a change in his plans.

His latest batch of recommendations to the Lamia in Francia regarding the dangers of the Strigoi brought all but one of them home to Rome. Only Teá, or Talia, as she preferred to be called now, rejected his recommendation, stating that her successful reclamation of her grandfather Godomer's lands could not be ceased. She claimed to have spent too much time in Époisses amongst various families of mortal rabble to be troubled with the Strigoi.

Mandubratius planned to go to her later, after completing the investigation, but now he felt as though the investigation could continue without his assistance. The inspector general was not a fool and could continue the investigation without him. Alone, even Julien would see the Strigoi for demons, or perhaps he would realize that they were blood-drinkers, sooner or later.

The court gossips' tongues wagged that Julien had protected the Imperial Majesty from some dire circumstance at one point and held the old man's ear, like many of the councilors. The word 'demon' from his mouth to the emperor's ear might dissuade Emperor Charles from defending His Holiness.

Interesting…

Mandubratius grinned at the thought of visiting Talia, and of course of the chaos which might ensue from his latest plan.

He started to dress, sensing the death of the sun as night neared.

He joined the others outside, squinting at the purple skies, and then Mandubratius cleared his throat.

"I have received word of a family emergency in Époisses. I need to leave at once. I leave my men to you, Inspector General. I will meet with you again in Aachen in a week or so. Then you can tell me and his Imperial Majesty more about these… beings who pillage the people of the Empire."

He witnessed the gendarme almost smile.

"Well, I hope your journey goes well and your family issues become resolved quickly, my Lord Emissary," Julien offered.

"Thank you," Mandubratius replied, taking the reins of his mount. He hopped onto the horse and took off in a gallop, hoping to put some distance between him and Auxerre before setting the horse free. Perhaps this would give him a chance to see the Strigoi as well. The memories from his mandrake-induced dream faded along with his ancient fears from his childhood. Mandubratius believed that he needed to see one with his own eyes in order to reinforce his earlier decision that the Strigoi presented a clear and present danger.

chapter five

Époisses

Talia lit the candles in the hallway. Her husband could be so cheap on necessities such as candles. Even with enhanced senses, she needed a light or two, as it would seem odd for people to see her walk about in the dark constantly. Besides, she enjoyed arguments with Guilbert regarding house expenses. A tug on her left sleeve garnered her attention.

"Yes, what is it, Ansere?" She turned to face one of her husband's major distractions, many of which resided within the 'nunnery' in town. The emperor had declared prostitution to be illegal, but if anything, the new laws kept houses of ill repute occupied with a constant stream of men. Even the gendarmes, who swore oaths to protect the empire's laws and its people, frequented the brothels.

Talia smiled at Ansere. She loved to annoy that poor, pitiful schemer. Ansere always attempted to usurp Talia's position, but she always failed. Seeing the woman's plans collapse offered much more entertainment than simply killing her. Then again, Ansere offered great blood, and the little fool never realized it.

"My lady, a gentleman is at the door who says he is a papal emissary and your cousin…" Ansere's almond-shaped eyes grew large and suggestive.

Talia clasped her hands to her mouth in order to keep from chuckling aloud. "Go get my husband, Ansere. It has been so long since my cousin Ma… Michael has visited." She almost flew down the hall towards the door upon seeing Prades take Michael's cloak.

"Talia!" her 'cousin' yelled as he laughed and then held out his ring, "the papal emissary has arrived."

She joined him in laughter before kneeling to kiss his ring. She tried to get a chaste kiss on his cheek, but he dodged her and instead kissed her lips.

"You are very, very naughty for not visiting me sooner," she purred, "and for kissing me in such a manner. My husband will be horrified." She squealed as he grabbed her backside. She looked around and noticed Prades. She then concentrated on his mind. "Forget this."

The servant nodded and lowered his head.

"You are very talented with manipulation and mind-bending," Mandubratius whispered in her ear.

"I know," she replied, glad that the manipulation worked. Sometimes it did not.

"We must talk, Talia. I am worried for your safety." Mandubratius took her right hand and kissed it. "I wish you would return to Rome, to our temple. The Strigoi are monsters."

"Oh please, Ma... Michael. I am safe here. No monster can keep me from my prize, and I am about to win. No more pesky children or grandchildren... no more doddering parents..." her words grew quiet for a brief moment. "Then I will gain entrance to more houses of Frankish nobility, and I will make my ancestral lands mine."

"Well, well, well," Guilbert prattled as he walked downstairs. "Did I hear you trying to steal my precious from me, Michael?"

"Not steal, borrow," Michael chuckled, turning on the charm. "My cousin's friends always ask about sweet Talia and why she never returns to visit. Such a pity."

Guilbert smiled. "I do believe it is because she finds happiness here with family and friends."

"Of course," Michael replied. "And if I were here, I would never want to leave this lovely home."

"The pope must be granting favors," Guilbert mentioned as he nodded to the ring. "You are running an errand for him?" he asked before waving at Ansere. "More wine." She departed and soon returned with the wine from the family vineyards and cups. She then filled the cups and passed them out.

"Try this. It is excellent," Guilbert boasted as he poured the wine for them. "And you will not take Talia from me. I need a wife to keep things in order." He smiled at them both, the ignorant bastard.

"Well, my love it is time for me to retire. Good night," Guilbert rose from his seat and then retreated to his chambers.

Talia smirked as the door closed. "What a lovely husband I have." She played with the remaining wine in her goblet.

Michael chuckled. "So, how close are you to fulfilling your goals?"

"I have convinced him to make me his sole beneficiary, which means I do not have to kill off the children of his dead brothers," Talia replied, finishing off her wine. "I would even receive his title. His lawyer actually believed this to be a smart move."

"Imagine that," Michael congratulated with a smile. "I wonder how he could have been persuaded... a woman with title in this day and age."

Talia chuckled a little. "Guilbert's two sons were killed in battle, even though I heard it was bad luck on horseback. His three daughters all died during the pains of childbirth with the same mysterious midwife."

"You have always had such a strong effect on those you love," Mandubratius drawled. "How long does this husband have left to live?"

Talia drummed her fingertips against the table. "I think one night on his way home from the brothel he shall die, perhaps because of a robbery gone wrong. Guilbert is horribly stubborn, Michael." She raised a brow, knowing that he loved this kind of game.

"That will be very sad news for you," Michael purred.

"Yes, very sad that we exchanged our last kiss over three years ago on our wedding night," she replied in a whisper.

"Oh yes, so sad," Michael agreed as he stood up. "Will you excuse me, sweet cousin? I must take care of some business."

"Excuse me," Mandubratius began after walking over to a drunk. "Can you tell me where the town nunnery is?" He loved using the now infamous word for an illegal brothel. How strange Christians could be.

The drunk pointed to what appeared to be a respectable and well-lit building. The sign over the red-painted door revealed flowers and animals.

Mandubratius tossed the drunk a denier before walking towards the brothel.

He opened the door and stepped inside. A loud series of giggles made him turn to the left. As he stepped through the door, it swung shut behind him. Mandubratius noticed several scantily clad women run through the halls being chased by men wielding false bows and arrows as if they were hunting. The advertisements along the brightly painted walls promised soft beds, gentle women, and the finest accoutrements in Époisses. A guard and a madam watched him from behind a desk. Mandubratius could barely make out the madam from behind her abacus and a ledger book.

"Well, are you here to pay or to look at the scenery?" the brunette madam inquired. Her once lovely face now displayed a sea of wrinkles from a hard life. He would have to return to get a sample of that life later.

"Ah yes," he replied, focusing on his purpose. "I wish to sample your finest cuisine." The strong smell of flowers and incense did little to cover the scent of copulation that clung to the sparse furniture and copious decorations in the entrance.

"Our finest, eh? Well, no silver sou, no coitus," she replied.

Mandubratius held up a purse and jingled it. He then opened it and tossed a sou onto the solid, oak table. "I am not without means, if that is your concern."

He watched the crone drool at the sight of coin.

"The finest," she began. "We have a few of noble wives who recently lost their husbands. They did not do their wifely duty, and so they were tossed aside. Would such a woman please you?"

"Yes, indeed," he answered. "Before you summon them, I have one other request. I am looking for a nobleman named Guilbert. He's old, balding, and rich." Mandubratius concentrated on unfolding the secrets in the old madam's mind.

"Oh yes," the madam answered with a smile, lost in his spell. "He is in number four on the left with his favorite, Hildegard. She will keep him entertained for a half hour or so." The madam snapped her fingers, and a young boy ran towards her.

"Bring us Brune, Marie, and Petrona," she ordered before turning back to Mandubratius. "They are our finest, and each costs ten sou."

"I already gave you the coin for all three," Mandubratius replied, concentrating on her.

The madam looked perplexed for a moment before saying, "Oh, yes of course."

"I have also included a nice bonus for you."

The old woman grinned at him. "That is most generous. Thank you…"

"Michael," he said.

She scribbled down his name just as the three beauties walked in. Two had hair of gold with brown eyes, and the other revealed blue eyes and honey-colored curls.

"Disrobe, please," he said.

They looked over at the madam, and she nodded her head.

They dropped their clothing and met his eyes.

"Lovely," he smiled at them, deciding these women would be a pleasant way to spend half an hour.

"Fifth door to your left," the madam said as he led his amusements down the hall.

Mandubratius walked out of the room, leaving the women in an exhausted, half-asleep state. He leaned up against the door of number four and heard snoring.

He then opened the door and witnessed a frightened brunette with a black eye lower her face into her hands as she sat in a large chair far away from Guilbert. Mandubratius clucked his tongue. He noticed the woman lower her hands. Then her eyes settled on him, and he motioned for her to move closer. After walking to Mandubratius, the woman squatted on the floor

"Let me see what he did to you," he whispered. He leaned over to flick a piece of candle wax off a blistered burn. "Your madam allows him to do this to you, Hildegard?" he asked as he tugged her to her feet and into the hallway. Mandubratius closed the door part way.

"He pays well for the privilege," she replied, sounding bitter and dejected. "He told her that he needs it, because his wife apparently will not take what I absorb. After all, this is what prostitutes are for, is it not? We take this abuse so the married women and young virgins can keep their virtue intact."

Hildegard gave Mandubratius a wicked smile, revealing the bruises lining her face. "At least he's passed out from wine, now, so I have some peace."

Mandubratius ran a finger over her marred skin, wishing he could relieve some of that pain. "What do you want to do to him, since he caused you so much pain?" he asked as he pushed easily into her mind. "Do you wish him dead? I am certain that you do. If someone did this to me, I would want him or her to die."

"Yes," she whispered.

He pulled her back into the room, marveling at what passed for good décor these days. "Do you have the means to kill him?"

"I have a knife," she whispered.

"Then you know what to do," he told her. "Do it now while he is asleep. It will be simple. He is face down in the bed. You can get behind him, but try not to stir the bed. Then you just need to grab him by the chin and slice his throat open. Keep his mouth shut until he dies," he informed her. That should be simple enough for her.

Mandubratius held open the door for Hildegard.

He watched the young woman amble through the door. Mandubratius followed the young prostitute and with gentleness closed the door behind him.

Hildegard drew a blade from a plate of winter fruit. The prostitute then strode over to the bed and straddled the other mortal.

Guilbert uttered a muffled moan.

Hildegard raised the knife and yanked back on Guilbert's head, keeping his mouth shut. It reminded Mandubratius of watching the clan butcher during his mortal childhood. His hunger and desire grew as the blood fell, coating the bed a deep, blood red. Guilbert struggled for a moment and then fell back into the mattress.

Mandubratius walked towards the bed. "You are free now," he whispered. "Well done, Hildegard."

He walked out of the room and closed the door behind him. Once again, he completed his work without the victim's blood on his hands.

Mandubratius returned to the table, and wrapped an arm around her shoulders. She looked up from her meal of blood and wine.

"I apologize for taking so long in the privy," he whispered in her ear, before kissing the top of her head. Mandubratius sat down next to her.

"I started to wonder whether I needed to check to make sure you had not fallen in," Talia replied. "Strange... mortals fall asleep in there sometimes. Do you need refreshment?" she asked as she pushed her cup towards him.

"I fear that I had too much... cousin," he purred. Mandubratius pulled away, hearing footsteps in the corridors.

Prades came to the table, pale and trembling. "My lady, I bring bad news from town. Your husband has been slain."

Talia's face grew somber. Mandubratius felt her hand clasp his for a moment before she stood.

"Take me to him, Prades," she said. "Cousin, please join me."

He followed her to the stable.

"There, there," Mandubratius soothed as he patted Talia's shoulder, although she continued to cry. As he expected, they found the prostitute's naked body next to Guilbert's. After finding the body, the guard would have taken care of Hildegard.

After a quick viewing of Guilbert's body, they returned to Talia's home.

"The town magistrates will arrive soon, my lady," Prades told her.

Talia turned away from Mandubratius. "Oh, this is a horrid and wretched business." Talia cried into her own sleeve and then blew her nose loudly.

"Is there anything I can get for you, my lady?" Prades asked.

Talia shook her head in a vigorous manner.

"Prades, you look exhausted. Go to bed," Mandubratius suggested.

"I am exhausted," Prades murmured. "I will go to bed."

He quietly dismissed the other servants with suggestions and then grabbed an unfinished cask of wine. "Now, I have given you freedom, Talia. Stop being stubborn and come home to Rome. I miss you."

Talia laughed and shook her head. "You lie, Mich... Mandubratius. You simply miss having me as your primary source for amusement."

He handed her a glass of wine. "You are right, of course, but Talia, the Strigoi are a real danger. Even Patroclus is scared of them, and nothing scares the Legate," he explained before chuckling a little.

"Seriously, he is scared of a race that most of us have never seen?" Talia asked with a raised brow.

"They are monstrous," he explained. "They draw forth their own insanity and place it in the minds of mortals and blood-drinker alike. I sent the Legate and Amata to make a truce with the Celtic lines."

"You are the mad one, I think. The Deargh Du will skin your poor sister alive and do something worse to Patroclus," she challenged.

"Talia…" Mandubratius could see a hint of pleasure in her eyes. "Stop thinking ill of Amata. Besides, my sister is quite good at putting on a sweet and docile face," Mandubratius replied. "I am certain she and the Legate will return with new allies. After all, the Celtic lines hate seeing mortals in pain. That is one of their many weaknesses." He began to pour wine into two cups.

"So, what are the Strigoi doing that is so dangerous to us, oh great sponsor?" Talia took her full cup and began sipping on her wine.

"The Strigoi are attacking small villages, defiling the churches, and murdering the priests. While part of me revels in this chaos, I cannot let the Strigoi take our lands or the power of our church. Nor can I allow them to take you either, Talia." Mandubratius approached Talia, took her cup from her hand, and then brushed his lips over hers.

Talia pulled back with a sly grin. She took off her trappings and hair coverings before twirling a gilded lock of hair around her finger. "I will think over this enemy, Mandubratius. However, this is my home. I have heard about these church attacks, but I want Burgundy to be mine as my grandfather meant for it to be."

She pushed Mandubratius against the wall and nipped his lips playfully. "Now, take me to bed. I tire of your teasing."

Ard Macha

"Hold there," a firm male voice said. Then a pair of blue eyes stared at them from over the wall. "Marcus? Máire?"

"Hello, Maon," Marcus replied. "That is you, is it not?"

The hinged gate swung open, and Maon, as well as several other guards, stared at them. The starlit skies lent little light on the gathered group, but with Morrigan's gifts, Marcus could see everyone with clarity.

"I am speechless," Maon whispered. "We heard the rumors, but none of us could believe them." He and the other guards fell silent.

"Are we to be allowed in or not?" Marcus asked.

"Poor Edward and Mac Alpin are still recovering from their journey over the seas," Máire said to the guards.

"Forgive us for such rudeness," Fianait offered as she pushed her way past the other guards. "Welcome home."

"I offer my apologies for such discourtesy, General. You, Máire, Claudius, Edward, and Mac Alpin may join the others," Maon stated with a nod. "However, I still wish to hear directly from Sáerlaith regarding your Lamia guests." Maon, Fianait and the other guards parted way for Edward and Mac

Alpin to join him.

Marcus turned to face Máire. "Take care of them," he said before tucking an errant plait behind her ear.

"I will make sure they are safe," she replied. He turned and walked through the gate. The guards then pushed the heavy gate closed.

Máire could hear Marcus and the others begin talking. She looked over their guests and started to pace about, offering them a small half smile. As she studied them, she wondered why Amata remained silent, seemingly content to stare at the night skies. The Legate joined Máire, but after a few turns about the open grounds, she sat down. "Rest," Máire advised the Legate. "This is likely to take a little while," yet Patroclus still continued to pace.

Máire turned her attention to the skies and then the dark village of Ard Macha, hoping the view would help settle her nerves. She knew why she experienced such mixed feelings about Ard Macha and Eire in general... Banishment, on pain of death, is what had kept her away all this time. However, the terms of her banishment had allowed her to return should the situation warrant it, and she hoped the threat the Strigoi posed would prevent her from being killed by her fellow Deargh Du. If only she had killed Aisling... Over a hundred years too late to worry about that. Now, according to messages Sáerlaith sent to Bath, Aisling had many friends, such as Conlan and his children-in-darkness within the isolationist faction.

Of course, this was her home. She was born in Eire, and she even became a Chieftain. Her father died here. Seanán died here. Her mother died here. Her uncle Fergus... Of course Aunt Sive and Sitara had died in Bath, but they too never returned to their respective homes.

Amata sat down next to a rock. Her movements distracted Máire from remembering her family in exile. At least Sáerlaith had convinced the council to permit the Cothromaigh to work outside of Ard Macha and Eire. Otherwise, Máire and Marcus would not have been allowed to participate.

She and Amata both watched Patroclus continue pacing.

Suddenly, Amata leapt to her feet and grabbed his arm.

Máire leaned back against the wall and listened to their whispered conversation.

"Stop pacing. Do you want our hosts to think us fearful and lacking in confidence?" Amata's eyes glowed red for a moment and then settled back to blue.

Soon after, the gates opened. Máire rose and dusted herself off. Marcus, Claudius, and a few guards walked out.

"My apologies for taking so long," Marcus replied. "You are given leave to enter our humble stronghold. However, I have been asked to blindfold you both."

"Are you mad?" The Deargh Du's voice echoed through the stone corridors. Máire watched Conlan grow red in fury. She glanced over at Ruarí, who shared the bench with her. The arch druid wore an amused yet patient smile.

"Conlan loves to argue," he whispered in her ear. "The young are so impatient, sometimes."

"Do I count as young?" she whispered back.

"Yes, and yes, you are impatient," Ruarí murmured with a smirk.

They grew silent as Marcus narrowed his eyes at Conlan.

"I said I support allying with the Lamia against the Strigoi," Marcus replied. "If they cannot hold them back, soon the Strigoi will come north."

"How dare you suggest we ally ourselves with an enemy!" Conlan raged. Máire watched his neck become scarlet. She wondered whether he had fed right before the meeting.

Sáerlaith stood up. "Conlan, you are out of line," she roared, looking much like a wrathful goddess. She began to turn crimson as well. "Please sit down and calm yourself," Sáerlaith advised. She seemed to steady her voice and her demeanor. Soon, she began to pale.

"Now, I admit that what Marcus proposes seems... unusual... given our history with the Lamia. However, one of the consuls of the Lamia has come to us in person, asking us to take up arms against a common foe who threatens possible expansion into Eire. These beings are tipping the balance in the continent and in other far-flung lands. They target the mortals and do horrible things to them. May I remind everyone that we have a duty to Morrigan, our creator, to maintain the balance at all costs? I believe that it is in our best interests, and Hers, to accept this proposal and form an alliance."

The room echoed in murmured exclamations.

"If you will allow your council leader to finish..." Sáerlaith challenged as she raised her hand. "Calm yourselves. This relationship will be guarded. After all, we will be wary because of our history with them, as I am sure our associates in Briton will be equally as wary." She nodded towards Claudius, Edward, and Mac Alpin.

"I call for a vote," Ruarí announced as he raised his hand. "All who accept this proposal shall hold up their right hand."

Máire raised her hand and then watched Sáerlaith stared at each Deargh Du, one by one. May the Goddess help them if she ever lost her place in the Council. More hands soon went up. After a moment of apparent indecision, all hands slowly raised.

"I hate those disgusting, vile, and mind-bending Lamia," Ruarí stated as he looked over a copy of Máire's scroll. "Yet, I must admit that if these Strigoi inspire such fear within them, the Strigoi must truly be horrifying." He then sat down across from her.

The new room for their small collection of scrolls and written words smelled sweet of honey, herbs, and earth.

"Ruarí, have you found anything regarding my personal issues," she asked.

"I again have found nothing. I am very sorry," the arch druid murmured as he patted her hand in a comforting manner that made her feel a little patronized. "Sometimes, things work out on their own, Máire. At times, I myself feel that spells and incantations force a lack of balance. The Gods balance. The earth, the stars, the sun, and the moon balance. Now look at a Deargh Du. We do not say a spell to heal our mortal victims, create beautiful illumination, or to draw down the darkness. We think it and it happens. It merely comes forth like the budding of the trees. We can manifest magics, but pulling forth the energies of the Otherworld sometimes doesn't sit right to me. I use the energies, of course, but there is a magic to us that is our own and that is what I prefer to use."

"Are you saying that I do not need to reverse that old hag's spell?" Máire asked. "She threw some nasty rotten fruit at me, and then my heart froze. She exuded such a powerful force that it made me want to shrivel up and cry. Then I killed her, and that feeling should have gone away, Ruarí. I felt things before then. Even when my aunt Sive died, I could not cry over her. Something is horribly wrong with me. I am not balanced, and I can feel it. Everyone feels it," she whispered. "I've tried to pull forth healing from the Otherworld, but it doesn't seem to work."

Ruarí stared at her. His eyes reflected the candlelight back to her. "Be patient with Them," he advised her.

"Please tell Marcus that. I loved him once, and it wounds him when I cannot tell him what he wants to hear. Even if it is not romantic love, he deserves some form of it, Ruarí. I still feel... nothing for him, or anyone."

"I doubt that. If you didn't care..." Ruarí offered before pausing for a moment. "We can look more, chroí. Make offerings to our Patroness, or Brigid the Healer, and Angus Mac Og. They will give you strength, and They love you." He leaned forward and anointed her forehead with mistletoe oil.

"Find peace within yourself, Máire. Stop forcing the matter. Then when you least expect it, you may find a return of emotion."

"Ah there you are," Sáerlaith said after walking into the room. "We have been looking for you, Máire. You and Ruarí dashed out so quickly after our successful vote. We just... need your support to speak to 'Them'."

"Máire loves the company of scrolls and writings," Marcus called as he joined them. "You should see her recipe collection." He turned to the arch druid and said, "Ruarí, thank you for your support. If I were in your place, I doubt I would be as forgiving. In fact, I'm not sure whether I can keep from removing Mandubratius' head should he and I cross paths."

Ruarí smirked. "Lucky for the Lamia, they sent two strangers to me, or I may have not been as supportive." Ruarí then looked back at Máire. "I wish you both well. Travel safely, and I will keep this extra set of scrolls."

He leaned in and kissed Máire's cheek winking at her.

"You old flirt," Sáerlaith chided as she patted his shoulder and then took Máire's arm. "Let's give our guests the good news."

Sáerlaith opened the door to the Lamia's guest quarters and then motioned the guards aside. Máire followed behind Marcus, curious to see the political movement game continued.

"Thank you so very much for your patience. You must understand the mistrust of many here," Sáerlaith began.

"Yes I do. You have been so very kind. I could not have anticipated such a warm reception, after what our line has done. I do not just mean you," Amata stated as she stared at Marcus. "Marcus was most congenial, as were his friends and family." Amata gave them all a dazzling smile.

Máire felt a strange, unmistakable charm exude from Amata. She smiled back at her, feeling rather stupid. Máire wondered whether that talent had been innate or something Mandubratius nurtured within his elder sister. Then again, it could have come from their father-in-darkness. She took a look at Marcus and noticed a smile light his face. The man did love being flattered, but they all seemed to love that.

"I have good news," Sáerlaith interrupted Amata's praise. "The council has agreed to assist the Lamia. I would like to send an expeditionary force to accompany you two to investigate the Strigoi. I know Claudius and Mac Alpin are sending messengers to the Ekimmu Cruitne Council and the Sugnwr Gwaed Assembly now, informing them of what has happened in the empire. If we see the need develop, we will send an entire army to assist yours."

"A wise decision," commented Patroclus. "Sending an entire army now seems premature and wasteful. The Strigoi have not massed in force... ever." His words grew soft.

Sáerlaith's eyes revealed mercy.

"What you survived is extraordinary. I pity those mortals who were and continue to be victimized. Such a sad waste. You must be incredibly resilient, Patroclus."

Amata nodded her head. "He is, Sáerlaith. That is why I trust him." She then cleared her throat. "So, when do we leave, and who will accompany us?"

"We leave tomorrow night, Amata," Marcus answered. "And it will be I, Máire, Claudius, Mac Alpin, Edward, and five other Deargh Du."

"Excellent. So travel preparations have been made?" Amata asked.

"Of course," Sáerlaith answered with a smile.

Amata sat down across from Patroclus in one of the room's chairs and rubbed her hands together.

"This is such a strange place," she murmured in Latin.

"How do you mean?" he inquired. "Except for some small rudeness from a few individuals, the Deargh Du and their Celtic brethren to the east seem most... warm." He lowered his voice further. "Yet, smiling faces can mask anyone. Can they be trusted?"

"I think so, Patroclus, but let us remain cautious, as they are."

"Where do you think Mandubratius is?" he asked.

Amata chuckled before pouring them both a serving of bloodmead. "I believe he would be in the empire now, perhaps speaking to Emperor Charles at this moment."

She watched Patroclus smile, but soon his smile faded, and a few worry-lines encroached upon his face. "I am not enthralled with the idea of going back to face the Strigoi, again."

"I understand," she said. "However, you have faced them once before and survived."

"If I face them a second time, Amata, I fear I will not survive," he whispered.

She stood up and walked over to him. She embraced him and felt him relax in her arms.

A pair of hands removed her blindfold, and Amata found herself outside of the Deargh Du stronghold. She shivered in the out-pour of rain and now wished she had plaited her hair as Máire had suggested. Amata pushed her wet hair out of her eyes.

"I forgot about the storms here," she said to Marcus. "Is it not storming so badly that we must postpone our trip?"

Marcus turned back, shook out his wet hair, and laughed. "Nonsense, Amata. We are leaving tonight. This storm will not stop us. No storms do." He pulled up the cowl of his cloak, and she watched as his eyes became green and gleamed at her. She found herself thinking that she needed to bed him again in order to get more information about the Deargh Du, yet the idea of traveling in this atrocious weather gave her pause.

"Are you mad?" Amata asked. "The seas are probably too high for any sane captain to sail."

"We will not be sailing," Máire's voice rang in her left ear. She felt the woman wrap a cloaked arm around her. Marcus' arm went around her right side. She watched Claudius and another Deargh Du grab Patroclus in the same manner.

"You cannot be serious," she bellowed, as the ground's settling presence disappeared from the reach of her feet. "Let go, no... do not let go!" She ducked her face into someone's shoulder, hoping to keep her meal from making a re-appearance.

chapter six

Francia

hey landed a few miles away from a village. Amata shook as her feet touched the grass. She then collapsed on the ground relieved, paying little attention to the scenery.

A chilled hand shook her shoulder.

"We must continue moving," Claudius informed her.

"Why?" she whined, yet she hated hearing that annoying tone in her voice.

"The sun rises soon," he commented. "Máire went to find food and Marcus, along with the other Deargh Du, is taking Mac Alpin and Edward to a root cellar. We expended a great deal of energy to get to Francia in one night. I hope you are not too choosy in selecting meals or accommodations."

Amata scrambled to her feet. Claudius started walking, and Amata began to follow him down into the large cellar of a nobleman's home.

"We are in Francia?" she asked Marcus upon entering the cellar. She looked on as he placed Edward on his cloak.

"Yes," Marcus answered. She watched him shake off the wetness of the storm before sitting down in between Edward and Mac Alpin. "We usually stop halfway and spend the day deep underwater, attached to the seaweed, but that would have been difficult for Arwin and Edward. This was our first time to cross both the Irish Sea and the North Sea with passengers."

Amata heard the door open, and a large party of perhaps a dozen people carrying blankets entered. Several sheep stared at her from behind a radiant creature that made her heart stop. She blinked back tears as realized she beheld Máire.

"They think I am an angel," whispered Máire. "I asked for assistance for weary travelers, but the glamoury blinds mortals sometimes. Do not overwhelm them." She moved over to Edward and Mac Alpin and then motioned for two mortal men to come forth. "We will let them feed first so they can regain their strength."

"Do you always take such good care of your meals?" Amata asked them. Edward and Mac Alpin started to feed.

"If we killed all from whom we fed, how could we survive?" Claudius asked. "I assume we will use the celebration ruse, right?"

She heard a murmuring assent from Marcus. Amata then watched him take a blanket from a mortal and start to feed. She now felt a little guilty, given that she had expended little energy during the voyage, yet the Ekimmu

Cruitne seemed to be almost comatose. She held up her hand to Patroclus motioned for him to come to her side.

After joining her, Amata whispered, "Let us allow them to feed first. They must have expended a great deal of energy to carry us."

"Of course, Domina," Patroclus whispered back in agreement.

"What is your plan after our recovery?" she asked Marcus aloud.

"I imagine we will convince these villagers and others to answer our questions," he suggested as he wiped the blood from his lips. She watched him place a hand on his meal's neck and close his eyes.

"You are... healing them?" she asked, surprised by this gift.

"It is something we can all do," Edward mumbled weakly from his bed.

Amata watched them feed and heal. When they finished, Marcus pointed to places for the mortals to lie down to rest. These Celtic lines could be so odd, and yet so beautiful.

Aachen

Julien rolled out one of the old campaign maps on his extra table and studied it for a moment before mounting it to a board. "Edel?" he called to one of the assistants. The gendarme Edel joined him.

"Yes sir?"

"I am going to list out villages that have witnessed attacks or sightings. Please mark them on this map with a red 'x'."

"Of course, sir," Edel replied before taking the rare, imported red ink and one of Julien's wring quills made from a shorn wing feather from a swan.

Julien started reading his list. "Torino, Passau, Bremen, Abbatial–" He stopped when a knock at the door interrupted him. The emperor then opened the door and strode into the room. In deference to his emperor, Julien began to drop to his knees.

"No bowing or kneeling," Emperor Charles chided with a chuckle. "I'm weary of dealing with people genuflecting to me. Kingship is enjoyable, but being emperor is too much work. Welcome home, Inspector General," the emperor greeted him. "Ercanbald has informed me of the map you are working on. May I see it?"

"We have just started it, Imperial Majesty," Julien explained as he held up the board. "I have visited nine locations with the papal emissary and his emissary, yet our reports say that there are upwards of one hundred sightings and attacks."

The emperor stared at the board and then placed his right hand on his sword.

Julien snuck a quick glance to see whether this was a regular sword or

Joyeux, the emperor's treasured sword. He tried not to be disappointed that upon further scrutiny, this sword did not appear to be Joyeux.

The emperor tilted his head to one side. "Please excuse us, gendarme," he said to Edel before folding his arms over his chest.

After the young gendarme bowed and left the office, the emperor returned to studying the board. "It would seem the empire is being invaded."

"I am not a military man like my older brother Reginald," Julien stated, "but I have drawn that same conclusion, Imperial Majesty."

"Yet, there have been no sightings of an army," Emperor Charles stated. "Certainly, not one as vast as what one might expect from all of these attacks."

"Yes," Julien answered. "It seems that these people..." he noticed the emperor raise his brows at that word, "...these people travel in small bands, and they only attack at night. They kill the priest and sometimes a few others, and then they desecrate the church with lifeless bodies of the victims. However, in Verviers they scattered the body parts of perhaps a dozen people in the church."

"How do you know it was a dozen, Julien?" the emperor asked.

"We weighed the body parts, and the night watch provided a detailed list of twelve missing victims. These attacks are always made on adults so far, thanks to God. Nothing appeared to be small enough to be from a child. Also, the killers do not discriminate against women or men. There have been just as many female dead as male." Julien stopped for a breath.

"So, as you mentioned in your letter, they effectively shut down the churches of my empire," the emperor reasoned as he stroked his beard.

"Yes. Not only do they defile the church with blood and other fluids of the victims, they always kill the priests. Always." Julien scratched his chin and met the emperor's gaze. "Or, at least I assume the priests are dead. We could not find the priest's body in the church in Verviers."

"What would you suggest needs to be done?" the emperor asked.

"I would advise priests avoid their churches after dusk. In fact, I would recommend a general curfew ordered for all villages. The army should be mobilized, and garrisons need to be built within the villages," Julien replied.

"And you are certain the attacks are only at night?"

"Yes, I am certain, Imperial Majesty," Julien answered with conviction.

"Is there anything peculiar about these murders?" Emperor Charles inquired as he began to pace about Julien's small office.

"In some cases, it appears that the bodies were torn and ripped apart. In other villages, it seems that the poor victims scratched out their own eyes. I found others with sticks wedged in their ears. I even believe some pulled out their jaws... why and how I cannot understand. Also, many victims display strange puncture wounds in their necks."

"What beast would do such a thing?" Emperor Charles asked. Anger and frustration laced his words.

"Imperial Majesty, I know it is blasphemous to say this, but I am familiar with some early legends of beings that drink human blood. These creatures can only travel at night, for sun is deadly to them. They are nearly impossible to kill. These beings feed on the unfortunate victims by making puncture wounds in their victims' throats and other parts of the body."

The emperor's pale features grew red. "You realize, of course, that by possessing this knowledge, people may believe you to be tainted by Satan." Emperor Charles took a deep breath and exhaled. "Yet, on the other hand, this knowledge may save us, and I know you are not one who relies on nonsensical religious ravings. I am not going to ask how you obtained this information, Julien. You must keep it to yourself. Otherwise, people like that Michael Tolomei will deem you a heretic, and then there would be nothing I could do to ensure your protection."

"If this legend proves true, Imperial Majesty, then I would sooner be killed as a heretic than be bled dry," Julien answered. "I would not tell many people about this intelligence, just those whom I can trust. So far, you are the only person who I have notified about this knowledge."

The emperor nodded his head. "Well, I will follow with your recommendations. Your investigation is well thought out. Be sure to ask should you require any other resources."

"A few extra men, horses, and bribe money," Julien answered. "I have paid out a few bribes with my own sou."

"Then I will assign you a detachment of guards and send Ercanbald with funds for you. I just remembered another question," the emperor said after placing his right hand on the door. "How are these attacks coordinated?" He turned back around to face Julien.

"I believe the distances between the attacks are too great to be between riders on horseback," Julien answered. "In other words, that is a question I still ask myself."

"These blood-drinkers of yours," the emperor asked as he bit his lower lip. "Are they the spawn of Satan?"

"I do not believe so," Julien replied. "According to what I have read, this is a sickness that is spread to men and women. They are not demons. Most of these legends are older than Christianity itself."

"Beware of the papal emissary. He may not agree with your deduction." Emperor Charles pushed open the door. "Thank you, Julien," he said as he left the office.

The only break in the dark skies came from the blissful, white circle of the moon. The streets of Aachen echoed a strange silence that broke only with the sounds of animals calling out in the dark. The night song of ravens or crows brought forth a strange restlessness in Marcus.

He followed the staggering drunk through the dim alleys, knowing that the elder's tainted blood would have a small effect on his senses, yet he could not be choosy. He would rather not have to break into someone's home. He caught up to the drunk and pulled him into the alleyway.

"We need to talk, old friend," Marcus said. That was one of the best ruses to use. Just a quick meal, and then he could return to the twelve others.

"Gris!" the slobbering old man called out. "How long has it been?"

He forced the drunk against the wall and then started to feed, gauging the amount of blood that would give him strength, yet give the drunk enough of a chance to get home and leave Marcus safe.

Such matters distracted him from the sound of a mortal running into the alley blowing a whistle. Marcus turned, a ready smile on his face, planning to present himself with as much glamoury as necessary to escape this mistake.

"Wait, you are not Gris!" the old man shouted, distracting Marcus. Then, a deep radiating pain circled his head, and he could see a broken plank of wood fall in front of him.

Marcus fell to his knees and then collapsed onto the dirty road.

Máire heard the sound of a distant whistle. Where could everyone in town be? While the movement of the moon pointed to the early evening, the streets echoed no town dwellers, just the footsteps of soldiers, which drew near. She took to the air and then stopped at a house. She paused, hearing one steady heartbeat. An open window allowed her access. She levitated into the room and found a sleeping man with an empty cup in one hand. He looked to be in his mid thirties. Dried tears covered his eyes.

She straddled him, placed silver coins on his bedside, and tipped his neck to one side. The raw loneliness lingering in his wine-laced blood almost made her cry. His family had suffered the ravages of the plague. Those images, mixed with the mental recollections of a wife dying in childbirth along with their son, made her pull away.

She heard a soft noise as he shifted under her embrace. She placed a hand on the wound and started to heal him. Once she had healed his wound, Máire stepped off the bed and then knelt on the floor next to him.

He blinked his eyes and then focused on her. His lips moved as if he whispered a secret.

She expended a soft glamoury before touching his hand. "I am the angel of mercy," Máire told him. "Your wife resides in our home of regal splendor with your children. She wished for me to tell you that you need to find happiness with a new love. Stop drinking. She wants you to find peace in life." She watched the stranger smile and then closed his eyes.

Máire made her exit through the open window and then landed on the roof. Soldiers marched below. After they passed, Máire flew above the rooftops towards the countryside farms on the outskirts of Aachen, heading for one farm in particular. When she arrived, Máire landed and then walked into the barn. "Is there a curfew in town?" she asked as she sat next to Mac Alpin. "I saw no one but soldiers."

"Did you happen to pass Marcus?" Amata asked, interrupting Mac Alpin's answer.

"No…"

The prisoner remained passed out in the pitch-black dungeon. Julien heaved a sigh of relief as he followed Edel out of the dungeon towards the lights of the palace. The city felt safe.

"Edel, contact Arnaud. I want a sketch made of our prisoner to be placed in the town square." He paused as he stepped out of the staircase. Edel followed him.

"Place a note on the sketch that offers a reward of 20 livres for any information leading to the capture of this person's associates. Anyone seeking the award is to contact me."

Julien paused mid-stride. "On second thought, see if Arnaud can make several copies of this sketch and post it around Aachen."

Marcus opened one eye and then rubbed his forehead. The scent of mold lingered, along with the smell of dirty mortals. He licked his lips, trying to ignore his hunger. How long had it been between his last meals? He rubbed his brow again, hating the interruption last night. The pain started to pass, so he decided to sit up on the floor. With his head now upright, Marcus felt strong enough to stand, so he rose. Once on his feet, he could see someone sitting in a chair, watching him in the distance from behind the small, barred window in the door. A torch revealed the stranger's face. A young man stared at him.

Marcus gazed at the soldier through the bars, wondering whether he should chance breaking the walls or pushing down the door, grabbing the stranger, feeding from him, and getting the strength to escape this dungeon. He sniffed the air and closed his eyes. Twelve mortals wandered the labyrinth of the cells.

Marcus walked over to the door and lowered his head so he could look through the hole. The young Frankish soldier met his stare.

Soon the stranger cleared his throat. "I am Julien de Divio, Inspector General of the Gendarmes. Whom am I addressing?"

"Marcus," he said as he considered whether giving his real name would add nothing but confusion to this conversation. "Marcus of Bath."

"Bath?" The inspector general's blue eyes gleamed for a moment. "I am afraid that I am not familiar with Bath." The gendarme rubbed his chin. Julien had a bit of a Frankish accent, but he spoken Latin well enough.

"Bath is in Briton. Actually, it's the Kingdom of Wessex," Marcus clarified. "I am not a subject of his... your lord, the Emperor Charles."

"Indeed. Do you know why you are here, Marcus of Bath?"

Marcus smiled, trying to gather up whatever glamoury he could muster. "I cannot say that I remember why."

"You were caught attempting to feed off the blood of a citizen of this town in an affront to God and man," Julien de Divio replied.

"You have been mistaken," Marcus explained.

"I know it to be true. I witnessed it with my own eyes," the inspector general answered. "Two of my men can also attest to seeing you about to bite the neck of your intended victim."

Marcus gave up on his glamoury. The amount of energy required to use it on a dozen men would be a waste. He decided to remain silent.

"I know you have others who hunt with you," his captor stated. "I believe that you and yours may be those who are murdering priests and poor vassals."

"I am alone here," Marcus replied. "My friends and family reside in Briton and Eire."

"Nonsense. We have heard of others of your kind, your family, committing murders all over the empire."

"As I said, my friends and family are not in the–"

"I know it was you and your friends," the inspector general exclaimed, interrupting him. "Tell me more so I can find them. I do not like the thought of torturing information from anyone."

Marcus walked over to his bed, sat on it, and reclined.

"Very well. I will hunt them down myself, with or without your assistance." His guest turned away. "I think the best torture at the moment is to leave you here without light or food. The guards here have orders not to come anywhere near the bars upon pain of death."

Marcus closed his eyes, deciding to conserve his energy. They would find him soon.

"Guess what I found?" Claudius asked as he walked into the barn holding a sketch of Marcus. "Not the best likeness I have seen, but it does resemble him."

Amata grumbled into her hands.

"So, somebody captured him." Máire wondered how a mortal could manage such a thing. "What do we do to rescue him?"

"I have been considering a plan," Claudius offered as he sat down next to her. He patted then Máire's shoulder. "We can borrow some clothes from the local guards."

"You plan on walking into the palace," Patroclus ascertained.

"Not really the palace," Claudius continued. "I had an opportunity to look at the palace during my trip to Aachen. The garrison is above the dungeon."

"You plan on us going into the garrison and talking our way into the dungeon," Mac Alpin reasoned aloud with a smirk. "That may just work."

Amata shook her head a bit. "There is an alternative. I know someone here. They can help us."

Patroclus shook his head. "I think we should try this first. You lovely ladies can stay here with the rest of the party while we four," he explained while motioning to himself, Claudius, Mac Alpin and Edward, "should take care of these mortals. The rescue should not be too difficult. Use your associate as our backup plan. You can put your plan into effect tomorrow night if we do not return."

"I have the distinct impression that you and I are outvoted, Amata," Máire said. "Do be careful. I do not think she and I will be able to dress as guards here. Try not to kill any of the mortals," she said, more to Patroclus than anyone else.

Julien moved upstairs into the garrison, dodging around the palace guards who marched through the process of handing over weapons to the sergeant of arms at the end of their shifts. However, a group of four standing together in the front of the line refused to hand over their armaments. Oddly enough, the four came from three different regiments.

Julien watched two of them in the midst of convincing the sergeant for keys to the dungeon.

"We are here to transfer a prisoner," one of them said.

Julien raised his brows. The dungeon only held one prisoner. "Halt," he said to the guards, willing to play their captain. If they were true guards, they would stare at him as if he were a fool. He watched the foursome turn to face him. "Why do you not relinquish your weapons?" he asked. Julien caught sight of the captain of the guards and nodded to him.

The captain watched the situation and then motioned for additional guards to surround the infiltrators.

"My apologies, sir," one of the infiltrators replied. "We were ordered to keep our weapons at hand."

The guards swarmed the strangers, and soon twenty swords pointed at their necks.

"Why do I not believe you?" asked Julien, impatient for the truth.

"We are here because you wrongfully captured our friend. Release him," The stranger's eyes turned gold for a moment.

Julien closed his eyes, arguing with himself about the prisoner. He then opened his eyes, ignoring the strange voice in his head, concentrating on the guards who now wielded heavy scabbards. "Who is this friend of yours," he asked the masquerading guards.

"Marcus of Bath," the bearded one answered.

"Oh, so you are his friends. You will see him soon enough."

The guards chose that moment to bash the four infiltrators over their heads, effectively knocking them out.

"Throw them in the dungeon along with their friend," Julien ordered.

Marcus started counting the guards again. Their numbers had increased. The scents of his associates mingled in with the mortals. He sensed the guards toss Claudius into the cell next to his.

"Claudius," Marcus whispered. "Claudius!"

"Marcus?" Claudius said, raising his voice so they could hear each other through the wall. "Is that you?"

"Shhhh… what happened?"

"We tried to get to the dungeon through the garrison, but we were caught, because we failed to follow protocol," Claudius answered. "We thought about taking time to study the guards' habits, but Mac Alpin thought that might be difficult if you could not fly out. Do you have the strength to escape with us?"

"Not without seriously injuring someone," Marcus murmured. "Frankly, I do not think that would be the wisest plan to follow. I have not fed in two nights. There are nearly forty guards here. I do not want to kill the emperor's men needlessly, though without feeding soon, I'll have little control. Besides, we may need them to assist with the Strigoi. What is the backup plan?"

Claudius chuckled. "This is the backup plan, Marcus. Oh, wait. Amata says she has contacts here. What should we do in the meantime?"

"Conserve your strength. It does not look like it will be easy feeding with so many eyes watching us."

"Very well," Claudius conceded.

Mandubratius wandered into the palace, just beating the daylight. He waved away his entourage, which fast approached him. "Tonight. Just let me have some rest until tonight," he said, hoping that manipulation and mind-bending would not be necessary.

He followed the secretary to his guest quarters and collapsed on the bed, grateful again for a windowless room.

Mandubratius awoke the next evening to the delirious and delicious sensation that women waited for him. It would probably be nothing more than a dream, but he did have his hopes. He inhaled and closed his eyes. One of the visitors could be Amata. The thin threads of recognition tugged at his memory and confirmed his suspicion. The other person must be a stranger.

Mandubratius walked into the sitting room in his linen, long-sleeved tunic that went to his knees. He smiled at Amata and then turned his gaze to the other woman. Dark red, flame-colored curls and green eyes met his stare and did not blink.

He smiled at Maél Muire and almost laughed as she gave up in their staring battle and turned away from his eyes as if she became shy. He tried to make his body behave. He had half a mind to send Amata outside and then pick up his long, lost treasure in order to spend the evening punishing her for her cruelty at their last meeting. The tiny pinch of anger that remained melted away at seeing her in a dress the color of a woman's tender blushes. He trained his eyes on the wall behind her.

"So," he began, feeling a smile purse his lips. "What brings you two dazzling goddesses into my midst?"

Amata opened her mouth and then glanced at Maél Muire.

"I wish I were here to rip out your heart and feel the blood trickling through my fingers," Maél Muire revealed with a slight grimace, "however, there is an alliance now between my kind and yours, and we need your assistance. When we first arrived in your quarters, I almost left, but Amata told me you would help us in our time of need. Let it be known that I am only here, speaking with you, to rescue my oldest friends. To give this long tale some brevity, I suppose I am here to kiss your arse," Maél Muire finished. He noticed her grimace fade into a resolved smirk.

"How fortunate for me that you and yours allied with us," Mandubratius purred. He sat down in a chair across from theirs.

"So, the both of you need help from me." He could but continue to smile.

"How was your journey, Amata?"

"Ma–"

"Michael," he interrupted her, holding up a finger.

He noticed Maél Muire stare at Amata as if confused.

"Excuse me," Amata said with a smirk. "Michael, this is Máire."

"Máire, what an odd name," he said. "Bitterness really does not suit you," he said to Maél... Máire.

"Neither does your new name suit you," she snapped, and then her mouth moved back into an uneasy smile.

"Are you not going to inquire as to what assistance we need, my Lord Emissary?" Amata asked.

"Of course," he answered, pretending to be distracted. "How may this humble servant of God assist you?"

He almost started laughing at the confused look upon Máire's face.

"It would seem that the inspector general of the Gendarmes has caught your old friend Marcus. They arrested him two nights ago." Amata folded her hands over her dress.

"Marcus! Captured by a mere mortal gendarme?" He started to laugh.

"Last night, while trying to rescue Marcus, Patroclus and three of our companions were also caught and imprisoned," Amata added.

Mandubratius continued laughing and shook his head, trying to control his outburst. "This is a wonderful tragic comedy of errors that even Plautus himself could not have conjured. Why doesn't Marcus simply knock down the door and release himself?"

He watched Maél... Máire open her mouth to answer.

"I know," he smirked. "Marcus wouldn't dare endanger a mortal. He's far too honorable to think such a thing. I suppose I could assist in arranging their executions."

"Michael!" Amata exclaimed through pursed lips. "This is not time for your games."

"Oh Amata, there is always time for games," Mandubratius drawled as he glanced over at Máire. "Honestly, I jest, I jest. I will see about arranging for their release."

"Thank you so–" his redheaded guest began to say.

"Ah, ah, ah," Mandubratius interjected with a smirk He rose from his chair and walked over to stand in front of Máire... such an odd name for a beautiful woman. "I have one condition that you must meet." He stared down at her green eyes, trying to stop imagining what pleasures her pouting lips could bring him. He stuck out his right hand instead. "Kiss my ring."

"This is… this must be a joke," Máire said. Her right brow lifted in a questioning arc. He vaguely remembered seeing the General in his days as a mortal make that very gesture. She must have copied her sponsor.

"Either my ring or my arse," Mandubratius replied, grinning down at her. "It is entirely up to you, Maél… Máire."

He watched her purse her lips. She then leaned forward, and he felt a soft brush of air on his ring finger. She avoided touching the gold, though of course he knew it was toxic to Deargh Du. As Máire sat back up, he noticed a pained expression on her face.

He then turned to face Amata.

She started to chuckle. "You do not expect me to kiss your ring, do you, Michael?"

He stuck his hand in front of her and stared into her blue eyes.

"I only do this because we do not have time," Amata groaned at him. She leaned forward and kissed it.

"Well, then it is settled. Now I must change into more courtly attire. The emperor and his courtiers do love dressing like their subjects, but they expect decoration from the visitors, and you two make me look very poor indeed." He went into the bedroom and began to dress.

Mandubratius emerged a few moments later. "Shall we go?"

"Oh how the mighty have fallen. Hello, Praetor."

A familiar voice swelled through the cell in Greek, making Marcus twitch a little as he sat up. The darkness cleared from his brain.

"Where have I heard that voice before," he muttered.

He could smell Máire and Amata. The third blood-drinker, a Lamia, remained a mystery for the moment. Marcus sat up in bed and stared back at Máire. Her face revealed strong displeasure. Then the stranger nudged her aside to look at him. The stranger's face grew familiar, and he realized he remembered the voice.

"Man–" he began.

"My name is Michael Tolomei," Mandubratius replied, now in Latin. "I am the papal emissary to the Imperial Court. I understand that you are Marcus of Bath. Perhaps we met during my visits to churches in Wessex. Oh and I must apologize, for I have brought your friends, Lady Amata and Lady Maél Muire to join me. Such lovely friends you have, Marcus."

Marcus watched the Briton smile at him.

Did he ever not have a game to play?

"Am I to understand that you and your cohorts are possessed by Satan?"

the newly renamed Michael asked him.

"Mandubratius," he drawled, "stop with this ridiculous game." He walked up to the door and peeked through the bars, ignoring his earlier orders to himself about wasting his remaining energy. He then placed his hands on the bars.

Máire pushed Mandubratius aside and reached for Marcus' hand. Her fingertips brushed over his knuckles.

Mandubratius pushed Máire aside. "I am not quite sure I believe you, sir," Mandubratius challenged with a smile. "Also, you mistake me for some associate of yours. My name is Michael, and the inspector general himself claims to have seen you preparing to drink the life essence from another man."

"The inspector general is blind," Marcus hissed. "He is mistaken. When will he finish this fool's game?" he addressed Amata and Máire.

Marcus watched 'Michael' wipe his face with a handkerchief. "My, you do not have to be so rude and spit in my face. You are quite the barbarian. If you will behave that way, then I will not help you out of here. Shall we, ladies?"

Marcus noticed stares exchanged between the women.

"My lord, I think these men do not appear to be the children of the devil. Perhaps this Inspector General is mistaken in what he witnessed," Amata countered.

Marcus rubbed his forehead, bewildered that Amata seemed to play along in this game.

"Mmmmm, perhaps," Amata's brother-in-darkness purred. "However, these men could be Satan's helpers. They can be hiding the truth. Perhaps executing them at first light will prevent further deaths in the empire."

He watched Máire turn to face Mandubratius. "You promised assistance. I kissed your ring, my lord. Do you mean just to jest again? After all, there are continuing attacks in the empire, are there not? Does that not prove these men are innocent?" She delivered her last words in a derisive hiss. "My impatience with this game has reached a summit!" she yelled in British.

"Oh very well," Mandubratius groaned as he stared at Máire as if disappointed. "We will discuss this matter with the inspector general. Perhaps he could be persuaded that he made a mistake. Will you ladies accompany me?" Marcus watched Mandubratius' green eyes turn cold, "or would you rather remain in this dark, dank dungeon?"

"I will go, Papal Emissary." A quick and false smile flitted across Máire's face. She turned to Marcus and leaned forward. "We will return with your freedom," she whispered.

They all backed away just when a guard approached them. "Get away from the bars!" the guard yelled at them. "You will be here for a long time," he shouted at Marcus with a sneer.

Marcus sat down against the wall adjacent to the other cell.

"It sounds like we may be leaving here soon," he said to Claudius.

"If Máire does not kill Mandubratius first," Claudius replied.

The execution orders lay on Julien's desk. He planned to update the emperor in an hour or two. He thumbed through the papers and then drummed his fingers on the table, pondering why the reports of 'devil' attacks seemed to increase in number over the last few nights. A knock at the door interrupted his thoughts.

"Enter," he said.

The door opened. "My lord," Edel said as he looked over at him. "The papal emissary wishes to see you. He is here with two companions."

"Show them in," he said as he set down his papers on his desk.

Edel exited his office. The door opened again, and the papal emissary walked into Julien's office. Behind the papal emissary walked two beautiful women. The one to his right had the loveliest pale blue eyes. The one on the left side stared at the books and scrolls behind Julien before meeting his eyes. He inhaled and tried not to blush like a young boy. Unlike the ladies of the court, the flame-haired stranger did not cover her hair. Whatever beauty the blue-eyed woman exuded paled in comparison to this other lady.

"It is a pleasure to see you again, my Lord Emissary," he said to Michael. "What did I do to deserve such loveliness in my office?"

The lady with blue eyes smiled at the compliment. However, the other woman seemed oblivious to the flattering remarks.

"The pleasure is all mine, Inspector General," Michael replied. "Allow me to introduce my relation, the Lady Amata Tolomei of Rome."

The woman on his right curtsied a little. In response, Julien bowed his head.

"And this is the Lady Maél Muire... of the court in Ulster," Michael announced as he looked over at his other companion.

The woman pulled out of her distraction and extended her right hand.

Julien chuckled as he extended his arm. She had cold fingers. "The situation in Ulster must be dire if women there check men for hidden weapons. I apologize. I have no idea where Ulster is."

He watched a flush of color grace Maél Muire's face, and he felt a moment of shame for embarrassing her.

"Eire," she answered. Her attempts to regain her confidence were obvious. "Ulster is in Eire, and yes many women must protect themselves from all matters of men, including those who pretend to be gentlemen." The beauty glanced at the papal Emissary. "Once again, my Lord Emissary, my name is

'Máire'. Maél Muire is my official name, but no one uses my true name," she added in her strangely accented Latin.

The papal Emissary grinned. "The people of Eire have most unusual and charming customs, Inspector General. I'm certain you've heard their poets expound on the late Queen Hildegard."

"Of course," Julien muttered, still staring into Máire's emerald colored eyes. He caught his breath and looked away. "Please take a seat. Now, how can I assist you three?" He found himself staring at the Lady Amata again.

"These ladies are acquainted with the individuals you mistakenly arrested for being the minions of Satan," Michael replied.

"I am mistaken?" He shook his head from side to side. "I am not mistaken. With my own eyes I witnessed Marcus of Bath attack a drunk man."

Máire met his eyes. "Please, my lord," she began. "These men are not demon spawn. I have known them most of my life. While they are boisterous and playful, they are also the truest of companions. Since my family passed on, Marcus and our friends have taken care of me."

He heard an impatient sigh from Michael, who seemed irritated with her comments. Then Michael's annoyance seemed to pass.

"How sure are you that you witnessed what you believe you saw?" Michael asked him.

"I am quite sure," Julien replied.

"How dark was it?" The papal emissary rose from his seat and extended his hands. "Was it this dark in the streets?"

Julien hesitated for a moment.

Michael walked over to the other side of the room and began to blow out candles. "Was it this dark?"

"No, darker still," Julien admitted.

The oil lamps grew dim, and their flames disappeared. Michael blew out all the remaining candles save one. The moonlight lit the stark room.

"Yes."

The figures of Michael and the ladies moved around in front of him.

Michael stopped in front of one of the ladies, who proceeded to kneel.

"Now, can you tell me what I am doing to Lady Máire?" Michael asked.

"I cannot say for sure," Julien replied, not wanting to admit what it looked like she did.

"What does your mind's eye tell you, Inspector General?"

"You are in an embrace of sorts," Julien admitted, keeping his mouth shut on how lewd the embrace appeared to be.

"Amata, would you be so kind to light the lamps I extinguished?" the papal emissary asked.

The room lit up, and Julien could see that Michael and Máire were not in an embrace at all. She knelt with hands folded as if in prayer. Michael stood about a foot away from her with his hands resting at his sides.

"So, you are saying that because of my state of mind, I saw what looked like a demon feeding from a drunk, and in reality it was someone trying to assist a wayward soul?"

"Yes, I believe that is what you saw," Michael replied.

"Hmm," Julien hummed thoughtfully. "What about his friends who tried to break into the dungeon to help him escape?"

"Misguided fools," explained Michael before laughing. "They believed that they needed to come to the aid of their friend, who had been wrongfully accused. It is a common custom in Wessex and Eire to perform this sort of activity for friends. As I said, they have most unusual traditions."

"Still, they were civilians armed within the confines of the garrison. That is an offense under the laws of this empire," Julien argued.

"But it isn't illegal to carry arms in this land!" Lady Máire sputtered.

"They were impersonating guards," Julien replied.

"Now, calm down," the papal emissary soothed. "Inspector General, if you tell the emperor that these individuals worked for you in secret to find the cause of these atrocious murders, there would be no need for them to remain in the dungeon."

"Why would I say such a thing?" Julien asked. "This second argument of yours does not hold water, Emissary."

"Because you made a mistake," Michael stated. "Not to mention that there is one person in the dungeon who has met these murderers without losing his sanity. His name is Patroclus. I am certain he would have much to teach you."

Julien looked back at the two women, giving himself time to think over the situation. For the first time, he wondered whether Michael could be sincere. He caught himself smiling at Máire again.

"Alright. I do need all of the assistance I can find in learning about this enemy," Julien reasoned. "I will claim that this was a clerical error and that they were under my authority," Julien muttered. "However, if I do this, from this point forward, they will be under my authority and released into my recognizance."

"That is most generous, do not you ladies agree?" Michael drawled at the two women with a smile.

"Very generous," Amata stated, giving Julien a seductive grin that made his heart race for a moment. He turned to Máire in hopes of calming down.

She pouted a bit. "These terms are acceptable," she mumbled, before sliding a hand over her hair. Julien lost his train of thought at that moment. Her hair seemed to lift and flow with an invisible breeze. Julien forgot his earlier annoyance with Máire.

"Very well," Julien agreed as he sat back down. "I will draw up the papers, and they will be released to my custody." He began to write out the documents.

"Before we leave, I have one last request, Inspector General," Michael said.

"Certainly," Julien acknowledged as he looked up to face the emissary.

"As a souvenir, I would like these death certificates you filed for the gentlemen. I see them on your desk."

He heard a harsh utterance from Lady Máire, perhaps in her native tongue.

Julien watched the papal emissary reply something to her, and then he turned to face him again.

Julien closed his eyes, as the papal emissary's question seemed to repeat itself in his head.

"Yes of course," Julien answered, holding out the papers. "Take them."

Amata followed Mandubratius a few steps behind Máire. The Deargh Du attempted to snatch the death warrants from him, a pointless endeavor if there ever was one.

"Would you stop with these childish games... Ma... Michael?" Máire asked in British. "I know very well what you plan. We do not have time for this! If you go through with this, the next time we meet, I will–"

"You will what?" Mandubratius turned around and continued walking backwards. An innocent smile played at his lips. "I remember once... you and I were sitting in trees together, the best of friends. I still have that raven you carved. Will you try to kill me again?"

Máire's face betrayed her raging emotions. Mandubratius always enjoyed playing games with people like that. Amata believed it easier to just hide her feelings around Mandubratius and pretend that nothing annoyed her. Otherwise, Mandubratius would simply continue with his amusements.

"Maél Muire is ignoring me now," Mandubratius drawled. "Do you know what her real name means, Amata?" He spun around and started walking normally.

Amata wondered why she allowed him to play these confounding games when they needed to pay attention to matters at hand.

Damn this male-dominated world.

There had been a simpler time in Rome when spreading her legs brought many men to their knees. Now, men just received some strange pleasure from the holy church.

"I suppose you will tell me," Amata replied. "Despite the fact that time is an issue."

She heard him grumble under his breath. "You two are not any fun. Maél Muire means devotee or servant of Mary."

He shoved the scrolls into a purse. "Now, are you going to be furious or not?" he asked Máire. "I have been wondering when I might expect you to stab me with a knife or a sword."

"When you least expect it," Máire replied. "I know what you plan to do, and it is a way to waste time."

Mandubratius stopped, turned around, and grabbed Máire's wrists.

"If you do not allow me to have my fun, I will destroy the release orders," he said to Máire. "I deserve this at the very least, and you will be silent, or do you want your beloved sponsor to die in the sun."

"Fine," Máire agreed in a forced but calm voice before pulling her arm away. "Have at your pointless game."

"Fine, I will," Mandubratius replied. He chuckled. "You really need to come up with fun activities for yourself... Máire."

The guards opened the dungeon doors, and they walked over to Marcus' cell. Amata caught sight of what appeared to be Mac Alpin waving to Máire.

"Guard, please wait by the other cells," Mandubratius instructed him.

"What took so long?" Marcus stared at them with otherworldly green eyes. Then he blinked and then stared at them with silver eyes. "I want out of here now." He came up to the bars and wrapped his hands around them.

"Of course," Mandubratius purred. "You will have your release soon enough." Amata watched him thumb through the scrolls in his bag and reveal the selected scroll to Marcus.

Amata rubbed her forehead.

"What's this?" Marcus asked. "This is what you call an order for my release?"

Mandubratius attempted a look of confusion. "Well yes. You do want to be released, do you not?"

Amata found her impatience growing to unsteady levels. "Michael, show him the real release papers! Then show it to the guards!"

"You mean I did not give you the real release papers?"

No one said a word.

"Oh dear," Mandubratius said as he looked over the papers in his bag. "I must have confused them. How embarrassing." He grabbed another scroll and held it up. This time, Amata recognized the release forms in his hand. "However, there is one condition to your release."

Máire clenched her fists and shut her eyes.

"And this condition?" Marcus asked in a faint voice.

"Your friends must pledge to help the inspector general investigate and thwart this horrible menace that plagues our people. So, do you accept my generous proposal for your release into the service of the inspector general? It seems a worthy cause."

She heard a whisper from the cell.

"I am sorry. I do not think I heard you clearly," Mandubratius addressed Marcus with a grin. Amata knew well that Mandubratius had heard exactly what she heard from Marcus.

"I agree!" Marcus yelled. "Now get the keys or the guards to open these damn cell doors so I can feed without destroying the garrison!"

"Splendid," Mandubratius agreed with a smirk. "Guards, I can release the prisoners. After all, we shouldn't frighten them with your horrifying eating habits," he addressed to Marcus.

Mandubratius took the keys from one of the guards and motioned for him and the others to leave. The main door closed, leaving them in relative privacy.

"Now, we have much to discuss, but you all smell wretched. There are wonderful baths in the springs nearby." Mandubratius opened Marcus' cell door.

Amata smirked as Marcus punched Mandubratius in the face, knocking him to the ground.

"Gods, do you ever shut up!" Marcus growled. He then grabbed Máire and pushed her against the wall, commencing to feed from his daughter-in-darkness.

chapter seven

Regensburg

he nights of flight ended, and the cold winds and rain of the north welcomed them with the sweet kisses of a long, lost lover. Seosaimhín landed and then wept with joy as the muddy lands claimed their ankles. This soft land could remind one of home.

Voices called on the winds, and the animals became silent in respect of those words. She crouched to the ground and crawled, hearing the language of insanity grow clearer.

"Nagirrom promised, and here you waited," Seosaimhín said to the elements. She closed her eyes and felt the drawing power grow as she neared one of the so-called Strigoi. "Now, we must learn your secrets. Nagirrom's knowledge will keep me from your onslaught." Seosaimhín could still taste the bitter dregs of the tea that Nagirrom had insisted she brew and drink. The disgusting potion made her head pound, but at least the Strigoi's mental attacks seemed to have little effect on her.

Seosaimhín moved in and then pounced on the unsuspecting fool, fangs stiff with promise. She began suckling the blood, and soon the visions began, ripe with color. The beginning origins showed embraces of jealousy and tasted of a lingering madness. The sweetness almost became sour in her mouth.

The vision of a God grew in her mind, yet not a God. An immortal blood-drinker reveled in Godlike powers, enabling him to control these beings.

The visual patterns and crossing scents created confusion as the Strigoi tore apart a mortal victim under the wooden stare of the merciful man on a cross. They took away the man holding a wooden cross with tears in his fearful eyes as he begged for assistance from a variety of Gods and immortal beings.

The roar of the pretend God's words rang in her ears with precision.

"Destroy the churches. Kill the priests and a few of their faithful," he raged with strange eyes the color of lightning.

She released the Strigoi, allowing the being to collapse to the ground, and then she wiped her mouth. A few moments later, the Strigoi opened his eyes and stared at her.

She stretched out her hand to him and smiled. His orange eyes suddenly seemed beautiful and heart wrenching.

"We are your friend," she whispered to him simply. "We will help you."

"Friend, yes, we are friend," he answered in a gravelly voice, which smelt

---

of death. A speck of drool from his mouth became a wet line as he started nodding his head.

"We want to see the bull of bulls," Seosaimhín said, leaning in to stroke a hand over the thin hair covering his bumpy scalp. While the Strigoi's skin paled into gray, his blonde hair seemed soft like the silk strands of the spider web.

"The bull is in the prairie, surrounded by heifers of the lesser bulls," the Strigoi's voice echoed around her.

"Let the grass sweep the bottoms of our feet as you lead us to your great bull," Seosaimhín suggested.

Omid grabbed the Strigoi's arm and shook her a bit. "How many people died in your arms," he asked, sensing his voice echo a bit. "How many priests are in our ranks?"

"What about the churches?" Omid continued, seeing his warriors struggle with his questions.

"We found others. Other blood-drinkers," the Strigoi mumbled as he placed his hands on the sides of his face and shook his head. "From the South they were. They speak in the old tongue."

"Latin? You mean they were Lamia?" Omid asked.

"Yes," another Strigoi whispered.

"And what happened?"

"Killed some, some escape," the first Strigoi answered, turning to stretch his arms toward the moon like a lost child beckoning to his mother.

"The Lamia will come in greater numbers. Create more of yourselves when you go to the South and West," Omid ordered. "Tell your brethren, now."

The Strigoi closed their eyes in silent obeisance.

"Thy will be done," the oldest one acknowledged.

Soon, a strange noise echoed in Omid's ears. The sounds of footsteps made him turn to his right, and he witnessed a charcoal-colored beauty with hair of silver stare at him from ten feet away. Her eyes glowed with a green light.

"You are Deargh Du, but not," Omid began, remembering the tales of other blood-drinkers.

"We are the children of the damned, the soulless ones, yet not damned and not soulless," the woman intoned with a clear voice which echoed. She then stepped closer. "We are not of Morrigan. Rather, we are of Nagirrom.

"And who is Nagirrom?" Omid asked as he moved his feet over the soft grass to meet her.

"Nagirrom is He who led us to you," the Deargh Du replied.

"To what end?" he asked, suspicious of this woman's intent.

"Nagirrom wishes to help the Strigoi," she said, allowing a beaming radiance to surround her. "Yes, He sends a mere woman to help them." The woman chuckled, revealing white fangs. "Wisdom is not achieved by burning a house one is within."

The stranger's voice became louder with her last sentence, and he sensed a growing strength from the woman. A strange darkness befell the land, and Omid's sight failed him.

"We have offered to help, though only if you treat women like men," she yelled, as her voice grew stronger… strong enough that he almost covered his ears.

Then the darkness cleared, and he could not see the woman.

"Will you accept us?" a voice behind him queried.

Omid turned around. This being had much to offer in his quest to destroy the raging beast that had destroyed his family.

"Yes, of course," he answered.

"Nagirrom is pleased," the dark beauty purred.

Époisses

Talia tried to keep quiet as she finished off the wine bottle. For once, she wished for a wake… an excuse to celebrate her dear husband's passing. Typically, she avoided funerals, as she found them so droll and morbid. Why have a boring and lethargic mass, mourning over death, when life could be celebrated with music, dancing, and drinking? How she missed those old days.

With no wake to attend, Talia felt some contentment sitting in her husband's chair enjoying the beauty of the stars and drinking his wine. Too bad Mandubratius could not remain to enjoy this leisure.

"Ansere! Prades! I need more wine," she called out, keeping up the appearance of a devoted and mourning wife.

When they did not answer, she stood up and noticed the smell of blood wafting in the air. Talia stood up and walked into the hall. When she arrived, she could no longer hear the night creatures' chatter, or the wind for that matter. The lands' silence overwhelmed her ears.

She turned to face the front door and then spied glowing orange eyes stare at her from what appeared to be Prades' fallen body. The thing smiled at her, and then the sky turned colors. Noises echoed in her ears demanding her suicide.

Talia fell to her knees and screamed as the colors turned to visions that felt as if the past had returned to reality. She watched her family torn to pieces by the Franks. Her first husband dragged her to the ground, screaming at her in Gaelic about his tortured soul.

Just then, the visions broke, and she watched the horrific being flinging his arms in an odd, comedic movement. Talia saw that an arrow had wedged itself in the being's back, and behind him stood her savior, a mortal guard. The Strigoi roared and then chased after the guard who had saved her.

Talia wrenched herself to her feet and then started to run toward Aachen. She would run all night, if needed, and if she could not reach Aachen tonight, then surely she would be there tomorrow night.

She heard herself screaming as the visions started again.

Aachen

Amata trailed a few steps behind Mandubratius.

"That was rather generous of the inspector general," she stated, "I mean, to give lodging and clothing to our wayward companions."

He smiled at her before opening the door to his quarters. Her eyes lit with what could be sweet innocence, but he knew better. "I am sure that the servants will provide for much needed sustenance."

They walked into the room. Amata closed the door and then regarded him with the same grin that he knew meant she watched him for any telltale signs of weakness. Thank the Gods that the world remained in the hands of men.

"How goes your manipulation of Pope Leo?" Amata queried.

"These attacks continue," he began, "not to mention, the emperor's efforts in proving that the matter is secular have not proven fruitful. Therefore, the Holy Father will be forced to send the papal army against Satan." Mandubratius shook his head. "I fear that Leo may not remain on the throne of Rome for long."

"And you plan on the next pope being someone more attuned to our needs?" Amata continued to grin at him. "I must compliment you on playing this game so very well, Man... Michael. I thought your one concern was the Strigoi."

"It is a concern, but we must examine the big picture," he said, wrapping an arm around her. "The future of Christendom must remain in the palm of the Lamia."

"What of Marcus, Máire, and the rest of our new allies?"

"Máire? Oh yes, I cannot believe she refers to herself with that name. Well, we continue with this quest for the survival of the western and eastern empire. Once the other races come out of hiding, sweetheart, they will be most grateful to their saviors. The Lamia have much to gain as the saviors of the other continental lines. You see, the Celtic lines believe in protecting the mortals and could care less about political machinations here. They are so small minded. We can take the credit that they would simply ignore."

A knock at the door interrupted his train of thought.

"Come in," he called out.

A messenger stepped forth.

"Well, what is it?" Amata asked.

"My Lord Emissary, there is a hysterical woman calling for you at the front gate."

"Hysterical, you say. Who is this woman who desires my attention?" Mandubratius asked.

"Lady Talia de Époisses."

Mandubratius scratched his bearded chin for a moment. "Very well, bring her in."

The messenger turned on his heel and left the room.

"Shall I go?" Amata asked. "They gave me very nice quarters, and I know that Talia abhors my company." She grinned at Mandubratius.

"No, please stay," he replied.

"Ave Pope Michael?" Amata teased with a chuckle.

"Oh no, I am not going to be stuck celebrating masses and all that dull pomp," Mandubratius replied.

The door slammed opened and then Talia ran in. Dried tears made her appear old. She fell to her knees and began crying anew. Talia slapped herself and swayed back and forth, singing a soft and querulous song.

Mandubratius sighed and then kneeled in front of her. "Talia, what happened?" he asked with what sounded to be empathy and patience.

"I escaped," Talia whispered. "The madness became unbearable."

"Shhhhh," he soothed as he helped Talia to her feet. "Everything will be fine. After tomorrow night, you will reclaim your lands. The Strigoi do not stay in one place for long, and they do not take property."

"I do not want to go back alone," Talia told him. "Will you come with me?" She turned, and seemed to notice Amata for the first time. "Hello Amata?" Her words seemed to be an uncertain query. Talia turned back to Mandubratius, who stared into her frightened eyes. "Please," she begged in an airy voice.

"If I do this for you, I want something in return."

"Anything!" she exclaimed.

"Well," he purred, "there are three of us, and I could not imagine a better way to spend my day."

"How is it Amata and Máire get their own private quarters, and the five of us wind up sharing this?" Claudius asked.

"I suppose it is because they were introduced to that gendarme as families of royalty, so to speak," Edward answered with a sigh, "while we are just ex-prisoners who he and the rest of this court regard as mercenaries."

Marcus turned on his side to stare at the others. His gaze fell on Patroclus.

"Did it not seem odd for your superior to be impersonating the emissary of Pope Leo?" he asked.

Patroclus pulled off his boots and reclined on his bed. "The Lamia have had long standing relationships with the rulers of Rome, whether they be Caesars or Popes. Even though the Rome we knew is long dead, the new Rome offers ample opportunities to continue our relationship with powerful and influential empires." He yawned.

"These accommodations are much better than the stone floors in the cell," Arwin commented.

"Yes, much," Marcus agreed with a smirk. "It's a very nice home."

"Speak for yourself," Mac Alpin grumbled. "This palace makes me feel confined, as if I were in that cell again. Give me a dirt bed under a tree."

"It feels a little like Rome in my day," Claudius muttered. "I find myself enjoying it, but I am also repelled by the lack of fresh air. These Imperial homes do feel as if they long for the old days of the republic and the empire."

Patroclus seemed to study them. "So, is it the nature of the Celtic lines to require fresh, chilled air and rain?"

Marcus watched the others grin for a moment.

"It's not required, but we prefer it," he said. "As we've noticed, the Lamia enjoy warmth. So, Patroclus, does 'Michael'," he drawled, using Mandubratius' new name, "wish to be the next pope?"

"It has not been uncommon in Rome's history for the Lamia to manipulate events in favor of one ruler or another. Some have in fact lost their heads. However, the Lamia do not directly rule Rome. It is much easier to take a step away from he who rules. That is where true power lies."

"How has that changed with the church?" Marcus asked.

Patroclus' face turned up in a small smile. "When the sand in the hourglass has been emptied, the glass will be turned over. Politics and religion always change, but they will never leave us."

Marcus shook his head. "The world of Lamia seems more akin to the backroom machinations of a senator than someone with your directness."

The Legate opened his mouth to reply when darkness settled over the room. Marcus closed his eyes and inhaled. He could sense the thrum of building ire and drawn magical energy grow. "Máire, you should be in your plush accommodations now." He smirked as he opened his eyes. Soon, the darkness lifted and faded like the gentle mists back in Eire.

Máire stood in front of them with her arms folded primly across her chest.

"I cannot believe what this society considers style," she raged. "You should have seen the horrible garments they gave me... heavy cloth that makes it impossible to stretch, veils for my hair... how can I wear such things?"

She continued her rant with typical aplomb. "I cannot find comfort in any of them. Then I decided to stretch my legs in my léine, and you never heard such a racket. Women screamed as if I were a leper in the halls. Men covered their faces as if they were ashamed. In fact, they acted as if I was Pandora's Box. I could not be seen for fear of their own sanity."

She became quiet, for a moment. "Then the guards had the gall to escort me to my quarters because I had caused such uproar amongst these genteel folk. Gentlemen, what happened to the days when a woman could go out in comfortable clothing without men guffawing or passing out in her presence?"

Máire grew silent before continuing. "I miss Eire... my Eire, sometimes."

"And you are naked because you are protesting this treatment," Mac Alpin ascertained.

"Yes. Is there a problem with that?" she asked. "It is not as if any of you have never seen me naked before."

"I do not believe I have had that pleasure before," Patroclus answered. Marcus watched the Lamia smile at her and raise his brows.

"Alright, so one man here has not seen me in this state, but you don't act as though it's an unnatural state," she argued. "I am very close to hoping one of those God-fearing guards sees me, an unwed woman naked, with five unwed men. It would probably cause their hearts to explode."

"You would be lucky if they do not throw you and all of us back in the dungeon," Edward commented as his eyes moved over her for a moment.

"I suppose you are right, Edward. I should return to my room and pretend to be a delicate woman."

"Sleep well," Marcus suggested with a wink at Máire.

"I will," she drawled. "You all sleep well too." Máire opened the door and walked out of the room without bringing down the darkness or utilizing her speed.

"Your child is very free-spirited," Patroclus said after the door closed. "She must make a most amusing companion."

Marcus smiled and then closed his eyes. "Yes, she is that," he responded, feeling sleep demanding his attention.

Mandubratius tilted his head to one side as the emperor rubbed his forehead and managed to look irritated as his arbitration duties continued. He looked over his shoulder and noticed the shabby little party of Celtic lines that Amata and Patroclus had befriended, though perhaps 'befriended' might be too strong a word.

The emperor began to pace a bit before heading towards the throne. The disagreement between the neighbors just became circular arguments, now, regarding whose father received what lands from Emperor Charles.

Mandubratius backed towards the group of blood-drinkers, who shuffled their feet and tried not to look bored with the proceedings. Some studied the tapestries on the walls or the sturdy palace itself. Marcus and the burly Scot began to nod towards the lovely young woman named Gundrada. Máire covered her mouth in a yawn.

"There are two ways to end such an argument," he muttered to Marcus in Gaelic. "The first would be those two fighting to the death, and the second and better alternative would be killing them both and taking back the lands."

"Enough!" the emperor roared. Both parties grew silent. Even Mandubratius had lost his tongue at the Imperial outburst. Emperor Charles' patience disappeared. "Because you cannot decide the boundary of your land, I shall buy them from you both for a livre per acre."

Mandubratius watched the two mortal's eyes light up at the promise of money for what was probably scrubby land or forests. He noticed Julien staring at Máire and tried not to laugh. Máire, once again, appeared to be oblivious. The inspector general then finally paid attention to the matters at hand.

One of the landowners cleared his throat. "Imperial Majesty, my family has been there since before I was born."

"Well, I could just take all your lands for nothing and throw your family out," the emperor grumbled before taking a seat.

"I would be happy to give up my land for the good of the empire," the other man replied.

"Good," the emperor grumbled. "So it shall be. What is next on the daily docket?" he asked Ercanbald.

"Per your request, Imperial Majesty, I have summoned Michael Tolomei, the papal emissary, and Julien de Divio, Inspector General of the Gendarme," the secretary replied.

The emperor stood up and moved towards them. His clear blue eyes studied them both. "Lord Emissary, how fares the investigation?"

"I am convinced the devil does indeed walk the earth," Mandubratius replied. He heard a sharp intake of breath and then glanced at the inspector general from the corner of his eye. He could not be more pleased to see anger and irritation on Julien's face. The inspector general did nothing to shield his rage.

"Please explain," the emperor replied.

"Every church in every village struck by these demons has been desecrated with dead bodies. Satan harvests these souls and rends the bodies to shreds. Those who witness these events are driven mad by sin and must be put down. The leaders of these villages generally order the execution of these survivors and their families to prevent the spread of madness. They are burned as heretics. I plan to recommend this as a universal practice to His Holiness." Mandubratius tried not to laugh. It could be so easy to pretend to be an extremist Christian. He just needed to claim everything to be the work of Satan. After all, the emperor and rest of the court expected this kind of attitude from Rome.

"Julien, do you agree with this proposed practice?" the emperor asked.

"I most certainly do not agree!" Julien seethed, though he seemed to calm himself a little after his outburst.

"Explain yourself." The emperor turned to face the mortal.

"We are no closer to finding out who is performing these killings. It is someone who wants to destroy the power of the holy Church and her leaders."

By the Gods, the inspector general's calm started to fade again. The mortal took a deep breath and continued.

"This does not mean the guilty party is Satan. It could be the Moors or the Saxons... it could be heretics, or it could be any number of people who count themselves as enemies of the church. You cannot say it is Satan without further investigation. Also, I feel it is a condemnation of the innocent to execute the family members of those who have been attacked or driven to madness. There is no evidence to suggest that these other victims are heretics or in league with the devil."

"They are demon spawn, not victims," Mandubratius interjected. He lowered his head a bit to hide his smile and silent laughter.

"They are your subjects, Imperial Majesty!" the inspector general insisted.

The emperor put up his hand.

"Why is it I can never enjoy my evenings as I used to? Lately, my nights have consisted of judgments," Emperor Charles mumbled, before rising from his throne pacing. The emperor's voice lowered as he muttered something about blasted imperial duties. Soon, Emperor Charles ceased his private muttering and turned back to face the court.

"I find myself tending to lean toward the inspector general's assessment. I will not have my subjects murdered because a family member has fallen to these desecrators. The people are scared of being hunted down by their emperor because their relations were slain. We cannot continue this practice, is that understood, Papal Emissary?"

The emperor's eyes glared at him. Mandubratius raised his head and nodded. He then smiled and bowed his head again.

"Yes, Imperial Majesty," Mandubratius answered.

"Julien, I realize you are not done with the investigation, but I need to do something... now. What do you suggest I do?"

The inspector general cleared his throat. "Extend the curfew to all nighttime hours. Order the army to set up garrisons in the center of the larger towns. Also request that the churches be locked at night. Have the priests stay at the garrisons."

"Finally, some sound advice for protecting us from this menace, but how do we combat and kill it?" the emperor asked.

Mandubratius heard a throat clear and then noticed Marcus step towards the emperor and Julien.

"If you will pardon my interruption, Imperial Majesty, but I may have a solution to this problem," Marcus said.

"Who are you?" the emperor asked.

"This is Marcus of Bath," Julien explained. "He and his associates were released into my custody to help with my investigation." The inspector general delivered his last sentence in a half whisper.

"I see. Well, despite the fact you are now working for my best Gendarme, inform me how you can help, Marcus of Bath." The emperor crossed his arms over his chest.

"My associates and I are hunters of a sort. We have dealt with similar problems of this nature in Scotland, the Anglo-Saxon kingdoms, and Eire."

The emperor chuckled. "They have such issues in Eire, Scotland and the Saxon lands? The poets and the instructors from the across the sea at our colleges in the empire say nothing about such problems. Are you mercenaries, or just the cause of these problems?"

"No Imperial Majesty, we are not mercenaries, and we have no involvement in these troubles," Marcus answered.

The inspector general, as well as the other mortals, watched the two men speak with interest.

"So, because you are not mercenaries, then you require no coin to deal with this problem?" The emperor smirked a bit.

"That is correct, we require no coin. However–"

"That is the exact word I was expecting to hear next," the emperor interjected before pacing about for a moment. "Please go on and explain this 'however', Marcus of Bath."

"We wish to have command over your soldiers whenever it is needed," Marcus answered.

"Command over my soldiers?" The emperor appeared incredulous, and continued to pace about the great hall.

"From what we have been able to discover, it is not a few men, but an army scattered throughout the empire, yet it is still an army. Imperial Majesty, I know well that it takes an army to defeat an army," Marcus answered.

"If I decide to go along with this, what makes you think you can command my troops?"

Marcus bowed his head. "I am not without experience in soldiering, Imperial Majesty."

"Really? Is this experience mastery over men or mastery over a weapon?" The emperor grinned again.

"Both, Imperial Majesty," Marcus replied.

"I would like to see a demonstration of your mastery. Are you up to it?"

"Of course."

Mandubratius watched the former Roman General smile with a gleam in his silver eyes.

"Splendid. Doolin!" The emperor turned toward his guards. "Join us, and bring forth your four best warriors."

The captain motioned to four of his men. They moved forward, dressed in jackets of scaled armor and heavy leather."

"Do you require armor?" Emperor Charles asked.

"No, I do not," Marcus replied.

"Somewhat foolish, but as you wish," the emperor pointed out with a chuckle. "Now, you may choose a sword from my guards."

"May I take two swords, since I did not take the armor?" Marcus asked as he marched over to a nearby guard to judge the balance of the sword in his hands.

"Very well, you may have two swords," the emperor agreed, nodding his head. "Now, there are five of you. You are to select one of my soldiers to command. The remaining three will attack. The objective is to defeat the enemy and for both of you to stay alive."

Marcus walked around the four soldiers and then picked the youngest of the four. Mandubratius could not help but raise a brow at that. He looked over at Amata and Patroclus, but they both shrugged and then returned to watching the activity in the center of the room.

"Hmmmm, I notice you did not pick my captain," Emperor Charles stated.

"Most interesting."

"Before we engage in combat, may I take a moment to speak with my new lieutenant?" The Deargh Du smiled at their host.

"Very well," the emperor agreed with a nod.

Marcus motioned for the young mortal to a corner and began to whisper in his ear. The emperor could not hear the conversation, but watched the boy's nervousness fade away. The young soldier appeared resolved. Marcus and his lieutenant then walked back towards the other three soldiers with their weapons drawn.

"Captain, are you and your soldiers ready?" the emperor asked.

"Yes, Imperial Majesty," the captain of the guards replied as he drew his blade.

"Marcus of Bath, are you and your new lieutenant prepared?"

"Yes, Imperial Majesty."

"Begin!" The emperor moved to the side and joined the other spectators.

The two other guards drew their blades and walked three paces away from their captain, who remained in the middle. Mandubratius strained to hear the quiet conversation between Marcus and the soldier.

"Amélien, they are going to flank us to our left," Marcus said to his lieutenant in a soft voice.

"How can you tell?" the young soldier asked.

"The captain and the one on his right are looking forward and the other is looking behind," Marcus answered calmly.

The lieutenant charged the guard to their left, and Marcus ran towards the captain. The guard flanking his captain's left side, moved back to charge Marcus.

Before either mortal could land a blow, Marcus sidestepped the captain and caught the flanking guard unaware, sliding the blade in his right hand under the guard's armpit. The smell of blood graced the air. Marcus withdrew the blade, and the guard fell.

Amélien held his own against the other guard flanking the captain.

Marcus turned to face the captain and then stepped back and raced around him. He and his lieutenant switched their opponents in the middle of a strike. The flanking guard slashed at Marcus. The Deargh Du dodged the attack and, with his left sword, he sliced the right side of the guard's face, effectively blinding the mortal in that eye.

Marcus blocked another attack and sliced through the guard's throat with his right blade.

This left them with the captain of the guards, the emperor's best warrior. Amélien, awash with confidence, moved on the offensive and proved himself quicker with the blade than his captain. Mandubratius saw Marcus smile as he watched the young mortal. Marcus could intervene, but he seemed to prefer to watch the battle. The elder captain of the guards appeared tired, and his defense became slowed. He stepped back from a cut he made too late, but the lieutenant stepped in with a thrust through the captain's mouth. When Amélien withdrew his blade, the captain's lifeless body dropped to the floor with a wet thud. He and Marcus then placed their blades on the bodies of the dead before bowing in the direction of the emperor.

The emperor appeared to be on the verge between anger and ecstasy, but ecstasy seemed to win out, for the emperor began to applaud, and the rest of the court joined in.

"It would seem you have earned your duty," Emperor Charles said, "and your freedom. You all are released from the custody of the gendarme, yet I am assured you will assist him with this danger stalking our lands."

"Thank you, Imperial Majesty," Mandubratius heard Marcus reply.

"There is, however, one more thing I must say before I toast to your and my new captain's victory," the emperor replied, looking in the direction of the blood-drinkers.

"What is that?" Marcus asked. He followed the emperor's stare.

"Instruct the red-haired woman in your company to kindly refrain from traipsing around my palace without benefit of proper clothing. Despite what the Basileus Irene believes, we are not barbarians here."

Mandubratius scanned the bloody bodies on the floor and noticed bloodstains on the clothing of the court and the emperor. Civility could be so fragile.

Marcus looked over at Máire for a moment with a gentle smile as if he prepared to chide her.

"I will chastise her later, Imperial Majesty," Marcus replied.

Mandubratius took a moment to look at Máire. She stared passively back at Marcus, trying, apparently, to hide the building anger within. He smirked at Máire, daring to hope that the chieftain would arise from her gentle form and tell the emperor about true decorum and say that he and the Franks were backwards, full of bloodlust, and lacked civility. Yet, she remained silent.

"It shall be done," the emperor stated before turning away from Máire. "Now, what is the next order of business?"

"The secretary spoke to me after the court left," Marcus said, taking a seat next to the rest of the party in the dark and somber inn. "He gave me assurances that when needed, I could command an army against the Strigoi."

"But, this would be an army of mortals," Edward replied. "We would have no use for them, would we?"

"Perhaps, perhaps not," Marcus answered, before taking a goblet of wine from of the women carrying a tray weighted with cups, "at least not in direct a confrontation with the Strigoi. However, it may be a useful tool to get information from the soldiers, and if necessary, prevent needless death of family members who may be related to a victim." He turned away and took a long drink.

"So, where should we go?" Mac Alpin queried.

"I am not sure yet," Marcus answered with a chuckle.

"What will we do when we encounter them?" Máire asked.

"All I think we can do is distance ourselves around the Strigoi and attack them from all sides. Hopefully, one would not be able to incapacitate all of us at one time," Marcus answered.

"I wish there were a better way," he heard Patroclus murmur. The others turned to look at the Lamia. "I am no coward, but I do not look forward to facing their madness once again."

Marcus sensed the approach of a mortal and then noticed the inspector general walking towards him.

"Madness, what madness?" the Frank asked, before turning to study Máire with a tender smile.

Marcus cleared his throat, partly to get the Gendarme's attention, but also to get Máire to control her glamoury. Once again, she seemed oblivious to mortals being drowned by her beauty. "Did your investigation indicate whether people in the vicinity of the murders grew mad with no obvious cause, Inspector General?"

"Yes," Julien answered. "That was an observation I made in my official documents, not that they will probably be seen by many. Not too many in the court or within the emperor's staff read very well." The gendarme laughed a little.

"We were just trying to determine how the madness is caused," Marcus explained. "Would you like to join us?"

"Yes, thank you." Julien slid on the bench and sat down across from Marcus. "By the way, do you have an official title that I should use in reference to you?"

"Suí ó gaisced," Máire murmured in Gaelic, giving his official title amongst the Deargh Du. She noticed the others stare at her, and she smirked for a moment.

"I am sorry," Máire added, "that means 'Master of Arms'. That is what others call him in Ulster and Bath."

"Well, you proved that in court. I found myself speechless at your superior display of command and fighting prowess. I should probably not say this, but your young lieutenant was not a very good guard. What did you tell him?"

"It was an ancient Roman motivational trick," Marcus replied. He watched Claudius and Máire look at each other and chuckle into their drinks.

"Oh I see. It is most effective." The inspector general appeared confused with the laughter at the other end of the table. "So, may I ask how you wish to track down this army?" Julien raised his brows.

"We intend to bait it, surround it, and kill it," Marcus answered.

"And would you perhaps require some official assistance?" the mortal queried.

"You are more than welcome to join us," Marcus replied.

"Thank you. I look forward to this grand adventure. When do we leave?"

"Tomorrow night at dusk. Where should we start our journey?" Marcus asked. "We are not familiar with this part of the empire."

"Based on their progress, they seem to move through the eastern half of the emperor's lands towards the west. I would say we should start towards the town of Divio. I know it has not yet been attacked. Neither have many of the villages in the west of Burgundy, such as Vézelay."

Marcus watched the mortal's eyes light up with mention of Vézelay. "Do you have any idea why they are going that way?" he asked Julien.

"They seem to be enveloping the empire from the east, almost as if a pincer threatened to squeeze the empire.

"A classic military maneuver," Claudius stated. "To close all paths of escape for an enemy, I mean."

Julien nodded his head. "Hopefully, we can find some way to prevent that from occurring." He rose from the bench. "I suppose we should all start preparing. I am certain Emperor Charles will insist on his soldiers and some of my men accompanying us."

"Of course," Marcus replied. "After all, he promised to allow me to command the forces we needed."

"I am certain he will wish to send us off with a formal farewell," Julien added. "We should all meet in front of the palace. Is the papal emissary traveling with us?"

"Doubtful. I believe he is taking care of some business elsewhere," Patroclus answered.

"Do you wish to meet at dusk?" Marcus asked.

"Very well, dusk it is." The gendarme nodded to them and then headed for the exit.

"I suppose this means we need to pack," Máire observed.

"Yes, that it does." Marcus grinned at his party. He began to wonder what they would encounter during this journey.

Máire began polishing her blades after deciding to stay in a comfortable and loose green léine... the desires of that pompous windbag Frank be damned. She oiled the first of her three swords. Two of them would go in one of the equipment wagons or pack horses, but her favorite, a simple one-handed sword, would stay with her. It balanced perfectly in her hand. This old-style Celtic blade looked similar to the gladii that Marcus and Claudius preferred. Their blades did appear odd next to the longer swords that the Franks used.

She placed the clean and oiled sword on the bed and began packing clothing, leaving the odd, discomforting clothes of this empire on one of the two spare chairs in her room. She found no use for them, yet wondered whether she should bring them along. Surely, they could be used as bandages or serve some other purpose.

A knock on the door interrupted her packing, and so she closed her eyes and sensed a mortal stood behind the door.

Someone must be lost. He or she will move along.

She turned back to packing and began to wrap up one of her spare swords. A louder knock drew her attention to the wooden door again.

"Who is it?" Máire asked.

"Charles," a man replied.

Charles?

There were only two men named 'Charles' in the court that she knew of. The first would be the emperor's little grandson, Charles. The second would be the emperor himself.

"What is it that you want?" she asked, deciding there must be more than two men named Charles.

"I wish to apologize to you." When the answer came, she finally recognized the emperor's voice.

"Very well," Máire said, before opening the door. She stood aside to allow the emperor in. For a man who insisted upon some formality within his palace, he appeared to be dressed as most of the Franks did.

"Please come in," she said, seeing that he waited until she gave permission for him to enter. "This is your home, after all. I am certain that you have leave to go into whatever room you wish, Imperial Majesty."

She closed the door after he walked in. Máire then sauntered back towards the table and chairs. She noticed that he remained silent.

She turned back to face the emperor and looked him up and down, trying to ascertain his age. He must be at least fifty, yet he embodied a strength that gleamed behind those blue eyes. The candlelight revealed his hair to be dark blonde, almost the color of honey, yet a few silvered hairs near his ears gave his age away. For an older man who had seen more than his share of battles, he seemed rather striking. Upon closer inspection, Charles now appeared to be taller than when Máire had last seen him at court. He even seemed to be as tall as Marcus.

"You may speak," she said, wondering whether she released too much glamoury. Máire grabbed a dagger and began cleaning and polishing it, relishing the chance to make an emperor nervous, though he seemed unfazed for the moment.

The emperor opened his mouth to speak, yet he said nothing, as if carefully selecting his words.

"You are a most unusual woman, Máire of Ulster," the emperor said at last. He began to pace a bit. "I am most contrite for embarrassing you in front of the entire court. I did pronounce your name correctly, did I not?"

She watched a slight grin tug at the emperor's facial features, causing him to appear even younger.

"Yes, Imperial Majesty, you pronounced my name perfectly," she replied, before putting down her dagger and returning to her packing. "I am a woman of Eire, and my customs must seem odd to most Franks. No apology is necessary. I was not aware of my social breach, and the correction has been made."

She put clothes into bags, knowing a stupid, childish hurt would be revealed in her eyes if she turned to face him now. Men had no right to dictate her clothing, or lack thereof. Perhaps living with her father-in-darkness and their roving circle of friends made her soft in some ways. She made her own choices and received advice only when she sought it.

"You speak with the detached coldness of a man," he noted. "Again, most unusual. However, I do like directness." She caught him looking over her clothing and the supplies she had packed.

"Most women in my country do not handle swords or wear such clothing as you pack in those bags," Emperor Charles added. "Frankish women depend on their husbands and families to carry swords and take care of them."

"War and Death in my country do not spare the women," Máire said as she turned to face him. "I am surprised the poets from my home do not tell you this. I suppose they only spout romantic tales of the mythic cycles, leaving out the raids, ravishing, and battles in the real Eire." She paused and considered her guest again, hoping he would not see her facts as a slight. "Once, during days not long ago, men and women of Eire were equals in all things. Even our legendary warrior, Cu Chulainn, received expert tutelage from a woman. I carry on those ancient traditions," she explained with a smile.

"Ah, but I have a feeling you are more than just a mere woman belonging to your friend, Marcus." The emperor's eyes regarded her again.

Máire laughed. "Marcus is my friend, yes, but I am not owned by him or are any of my other friends. And, yes, you are correct, Emperor Charles. Once I was a chieftain of over one hundred souls." She picked up another sword to polish.

The emperor smiled. "So, you are royalty in Eire? I must have the poets of your home write of your eyes and lineage. One wrote a most beautiful poem for my poor departed wife, Hildegard." He took a few steps closer to her.

"Imperial Majesty, I am afraid you do not understand. Royalty here implies that someone is selected by the... I mean God. Rather for me, it was the people of my home who selected me to lead them. My uncle and my father both did the same." She smiled a bit before taking a step back and returning to polishing her sword. She wondered whether she could be royalty. Morrigan chose her, after all.

She heard a soft, breathy sigh and the racing of a heartbeat. Charles knelt at her right side. She set down her sword and turned to face him. When she looked in his direction, the emperor stared up at her.

"Excuse my rambling. The fact is that when I lost Hildegard, I thought I would never see someone else with whom I would feel an interest. My marriages have been mostly for political alliances. My last wife was a lovely woman, but we had little in common. Yet, I am drawn to you like a moth to a deadly flame. I want you," he purred in Latin.

"When I saw you in my court, I must admit that I felt a twinge of jealousy towards your associates. I brought up your strange clothing and customs to have the excuse to speak with you privately. Please stay here with us. I feel that I can gaze upon you and be at peace. You won't be sorry for staying. I can give you more than any mere mercenary." He fell silent for a moment while he seemed to study her. "However, I see in your eyes little interest in such things. You seem a most unusual woman, Máire. You will probably leave in search of adventure tomorrow night."

He took her hand in his, and the scent of his blood grew stronger. "If you leave tomorrow, I still wish to share your bed tonight."

"Imperial Majesty," Máire cooed as she leaned forward and cocked her head to the left, "what if I said you could not share my bed?" She desired to see what his reaction would be to such rejection, and she tried to keep from smiling.

Emperor Charles rose from his knees. "I would find ways to make you more willing," he said as he arched his brow. "I do not take 'no' for an answer easily, Máire. I think you will find my countrymen and me to be most stubborn. I'm sure you have some weakness, and I shall find it and exploit it," the emperor continued with a smirk, "whether the weakness is jewelry, weapons, or your own stubbornness."

"You would take advantage of my weaknesses to make me pliable to your advances?" She took a few steps closer, allowing her hips to sway, knowing it might make him even more demanding of her affections. However as much as she hated Mandubratius' manipulative games, playing with this mortal, without resorting to glamoury, could offer a great deal of entertainment and pleasure. Máire stared into the emperor's eyes for a moment. The smell of strength and power in his blood made her hunger rise.

"I don't think I need any extra men to subdue you," he answered, before moving in closer to her. "I can tell enough about you already."

"So, are you man enough to take me?" Her words became a soft lilt.

She ducked away as he reached for her.

"I believe myself to be man enough to handle a woman like you," the emperor boasted with a smile.

"And have you seen a real woman before?" she murmured as she pulled at the sleeves of her léine, allowing it to fall to the floor.

She studied him as he stared at her body.

"No." His words were a breathless hiss. "Not a woman like you."

She took his arm and began to undress him. His hands slid over her as she pulled off his tunic and then took off his linen shirt, breeches, and boots. The emperor seemed almost in shock as she led him towards the bed.

He pushed aside her packed bags and swords at the last moment and lay down, patting the bed beside him. A sensuous grin played at his mouth. She watched his eyes light up in surprise as she straddled him. Most Franks seemed to share the beliefs of their church about women taking the lead in bed.

She leaned in and kissed him. His arms slid around her, and he tried to roll her onto her back as she deepened the kiss and nibbled gently at his lower lip.

"Imperial Majesty," she cooed, with a smile as she stared down at him. "Please allow me to show you how we please our men in Eire."

The red-haired beauty smiled down at the emperor and moved off him before rolling onto her side. He wrapped an arm around her and then pulled her in for another kiss.

After the kiss, he released her. Charles felt sleepy and content, but he kept her hand in his. "You may walk around my palace naked any time you wish, Máire. In fact, I would prefer it that way," he said with a chuckle.

"Thank you, Charles," she purred. "I hope you do not mind if I continue to pack." He watched her slide out of bed.

"I do not mind, if you do not mind my watching you like an adolescent boy staring at a beautiful girl." He smirked before yawning.

"Just do not act like one," she replied. He heard her soft laughter and her strange words in her foreign tongue. The words seemed like a gentle song in his ears. Soon Charles drifted off to sleep.

Sometime during the night, he awoke to her joining him back in the bed. Her cold arms sent a chill through him, yet after a brief prelude of pain, a feeling of utter joy overwhelmed him.

chapter eight

o you think the emperor requires the trumpeters to signal his arrival and departure at the latrine?" Mac Alpin asked amidst chuckles.

"Who can tell," answered Máire with a smirk.

Claudius studied the official court waiting on the mortals in their party to finish their packing duties. Marcus seemed to exude a quiet patience as they all waited on the horses.

The emperor looked over at Máire. He caught a half smile play at the old man's lips.

"This display is nothing, really," Claudius countered. "Every time Julius Caesar headed for the latrine, a thousand bulls were sacrificed.

"And I heard when Vercingetorix took a moment to get relief, fifty Romans were sacrificed," Arwin interjected as he grinned at Máire. "How was he?"

"Boys, does this game ever get old?" Máire inquired.

"Chroí, you know well enough that we never get tired of this game," Mac Alpin argued.

"I have to wonder how long he begged," Claudius quipped. "Be grateful, Maél Morrigan, that you are not traveling with a group of bickering, backstabbing women. At least with us, we will tell the truth without sugaring it or whispering it behind your back."

"I daresay that is probably Amata's job," Máire replied with a laugh.

"I think they are done," Claudius muttered. "Perhaps we should become silent so the Franks can give us a speech about honor, victory, and God. Let us get a closer look." They walked towards Marcus.

The gendarme nodded at the emperor and then looked over at the party.

Claudius noticed Julien stare at Máire and Amata for a moment as if confused. He then marched towards them. Claudius almost laughed outright at the sight of the inspector general marching, much like how Marcus would stomp whenever his mood demanded being in a snit, or at least looking the part.

"Uh oh, somebody is not happy about the female portion of our regiment," Arwin muttered in Gaelic.

"You are bringing your women with us?" Julien asked.

"Yes–" Claudius began, before being interrupted.

Máire elbowed Claudius in the ribs to push him away. "I am no one's woman, and I am certain Lady Amata feels the same way."

"But..." The Frank still managed to look confused. "We need warriors on this journey."

"Inspector General, I am a warrior, and I take offense to your tone, sir," Máire replied.

Claudius tried to stop grinning, hoping that Julien would be prepared for the pain. Máire hated being treated like a frail female.

Another mortal interrupted the ensuing fray. The emperor cleared his throat. "Is there a disagreement between you?" he asked as he looked at them both.

"Imperial Majesty, the ladies wish to accompany us," Julien de Divio explained, though he still managed to sound incredulous.

Claudius swallowed his laughter upon seeing the emperor studying Máire. No, that would be worshiping. It vaguely resembled the same stares that Julien gave her. Claudius nudged Arwin and held out his hand.

"Then I am certain their presence will only help bring about a successful conclusion to this campaign," the emperor replied.

"Yes, Imperial Majesty," the gendarme acknowledged as he lowered his head. He then returned to his place at the head of the columns of the fifty soldiers. He took the reins of his horse and leapt on, joining his four officers.

Mac Alpin rolled his eyes a bit.

"Yes, yes, we all realize what great horsemen and huntsmen the Franks are," Edward muttered as he nudging his horse towards them. "Must we all be subjected to their acrobatic antics?"

"Edward, I forgot you did not like horseback riding," Máire added as she adjusted the stirrups and then swung herself into the saddle.

"Horses can be skittish," Edward admitted. "I am not. I don't have your ease with them or Claudius' ability to speak with them."

"So, Claudius, what did you and Arwin bet on this time?" Máire asked after taking the reins of the horse.

"After the emperor complained about you last night, I thought it seemed an obvious ruse to bed you," Claudius answered. "Arwin thought he just wanted to be rude to foreigners. So Arwin owes me–"

"Two sou," Mac Alpin groused before passing over his bet.

"So, was his Imperial Majesty good in bed?" Claudius queried Máire while placing his winnings in a purse.

"He was not bad," she replied. "On the other hand, I was good enough to be allowed to ride with you."

Claudius shook his head and chuckled again, before noticing that the four officers and the inspector general had drawn their swords in a salute to the emperor.

Emperor Charles held up a hand to quiet the soldiers and his court. "May the Lord protect these men and women who go forth to eradicate the great evil stalking our land. We pray these warriors ride swiftly and be a beacon of justice to others."

The emperor then dropped his hand to his side in a swift motion.

"Forward!" the inspector general ordered. The flare of trumpets and drums echoed around the palace, and then the columns advanced.

"So what shall we wager on next? Amata and Marcus? That should be very entertaining," Arwin stated.

"I think he is very wary of the Lamia in general," Claudius answered. "I feel that such a coupling between the two of them would be quite unusual." Their conversation died down as they caught up to Marcus.

"What is the wager this time?" Marcus asked with a knowing smirk.

"Nothing at all," Arwin answered before nodding to Claudius.

Époisses

An impatient Mandubratius led Talia through her home.

"See, they are all gone, just as I said they would be," he chided as he patted her hand and smiled.

"Please stop patronizing me," Talia said. "The things they showed me," she shuddered a little. "Strange, I do not smell blood."

She stared down at the floor.

"I imagine your vassals cleaned the floors," Mandubratius pointed out. "How noble of them to continue with their obligations to you."

Talia nodded her head. "I shall need more servants and vassals to work my lands. I also will require a small army to protect me."

He noticed a fierce determination enter her eyes. Already, her plans helped diminish her fears.

"Perhaps I will even sponsor some of my guards," she added.

Mandubratius laughed outright and then shook his head a bit. "You will make a most charming noble lady, Talia."

"Well, what will the noble Michael Tolomei do during my recovery and my mourning?"

"I am bound for Rome in a few nights," Mandubratius replied. "I cannot wait to arrive."

"That sounds most entertaining," Talia stated. "I wish our ambitions did not lie so far apart."

"Tonight, our ambitions lie in the same bed," he purred before taking her arm and leading Talia towards her quarters.

Outside Aachen

Julien snuck a peek inside one of the foreigner's tents out of curiosity. Early this morning, he watched them split into four groups of three each. Amata and Máire seemed oblivious to the quiet jeers of the soldiers who watched them walk with their friends into those tents without a second thought.

He studied the interior of the tent and noticed three small tents created with heavy blankets covering two chairs. He wondered whether that would help him sleep during the day. He then moved out of the tent and back towards two of his lieutenants.

"They have individual tents within the larger tents," Isore said to Edel.

"That is so strange," Edel replied as he drank water from his pouch.

Julien cleared his throat, and the two men stood at attention.

"As you were," he said. "As you are well aware, our traveling companions are attempting to duplicate the patterns of our prey so they can be more effective in the hunt." Julien warmed his hands over small fire. The early spring chill lingered in the early afternoon. A beautiful mist had faded into the thick forest earlier that morning. The sun heated the land, but did not entirely defeat the cold. "I find their method of blocking the sun to be rather ingenious. I plan to try the same technique in a few hours. Perhaps you two should try it as well. At the very least, it would keep you from gossiping about their oddities like old women."

"Yes sir," they said in unison.

"Isore, you have watch in three hours… get to sleep. We will be up and moving by sunset. We have a long night ahead," Julien ordered before he headed for his tent, hoping for sleep.

Julien rushed out of his tent, sensing something might be wrong.

"Isore?" He looked about for the other gendarmes. The camp seemed to resonate a growing, chilled silence. He took a quick peek within their foreign associates' tents, which appeared deserted.

Julien heard a noise, turned, and then jumped when he spied a shadow. Instead of a murderous beast, Isore stood over his shoulder.

"Where have you been?" Julien demanded, hating to reveal his nervousness.

"I was taking care of some business in the woods," Isore replied. "I am sorry I left my post sir. Edel promised to take over for me."

"I cannot find Edel," Julien stated. "Where is everyone? Where are Drogo, Engilbert, Gerold, Marcus, and his associates?"

"Sir, I have not seen them," Isore replied. His eyes seemed to turn blank for a moment.

Soon Edel and Gerold walked through the camouflaging leaves of green.

"Where have you two been?" Julien asked them.

"Sorry sir. Nature called," Gerold replied.

Julien shook his head. Something seemed very strange. He stepped through the forest and noticed a small grove of well-tended apple trees breaking from the wilder stand of trees. He stepped into the grove, searching for anything out of the ordinary, when the sound of flapping wings broke his concentration. Several of the soldiers and gendarmes sat under the trees staring at nothing, baring blissful smiles as if caught in the throes of a beautiful dream.

"What are you all doing here?" he asked them.

The soldiers and gendarmes rose to attention.

"Just tending to personal business, sir," Drogo answered.

"Then why were you all sitting under the trees with strange, satisfied smiles upon your faces?"

"I am not sure," Drogo answered. "I just feel very… satisfied. Perhaps I had too much water to drink."

The others nodded their heads, agreeing with Drogo's explanation.

Julien said nothing as he pushed his way through the trees to find their traveling companions saddling their horses after packing their two tents, while his men wandered about in a strange haze, peacefully smiling at everyone they came across. This annoyed him to no end. Even Máire and Amata seemed prepared for their journey.

"Anyone who is not in formation in five minutes will have to run laps around us during our next two hours of travel," Julien ordered as he saddled his horses.

His men started scrambling to pack their tents in a flurry of activity. He heard soft chuckles from Marcus' party but decided to ignore him.

Five soldiers ran laps around the moving forces. Julien slowed down to allow the northern contingent to join him.

Claudius, Arwin Mac Alpin, and Máire trotted past him, chattering away in some strange language. He stared at Máire's back.

He then heard a throat clear, and so he turned to face Marcus.

"You must be quite pleased to lead troops into battle, so to speak," Marcus stated. The older warrior raised a brow as he looked over at the red-haired woman with a somewhat rude familiarity.

"Why do you say that?" Julien asked.

"Well, I presume that you have two older brothers… one who now controls the familial estate lands within Divio and carries on the military duties of your father, while the other is likely a priest or an abbot, perhaps. It is very difficult to rise to leadership when one is the third-born son. You probably never expected to lead such a large group men, and you probably had to fight for your role as Inspector General."

"You are most perceptive. I have an older brother, Reginald, who resides in Divio. Our brother, Aldabert served at Prüm Abbey, though he died two years ago," Julien replied, wishing to forget poor Aldabert's death. "What place do you hold within your family?"

Marcus stared at him with those strange, silvery eyes for a moment. "I was the only son and only child," he commented. "However, I think I prefer my current family." Marcus grinned and nodded towards his friends. "So, I was right about the two older brothers. Do you have any sisters?"

"Yes, I have a twin sister, Lirienne," Julien replied.

"Twins… how lucky for your family."

"So, how did you meet your current family?" Julien asked.

"Claudius, Arwin, Edward, and I fought many battles together in the past," Marcus began. "Amata and Patroclus I do not know as well, but they are well known within our circles of friends and acquaintances. Máire and I are hard to explain. We are not really related, but sometimes circumstances create family. So, do you think you will be able to continue this position of leadership within Emperor Charles' court?"

Julien wondered for a brief moment whether he needed to keep his thoughts to himself, but he decided that something must be done during the long night. He could see little beyond the torches of the foot soldiers.

"This is an experience I never thought possible," he began. "However, my current situation is an indication of how dire the circumstances are. We face an enemy that many here believe to be demonic. At the very least, it is an enemy that we have yet to kill. I am not sure how long it will last, but I will appreciate it. Besides, the truth is gendarmes are paid quite well. The only other option in terms of work for me would be holy orders, and I think I would be ill-suited for a career within the priesthood." Julien chuckled as he considered how miserable he would be serving some abbot in a far-flung abbey.

"Perhaps this situation is an indication of the confidence that the emperor has in his Inspector General," Marcus replied as he leaned forward to pat his horse, which had turned and shook a bit at the sound of an owl.

"Thank you. I am curious myself about why a man from Bath would wish to help us without monetary compensation." Julien looked up at the clouded skies for a moment. The clouds obscured the clear white eye of night and then passed, allowing the moon grow full and bright again.

"We are members of an order of warriors called the Cothromaigh," the Briton replied. "Our mission is to guide and maintain the balance between good and evil. While I highly doubt the demonic nature of these beings, the truth is that there is evil in this world, and these murderers are most certainly evil."

"I concur on that," Julien agreed with a smirk, hoping these warriors would not become bogged down in thoughts that the attacks were guided by Satan or something similar. "What about the ladies in your party?" Julien could hear the incredulity in his voice. "Surely they are not warriors."

"Amata is not of our order," Marcus replied, "but Máire is a warrior, and she takes her duties as one seriously."

Julien chuckled. "What order would allow a weakling woman into their ranks?"

Julien's horse neighed as Máire wheeled her mount around and charged him, before stopping only a few inches from his horse, blocking his path. Her eyes seemed to grow dark with rage. Julien almost felt a strange fear well in the pit of his stomach, but soon it passed and he glared back at her.

"I have absorbed the last insult I will entertain from you, you Frankish... imbecile! Either accept my challenge or go cower from the face of this 'weakling' woman!" Máire practically roared. The beautiful woman from the palace had disappeared, replaced by something unnameable, hard, and with plaited hair instead of soft curls.

The entire force stopped, and he could hear muted laughter behind him. "Silence!" he yelled to his men.

"I accept your challenge, as long as you promise not to cry when I take your sword," he countered to Máire before dismounting and then bellowing to his men. "Set up perimeters and light more torches."

When he unfastened his shield, Julien heard talk amongst the foreign band of warriors that sounded as though they were placing bets, though not on whether his female opponent would win, but when she would win.

Máire unsheathed her sword and appeared to check the balance and condition of her blade. She then took a shield offered to her from one of the soldiers before she sheathed her weapon. She then pushed her plaited hair away from her face and behind her ears.

Julien joined her within the perimeter, unclear whether he should attack or defend. Máire met his eyes, and the light of the moon and the torches made her eyes appear as vivid as emeralds. Julien decided to wait for her to make the first move.

After another few seconds that seemed to stretch into minutes, he felt a strong, unyielding pain extend down his arm. Julien realized she had slammed her shield against his. His arm ached, and he pulled back a moment to shake it out. She stopped, as if waiting for him to strike.

He stepped in, feinting with a thrust and then cutting at her right arm. Máire stepped back and deflected the blade with hers. Then she smashed her shield against his again, breaking both of the shields and eliciting more pain down Julien's arm. Máire tossed aside her shield and appeared to wait for him to do the same. Julien took time to shake out his aching arm again.

Máire switched to a two-handed grip and led this time with a low right to left cut. Julien moved to parry the cut, but he realized too late that it was a feint.

The woman warrior stepped to her left and arched her sword, aiming for his exposed midsection. Julien waited for death, but he instead felt the flat of the blade hit his side. A strong hand then gripped his throat. Máire squeezed her left hand a little, and he felt her right knee move against his left. His knee gave out and then Julien fell to his knees, dropping his sword on the way down. Máire's leg connected with his shoulder, and she pinned him to the ground with her right knee. She then kicked away his sword and pointed the tip of her blade at his face.

"Do you yield, Inspector General?" she asked.

"Yes," he squeaked.

"Very well," she acknowledged before shoving her sword in the ground. Máire moved her knee and then released his neck and shoulder. She then gripped his arm and pulled him up.

"Can you walk and ride?" she asked.

"Yes," he answered.

"Good," she stated as she picked up his sword and handed it to him, hilt first.

Julien took it and watched her pull her own blade from the ground, wipe off the dirt from it, and then sheath it.

The gathered soldiers remained silent as she mounted her horse. He watched Claudius, Arwin, and Patroclus hand over money to Edward.

Julien shook his arms out for a moment, sheathed his sword, and jumped onto his horse, hoping he did not look too flustered. He then nudged his horse toward his lieutenants. "Form up for the march," he ordered, allowing them to yell and relay the order to the rest of the men.

The force assembled and disembarked once again. As he rejoined Marcus, the elder Briton grinned at him.

"She does not like to be treated like most Frankish women, Inspector General. Things are very different where we come from. In Eire, a woman must be all things men are, and more." He chuckled.

"It must be a very harsh land," Julien replied. "Call me Julien." He noticed Máire slow her horse and pull away from the other warriors to join them.

"It is harsh, but beautiful," she said. "However, it is always a land of contradictions."

"Indeed," he said as he nodded a little, thinking she seemed a great deal like the description of her home. "I am most impressed with your order of warriors. I apologize for the insult, my la… Máire."

"I accept your apology," she acknowledged with a nod before smiling at him.

Julien grinned back at her, hoping that would not lead to more trouble. Máire turned away and then pushed aside her hair from her face again with a strange series of movements that made Julien almost forget himself. He realized he was staring at her, and tried to think of something to talk about.

"What does your name mean?" he asked Máire. "I have not heard anything like it."

He could hear Marcus chuckle. The Briton slowed down and allowed Máire to move in closer to Julien.

"'Bitter'," she replied softly.

"Bitter what?"

"Just 'bitter'," she repeated. "Some say it means, 'bitterly wanted'. It depends. I kind of prefer bitter." She smiled and then looked ahead.

Époisses

The new servants wandered about Talia's home cleaning and preparing to move some of the old furnishings out to their huts and farms. Candles lit the dark corners, warming the surroundings and giving them a bright glow. Talia allowed herself to smile before taking a long draught of wine.

Mandubratius sat down across from her. "I must admit to having second thoughts about allowing you to remain here, Talia," Mandubratius commented as he motioned for the servants to leave. While they shuffled out of the room, Talia could hear their soft whispers of gossip, and she tried to remain calm.

"I am here to protect my holdings," she replied.

"But this is so… pointless," her sponsor remarked as he leaned across the table and poured himself a cup of wine. "Return to Aachen, use your talents on the illiterate emperor, manipulate him and his associates, and you can rule all of the empire with a puppet. The way you do things is not the way of the Lamia. Go to the head of the snake, not a scale. Why would you even bother with marrying these dull Franks?"

"Because I want the Franks to suffer!" Talia answered in a terse hiss.

"Then make them work for you," Mandubratius replied. He arose and began to pace.

Talia slammed her fists against the table. Once again her sponsor had annoyed her.

"This is my goal and mission," Talia answered. "You knew it when you transformed me, and you've never once offered any kind of assistance!"

Mandubratius continued pacing. "I believed that it was only your lack of sophistication, Talia. I believed it would fade away when you gained a better perspective of the world. I tried to teach you, but you are so stubborn."

"I will not change my course," Talia yelled at him. "I will make them suffer for what they did to my poor grandfather!"

"Fine," her guest hissed, "do it your way, but don't expect me to assist you when you mess it up. Have fun with your useless game." Mandubratius began to walk towards the front door.

Talia ran towards him and began pushing him out.

A servant opened the door as Mandubratius moved onto the threshold.

"Useless!" Talia spat. "So my game is like your ineffectual diversion with my niece!"

She heard Mandubratius start to laugh, and the very sound of it annoyed her.

"Oh, I'll prevail at that pointless diversion," he answered. "It's too much fun to give up on it."

Talia slammed the door in his face. "Make sure he does not come in again for at least a... month!" she growled at the servants. Talia took a deep breath before smoothing her dress. "Unless he apologizes," she added. "I need another drink and new amusements." Talia looked up at the female servant attending her.

Prades' eldest daughter refill Talia's glass from the jug of wine she held. The young mortal appeared to find her duties to be tiresome, although Talia had called the young woman back from her service in Aachen.

"Rosamund," Talia said as she pulled her goblet away, "I know you must miss your old obligations in Aachen, but I do need your assistance. You must be very wise about the court there. The lady of the lands needs protection in the form of a husband. As much as I hate breaking forth from my mourning, I must seek security."

"Of course, my lady," Rosamund replied. "How may I help you?"

Talia smiled, finding the keys to unlock Rosamund's mind. The young woman stared back at her as if entranced.

"Tell me, Rosamund. Which of the emperor's male relations are unwed now?" Talia took a sip of wine.

"Unfortunately, Lady Talia, they are all married now."

"Are any of these relations of Emperor Charles likely to quietly divorce their wives anytime soon?" Talia asked.

"Well, it has been rumored that the family of the emperor goes through wives like a normal person goes through cases of wine. The emperor himself lost his official wife last year, but I think he prefers to spend time with all of his concubines and mistresses, as opposed to choosing just one," Rosamund explained with a smile.

"So, tell me about his relatives who have lands within or close to Burgundy," Talia requested. "Sit," she said, pointing to a chair. "Pour yourself a glass of this wine. It is excellent." She smiled.

Rosamund poured herself a cup, sat, and then sipped at her wine. "There are several who have barren wives who were brokered through old alliances long since passed. They have need of women who are of child-bearing age," Rosamund answered. "I know that the emperor's cousin Eustache owns lands in Beaune. Hamund and Burchard are the lords of Macon. Perhaps even one of the emperor's sons might be interested. You could be queen over an entire realm."

Talia raised a brow. "While being a queen would be an honor, I feel it is one above my station." As if she cared about the rest of Francia or the Empire. She needed a husband with lands in Burgundy to continue in her plans.

"Beaune is close, but other villages are closer. I'd prefer an alliance with a neighbor," Talia continued. "However, tell me of this Eustache."

"He is very wealthy, but older… not too old though, my lady. He grabbed me once."

Rosamund's face became red, and Talia could smell the blood waft through the air, as if it were a delicate perfume.

"Excellent, Rosamund. Would you care to join me at court?"

Rosamund stood and curtseyed. "My lady, you honor me by asking me what I wish to do."

"Nonsense, my child. I feel a great amount of guilt with your father's death, what with his long and faithful services to my departed husband and myself." Talia stood up. "I need to be more generous to the surviving families. You will help me with that as well. My husband, while a good man, seemed preoccupied with other matters."

Rosamund nodded her head. "It would please me greatly to serve you in these matters."

"Now, I need some help with this dress," Talia stated as she motioned towards the half-finished dress. "Call in the others, and we can finish it."

Outside Aachen

The fifty soldiers marched in a slow, drifting cadence, with the exception of the frequent jumping at every possible noise. Edward grumbled and shook his head. Why did Marcus agree to have these men accompany them? The Strigoi could overwhelm these mortals so easily.

He inhaled and exhaled, imbibing all the scents that carried from the mortals, blood-drinkers, animals, and the earth. He loved being an Ekimmu Cruitne, but sometimes the overwhelming gift of scent could drive one mad with the sorting of various essences. The smell of mortals tangled with the external scent of blood-drinkers, and of course their own line's shared smell. While every individual blood-drinker exuded a unique aroma, they shared many common fragrances. For instance, the Sugnwr Gwaed smelled of pine, fir trees, and the forests. He and MacAlpin exuded a sharp, wild smell of roots and herbs. The Lamia smelt of strong incense… incense so strong, it almost made Edward's nose itch, but he could become used to it. Marcus and Máire gave off the flavors of mistletoe, wildflowers, and honey. However, he could not describe the scent of Strigoi.

Edward stretched a bit. While such perception had its usefulness, it could also make stinky herbs smell truly horrific.

Arwin, Marcus, and Claudius gabbed in Gaelic about their conquests of females during their mortal days. He then heard the sound of female laughter, and he watched as the inspector general smiled after making Máire giggle… a difficult task, but not entirely impossible.

Edward's eyes gazed upon the Lamia contingent in the group. Amata wore innocence like most women donned clothing. She stared ahead at the long line of people before her. Edward wondered what plans Amata calculated during these early spring eves.

To Edward's eye, the Legate Patroclus could not steady himself. His eyes darted at the small noises of the dark night, as if frightened at the hidden world. Did his experience with the Strigoi lead him to such anxiety? He seemed oblivious to Amata as he searched the woods for unseen attacks.

"What is wrong, Patroclus?" Amata asked him after nudging her mount closer to his.

A strange scent caught up to Edward. He nearly gagged at its pungent quality. He saw his father-in-darkness make a face of disgust. The Deargh Du and the other Celtic blood-drinkers also stopped their horses and sniffed the air. The mortal soldiers, having not received the order to halt, collided into each other, making noise as they tried to collect themselves.

"Battle formation," Marcus called out. "Two ranks, right of column. Move!"

The mortals stared at each other in a moment of indecision, but they quickly started to comply.

Edward shook his head a bit. Marcus could never give up 'command'. He dismounted and joined the other blood-drinkers.

"You five," Marcus thundered in Gaelic at the Deargh Du whom Sáerlaith had assigned to accompany them to Francia. "Take the right flank. The rest of us will take the left."

The five Deargh Du turned and rode to the right side of the ranks.

The inspector general nudged his mount away from Máire and headed towards Marcus. His face appeared to be burning with fury.

"How dare you presume to give orders to my men?" Julien hissed at Marcus in a fierce whisper. "You have control over the contingent of Imperial forces, but the gendarmes are mine to command."

"My apologies, Inspector General, but we are under attack. I suggest you get in a position so you can lead your men," Marcus murmured.

The gendarme muttered to himself in Frankish, possibly criticizing obstinate Anglo-Saxons. The inspector general dismounted his horse and joined the middle formation.

The forces drew their blades, and Edward gathered his supplies. Shouts and cries from the right of the column interrupted his preparations. Mortal men bowed over and writhed in pain. They began to clutch their foreheads, and he felt nauseous as he saw some of the men begin to gouge out their own eyes.

He remembered Patroclus speaking of that effect on mortals, but witnessing it for himself merely brought out his own growing terror.

He heard shouts in Gaelic ordering the Deargh Du on the right flank to attack. Claudius tugged at Julien's sleeve.

"Tell your men to pull back from the fallen, quickly," Claudius yelled.

"Why?" the inspector general asked. "We have come here seeking this enemy, and I shall not leave until I identify whom they are and what they are doing."

"Your men are dying and killing themselves," Marcus shouted over the din of screams, as he joined Claudius and Julien. "They need to back off and allow us to take care of things."

"Left flank, pincer to right," Marcus yelled in Gaelic over his shoulder. He looked at Amata and the Legate and then gestured for them to follow the left flank.

Edward turned back towards the right flank upon hearing echoes of growing screams and cries.

The sounds finally got to the head gendarme, and he began calling for his forces to withdraw from the wailing mortals.

Edward could no longer see the Deargh Du on the right flank of their forces. He rushed towards that flank, but his senses reeled as he smelled a growing stench. He ducked around a few trees before taking to the air, hoping no mortal witnessed his ascent. Edward followed the disgusting smell. Soon he spied a monstrous being feeding from a Deargh Du whose eyes were closed.

Edward grabbed one of his tiny incendiary ceramic jugs of black powder and threw it at the Strigoi. The jug shattered, covering the Strigoi in chemicals. The ugly blood-drinker scratched his head as if confused and then dropped his victim. Edward thanked the Gods that it seemed oblivious to his aerial attack.

Edward palmed another ceramic jug and threw it at the Strigoi's chest, grunting at the exertion.

The powder-filled jug lodged into the Strigoi's ribcage and exploded in a massive fireball, shooting flame and body parts everywhere. A small fire lit amongst some dry grass. Another movement caught Edward's eyes, and he followed yet another Strigoi, which loped away from the fire in a strange, gangly gait.

Edward threw another ceramic pot at the Strigoi's feet in an attempt to ascertain its direction. He missed, but he noticed another fire start. Edward then tossed an extra one at the Strigoi, and this time the jug hit between the monster's shoulder blades, turning it into a screaming and furious blood-drinker.

He smelled a different Strigoi. Edward turned and flew over a few trees, coming to a clearing. Patroclus, Amata, and Claudius stood immobile within the forested clearing. He attempted to focus on the Strigoi again. He finally found it, hiding in scrubby bushes, staring at the three other blood-drinkers, seemingly unaware of Edward's presence.

Edward threw the jug, and it hit his mark in the left shoulder blade. The Strigoi erupted in flame. Amata, Patroclus, and Claudius finally seemed to break free of the spell.

"What do you think you were doing?" Marcus asked him as he landed. "We set a trap, and they were the bait." He motioned towards Arwin and Máire, who peered at him from the bushes.

"I believed the others to be immobile," Edward grumbled. He hated being blamed for trying to assist.

"We were," Patroclus replied, "but that was part of the ruse."

"Arwin, Máire, and I were going to knock out the Strigoi so we could understand it," Marcus added.

"Well, I killed two others," Edward grumbled again, pointing in the direction of the dead Strigoi.

"So, did you kill both of them with your fire pots?" Marcus asked.

"Yes, but my accuracy was not very high," Edward admitted, now feeling foolish. He could see Mac Alpin sniffing the air and closing his eyes.

"So, how many did you throw?" Claudius asked.

"Five," Edward answered.

"This forest is on fire," Mac Alpin stated, "all the way back to the road, and it is spreading. We are cut off from the mortal troops."

The sounds of screaming tore at his ears unlike anything he heard before. Julien closed his eyes, willing the strange images to flee and be replaced by the running stream near his mother's home in Vézelay. The soothing stream did nothing more than bubble over the smooth stones that lay in its bed.

"Sir, sir!" An insistent plea pulled him from his dream. "We must take in the wounded," Edel told him.

"No," Julien answered, opening his eyes. Marcus' stern warning echoed in his mind, but the scent of smoke and the sight of a burning tree canopy made him change his mind.

"Never mind what I said," he told the young soldier. "Take only the living," he ordered his men. "Pull them to the old Roman road."

"Sir, what about the mercenaries?" Gerold called out.

Julien ignored the question as he tossed aside his shield and sheathed his sword. He moved towards the fallen, some of whom crawled towards him, though others remained motionless and silent in death, still clutching their swords. A few sat on the ground, and wailed while covering their eyes. Julien crouched down next to one and tried to remember his name. The mud soaked through his clothing.

The young man spoke while covering his eyes. "Tell the birds to go away. They wish to have my eyes," he whispered to Julien in a strange, singsong plea. "Stop the world from spinning. It is night, yet the colors burn too brightly. They burn into my eyes. The voices tell me to do things to myself... unspeakable and monstrous things."

"What have they told you to do, Gilles?" Julien asked, believing that he had correctly remembered soldier's name.

"They tell me to pull out my tongue and slice it with my knife. They want me to tear out my jaw. They say to rip open my stomach with my sword to see whether I experience any pain. Then they beg me to deafen myself and then slice my throat," Gilles answered. "But I beat them."

Julien tried to find his voice. "Gilles, I congratulate you for beating such overwhelming evil. Let me help you up." He rose to his feet and started pulling up Gilles under his arm, but it appeared to be covered in blood.

"No, no," Gilles yelled, still covering his eyes.

Julien forced Gilles hands away from the soldier's face.

"Holy mother," Julien cried out as he backed a step away from Gilles upon seeing empty, bloody eye sockets.

Gilles held out his eyes in his hands and then started to laugh. "I guess the birds won after all." He pulled out a hidden dagger and then stabbed himself in the chest.

Julien took another step back and fell over another body. He stared into another eyeless face and gagged at the sight of the gore and entrails lying next to the soldier's body. He shivered, hearing the sobs of grown men over his shoulder. The sounds and smells of death overwhelmed him until the smoke made him look up at the inferno that rushed towards him in an effort to gobble up the dead.

He turned and found another unaffected soldier trying to drag away one of the unfortunate dead.

"Leave him," he ordered. "It is too late." Julien rose on his shaky feet. "We will retreat now and return later."

None even looked up at his words.

"Go now," he yelled as he stared at the raging fire. When no one yet moved, Julien kicked one of the soldiers. "Get up, all of you. We can do no more."

He shook Drogo.

"What did this?" Drogo whispered.

"Perhaps Satan does walk this earth," Julien answered, hoping to scare them into moving. "This is what happened in the villages... death and insanity. Where are Marcus and his party?"

"They have not returned from chasing the murderers," Gerold answered.

"We will go and allow them a chance to catch up." He then noticed his lieutenants staring at each other as if doubting his hope of their companions' survival.

"The silent fool did this? Flay him!" Amata hissed as she tugged on Marcus' sleeve. "He has put us all in danger."

The fire raged and belched smoke, surrounding them, and obliterating any chance of an escape by flight.

Marcus shrugged away from Amata's grasp and then wrapped an arm around his daughter-in-darkness.

"We have need of a Druid's rain," he suggested to Máire.

"Yes of course," the other surviving Deargh Du replied.

Máire pulled out a small pouch from her belt. She then extracted a black substance from the pouch and blew it into the air. Some of it landed on Máire, but the rest of the dusty soot seemed to float upwards.

Amata stared at the other woman as she began to chant something that grew louder with each repetition. Amata clutched her arms as she witnessed Máire's eyes begin to glow. She tried to control her fright, but her mind did not listen and obey. The sound of thunder made her look up at the sky. The nearly full moon disappeared as clouds rolled past. A few raindrops pelted her face before the rain railed forth in steadily increasing torrents, which soaked her clothing. Soon, however, Amata heard a hiss as the rain drenched the fire. She could find no words to explain her confusion and astonishment.

"Is this a mere coincidence or true magic?" she asked. Claudius and Arwin merely grinned at her. Máire and Marcus tipped their heads up to allow the rain to soak them completely. The Deargh Du could be so strange.

The rain continued unabated.

"Let us try to rejoin the inspector general's troops," Marcus suggested, finally breaking his silence. He motioned for the others to follow him. As they walked, the stench of burnt human flesh made her turn in disgust. Edward and Mac Alpin backed away, covering their mouths.

Máire handed them a set of cloths that she had drenched in some strong peppermint. Both Ekimmu Cruitne tied the cloths around their faces and rejoined the others.

She noticed Marcus digging at the ground with his hands. The others, even her legate, joined him in burying the bodies. She wanted to ask why they wasted time, and then she finally found words.

"Why?" she asked Edward, who stood the closest to her.

He shrugged a bit. "Christians like to be buried," he stated. "It seems to be the respectful thing to do."

Amata rubbed her forehead as Marcus fashioned some crosses out of wood and placed them at the front, middle, and far edge of the grave.

"Dawn comes soon," Amata warned, despite her knowledge that they knew this as well as she. "Where will we sleep?"

"You have never slept in the ground?" Claudius asked while raising a brow.

The others, save Patroclus, stared at her as if she were a fool.

"Yes, I have… but only in extreme circumstances," she told them. She looked on as they started digging holes for themselves.

"I do not like to get dirty," Amata added.

She heard Marcus laugh.

"Do not fret, Amata. Máire can call forth the rain again tomorrow night. It will remove any dirt from us."

Julien wiped away the rain that had soaked through his cloak. The deluge seemed to wash away his and his men's earlier fears.

"This rain may spare our companions," he said in order to reassure himself that they would not have perished in the fire. The thought of the warriors dying in the smoke and flame filled him with a strange sadness.

"Where are we going, Inspector General?" Edel asked.

"Vézelay is but five miles," Julien answered. "I recognize these forests. We will stop there and wait for our foreign friends. There is a garrison there, and my family has a home outside of the village. We will rest and give the men a chance to recover."

"Sir, surely our traveling companions are dead," Drogo stated. "How could they survive the fire?"

"I..." Julien began, though he could not find the words he desired to express. Instead, he said, "Something tells me that they are not easily killed, Drogo. We will give them an opportunity to catch up with us."

Drogo and Edel nodded. Julien then nudged his mount to a trot, wanting to find peace and serenity in the bubbling stream.

chapter nine

Aachen

"How do I look?" Talia asked Rosamund while playing with her jewelry. The carriage wheels rolled over stones, causing the riders within to bounce.

"You will make the ladies at court look like poor vassals, my lady," Rosamund complimented with a grin. "You have exquisite taste, and you have picked well. All eyes will turn to you."

Talia closed her eyes as the carriage came to a stop at the palace. "Beauty, grace, and wit will win them all," she informed herself.

"This feast will celebrate the upcoming hunts in the spring," Rosamund informed her. "Be prepared to hear tales of the hunt. Try to be enthralled." They entered the palace and neared the great hall that served as the emperor's throne room.

Talia nodded as the emperor's secretary came forward to take her name. Rosamund pulled away to join her equals.

"Lady Talia of Époisses," the secretary stated to the official greeting line. She received kisses from other genteel, land owning guests, and she curtseyed to Emperor Charles and his family. The emperor then brought her up for a proper kiss of welcome, before turning to his next guest.

She watched him with some amount of curiosity. Perhaps she should forget her plan to find a new husband and instead focus on the head of the snake.

Damn that Mandubratius for making sense.

Talia took a goblet of wine and walked around the room as she listened to the gentle music play. The mortal conversations buzzed in her ears like annoying gnats. She attempted to decide which conversation to join. They seemed to mostly deal with hunting, the favorite pastime of the Franks, save drinking wine and arguing. How like the clans of Eire they seemed.

She then spotted Rosamund and took her arm.

"The emperor intrigues me. Tell me all you can about him," Talia ordered her new servant.

Rome

Mandubratius stopped the horse outside of the Lateran Palace and wiped the dust from his clothing. He then walked towards the guard and said, "I am His Holiness' emissary, Michael Tolomei." Mandubratius displayed the ring to them. The guards snapped to attention and allowed him to pass.

"I am here on an urgent matter. I must see the Holy Father," he said to the guard, as he concentrated on unfolding the guard's mind. The guard's mouth dropped open, and after a moment of indecision, he nodded his head.

"I will inform His Holiness. He will await you in the receiving room." The guard motioned for Mandubratius to follow him.

Mandubratius smiled and then trailed behind the guard towards the receiving room. When he arrived, Mandubratius began to pace, allowing peace to stretch through his mind, conserving energy to use later on the Holy Father.

Soon, His Holiness stalked through the doors with a clerk and the guard behind him.

Mandubratius inhaled and then smiled. The pope smelled of everything but incense.

"Michael, you are the one who takes me away from a good... book?" Pope Leo raged.

"My apologies, your holiness," Mandubratius began. "I bring grave news from the empire."

He heard soft laughter, and then the pope covered his mouth with a bejeweled hand. "This better be grave news."

Mandubratius stared at the pope and concentrated on bending the holy man's mind to his will, though their connection and his control over Pope Leo faded with time and distance.

"Indeed," he observed. "It is most grave, Holy Father. I discovered Satan truly walks the earth. The devil spawn have defiled many churches and killed their clergy. They destroy the minds and souls of innocents. Many innocent Christians also kill themselves because of Satan's madness. Despite these demonic horrors, that Frank still does nothing to fight them off!"

"Nothing, you say?" Pope Leo's eyes grew wide.

"There have been riots of God-fearing men, crying out for the Church to do something, Holy Father. They cannot go to mass or celebrate the sacraments," Mandubratius informed him as he wrung his hands in an attempt to appear concerned.

"These are most dire tidings," the pope replied. "You have done well, Michael, to wake me and bring this situation to my attention."

"I came as soon as I could," Mandubratius answered as he met the pope's eyes.

"Have you seen the devil spawn yourself?" Pope Leo asked.

"Yes, I have. I even came close to losing my sanity, but I was fortunate in that there were no lasting effects. My faith has kept me alive," Mandubratius lied.

"It would seem that you have accomplished your mission," the pope stated. "This menace is a spiritual matter. Therefore, it falls to me to raise a holy army in order to fight this darkness and protect Christendom. I will call forth all those who can fight, and I will lead this army myself. Will you join me, Michael? I could use a warrior of God as one of my generals."

"I do wish to serve you, your Holiness," Mandubratius replied with a ready smile. "However, I wish to serve you as a general of a light cavalry division… a small one of one thousand men."

"One thousand men…" Pope Leo murmured. "That is an excellent idea. You will be our guest here until our forces have gathered."

"Thank you, Holy Father."

"You are dismissed, emissary." Pope Leo extended his hand.

Mandubratius bowed and kissed the pope's ring. "Enjoy your manuscripts and scrolls," he cooed. "I have arrangements to make. I shall return soon." He bowed and then left the receiving room. He needed to pay a visit to the temple.

Vézelay

Julien and the surviving soldiers and gendarme arrived at the garrison mid-morning. The low morale concerned him, as did the weather. The sun seemed dismal, even though the rain had disappeared. The thought of leaving the dead and dying behind weighed on his mind still. Julien wrestled with the idea of Satan arriving on earth, bringing the fires of hell with him. It went against all his rational beliefs. There were certain things he accepted without reservation, such as his mother's whispered teachings in the secret grove, but Satan seemed a vague force. People did evil on their own, yet nothing else could explain what had happened last night. Should they have continued after their traveling companions, or should they have left the warriors to their assault on the band of murders?

"My lord," the garrison commander said as he saluted.

"Dreu?" Julien acknowledged as he returned the salute.

"Yes sir. Ayol died a few months ago in a hunting accident."

Julien nodded. "I have a most loyal troop of soldiers and gendarmes who need food, water, and sleep, Dreu."

"I will see to it personally," the commander replied. "Will you be going to your familial holdings?"

"Yes," Julien answered, "And Dreu, if by chance a party of foreigners arrives, would you extend courtesies to them? Point them toward my mother's home." Julien watched the commander nod and then walk away.

Julien then nudged his horse towards Drogo and Edel and announced, "I am going east. My family has a home here and I wish to rest there. It is about a mile from here. Prepare to leave tomorrow at sunset."

"Very good, inspector general," Edel and Drogo answered. They dismounted and then headed towards the inside of the garrison.

The blood-drinkers landed a half mile away from the quiet garrison and began to march towards it. The smell of the forests and wilderness faded as the scent of mortals grew stronger. Marcus cleared his throat and held up his hands in a sign of peaceful entreaty as they approached the garrison.

"Drogo," he said to one of the inspector general's lieutenants whom he recognized.

"God be praised! How did you all manage to survive?" Drogo asked as he waved the guards to lower their weapons.

"We met up with some of the murderers and managed to kill three, but we also lost three," Marcus explained.

"So, are they demon spawn?" the lieutenant asked in a whisper.

Marcus leaned in closer. "No, though I can understand why they seem that way, but they are not demon spawn."

"How did you escape the raging fire we heard about?" another soldier asked.

"A thunderstorm saved us," Patroclus replied.

"We also buried your soldiers. The graves are marked, so a priest can return to give them a proper burial," Claudius added.

"Thank you," Drogo said.

"Where is the inspector general?" Arwin asked.

"His mother's family owns most of the land in the village. The inspector general is visiting his mother's home," Drogo answered.

"May we see him?" Máire asked.

"Of course," Drogo agreed with a chuckle. "He was quite concerned about your survival. The house is about two miles to the east."

"We will split up," Marcus said. "It is far too late to wake up the house now. We will sleep out here and meet with Julien tomorrow."

"Orders, orders, orders," Amata grumbled under her breath. "Sorry," she said, noticing the sour looks.

"We are near a grove," Máire stated. "We can sleep there. It looked very clean, as if someone took care of it."

"I hear a stream," Claudius reported.

Patroclus nodded. "I smell fresh blood."

"Alright, the three of you will find some sort of livestock that can withstand the seven of us. Edward, Claudius, and I will make sure that this area is free from the Strigoi. Máire, you check the grove and stream to make sure they are suitable to meet our needs."

The six others turned away to fulfill their duties.

Máire walked towards the sound of the stream and found herself in a silent grove lit by the gentle moon. An ancient stone altar seemed to whisper to her. She placed a hand on the stone and closed her eyes, feeling a growing strength leap into her fingers.

"Not yet," she said. The Strigoi had left a hardened crust of evil and unbalance that caked on her skin and soul.

She moved towards the far western edge of the grove past a few ancient trees. She then kneeled at the bubbling stream and placed her right hand in the water. Before she could think of reasons to wait, she undressed and then waded into the water, feeling the residue leave as the water rushed around her waist. She went back to the solid land for her rope belt and looped it around her left foot.

Máire tied the other end to a thick branch that dipped its leaves towards the water like a hand reaching for a drink.

She reclined in the stream under the water, closed her eyes, lifted up her legs, and allowed the current to drift around her body, taking away the repulsiveness, leaving her soul refreshed.

"Lirienne!" Heloise called over her shoulder. "Lirienne, hurry," she grumbled under her breath as she gathered their supplies and honey cakes.

Lirienne marched down the stairs in her robe. "Settle down mother, we have plenty of time." Her daughter looked around as if to make sure none of the servants were about to hear.

"Do you have the offerings?" Heloise asked as she grabbed her daughter's arm and led her towards the back of their house and then outside. Sometimes, her daughter seemed less interested in their beliefs than she was in the feasting after their rituals.

"Yes, mother," Lirienne replied. "I have the figs and the wine." Lirienne giggled. "Should I tell Ermengarda that Julien is here?"

Heloise chuckled. "Your poor brother deserves some rest, Lirienne. Let me tell her, or else she will demand to come over and feed him herself. Oh, look at the beautiful moon," Heloise observed as soon as she stepped outside. She stopped Lirienne, and they both stared up at the moon, engrossed. "The

Goddess will bless us tonight," she whispered. "It is so bright tonight. I doubt we will need torches or candles."

Lirienne nodded, silent in revered awe, for once, as they neared the altar within the grove.

"Motherwolf," two of the other women greeted Heloise, calling her by her secret name. She embraced them.

"My friends," she said, as she watched other cloaked women join the growing circle. "I give you welcome to our celebration of the rebirth of spring as winter fades." She then turned to Lirienne.

"Nightingale, the words are the key to the entrance." Heloise hoped her daughter would not forget the code words to join her circle of worship. During the days of Gaul, the Druids had carried on these activities. Today, men found new promise and power within the Roman church. Now, only women seemed to find comfort and joy in this circle. She contemplated asking the others to allow Julien to join them, but the comfort level might disappear with any man's arrival. Her youngest son seemed happy enough to worship nature on his own or with her and Lirienne, yet his visits to their grove grew ever more seldom with his new duties in Aachen.

"I offer my unending love to the circle, and I remain silent with its secrets," Lirienne whispered in her mother's ear.

Heloise kissed her daughter's cheek. "Well done," she purred, before moving on to Elder Oak. A strange energy seemed to increase within the grove as the moon moved higher in the sky.

Máire tensed in the water and sat up. As she squeezed water from her hair, she heard a song asking for the blessings of Brigandu lilt to her ears. She smiled for a moment, wondering whether the singing could be a beautiful dream or perhaps she heard fae whispering their tidings in her ears.

Máire unknotted the rope encircling her foot and stood in the stream. The smell of mortal women grew with the volume of the song. A voice in her mind bade her to go to join them and sing the chorus with them. She moved past her clothing, forgetting that they may be needed or necessary. A force overwhelmed her, and so she stepped forth from the sylvan path, twining her way around the oaks. As she neared the altar, Máire witnessed fifteen disrobed women, but she said nothing. Máire shook her hair a bit, brushing away the chilled water.

She then realized that this circle of women represented the last vestiges of the Gallic Druids. Most of the women did not see her, but the eldest woman in the group did. She stared at Máire in awe.

Soon, Máire heard a voice that was not hers come from her throat. "I am the triple, three in one, I guide the waters and bless your fires," the words echoed. "You called for Brigandu, yet her sister answered the call instead."

"Her eyes, her eyes," the eldest whispered, continuing to watch her. The other women then glanced at Máire before lowering their heads in respect, or perhaps dread.

"Fear not, for I bring blessings of spring and creation too. I may be known in darkness, but without darkness, there could be no time for rest, sisters, and there would be no need to celebrate the return of the light."

The strange feeling passed. Máire placed her hand on her forehead and wondered whether Morrigan had again usurped her body.

"I..." Máire began, "I am Máire Ní Conghal of Eire." She kneeled before them. "I was in the stream and heard your song, which brought me forth."

"Are you a Druid?" the eldest asked as she moved forward and took her hand. Máire looked up at the stranger. Something seemed familiar in the smell of her blood.

"Yes, I am," she answered. "I apologize for interrupting your–"

"A Druid comes to us from Eire? The land where our ancients sought tutelage?" The woman's voice grew joyous. She smiled and leaned down to kiss Máire's cheek.

Máire looked at the other women who now smiled at her, seemingly forgetting their earlier discomfort.

"I apologize. We are not used to guests that come out of the moonlight during our chants, spouting the words of the Gods and Goddesses. You can understand how you appeared. We believed you to be Brigandu. I am Motherwolf, here, otherwise I am known as Heloise of Vézelay."

There were a flurry of introductions and several mispronunciations of her name.

Heloise pulled Máire to her feet. "You must help us complete this ritual of the celebration of spring."

Máire smiled and said, "I would be honored."

"Sheep always make a most pleasant meal," Patroclus commented, before making a bit of a sour face.

"Could be much worse in my days in the army–" Marcus began.

"We know," Amata interjected. "Caesar made everyone eat grass and you were happy for that grass," she said after wiping off her mouth. "And Patroclus will then say he ate dirt for Trajan. I still find this meal to be most disgusting." She looked over at Claudius. "Oh, and do not start with your stories of glorious battles."

"So, where are Edward, Arwin, and Máire? We should share this magnificent bounty," Claudius added. "Oh, here comes two of the three I mentioned."

"Was she at the grove," Marcus asked, "or did she decide to walk around and explore?" Máire tended to wander off at times.

As soon as Mac Alpin and Edward joined them, Edward said, "Well, she could be with all the women– oof," before Arwin elbowed him.

"You were not supposed to mention the women, lad," Mac Alpin chided with a chuckle.

"Women? Women where?" Claudius asked.

Amata shook her head in obvious annoyance.

"We saw–" Edward began.

"Nothing, we saw nothing," Arwin interjected as he nudged his child again.

"At least they were wearing nothing," Edward added.

"Edwina, keep quiet! I wanted to go back unobserved," Arwin pouted.

"Naked women? You must be joking," Marcus suggested with a smirk. "I wish to see these naked women."

"This is no joke," Mac Alpin challenged. "We saw a dozen or more naked women in that Druid's grove, and I smelled a Deargh Du in their ranks. Edward wished to immerse himself in their company. Apparently, he is more desperate for female companionship than me– oof!"

Edward nudged his father-in-darkness at that remark.

"Was this an ancient Sapphic rite?" Claudius asked with a chuckle.

"Oh really, Claudius," Amata chided. "You men are horrible."

"It looked to be similar to the Druidic rituals we celebrate," Edward answered, "but different in that only women were there."

"Imbolc is soon," Arwin said. "Perhaps, they celebrate it here too. Let us go make sure Máire is safe."

"Alright, but we need try to keep quiet. I don't want to scare them or offend their Gods or Goddesses." Everyone save Amata started to leave before Marcus could say 'but'. Only Amata waited for him to finish.

"Do you wish to join us?" he asked her.

"Of course. Someone has to make sure you boys behave," Amata teased. "Then again, I doubt Máire needs any sort of protection. You look impatient, Marcus. Go run along to see these naked women, and I shall follow you. I know you do not wish to miss any of this ritual."

"Arwin, what are you doing?" Claudius asked in a whisper. Marcus glanced over at the Scots warrior in the middle of disrobing.

"I thought I could fall out of the sky as Brigid's consort and join in the fun," he answered.

"You boys are horrible," Amata hissed, "pretending to be Gods just to get sex. That's pitiful!"

"Oh, as if you have not done something similar. I will wager you have been 'Venus' on any number of occasions," Arwin replied, trying to remain quiet.

"So, can we watch them until they leave?" Edward asked.

"I have never understood men's fascination with nudity," Amata whispered. She then exposed herself. "There. Was that so important?" She slid away from their hiding place. "Such immaturity," she muttered.

"If it was not for man's immaturity, the human race would cease to exist," Claudius quipped.

"There's a better place to view them here," commented Edward.

"Oh, by the Goddess, they put on their robes," Arwin grumbled.

Marcus moved to their vantage point to get a better view. The ceremony appeared to be finished. The majority of the women left the grove after embracing each other, leaving only Máire and two other women.

"Lirienne, go back home and make sure your brother is still asleep," the elder woman said.

The striking brunette turned away from the altar, after embracing Máire, and walked towards the house.

Máire and the elder stared at each other from opposite sides of the altar. Máire's face beamed in a serene smile. She always seemed pleased after the conclusion of her rituals.

"Tell me what you are," the elder asked. "You said you were a Druid, but I saw your eyes. I know you are more."

Máire stared at the ground for a moment, as if she were not sure what to say.

"Do not worry, for I will not tell the others. You are more beautiful than anyone I have ever seen," the woman praised before growing silent, for a moment. "I feel as if I have witnessed a Goddess participate in a ritual with me. Nothing pleases me more. Your eyes, when you first spoke to us, were black as midnight, yet now they are green as the soft grass that waits to rise from winter's ice and snow."

He watched Máire smile, and her glamoury grew. She revealed her glowing green eyes before blinking them away. "I am Deargh Du, a brood of Morrigan, for she is the Phantom Queen of my home."

The elder women dropped to her knees.

Máire walked around the altar and dropped to her knees in front of the women. "I will not harm you," Marcus heard her coo.

"I know," the other woman said. "I have read stories of the Deargh Du. My ancestors wrote down these legends and passed them to me to keep them safe.

"Do you know of the madness that stalks the empire?" Máire asked.

The elder woman's eye sparkled for a bit, radiating a blue strength. "My son is the Inspector General of the Gendarme. They are a policing group that catches criminals in this empire. He told me about these brutal murders during our meal tonight. He said foreign warriors traveled with his soldiers, and that they had disappeared during a battle with the enemy. According to him, one was a woman of such exquisite beauty that words were insufficient to describe her. That must be you."

"Perhaps," Máire said. "There is another woman in our party, but yes, we are those foreign warriors your son mentioned."

"Julien will be relieved. He was quite worried. Where are the others?"

"They are close by," Máire answered, looking towards them. Marcus could feel her eyes find him.

"Are they Deargh Du as well?"

"There are some Deargh Du with us, though others who travel with us are not Deargh Du. They are similar, you see. Just as there are different races of mortals, there are also different races of blood-drinkers, all of whom subsist on the life essences of mortals and animals. We feed on the blood of the living, and we do not kill our donors. As you probably know, Deargh Du try to remove the traces of feeding from the body and mind of the mortals. Most blood-drinkers do this in some way. Would you like to meet my friends?" Máire asked.

Heloise nodded her head with a wordless smile.

"You boys can come out," she called. "Marcus, could you please bring my clothes?"

Marcus hesitated for a moment before speaking. "Well, go on," he urged the others. "It seems we have been invited." He walked towards the flowing stream. He and gathered her clothing before walking back towards the altar. He found everyone sitting on the grass, looking to be at peace and relaxed, though Máire's hair still appeared to be dripping. Amata had just begun recounting the story of the Lamia.

He handed Máire her clothes and then waited for the story to end. While he waited, Máire pulled on her tunic and brocs, but she remained barefoot.

"Thank you," she whispered and then gave him a big grin. "Marcus, this is Lady Heloise of Vézelay," she said in a louder voice. "She is also the inspector general's mother. Lady Heloise, this is my father-in-darkness, the one who made me Deargh Du."

Marcus bowed to her. "I am sorry to interrupt this retelling of legends, but we have a few hours until sunrise. Have you fed?" He asked as he looked at Máire.

Máire shook her head vigorously.

"You look pale," he said. "Lady Heloise, may we stay here in your grove."

"No, you will stay in my home," Heloise answered. "I have a cellar that is windowless. I grow mushrooms there, and it is very dark. You can sleep there."

"Your son does not know what we are, my lady, perhaps–" Arwin started to say before being cut off.

"I can keep that secret from him if you wish," Heloise acknowledged. She then took Patroclus' hand and stood up. "Máire can feed from my servants, me, or my family, as can the rest of you. You are my guests, and I know that you will not seek to harm those who shelter you. They will not realize what has happened, right?"

"That is correct," Marcus replied, offering a hand to Amata.

"As long as my family and servants are safe, then you will honor me," Heloise replied. "I have plenty of spare blankets and cots."

"Thank you," Marcus replied, relieved at the offer of a warm bed and a day of darkness.

Julien wandered towards the table and looked on as his mother's servants scattered around the kitchen.

"Alesta?" he asked, believing he recognized one of their faces.

"Alais, my lord," the young woman corrected with a curtsy. "My older sister is Alesta. She is married to the blacksmith, now."

"Oh," he muttered, embarrassed that he could remember her name. "My apologies, Alais. Are my mother and sister–"

"Right here," his mother interjected with a smile before walking into the room. "Alais, feed this poor skinny boy," she requested before pulling her son into a seat. Alais started working on breakfast.

"Lirienne will be down soon." His mother beamed as if she held the secrets of the universe in the palm of her hand.

"Why are you such a pleased cat?" Julien asked his mother.

"Your friends managed to find our home late last night," she replied.

"Which friends?" he asked.

"Marcus, Claudius, Arwin, Patroclus, and the rest, including your lovely la roux," his mother teased.

"I am so hungry, I could eat ten eggs," his sister boasted as she walked to the table. "Hello, little brother." Lirienne leaned over and patted his hair.

"They survived?" Julien tried to dodge his sister's patronizing gestures. "They survived both the madness and the firestorm?"

"I…" Heloise started to explain before pausing for a moment. "From what I heard, not all of them survived." He watched her frown.

"I need to speak to them," he said before standing up.

"Sit," his mother said, firmly. "They are sleeping in the cellar, Julien. Let them rest."

Julien sat back down, feeling a bit cowed. "Of course, I just would like to know the secret of their survival. How was the ritual?" he asked in a half-whisper.

"It was wonderful, magical, and utterly glorious. If you wish we can have a family ritual tonight," his mother answered. "Anyway, Máire appeared from the woods and joined us in our celebration."

"Yes, it was so strangely beautiful," Lirienne added. She smiled, beaming like their mother. Lirienne giggled as the plates arrived in front of them. "Thank you, Alais."

His mother and sister started chuckling together, but Julien tried to ignore them.

"Have you heard anything from Flor?" his mother asked.

Julien began choking on his water. His mother began hitting him on the back, and he soon regained his breath.

"I have written correspondences, but have not had the time to secure a messenger," Julien replied.

He noticed his sister smile.

"Surely Reginald respects her now," his mother said. "Two strong sons and beautiful Tildy."

"I sincerely hope so," Julien replied, "but Flor is not as strong as she likes to pretend she is."

"No, she's not, but not every woman is like your la roux, little brother," Lirienne teased.

Julien did not want to admit that he believed he could simply compare every woman to the red-haired warrior in the cellar and find them somehow lacking. Even Flor could not compare.

"Julien, wake up. It's after sunset."

A gentle hand shook him awake. He opened his eyes and saw that his mother stood before him. His dreams faded into memory.

Julien sat up and rubbed his eyes. "This reverse sleeping schedule seems to make me sleepier," he said while yawning.

"I am sure you will get used to it soon," she replied. "Be quick. They are waiting on you." His mother left his room, leaving the candle behind.

He dressed and then walked downstairs. Upon entering the main level, he heard a voice singing in some foreign tongue. As he walked towards the singing, Julien noticed traveling gear, which lay strewn about in the middle of the room, and then he saw the source of the singing… Claudius. The Briton noticed him and stopped singing. The others turned to regard Julien, and he looked on as a few of them toasted him.

"How did you escape?" he asked, before noticing Máire turn to regard him. He tried to stop smiling, but he could not help himself. The very thought of her standing naked in the grove made him forget most of his other questions regarding their escape and survival.

"Luck," commented Mac Alpin.

"And rain," added Edward.

"Thank the Gods for that," he murmured, before realizing he should have offered thanks to God or Jesus.

He watched Máire smile. "Lady Heloise tells me that you are a man of the old faiths."

Julien felt his face heat. "I…" he stammered as he looked over at his mother. Both she and his sister smirked at one another. "I… yes, that is correct, at least I am that more than I am a Christian."

"Fear not, for none of us is Christian," Marcus stated. "We certainly will not turn you in to the pope, or his Imperial Majesty, for that matter."

"But," Julien asked as he looked over his guests, "what about the papal emissary, Michael Tolomei?"

Marcus' eyes turned towards Amata. The lady shrugged and smiled.

"The enemy of my enemy is my friend," Marcus answered. He said nothing more regarding the papal emissary.

"And who is the enemy?" Julien asked.

"The murderers we seek," Marcus answered.

He watched Patroclus stare out through a window.

"We should return to the garrison," Patroclus said.

"We took the liberty of saddling the horses," Claudius added. "Then the promise of wine and lovely company made us grow lazy."

The party of warriors soon began to gather their supplies. As Julien watched Máire going about her packing, he saw her drop a flask, and then red liquid spilled onto the floor. Alais must have noticed the spill, because she arrived and started to clean it. Julien then noticed that a strange scent of wine mixed with something else infiltrated the house.

"I fear the wine has made me clumsy," Máire said with a chuckle.

His mother and sister started on their farewells to their guests, and he watched the group of foreigners kiss them and wish them well in other languages. He wondered why they aided a Christian ruler and the pope. Then his mother interrupted his musings by embracing him and kissing his brow.

"Be careful," she warned him. He noticed his sister and the surviving foreigners chuckling and elbowing each other, and then he felt his face flush. His mother always had to do that.

From outside, Julien then heard racing footsteps move towards them.

Everyone ran outside to look at the commotion. He then saw Dreu and a small company of men running up to the house.

Dreu stopped running. He seemed to need a moment to catch his breath. "My lord," he squeaked. "People are running from the village of Sant Pere. They were attacked, and the beasts are headed this direction."

Marcus watched the Legate and Edward walk solemnly through the forested grove, and he sensed Claudius flying overhead. The rest of the village remained as dark as the skies above. The local vassals, merchants, and priest remained in Lady Heloise's home with the inspector general, the majority of the garrison, and a few of the stronger vassals, who served as guards.

Marcus hoped that this new plan would work. After all, it did make some sense. They would detect the arrival of the Strigoi. The archers behind himself, Mac Alpin, Patroclus, and Edward, would attack the Strigoi. The wounded Strigoi would find their concentration lacking, and therefore they would be unable to use their mental attack.

"Are you certain it's wise to have the archers behind us?" Mac Alpin asked.

"Which part of this plan do you question, Arwin?"

"Well, I'm not questioning anything, Marcus. I'm just wondering whether you've considered the skill level of these archers you placed behind us. Aren't they usually farmers? I'd prefer to not to be struck in the head with an arrow. That would be most annoying."

Marcus chuckled. "If you are so frightened of arrows, you can go back to Lady Heloise's and do lady's things with Máire, Amata, Lirienne, and Heloise." In reality, the 'lady's things' consisted of protecting the survivors of Sant Pere.

"Roman swine," Mac Alpin scoffed, though jest shone in his eyes. "I'll stay here, thank you, even if it's just to see your plan fail."

Silence descended, and even the animals ceased their conversation.

"And another thing—" Added Mac Alpin before Marcus cut him off.

"For a man who isn't questioning my plan, you have a lot of questions,"

Marcus stated, feeling bemused, yet somewhat annoyed. He stared at the other blood-drinker for a moment.

Mac Alpin chuckled and then shook his head.

"Speak your mind, Arwin."

"I just think that our points are too close to us." Mac Alpin motioned to the others.

Marcus looked at Edward and Patroclus. "If something happens, I wish to be close in order to help them. You wouldn't want Edward to suffer at the hands of the Strigoi, would you?"

"I suppose that makes sense," Arwin answered. With the debate over, they moved towards a copse of woodland.

"And I'm so happy you approve–"

"Stand fast!" Edward called out, interrupting him. Everyone stopped. Marcus watched Patroclus and then Edward fall to the ground.

"Archers! Fire towards the trees," Marcus yelled.

He heard the snap of arrows leaving the bows, and then he ran towards the trees, ignoring the potential danger of flying arrows.

"Keep up with us," Marcus yelled. He heard a loud thump and decided to risk a glance behind himself. Claudius lay unconscious in the grass.

Marcus could see a few of the Strigoi outlined against the trees. He heard others behind him fall or turned back. He growled his frustration, realizing that so many of his forces had fallen. Alone, he chased after the Strigoi.

They stood, many of them leaning against the trunk of the tree, and stared at him, unblinking. Their eyes showed nothing more than a maddening, orange glow. A lust for blood exploded within, and so he drew his two gladii and then began cutting down the Strigoi. Vitae and tissue congealed over his arms as he slashed his way through the Strigoi. Marcus felt blood coat his hair and drip onto his face. Then he experienced the strange awareness that his movements slowed down. His swords grew heavy, and soon a stabbing pain pounded at his temples.

Marcus stopped fighting. A gentle weakness embraced him, and soon a desire for rest grew within. He collapsed to his knees, but he managed to brace himself with the swords.

The remaining Strigoi stared at him. Their orange eyes penetrated his soul.

The sky brightened, and the sun arched in the heavens.

He remained cool and in one piece. He glanced down and saw a chestnut horse beneath him. A woman guided his mount with a gentle hand. Her golden hair lay straight down her back. He watched the woman turn towards him with a gentle smile. His mother stared at him with her beautiful, silver eyes.

"You look worried, my love. Do not fear. All will be well and as it is meant to be,"

she addressed him in the Gallic tongue before patting his knee.

A strange question dwelled within. He gave in to his compulsion to ask her. "Mother, how did my father die?" he asked.

"He died in battle against those barbarians to the south… those vicious Romans," his mother explained.

"Why don't we stand and fight the Romans?" he asked.

"Another day, my son," she answered, smiling at him. "For now, we cross Gaul to find our new home. That vile Julius Caesar has decided to let us pass, at least he gave his word he would do so. We'll see how much Caesar's word means, but it would be shameful to kill the ancients, women, and children."

"But what if they do come?" he asked in the querulous voice of a child. His tiny hands rested on the reins.

"Don't worry, the women will fight back," she told him. "Romans are afraid of women who go into battle." His mother patted the golden pommel of the sword hanging from her belt. She then pushed back a few blonde hairs from her face.

"How do you know so much about them?" he asked his mother.

"I was forced into slavery once, after I married your father," she explained. "I pretended to be docile, and they placed me in a household. I learned much from watching them. The Romans are a depraved and cowardly lot. They think nothing of beating their slaves and forcing them to…" She frowned, and her eyes revealed pain. "Anyways, one night, your father attacked the household and found me."

His mother seemed to force the pain from her eyes and smiled at him. "I will never allow you to be forced into such a life."

The sky above Marcus flashed dark again. He struggled to raise either of his swords over his head. The radiating pain swelled through his body.

The sky cleared to a sunny brightness again. He found himself back on the horse. A wind gust made the trees of the forest whisper. Then an abrasive, guttural war cry made him tremble. He forced himself to stop being fearful and instead protect his mother.

Red shields emblazoned with gold pushed through the brush and undergrowth. The warriors seemed to gleam with a blinding light as a red flood washed over the landscape in a torrent of blood.

A gentle sound of wind settled on his ears, but then he watched his clan begin to fall as arrows pierced them. Children screamed in fear. His mother released the reins as an arrow hit his mount. The horse bucked in pain, flinging him into air.

Another rain of arrows crashed around him. His mother protected him for a moment with her arms. Lucilla picked him up and then raced for the forest. Cries of victory and screams of agony echoed behind him. He heard a soft grunt, and suddenly, his mother fell to the ground, and he landed in the dirt.

She struggled to turn her prone body so she could reach the arrow that he saw embedded in her, but she managed to yank it from her leg. She then stared at him.

"I will slow you down," she whispered. "You must run for the nearest village. Show the chieftain your father's torc and tell the chieftain what Caesar's word means."

The skies grew black and ominous again. Marcus gasped and wondered how he witnessed images of pure imagination. He had never lived in Gaul with his real mother.

Marcus pushed aside those fantasies and caught sight of the Strigoi under the trees again, staring at him with hate-filled, orange eyes.

He continued to raise his swords. To stop the dreams, he had to destroy the wielder of the dreams. He prepared to throw his right gladius at the Strigoi.

"Run!" his mother whispered as the sun and the blinding light of the warriors coming towards her. She stood on shaky feet and prepared for battle.

He stood up and began to run, but glanced back upon hearing a scream. A huge figure in a red cape knocked his mother down, kicked away her meager weapons, and then stabbed her repeatedly.

She gurgled a soft warning that he ignored. He screamed and grabbed the only weapon he found on the ground, a loose arrow. The boy raced towards his mother and stabbed the warrior in the leg.

The warrior groaned in pain and looked down at his blood-soaked appendage. He stared up at Marcus and growled in fury, but then Marcus backed away, seeing his own fierce visage under the Roman helm of the warrior.

He felt himself pushed to the ground next to his mother.

She stared at him, betrayal written on her face.

The pain of the blade brought him out of the living nightmare.

Marcus threw the sword at the Strigoi and watched the blood-drinker flinch as the blade slashed into the nearby tree trunk.

The fear grew in his opponent's face as Marcus pushed himself up and prepared to launch his other sword at the Strigoi. The Strigoi shuddered and turned away, loping into the distance.

The throbbing pain in his head began to subside, but something still ached from within. Marcus begged for release and unconsciousness, but he remained awake and aware of the surroundings. Why would he see himself as a boy in this vision? Why would he kill himself or his own mother?

A weight in his hand drew his attention, and saw that a torc glimmered under the starlight.

A vague memory of stripping a torc off the battlefield from a dead boy grabbed his attention. He could see the field of the dying Helvetti, consisting of old men and women, children, and their mothers.

The bloody field, littered with broken bodies, stank of vicious crimes.

Marcus stood up on shaky legs and began to walk amongst the bodies. He counted the silver-headed and the young women clutching children.

Marcus knelt in shame, knowing the truth behind Rome's victory was a group of harmless Gauls that only wanted to find a new, peaceful home. Caesar needed gold to finance his political schemes, and so he had sent his legions after innocents. Their defeat would give him an opportunity to appear as a successful General.

Marcus' bloodstained name would not be an honorarium anymore. It only revealed the depths of darkness within his soul. He accepted that honorarium of 'Helvetticus' with all pleasure once. However, deep within, he knew that he'd wronged his own people. That knowledge would torment him now. The pain of that realization made him begin to weep.

Soon, a warm and gentle hand moved to his shoulder. He turned his head up and saw the silhouette of a woman between him and the sun. Despite the brightness of the sun, he could recognize the form of his mother. Her golden hair gleamed, blinding him.

"Remember, my son, this was your doing," Lucilla murmured.

The night overwhelmed the day, and he looked back to his mother, though Máire stood in her place.

"Where's my mother?" he asked as he scanned the forests and fields of Vézelay from his kneeling form, frantic. "Where did my mother go? I didn't kill her! I didn't kill my mother!"

Máire rubbed his shoulder, unsure of what to do at first. She'd joined the party outside again after four hours passed. Now, all the mortals lay mutilated, and the unconscious immortals remained insensate.

Marcus tugged at her tunic. While she returned to rubbing his shoulder, Máire knew that she needed to return to the great house and gather assistance.

"I didn't kill my mother," Marcus whispered into her tunic.

She stroked his hair. "I know you didn't," she whispered. Marcus had done many horrific deeds, but he had never mentioned such an appalling act.

She could not imagine how he managed to stay conscious, but he remained on his knees, grasping one of his gladii. Máire had seen that its sister remained lodged in a tree in the distance.

"I'll be right back," she whispered before kissing his brow. She walked over to the tree, yanked out the sword, and wandered back to Marcus. His eyes followed her and now watched her with a frightening intensity. She set down his other sword and touched his shoulder again.

"I know you didn't kill your mother, Marcus. The Strigoi hurt you, but you can still stand. The others have fallen."

"Fallen like the Helvetti," he answered. "Dead like my beautiful mother."

Máire knelt and grasped his face with her two hands. She then stared into his eyes.

"I need you to focus on me now," Máire instructed Marcus.

He stopped speaking, but his still lips moved. Then his eyes settled on hers, and their color moved back and forth between unsettled blue and gray.

"Marcus, our family survives, but they are helpless now. I must get assistance from our mortal friends. I need you to stay here and protect our family."

Máire released him and reached for his other sword.

"Here, you always liked having two," she whispered. "I could make very witty jokes about a man with two swords, but I will save my jesting for later."

She felt for his free arm, grabbed it, and placed the pommel of the sword in his palm. She then enclosed her hand over his.

"Can you do this for me? Can you do this for our family?" she asked.

His eyes focused on hers again. "Yes," he affirmed, though his voice strained at the effort.

"Thank you." Máire kissed Marcus' cheek. She walked away and began hiding the Strigoi's bodies in the forest. She could not explain the Strigoi's appearance to the people of Vézelay, nor to the inspector general. They would not comprehend.

After completing her duties, Máire flew away.

She returned with the mortals of the village, guiding one of the carts into the field. Máire found Marcus standing in the distance by the trees, staring into the forest.

She heard mortals crying behind her, and so she turned and watched them holding onto their loved ones and carrying their remains to the carts. Máire then turned back to watch Marcus.

A hand rested on her shoulder, and she recognized the herb-infused scent of Lady Heloise.

"What happened here?" she asked gently. Lady Heloise's hair streamed towards the west in the moonlit breezes.

"The demons attacked," Máire answered. She wished to tell Heloise the truth, but she could not, because the truth would frighten everyone who understood Latin.

"They're not demons remember?" Julien stated as he helped Dreu, the head of the garrison, carry Claudius. They lowered the Sugnwr Gwaed into one of the carts.

"Some were killed, some are unconscious, one is awake," Máire said, ignoring Julien's correction for the moment. "Marcus must have driven the so-called demons away. He kept a vigil while I summoned help."

"Where is Marcus?" Heloise started looking for him.

Máire pointed him out. "He's standing over by the eastern edge of the forest, watching us, Heloise."

She watched the elder mortal stare in Marcus' direction. He was not moving at all. At this moment, he resembled a statue.

"Well, how is it he stands..." Heloise paused. "Oh," she muttered. "Of course." Her words dropped into a whisper.

"Lady Heloise, we are ready to leave," Dreu said.

"I am glad to hear that." Heloise rubbed her hands over her arms before looking over at Máire.

"Will Marcus be joining us?"

"I'll go ask–" Máire began to answer before someone cut her off.

"Don't bother to do so," Marcus said. Máire turned to find him standing off to the side.

She studied him, and she could tell that he twitched a bit and his eyes still darted about. She walked towards him and placed an arm around Marcus.

"No, stay with the group," he murmured. "I will be fine. Someone must watch the back of the carts and assure that you reach the house." Marcus motioned for Lady Heloise, Dreu, and herself to leave with the others.

Máire nodded her head. She felt guilty for leaving him after such an attack. She wished to know how Marcus managed not to fall, and of course, what his babbling had been about, but perhaps he would talk to her about it later. She turned away and heard him jog towards the perimeter of the road. He then ducked into the trees and undergrowth.

 arcus watched Máire tuck another blanket around Edward. He could also hear the inspector general muttering to himself in one of the obscure Frankish dialects upstairs, though the rest of the house remained silent in rest.

"It is time to tell him all," he said as he placed a hand on her shoulder. "Join me. Julien will take it better if he hears it from the two of us, especially since he really likes you. The body waits in the grain storage."

Máire turned around and nodded.

Marcus and Máire walked upstairs to the first floor and stood as they watched Julien pace about the room.

"How are they?" Julien asked.

"They are recovering," Marcus answered. He watched as the inspector general's eyes studied Máire for a moment. "We cannot sleep. Do you care to join us for a walk?" Marcus asked.

"It was our habit at home to study the night sky before going to sleep," Máire added.

"Alright, perhaps the night air will give me answers to the questions plaguing my mind," Julien agreed before following them outside. Once they stood beyond the entryway of the house, Marcus lit the torches he had brought with him and gave one to each member of the party. They then ambled towards the eastern side of the house.

"So what troubles you, Julien?" Marcus asked as he turned his head to glance at the mortal.

"I just cannot understand what happened to the bodies of our enemies," Julien answered with a nervous half-chuckle. "Do not tell anyone this, but I have to wonder whether they were indeed the spawn of the devil. They seemed to have disappeared. The people of Vézelay and Sant Pere have every reason to be frightened. I find myself speculating on the most ridiculous and outlandish ideas." The inspector general shook his head. "Nothing sane and rational answers the question anymore."

"I have an answer for you," Marcus replied before he turned to the left and grabbed the door of the grain store. "I want to show you what we are fighting." He opened the door, walked in, and stood over the covered body. He then handed his torch to Máire.

"Witness the face of our enemy, Inspector General," he said before pulling away the cover from the body, exposing the body and its severed head.

He watched Julien blanch and back away. He could smell heady fear overwhelm the mortal.

"Dear Gods, what is that thing?" Julien asked. "Is that a demon? It must be a demon."

"No, it is not," Máire clarified.

"While this man looks devilish, he is not a demon, but he is dead now and cannot harm you. He is a Strigoi." Marcus looked back to Julien. "A Strigoi is... well, Inspector General, it is a long story."

Julien curiously touched the Strigoi's arm, regaining some his inquisitiveness. "I have time," he said in a near whisper. Julien cleared his throat and then seemed to find his voice. "Please tell me about these Strigoi."

"Have you heard tales of beings that are not mortal, yet walk the nights feeding on the blood of the living, Julien?" Marcus asked. "Almost every culture I have come across tells tales of these beings. Some are seen as demons and pure evil. Other kinds of blood-drinkers are seen as good, or at least neutral. That is the simplest explanation I can give. The Strigoi are evil and insane, and they draw out the worst in mortals and other blood-drinkers. They mentally attack anyone and bring forth living nightmares." Máire drew closer to him as they both turned to regard the mortal. "I am certain you must have questions as to how I could know of these matters. The answer is this, our associates, and we, are blood-drinkers."

Marcus allowed his eyes to glow, and he noticed Máire reveal her fangs a little. They both allowed their glamoury to surround them and create a soft glow of beauty in the dark grain shed.

Julien yelped and then drew his sword. His face and his racing heartbeat revealed fear and shock. Julien stared at them as if waiting for an attack, but soon he began to calm.

"That..." he stammered as he sheathed his sword, as if realizing there would be no attack, "that makes sense," he whispered. "All of the traveling at night, the fact that you never eat, the strange substance in your flask Máire, and then Marcus, I did see you trying to feed that first night in Aachen."

"Yes, I did try to feed on that drunk," Marcus admitted. "But I feed from several mortals or even animals every night so I do not have to take all of the blood from one. As a rule, we do not kill our donors."

"So I was not blind," the inspector general said. "You lied to me in Aachen, but I suppose that was for the better. I... I believe that you are not demons, so what are you?"

"We are Deargh Du," Máire answered. "We are the children of the Goddess Morrigan of Eire. She has given us the task of balancing good and evil in the world from night's tender shroud."

"Morrigan is our Queen of blood, battle, and rebirth. She seeks to challenge the warrior within us all. She grants us gifts for our duty to Her and to mankind," Marcus added. "Yet, we are not the only ones who walk the night. In fact, now Máire and I are the only Deargh Du in our traveling party. Our associates represent different races of blood-drinkers. Claudius is a Sugnwr Gwaed, and Edward and Arwin are Ekimmu Cruitne. Those two races are from Briton... excuse me... what are now the Saxon kingdoms, Scotland, Pictland, and what used to be Dalriada. Amata and Patroclus are Lamia from Rome. We all have different abilities, talents, gifts, and weaknesses," he added.

"We recently formed an alliance with the Lamia after many centuries of battle. The Strigoi attacked them and several mortal communities, and so they asked the Celtic lines for assistance," Máire added.

"Yes, as I said earlier about an old Roman saying, it goes, 'the enemy of my enemy is my friend', " Marcus quoted with a grin. He grew silent upon seeing the growing questions in Julien's eyes.

"If you are immortal, why is this being dead?" Julien asked.

"We are immortal to a certain point, to be honest," Marcus replied. "If you burn us, trap us under the sun, or behead us, we will die."

"How old are you?" the inspector general asked next as he came in closer as if to study them.

"My name is Marcus Galerius Primus... Helvetticus," he answered, though he had experienced some trepidation stating his honorarium, given his recent Strigoi-induced nightmare. He lowered his head for a moment before squaring his shoulders and meeting Julien's gaze. "I became Deargh Du in what would be 55 B.C. I later transformed Máire in 564 A.D."

"Arwin is the eldest of our party, and Edward is the youngest... well, he was transformed two years after me," Máire added with a slight shrug.

"Can anyone become as you two are?" Julien asked.

"Yes," Marcus answered. "There is more to it than just that, but we will save that for another night."

"And you do not have to kill?"

"No, we do not. In fact there are races of blood-drinkers who prefer to feed on animals, and even then, most of those animals survive," Marcus answered.

"Why kill something that can survive to feed you another time?" Máire added, before pacing a bit. "The sun wakes soon. We need rest. Will you be alright?" she asked while looking at Julien. "You realize, now, that we will not harm you? The Deargh Du even heal those whom they feed upon. If we wished you harm, you would have been dead long ago."

Julien nodded his head. "This is much to digest, but it does make sense now." The gendarme revealed a wide smile. "What you told me is most fascinating, and this new revelation has opened my mind."

"Your mother knows of our kind," Máire added. "We can talk more about this after sunset."

"Your friends will be well then, right?" Julien asked as he opened the door and held it for them to pass.

"They will recover soon," Marcus answered, hoping he was right. "Please do keep this as a secret," he added. "I am sure our companions will not mind, but I have no desire to be burned as a heretic by your vassals."

"I will not say a word, and I would not allow such a thing to happen," Julien answered, as they walked towards his home.

Marcus tried to not chuckle when he noticed Julien gazing upon Máire again with his normal, mortal lust intact.

Rome

Mandubratius yawned and then shook his head at the lack of entertainment here. He began to toy with the idea of manipulating the servants into kill themselves in combat for his amusement. However, the sounds and smells of another Lamia made him retreat from the creative confines of his mind and face reality. He turned around to see Hieronymus waiting for him.

"Dismissed," he yelled as he waved the servants away.

"Have you called forth all of the Lamia, Hieronymus?" he asked.

"Sir," Hieronymus acknowledge him and saluted, "the two hundred are assembled and are ready to participate in this plan."

"Excellent!" Mandubratius smiled at his lieutenant. "The papal army grows by leaps and bounds. Eight thousand men have amassed. My light cavalry will consist of one thousand. I feel that the two hundred will be able to transform one thousand within a night."

"I would agree," Hieronymus replied. "We all feel that this plan is most ingenious."

Mandubratius chuckled, but he quickly stifled his laughter. "Of course, Hieronymus… that is because it is my plan. Could you send over some of my personal slaves from the temple? I seem to have an abundance of energy, and I feel a little amorous."

Outside Chagny

Seosaimhín walked through the milling Strigoi and examined them as they backed away from her. She felt her smile turn predatory and widen. The Strigoi averted their eyes and physically turned, as if fearful. She neared the large noble house that served as Omid's residence. The Strigoi had returned from an attack several hours ago, yet the lumbering Ekimmu could not seem to find the time to address his pack. Instead, he remained with his harem of vile concubines.

The unwavering smile offered to every Strigoi made them turn, boosting Seosaimhín's confidence. She pushed through the main door, ignoring the guards posted throughout the elegant house that now smelled of blood and entrails. She moved past the maze of halls and reached the lord's chambers. Seosaimhín stopped at the oak door and then pushed it open, revealing Omid and four Strigoi females upon the great bed in the center of the room.

Seosaimhín chuckled at the sight of the Strigoi... naked, leaving no clothing to hide their repulsiveness. At least one of them she thought appeared to be male.

The hidden dagger in the palm of her right hand felt heavy in her grasp, but soon it would be time for her to use it. Seosaimhín walked over to the side of the bed and prepared to strike.

Omid opened his eyes and smiled at her. He then sat up as she leaned in close to him.

"Did you finally decide to join me?" the Ekimmu cooed with a grin, revealing his fangs.

Seosaimhín said nothing as she grabbed the back of his hair, exposing Omid's neck, and struck with her dagger. Blood splattered over Omid's Strigoi as she sliced her blade through his neck. The Strigoi began licking at the flecks of blood dotting their limbs. Omid's body became slack as his vitae flooded the noble bedding.

Seosaimhín tightened her grip on her dagger and began sawing at Omid's head. At long last, his head parted from his neck. Her arms and hands reflected back the beautiful black and copper color of torch-lit blood.

She could sense the entire pack of the Strigoi watching her from the door to the room and from the crowd that had gathered outside. Seosaimhín then held aloft her bloody trophy to the Strigoi in the room and to those outside of the window. She then licked the silken edge of the knife, loving the caress against her tongue.

"We lead you now," she informed the gathered masses. "We shall make you better. You will abide by the absolute will of Nagirrom."

A harsh caw interrupted Seosaimhín's speech, yet she smiled when she noticed Nagirrom flying into the room from an open window. The Strigoi dropped to the floor, and the soft chant of Nagirrom's name began to echo in her ears as the Strigoi repeated His name in a chant.

Seosaimhín chuckled. "All for you, ivory-colored, feathered friend."

Soon, a strangely cloying scent of honey, mistletoe, and male essences caught her nose. She sniffed again. The smell reminded her of someone she had met long ago, but whom.

She moved past the blood-drenched concubines, through the Strigoi gathered at the door to the room, past the hallways, and into the general crowd outside. The scent grew in potency with every step. She then found the Strigoi that exuded the sweet wafting perfume. Seosaimhín grabbed the Strigoi and rotated its body so she could see into its haggard eyes.

"Share with me your memories," she whispered in the Strigoi's left ear. Her fangs grew and soon blood swam as she bit into its flesh. Mists parted, and she watched as a soldier of Rome cried over his own body. Flashes of images revealed a boy and his mother. Then the moonlight lit the soulless one of Rome's face.

Seosaimhín pulled back and smiled. "So, returned have you to the continent and the lands you and yours pillaged in your mortal days," she whispered before turning back to the Strigoi.

"How I wish I could have been there. We all wish to give the soulless one of Rome nightmares. Alas, I must live through you as we continue to plague him with lurid flights into his past. Perhaps we can meet him again soon and reveal we have twisted his mind thus."

Seosaimhín embraced the Strigoi and then kissed it on its left cheek.

Máire stretched for a moment before she sat down in the grove. She studied the stone altar for a moment, wondering whether it had stood here long before her transformation. Perhaps this altar rested on the earth before the Franks, the Burgundians, the Romans, or perchance even the Gauls walked these lands.

The others still recovered in the basement. She wished to escape from the fearful murmurs of her friends and allies. To her knowledge, no blood-drinker had suffered terror to that extent before. Perhaps if she loved them, she could remain there for them and whisper, 'there, there', when they called for their mortal mothers.

Love again seemed like an unfamiliar and abstract concept that loomed behind her memories of joyous and spontaneous declarations of affection. Had it truly been that easy?

After spending an hour pondering the origins of the grove, and her own emotional peculiarities, she could sense a mortal walking through the grass. The delicate scent of Lady Heloise overwhelmed any of the other smells emanating from the grove.

Máire decided to remain silent. Perhaps Heloise wished to escape her numerous guests.

The elder mortal walked around her and then turned to face her. The woman's eyes crinkled at the corners, revealing not age, but grace, resolve, and a timeless beauty.

"What are you doing here all by yourself, Máire?"

Máire studied the mortal's eminent concern. "I didn't want to be with the others," she admitted.

"I'm sorry," the lady of the lands replied. "I didn't realize that you wanted to be alone. I'll leave you in peace." Heloise started walking back to the house.

"Wait," Máire replied. The other woman stopped and turned to face her. "I would love to have company," Máire added.

Lady Heloise sat down across from her and stared into the sky. After a few moments of silence, the mortal spoke again.

"It would appear that my son holds tender feelings for you."

Máire sputtered in shock. "I'm sorry… I'm flattered, but I think you…" she paused, unsure of how to end that sentence. Instead, she concluded with, "I have noticed no such attraction."

Lady Heloise's eyes met hers. While she and her son shared many common features, their eyes were different. Heloise had grayish-blue eyes, while her son's eyes reminded Máire of the blue oceans in her mortal days.

"It takes a mother to see these things," Heloise replied. "He tends to keep those thoughts to himself, primarily because he feels he has little to offer a woman. However, he watches over you."

A sudden discomfort settled over Máire.

Heloise tipped her head to the left side and smiled again. "Although, I'm certain many watch over you. Do you have a lover?"

"Wh… what?" The question surprised Máire.

"It is a simple question, and the answer would not shock me. I enjoy being an unmarried widow," Heloise replied. "The men tell me that things are different between the blood-drinkers."

"That is true," Máire admitted. "There is little jealousy between lovers in the Celtic lines. It's very difficult to explain to another race, let alone a mortal. However, for one to have lovers, one must love." She turned her face skyward and wiped away wetness from her cheek.

Heloise moved closer to her. "What has befallen you, my child? Why do you feel that you have no love to give?"

Máire's reluctance to admit the truth rose, along with the mild amusement that a woman much younger than herself called her, 'child'. "I don't wish to trouble you with a burden that is over two hundred years old," she answered.

"You've felt this way for that long?" Lady Heloise queried.

Máire nodded her head. "I'm cursed."

"Cursed?"

"It's a long story," Máire answered, "one that probably won't interest you."

"Nonsense," Heloise disagreed. "I rather enjoy the stories the blood-drinkers tell about their pasts, except for the ones involving nothing but battle. I'm sure there is more to your story that the others tell me about the war between the Lamia and the Celtic lines. Perhaps you can tell me the rest of the tale, or we can stare at the stars if you'd prefer not to say what happened to you. The stars are indeed breathtaking tonight." Heloise leaned back and stared up at the skies, pushing away the veil covering her hair.

A nagging impulse to blurt everything out swelled within.

"You may as well know," Máire began. "I killed my husband-to-be at the altar during our wedding ceremony. Connor, my last betrothed, had murdered my beloved betrothed before that, and he had involved himself in the war between the Lamia and us. He was also complicit in other activities against my family, clan, and friends as well."

Máire sensed Heloise pull away from her. The woman's eyes grew large.

"You killed him?" Lady Heloise asked in a whisper.

"He was an evil man," Máire answered. "Poor Seanán died in a most brutal and gruesome manner. In those days, I had every right to destroy the man who had done such a thing." She stopped herself from giving more details.

Heloise moved even closer. "Do you believe that you cannot feel love because of the way your husband-to-be betrayed you?"

"No," Máire answered, giving her hostess a wry smile. "I was very much in love with my father-in-darkness then. However, soon after, I became cursed. Connor's mother was a druid with knowledge in the ways of death. She focused on death instead of the balance. Seosaimhín placed a curse on me that has prevented me from feeling love in my lifetime. As I am Deargh Du, a lifetime is a long time."

"Have you tried lifting it?" Heloise inquired as she placed a gentle hand on her shoulder.

"My friends and I have tried," Máire answered. "However, most druids do not practice curse removal. Besides, most of my friends are warriors and not druids. On some occasions, we petitioned the Tuaths and other Gods or Goddesses for assistance. Sometimes they acted, while other times, they chose to let us work on the problem ourselves."

A breeze made the trees whisper to one another. Heloise shifted a bit and began rubbing her hands together in an apparent attempt to keep warm.

"It is a shame that my circle is not here. The Strigoi have scared many of us indoors," Heloise observed before turning to stare at the altar.

"What do you think your friends could have done?" Máire asked.

"Our practices include workings that may lift curses," Heloise explained as she met Máire's eyes. "We have used herbs and incantations to lift curses before."

A silence fell between the women for a few moments as Máire turned away to study her bare feet.

"Do you need the others to perform the incantation?" Máire asked.

"I suppose not," Heloise answered. "Would you like to try it?"

Máire grinned. "It can't hurt or make the situation worse," she stated, before pulling her knees toward her chin.

Heloise rose and then dusted herself off. "I'll gather what I need." She began to walk towards her home.

"Is there anything I can do to help prepare?" Máire asked.

Heloise turned back and smiled. "Just look at the stars and don't think about the curse," she answered.

Máire lowered her back to the ground and stared into the night, sensing Heloise fade into the distance. She closed her eyes and drifted into some kind of half-sleep.

A few moments later, the sharp smell of incense woke Máire. She sat up and turned, noticing Heloise and Lirienne approaching her, carrying several baskets.

"I thought it best that you rest instead of helping me with preparing the incantations," Heloise explained. The two mortals settled their baskets behind the altar and began placing oatcakes, honey, beeswax candles, and incense at the altar's center.

Máire nodded her head and remained silent as the women began to speak in Frankish. A few words rang familiar as they called forth guardian spirits, Gods, and otherworldly beings, though the rest of their words seemed to be a garbled, yet beautiful incantation.

Soon the mortal pair of mother and daughter almost became indistinguishable in the light of the stars and candles. A strange sensation pulsed through the earth and wind, revealing that a link between worlds existed. The candle flickered in time with the mortal heartbeats, and the sound of flowing water echoed in Máire's ears.

Heloise motioned for her to kneel, and so Máire rolled onto her knees and lowered her head, feeling her hair and plaits swing towards her face.

She heard Lirienne's heartbeat as the other mortal walked behind her.

As Heloise's arms hovered over her head, incense billowed around the three of them. Her words became a loud crescendo, and the earth and air vibrated in time with each syllable. Hands settled on Máire's hair, and then she heard the earth sigh like an ancient and eternal mother.

Heloise and Lirienne backed away from her. Máire looked up and witnessed them sending back the vibrations of energy to the Otherworld, or to whatever destination that created and set loose the forces in the ritual.

The two mortal women then sat down in front of her, holding food and a cask of wine. They both beamed radiant smiles at her. Máire returned a nervous grin, wondering whether she needed to feel anything. Mostly, she felt at peace, but she experienced a little confusion as well.

"It is done," Heloise said, in Latin.

"I wish I knew your language better," Máire replied. "Thank you both."

"I hope it worked, but it may take some time for the energy to take hold." Then Heloise's smile faded. "We must be patient for these workings." The two mortals then broke apart one of the honey-drenched oatcakes to share.

"What did you say during the incantation?" Máire asked.

Lirienne swallowed her food and then spoke. "We created an opening between this world and the hidden one," she began as she poured cups of wine for them. She passed one to Máire. "We asked those who dwell there to remove the curse from a woman who has suffered for far too long."

"That explains much," Máire replied, before sipping at the dark, red wine. She peeked at Lirienne and Heloise over the rim of her cup, noticing that they had finished their meal. The honey sweetened their scents.

Lirienne's eyes revealed a quiet awe. "What is it like? To be Deargh Du I mean."

Máire coughed on a sip of her wine. "It is enjoyable to serve Morrigan. I've traveled to distant lands, studied places forgotten in the mists of history, and met many mortals and immortals of various cultures and races. However, service to Morrigan is seldom effortless."

"How so?" Lirienne asked.

"When I'm not traveling by myself or with my family, there is conflict," Máire admitted. "I've witnessed and participated in more battles than most of the soldiers in Emperor Charles' army, and even the emperor himself. In addition to that, Marcus and I are outcasts amongst the majority of the Deargh Du."

"Why is that?" Heloise asked. "After all, Julien has told me about the battle at Ch… the court. I would presume that your father-in-darkness would be an esteemed Deargh Du. Besides that, he is likeable and tells excellent stories."

"Marcus is an outcast because he's Roman. He is half Gaul, but that is not good enough for most of the Deargh Du," Máire explained. "I'm an outcast, because, instead of requesting that a Deargh Du of proper lineage transform me, I asked Marcus to do it."

"It still sounds like an exciting life," Lirienne stated. "You get an opportunity to serve your Goddess and live forever."

Máire shrugged. "I could still die," she answered. "However, if my head remains attached to my neck, and I'm not exposed to the sun, then I could live forever."

"What was it like to become Deargh Du?" Lirienne asked.

Máire smiled. "I remember asking Marcus that when I was mortal. He informed me that it was very painful, but those words do not suffice in describing what a Deargh Du experiences in their transformation. Your physical body changes and you lose your teeth. Then you experience fae-madness for the first night."

She noticed Lirienne cringe.

"It was not that bad," Máire added. "I was fearful a Lamia would try to transform me. I decided that the pain of becoming a Deargh Du was better than the horrible fate that awaited me as a Lamia." She then rose to her feet.

"And I did transform into this," Máire explained as she flourished her hands from head to toe. "I was shorter, and I certainly was not this pretty. However, Morrigan's other offerings are worth so much more than mere beauty. All of the blood-drinkers have gifts… some gifts we share in common, and some are unique to a specific line. The Ekimmu Cruitne, for instance, have the best sense of smell of any blood-drinkers. The Sugnwr Gwaed have an innate connection with animals, and their singing is lovely. Just don't let Claudius know I said that." Máire chuckled. "The Lamia's talents lie in manipulation, yet the Deargh Du wield glamoury, and I prefer that gift instead of manipulative skills."

"How does…" Lirienne hesitated before asking, "how does one become Deargh Du, or any of the other races, for that matter?"

"Lirienne!" Heloise exclaimed before closing her eyes and smiling. "Let's leave our guest to her thoughts. We can speak of these matters at another time. Máire needs to reflect on her wishes."

Heloise rose to her feet and helped up Lirienne.

"Very well," Lirienne agreed with a smirk. "However, I want to know what how one becomes a blood-drinker." She turned her gaze back to Máire.

"You and your little brother's questions will drive me to the abbey!" Heloise yanked Lirienne away from the grove. She then stopped and turned back to Máire, walked towards her, and kissed Máire's left cheek.

"Be at peace," Heloise said.

She rejoined her daughter and wrapped an arm around Lirienne. Máire watched them walk through the circle of trees towards the torch-lit house in the distance.

She wondered whether the incantation would have an effect. Perhaps tomorrow night, she would commence on workings of her own. Surely, the others would still be recovering tomorrow night.

Rome

The barracks smelled of leather, pong, and dung, yet Horatio learned long ago to ignore the worst of smells and steel his nose on the delightful ones. Sometimes, he could smell wildflowers in the distance, reminding him of his family's small, lush estate. He then turned to his oldest friend, Renatus.

"How does my beard look?" Horatio asked as he ran a hand over his nearly hairless chin.

"It's the most pitiful beard I've ever seen," Renatus quipped. "My mother has more of a beard than you."

Horatio chuckled as he began tossing his friend's leather armor at him. Renatus caught each piece.

"Did you hear why we're getting into parade formation in the middle of the night?" Horatio asked. Other young soldiers prepared to join the formation on the field.

"I heard that the major wishes to impress the new officer in charge of the cavalry." Renatus laced the sides of his leather armor and then tossed Horatio's helm to him.

"I wish they could have waited until morning," Horatio whispered.

The door opened, and their lieutenant marched into the barracks.

The soldiers all fell silent and stood at attention.

"Continue with your preparations, but listen to my words," the lieutenant said. The soldiers broke ranks, but everyone watched their superior as he began to pace the room. "The cavalry has been granted special honors. We will join an elite order in the army."

"I believed we were already elite, sir," a soldier stated.

"We are, but ours is not the highest order," the lieutenant answered. "Only our regiment has been selected for this honor. You should be proud for earning this tribute. Now, finish up and join us on the field."

"Yes sir!" Horatio heard himself shout, along with everyone else. Their commanding then officer left the room.

"Did you know there was a higher order?" Renatus asked.

Horatio shrugged before motioning Renatus in closer. "Your armor is crooked," he teased as he tugged at an edge.

"And you stink," Renatus replied. "Do you think there will be promotions?"

"If they promote anyone, it should be me," Horatio boasted.

They left the room and headed towards the stables.

Horatio walked towards the grooms and took the reins of his horse, before quietly passing over a small coin to the groom. They paid the soldiers little, but they paid the grooms even less.

"Thank you for taking good care of Amadeo," he whispered. Horatio shoved his foot into the stirrup and hopped onto his horse.

He nudged Amadeo towards the assembly and then settled himself next to Renatus.

As the horn of assembly bellowed, a few sleepy horses seemed to wake at the loud noise.

The major then trotted out towards the gathered soldiers.

"I've called you all here to announce that you've all been chosen to join an elite cadre of soldiers in the service of the Holy Father and Lord Jesus Christ," the major shouted. "I'd like to introduce you to your new commanding officer, General Michael Tolomei."

Horatio looked over the new general, who seemed to be a bit clumsy in the saddle. He tried not to smile, remembering his training. Then Horatio sensed the new commanding officer's gaze settle upon him for a moment. The general's gaze and demeanor made Horatio forget the man's awkward seat in the saddle. His disposition seemed formidable, and Horatio felt a strange fear well within the pit of his stomach. He even shivered a little, but he could not understand why he felt so fearful.

The general then turned his gaze to the other members of the cavalry.

Horatio wondered whether a long, drawn out speech would commence.

"Tonight, you shall become something greater than men. You will be elevated to the status of angels in God's most holy army," their new general announced.

Horatio turned his head slightly to look at Renatus. His friend continued to stare at the general.

Why does this sound so insane, not to mention blasphemous?

Yet no one else said anything. They all seemed transfixed. It also seemed strange that hooded strangers, perhaps monks or priests, surrounded their regiment. Soon, however, Horatio's worry about the profane and sacrilegious statements of General Tolomei began to fade. After all, the Tolomei's were one of the richest families in Rome, and a large number of priests, bishops, and cardinals came from their family. Why would one of their personages say anything so bizarre if it were not right and true?

"Do you choose to accept this gift that I offer?"

Horatio heard the loud affirmative reply echo around him. Amadeo shifted and played with the bit in his mouth as if sensing Horatio's nervous state.

"Then follow me, and I will lead you to the sacred place where you will join God's most holy order," the general informed them.

The cavalry cheered, and Horatio found himself joining in the ovation, although he felt confused by his behavior, but it seemed right.

The major gave the orders to advance before beginning to lead the cavalry to the center of the old town.

Ruins of the ancient and powerful city gleamed in the moonlight. It almost seemed beautiful.

Horatio joined up in one of the columns, following Renatus silently. The horses moved in a slow jog until they reached an archaic temple dedicated to one of the old Pagan Deities of the city.

"Dismount!" he heard the major order.

Horatio tied Amadeo's reins to a large tree. When he finished, Horatio noticed the hooded monks again. The general soon came back into view and then leaned in to whisper to the major.

"Follow me!" the major then yelled as he headed towards a dark corridor within the dilapidated temple.

Horatio could see torches in the distance, lighting a dark tunnel. As he neared it, strange fears nearly overwhelmed him and grew greater with each step. At the edge of the dark tunnel, he realized it was a staircase. The torches seemed to offer barely enough light to avoid tripping. Soon, darkness surrounded him, and the meager flames made strange fantasies possible. He could see another group of monks waiting ahead. As he neared them, Horatio wondered where their rosaries were, yet he felt a great deal of relief upon taking the last step.

Horatio then noticed that the monks lead Renatus and several of the other lower ranking soldiers into a dark chamber. Horatio stopped as he and the last five members of the cavalry stood in front of the closed door. Horatio sensed a presence behind him, and then he felt a strong hand clasp on shoulder.

A painful squeeze made Horatio inhale a little. Strange noises behind the door alerted him to imminent danger.

"Do not fear," a voice murmured. "Your path lies ahead of you."

Horatio felt emboldened. This was just a test to prove his bravery and worthiness. After all, soldiers proved their mettle every day and night. He watched one of the monks open the door, and then he passed into the chamber, seeing little other than darkness.

The door slammed shut, and Horatio looked around. Horrors met his eyes, unspeakable bloody horrors that he had never witnessed on the battlefield, or anywhere else, for that matter. Monsters with red eyes and fanged smiles fed on his friends and superior officers, who could no longer move. Eerie, otherworldly gazes stopped Horatio's screams before they could escape his lips.

Horatio crossed himself and turned to flee. He then noticed Michael Tolomei standing in front of him.

The man-monster revealed his teeth in a feral smile.

"You'll do nicely," the general cooed as he stepped forward.

Horatio's world faded into gray and then turned as black as a starless night. He could almost smell wildflowers on the non-existent breeze.

Máire sat in front of the stone altar and closed her eyes, willing herself to remember the past and bring it back to the present. The scent of plants beginning to bud aided her memories of sweet kisses and shared embraces. She could hear a soft hum and recognized herself singing about Deirdre lamenting her lost lover. She leaned over a small cauldron and started a fire, placing the sponnc within the cauldron. Smoke drifted into the air. She inhaled and exhaled, wishing to enhance the memories of mortal love and remember the actual emotion.

After a few moments, the sponnc made her dizzy, but it gave her no further assistance.

Máire rose to her feet and began to pace around the fire. Soon, the pacing gave way to a spirited dance.

This will work. It has to work. Perhaps I need to be the one asking for aid.

"Lord of youth and love, hear my lament and be merciful to me and to those searching for affection," she called out to Angus Mac Og. She rubbed her forehead before pulling out a flask of bloodmead, hoping the offering would be suitable. After all, their supply of mead grew scarce, and the Gods always appreciated a personal sacrifice. The smoke soon overwhelmed her senses.

As her circles grew larger, she wandered into unprepared ground and tripped over a solid tree root. Máire fell onto the hard earth. She then realized that Arwin stared back at her. His face revealed a grin.

"Trying to remember past loves?" he asked.

"What? Why did you sneak up on me like that?" She gave a nervous chuckle.

"I did not. I have been sitting here for nearly ten minutes. I even said something to you, but you ignored me," he complained as he sniffed the air. "Sponnc. I have no idea how you can deal with it. Are you seeking past memories of love?" His face grew serious.

She could say nothing, as she felt flustered and a little embarrassed. Máire decided to sit down and cross one leg over another. "I see you are feeling better. I'm glad. I worried for all of you."

"Edward, Marcus, Claudius, you, and I are like a strange family, Máire," Arwin said. "You are Banbh Ceanúil, our endearing piglet, and we worry about you too."

"I know," she agreed before smiling back at him. "As much as you and the other boys tease me, we are a family. Families are created from the strangest of situations. I feel closer to you, Edward, and Claudius than I do with most Deargh Du."

Arwin smiled. "Is this petition you make to Angus Mac Og regarding the curse that settles on you?" he asked.

She nodded her head. "I found the memories, yet I cannot remember the feeling. It is as if the honey has no flavor, but I can see it and touch it. It is thick and golden, but the taste is gone."

"What have you tried lately to remove it?" he asked.

"Lady Heloise and Lirienne tried a ritual that did not work. Ruarí had searched the library again. Marcus searched his memory, and I had tried to talk him into working with me, yet he says I wield magic in our family and that he does not have the talent for it. I considered the idea tonight of speaking to Angus Mac Og and asking for his assistance."

"Are you sure the problem is not yours? Are you perhaps the cause of this lack of emotion?" he asked.

A general confusion overcame her, and Máire felt her face furrow.

"Let me explain further," Arwin said. "You went through more trauma within one week than most mortals might encounter in a lifetime. In short order, your uncle died, you changed into a Deargh Du, and you suffered from a period of insanity. You then channeled the wrath of an angry Goddess. How could these experiences not have affected you?"

"If those were not reason enough for me to lose the ability to love, then I should have recovered a century or more ago, Arwin. Instead, my loveless state persists to this night, and there is no possibility in my mind of it ending until the curse is lifted or I depart this life for the next. Those are the only two ways I feel that I can love again," Máire answered.

"I suppose you have noticed Julien's advances toward you," Mac Alpin stated. Máire did realize it, but she had no stomach for romance.

"Again, with this foolish talk?" She leaned forward a little. "Heloise said something about that, but I see not his advances or his tenderness."

"Oh? So you do not know why he stares at you like a sniveling adolescent and wishes to please you as if you were his first sweetheart. It's rather cloying, yet Marcus and Claudius find it amusing. You have not even noticed that Julien seems jealous whenever one of us takes your time? His pouts are most humorous. Even Heloise and Lirienne find it comical. They have taken to teasing him about his la roux. However, the effects of his mother's and sister's taunts make it all the more amusing."

"I suppose you are right," Máire stated. "I have been so focused on being rid of this curse and the Strigoi that I have not seen what seems to be obvious to everyone else."

"So what will you do now that you know of his attraction to you?"

"I have no idea. I can appreciate his affection, and I admit that he is interesting, but I have no feelings for him. I would feel awkward if he continued to woo me while I am unable to reciprocate. Besides, I'm sure Julien has any number of lovers in Burgundy and wherever he travels. He's very attractive. He has very nice eyes and a most appealing smile."

"Perhaps you should dissuade him from expressing anymore affection for you," Arwin advised with a chuckle. "His attraction to you could distract him too much from his current duties."

"But that would be very harsh," she suggested. "It would be cruel for me to say such things. You tell him."

"What?!" Arwin yelled while meeting her eyes.

"Please tell him for me as I do not wish to cause him any pain, Arwin." She scooted in closer to him.

"Some battles a man has to fight alone," he answered gruffly.

Máire leaned closer and punched Mac Alpin's shoulder. "I am not a man! I'm your Banbh Ceanúil!"

He rubbed his shoulder and scowled a bit. "You could have fooled me."

"Please do this," she said. "It would mean so much if you did this for me. We have fought side by side often… just please do this."

"Alright, Máire," he purred, "I will tell him, but you will owe me."

"Thank you," she said, feeling a smile turn up the corners of her lips.

"I will discuss this with the others," Mac Alpin said as he stood and brushed himself off. He then left the grove, shaking his head and talking to himself.

chapter eleven

"We should try this now, before he gets caught up with his duty or with her again," Claudius muttered.

"Should we use the patrol excuse?" Mac Alpin asked.

"That was your idea and you cannot even remember it?" Claudius countered as they exited the cellar.

"Inspector General, join us on patrol," Arwin requested as he motioned for the mortal to come towards them.

Julien sheathed his sword and then grinned. With the Strigoi out there somewhere, Claudius could understand why a man would run around his own house carrying a bare blade.

"What about the others?" Julien asked.

"Edward wants to work on his projects, and Patroclus is still recovering. Besides, I am tired of reliving the pains of the attack. Let's leave the ladies to caring for them," Claudius expressed with a chuckle.

"Very well, I have found things quite stuffy myself."

Claudius patted Julien on the shoulder before opening the door and motioning them out.

"Did you two ever meet on the battlefield as mortals?" Julien asked, before stopping and closing his eyes. "I hear music."

"It sounds like it is coming from the tavern," Arwin suggested. "And no, we have never met on the battlefield as mortals."

"But that would be against the curfew," Claudius pointed out. While he appeared shocked and horrified, something about his face suggested to Julien that some jest floated in the air.

"I assume that this is a sound reason for us to investigate who is at the tavern and who is singing," Julien suggested. He too tried not to smile, though, for some reason, the pretense sounded hollow. Why was he even smiling? "It almost sounds like a celebration," he announced in a quiet voice as he neared the door of the inn.

"Well, I say we arrest these diabolical criminals," Arwin recommended, while poorly attempting to hide his smirk.

Claudius drew his sword and advised, "I'm with–"

"I am the law here," Julien interjected. "I say when we arrest people."

He drew his sword. Whatever these foreign blood-drinkers were carrying on about, Julien wanted no part. He then opened the door and looked inside the inn, only to see Marcus turn to regard him, holding a cup in his hand. Marcus stopped singing, and then eight beautiful women, who surrounded the Roman and wore flattering attire, cheered.

"I met these lovely women in a few villages nearby, and they thought it might be entertaining to join our celebration," Marcus cried out, before guzzling his drink.

Two of the women, prostitutes, walked over to Julien and pulled him towards the table, allowing Claudius and Arwin through the door. The innkeeper's daughter arrived carrying more cups of wine. One of the women gently sheathed Julien's blade.

"You can sheath another sword in me later," she purred in his ear.

The women tugged him to the bench by Marcus, and he sat down. Claudius and Arwin seated themselves across from him and then grabbed cups from the innkeeper's daughter.

"You will share a drink with us, correct?" Marcus drawled as he pointed to his cup for a refill.

Julien took the goblet and then watched as the three blood-drinkers began to drain their cups. "You know you are violating curfew," he stated, though he jumped a bit when the warriors slammed down their empty cups.

"I was hoping you would make an exception in this case," Marcus said. "Drink up, drink up. After all, I spent many coins to pay for this celebration."

"What are we celebrating?" Julien asked.

"Survival," Marcus roared, "and I, for one, want to forget that horrible nightmare the Strigoi set upon me!"

"The wine is to settle our nerves," Arwin added.

"Drink," Claudius bade Julien. "The village will be safe tonight, and we must celebrate!"

Julien sighed. "I should be out with the rest of the gendarme, the soldiers, and the garrison."

"So should we, but the balance requires that we have some celebration to make up for the loss of life. It is only fitting that we observe a wake for those who died," Marcus explained before patting his lap. One of the prostitutes planted her backside in Marcus' lap, and then he wrapped an arm around her.

"Do you have wakes here?" Claudius asked as he faced Julien.

"Of course they don't," Arwin replied. "Such a feast would only be interesting to the lower classes. The rest of the civilized Franks would spend their days and nights in the church."

"Enough," Julien protested before drinking down his wine, though he stopped after a few swallows upon realizing something about the wine tasted different. "This wine tastes funny," he complained.

Marcus grabbed his cup, sniffed its contents, and then shoved it back into Julien's hand. "Smells good to me," he countered.

"Oh, he's probably wondering why the wine isn't spiced or watered down," suggested Claudius, "am I right?"

Arwin chimed in, "This is what wine tasted like, boy, before sobriety became a virtue. Now drink up... Marcus paid many sou for that heathen wine you are drinking."

Julien considered the wine he held in his cup, and he decided that this wine tasted better than any he had imbibed before. He then finished off his cup and then ordered another. While waiting for his second cup of wine, Julien tried to remember the subject of their conversation. "Oh yes... tell me more about these wakes!"

"It is a feast to celebrate the dead, and it allows the living to enjoy what the dead cannot," Arwin answered before emitting a loud belch. "We all drink, dance, argue, feast, and fuck, with as many beautiful ladies as can be found." Julien watched Arwin wave over another prostitute, pick her up, and place her on his lap.

"It is a true shame your people do not get to enjoy such celebrations," Marcus commented as he fondled one of the breasts of the prostitute who sat upon his lap.

"Perhaps we need more of these customs," Julien considered aloud as he finished his second cup of wine. He then held it up for a refill.

Julien wandered back towards the bench and then tripped over his feet. The giggling girls at either side of him smiled as they staggered together towards their friends. Claudius tossed one young woman over his shoulder and proceeded to tug another to the back room. He soon rejoined them, unescorted, when he yelled over his shoulder, "I will return in just a moment." He then returned to the table to gather several cups of wine.

"This is the best celebration ever," Julien drawled. "I want this kind of festivity again. Marcus, you are in charge of all merriment this village celebrates from now on." He sat down on the bench and then grabbed another cup. Julien closed his eyes and started to drink another goblet of wine. After he finished, he felt a hand clasp his left shoulder, and then Arwin sat down next to him.

"Lad, you know why we invited you here?" Arwin asked in a serious tone.

"For the wake, or because I'm almost as amusing as Edward. or perhaps you hoped if you shared drink with me that I would not arrest you for violating the curfew?" Julien asked with a slur.

Marcus hiccupped and then started laughing. "Stop avoiding the truth, Arwin. You promised Banbh Ceanúil to do this."

"Wait, what does 'Banbh Ceanúil' mean?" Julien inquired.

Mac Alpin glanced at Julien and quipped, "It means 'endearing piglet'," before regarding Marcus, once again.

"Who or what is–" Julien muttered, before Claudius interrupted him.

"That is what we call Máire," Claudius clarified.

"You told!" Marcus shouted after turning to regard Claudius. "Now she is going to kill you!" Marcus then regarded Arwin. "Now shush, Julien. Arwin, you are avoiding the truth… tell him!"

"I am not avoiding the truth… I am merely finding the best way to tell him this." Mac Alpin then turned back to Julien. "I was asked to give you some sorrowful news."

"Sorrowful news? What news?" Julien asked, unable to see the reason for dour looks.

"Máire doesn't love you," Arwin blurted out.

"She does not?" Julien asked, though he thought he might have heard the innkeeper say, 'we are out of wine', but that could not be.

"No lad, she doesn't love anyone," Arwin answered. "At least that's what she claims."

"Not even him?" Julien queried as he pointed at Claudius.

"No." Arwin chuckled, though he could not figure out why.

"You?" Julien asked while pointing at Arwin.

Mac Alpin shook his head.

"Him? He made her Deargh Du!" He motioned to Marcus.

"No!" The three other men answered in unison.

"Oh." Julien burped a little. "So why doesn't she love any of you?"

"She does not love anyone," Claudius replied. "It's just Máire."

"Well, why doesn't she?" Julien asked, hearing a little impatience in his voice. How in the hell could a woman not love someone? It seemed baffling. Unfathomable.

Where did those prostitutes go?

Marcus opened his mouth to answer but then said nothing. He then motioned for Julien in closer. They all stood, moved to the open floor, and then moved in closer, like a four-way test of strength, with arms locked over shoulders and heads together.

"It's my fault," Marcus answered.

"No it is not," Claudius disagreed.

"Some of it is," Arwin whispered.

"What do you mean?" Julien asked.

"Well, she lost a father," Marcus explained.

"She lost her betrothed," Claudius added.

"She lost three all together," Arwin clarified.

"She was raped," Marcus contributed.

"She killed the man who raped her and killed her second betrothed," offered Claudius.

"Do not forget, she lost an uncle," Arwin interjected.

"Two, she lost two… I think," Claudius corrected.

"And of course, I made her Deargh Du."

Julien glanced at the three blood-drinkers, wondering whether that could be the end of their discourse on matters concerning Máire. He waited to see whether they had anything else to say.

"Oh yes, there is the curse too," Arwin stated. "Did we say that already? A Druid cursed her never to love again. That's what she believes caused this. She takes it very seriously."

Julien heard giggles and deduced that the women had wandered back into the main room of the inn.

"Um… how do we get out of this position?" Julien asked his drinking buddies.

Mac Alpin replied, "It's easy, laddie! Just step your right leg in and push out with your arms." Julien tried, but he was not able to get out of this strange embrace. "You are doing it wrong… oh, wait. We all need to do it at the same time… now." Julien stepped and pushed at the same time as the others, and then all four men resumed standing.

Julien grabbed another cup of wine and finished it off. Despite the fuzz of wine in his head, he felt some amount of clarity. "I can understand why she has trepidations about love. I suppose I can pay heed to these detrimental experiences she has had and leave her alone, or I can ignore everything you have told me and try to chip away at the stone fortification guarding her heart."

He heard the women start to coo.

"That is the sweetest and most poetic thing I have ever heard a man say," one of the women murmured. She then turned him to face her And asked, "Are you ready for another… round?"

Mac Alpin drank another goblet of wine. "So, do you think we got through to the lad?" he slurred.

Marcus wiped off his mouth and then challenged, "I will bet you ten silver sous that that stubborn Frank will continue to go after her, and the best of luck to him in getting her to notice anything." Marcus chuckled. "So, will you take the bet?"

"Marcus, even I am not drunk enough to accept that wager."

Claudius stared at them with half-closed eyes. "And neither am I," he said in an attempt to mimic Arwin's brogue. He then fell face-forward onto the table.

Arwin grumbled before passing over the two silver pieces to Marcus.

"I told you... Claudius lost his tolerance for wine." Marcus chided.

Amata paced back and forth in the basement for a few minutes. She woke up half an hour ago and found herself a little bored. The boys had not awakened her for their festivities. She had heard them whispering about it last night, and yet Marcus, Arwin, and Claudius had not offered invitations to her or to Máire, although she had heard them speaking to Edward about some 'wake' for the lost. Edward had muttered something about needing to make more supplies. That had piqued her interest, more than any celebration that just involved wine, women, and song.

While Amata paced about the room, Edward and Máire tended to Patroclus.

"How is he?" Amata asked after wandering over to them.

She watched the Legate's eyes open, and then he reached for Máire's arm.

"Hungry," Patroclus whispered, as he opened his mouth to feed.

"I gorged myself earlier," Máire said, wincing for a moment as he bit into her bare wrist. "Edward, perhaps you should heal him again."

She watched Edward touch the Legate's arm and close his eyes for a few moments. Everything became silent, except for Patroclus feeding.

Máire soon yanked her hand away from Patroclus. "Sorry, but I need enough for myself. I will go feed again later."

"I've got to work," Edward murmured. "I'll leave you with the ladies," he said while facing Patroclus.

The Legate nodded and then closed his eyes. "Tell me about your tribe," he said after turning his head to face Máire. "I still hear the Strigoi sometimes... listening to another voice helps me focus,"

Amata noticed Edward head towards the staircase.

"Well, my clan is from the western side of Eire," Máire began. "We weren't the most powerful clan in Connacht, but we did own enough animals and lands to keep ourselves happy and fed. I miss visiting there sometimes. I've never been someplace else where the grass could be such a lush carpet of green, even under the moonlight."

Amata strolled away to pull on her boots, but she could still hear Patroclus' conversation with Máire.

"Yes, I remember that," Patroclus answered. "That grass and those trees," he whispered. "It almost made up for the constant rain and cold."

"I imagine so." Amata heard Máire chuckle.

"The Lamia abhor the cold and wet," Patroclus stated.

"Tell me about your home... not the Temple, but the home you grew up in, and no war stories," Amata heard Máire ask.

Amata stood up and then decided to try to follow Edward. She could sense him in the distance. As Patroclus began to talk about his family's estate outside of Rome, she started walking faster.

Amata smiled as she traipsed silently through the grass. She pulled her cloak in closer in an attempt to fend off the cold. Gaul never seemed to warm up. Amata shivered and almost groaned in annoyance.

She followed what she thought was his spoor to a barn hear the house. Since Edward seemed to have very astute senses, Amata reasoned that he could probably detect her outside.

As if to confirm her reasoning, she heard Edward call out from the barn. "You can come in if you wish, Amata. I've covered everything."

"Nose," she whispered to herself, now remembering what Edward had blurted out on their first meeting.

The Ekimmu Cruitne have talented noses.

Amata cleared her throat and then asked, "Is that an invitation to join you?" She tried to hide her irritation at his discovery.

She heard some laughter. "It is what it is, Amata."

"Where are you? Are you in one of these stalls?" she asked as she walked into the barn. The smells of hay and dung masked his scent. The horses stared at her, as if curious.

"No, I'm in the tack room," Edward answered.

As Amata moved past the stalls, she heard a mortal arrive behind her, perhaps planning to take the horses to field. She ignored him and continued towards the center of the barn. She then found a wooden door, slightly ajar, and decided to peek around it. She saw Edward smile at her, and she also noticed that blankets covered a bench behind him.

"Edward, we are allies. Why are you hiding something from me?" Amata removed all guile from her eyes, hoping she could handle the innocence routine, though she knew she could not match Mandubratius.

"Yes I am, and you know it," Edward answered. His eyes reflected the color of lightning back to her before returning to the color of cornflowers.

"You wound me," Amata drawled. That was another of Mandubratius' favorite phrases. "I was curious, but not that interested in what you're doing." She moved in closer and then batted Edward's chest in a playful manner.

"I'm busy." Edward chuckled. "Why don't you go to the party?"

"What is it a party for exactly?" Amata asked.

"It's a wake to celebrate survival. However, Arwin said something about cheering up Julien. Perhaps they'll tell him Máire doesn't notice his attempts to get her attention," Edward suggested with a shrug.

"I noticed that," Amata agreed. "Why doesn't she use that to her advantage? He's a powerful man, even if he's just a gendarme with a somewhat more impressive title." She then smirked at Edward.

"Máire is ignorant of men's advances most of the time, or she may simply disregard them. She believes herself cursed in matters of the heart," Edward replied.

Amata started to laugh. "She actually believes in curses?"

"Curses do have power sometimes," Edward said, "especially when someone allows it to have power over them. She does have passion, but I think she's afraid of losing her family again. It's easier to face something like the Strigoi when you are convinced you have no one to worry about."

"That is most perceptive," Amata replied. "You are much smarter than I believed you to be."

Edward chuckled before backing a step away from her. "Thank you. I will try to think that you are not as manipulative and monstrous as your brother-in-darkness."

"Mandubratius is not that monstrous," Amata posed, "but I do think you will find that I am very different from him." She smiled at him. "I would rather spend my time with someone like you than waste it while letting drunken blood-drinkers paw at me." She purred softly before moving closer to Edward.

"Really Amata, this acting of yours is the sort of game I'd expect Mandubratius to engage in."

"Augh!" Amata strained her voice in frustration. "I'm trying to explain my feelings for you, you dim-witted Briton, and you... insult me." Amata lowered her head and allowed her dark hair to drape her face. She peered at Edward through her black veil of tresses.

"Please stop this, or I will start laughing," Edward said. She could see that his smile had faded into a serious stare.

Amata tossed her hair over her shoulder and then pulled at the pins of her dress. "All I wish is for us to enjoy each other," she stated.

Edward looked a little bored. "If that is what you wish, I'll make due." She caught sight of his lips twitch as if he attempted to hide a smile. Amata took this as a sign for her to move in closer.

"However, I do have one condition," Edward remarked.

"You make conditions on my love?" Amata asked, allowing a pout to pucker her lips. Men loved pouting, but she feared it made her look foolish and childlike, so she stopped. "Fine, name this condition." Amata placed a hand on his arm.

"You must swear that you won't look beneath that blanket."

"That is your condition?" she asked. "I would have expected something that involved me begging or you beating me."

She noticed Edward make a face.

"I don't require those kinds of concessions," Edward replied.

"Truly?" Amata queried. "This coitus sounds to be the height of boredom."

She watched Edward smile at her with a crooked grin. He leaned in closer, and then she felt a strange sensation warm her while Edward still beamed at her. Did the Ekimmu Cruitne wield other secrets as well?

Amata wondered how long she lay on the pile of blankets that smelled of horse and why she didn't care. She closed her eyes and allowed herself to slip into a deeper state of relaxation. She couldn't remember the last time she had experienced satisfaction such as this. Could it be the feeding or simply the coitus? Did it even matter? She hated admitting that this elicited such pleasure and contentment.

"I need to bathe," Edward murmured into her ear. She felt his lips hover over her cheek for a moment and then lower. After Amata sensed Edward stand and leave, her curiosity returned. Her sensations wavered as he moved farther from the barn. She pushed aside her feelings and stood. The secret of his alchemy summoned her with a beckoning finger.

Amata yanked aside the blanket on the bench, only to reveal tools and hardware used to repair leather work. She cried out in frustration.

"You broke your promise!" she heard Edward yell from the east. She could even hear laughter from inside the barn.

Amata turned and faced the empty door. She sighed and then gathered her clothing, deciding to find someplace where no other blood-drinkers or mortals would disturb her.

The walk towards home seemed to be longer than the walk to the inn. They managed to dodge the objects thrown at them from the scattered homes.

"Does no one here appreciate a good song?" Claudius asked out. "I am told I have an excellent singing voice."

"Yes, yes, we all know the talents of your line and–"

A group of soldiers surrounded them and drew their swords, effectively interrupting Marcus.

"You are in violation of… oh it is you, my lord." Gerold bowed slightly. "Sorry, but I did not recognize you. We heard reports of noisy brigands. Obviously, you are not brigands."

Julien nodded his head. "Carry on, lad. We will not sing anymore," he drawled, copying Arwin's brogue. They all started laughing as they stepped forth again towards his mother's home. "So, what else can Deargh Du do?" he asked as he faced Marcus.

"I believe it is time to get a close look at the birds," Marcus answered.

"That sounds like a good idea," Mac Alpin chirped.

"No, no, that sounds like a horrible thing to do," Claudius grumbled.

"On the count of three," said Arwin.

Julien heard them count to three and then he felt the wind hit his face as they lifted him so high that he could see the trees and distant muddy fields under his feet. He could find no words until they landed. Julien emptied the contents of his stomach and then sat down.

"Are you feeling alright," Marcus asked.

"Better now," answered Julien as he wiped vomit from his mouth.

"Remind me not to do that again when I am drunk," Arwin grumbled before dragging himself towards the door to the house.

"For the thousandth time, yes!" Claudius yelled after rubbing his forehead.

"That was fun," Julien quipped as he stared at the three inebriated immortals. "What else can you do?"

Marcus turned and smirked. "This," he answered. Everything became black. Julien stood in surprise, but soon the darkness faded away. Arwin and Claudius leaned against the house, but Marcus had disappeared with the dark clouds.

Julien looked up to study the sky when something hit his head. He then noticed Marcus hovering upside down, directly above him.

"So, what do you think of that trick?" Marcus asked.

"Fascinating," Julien observed as he rubbed his forehead.

"Aye, it's great in a crowded inn where there's no room for sitting," added Arwin. "However, it doesn't work well when you try to drink."

The door then opened and hit the side of the house with a thunderous bang.

"You three stink!" Máire yelled. "You have woken up the household and the entire village with your caterwauling! Go take a bath, now!"

"The sun is almost up, Máire," he heard Marcus reply.

"Are you sure you have feelings for her?" Claudius asked. "She can be very loud and rude."

"You three should be able to bathe quickly enough before the sun burns you. Now, take a bath. And you," Máire exclaimed as she pointed a finger at Julien, "you do not need to rush, but you smell the worst." He heard the blood-drinkers start running for the river.

"Woman, I am exhausted," he drawled with a yawn as he pushed his way into the house. Before he could go too far, a hand latched on his wrist and tugged him back towards the door.

"Inspec... Julien, if you do not go take a bath, I will drag you to the stream, rip off your clothes, and throw you in myself. You stink of wine, women, and vomit," Máire grumbled. "On second thought, your clothes could use a good wash too."

"No, I will not go," he answered while crossing his arms over his chest. "I'm not–" He forgot what he intended to say, as Máire began dragging him towards the river, and before he could demand his release, she threw him in.

"This is freezing and humiliating," he yelled at her, feeling his desires to express something sweet to her disappear in the chilly stream.

Máire smiled and shrugged before turning towards her friends.

"Lads, the sun will be up soon. Finish washing up," she called to Marcus, Claudius, and Arwin.

Julien watched them race for the door. He took some more time and then followed them. He saw the lot of them stopped at the door with his robed mother pointing at the men's clothing. He chuckled upon hearing her yell about the wet floors.

He ambled over towards her and watched the three naked figures race indoors, leaving his mother and Máire holding their clothing. He watched Máire blink her eyes as she shielded her face from the sunrise, and then dart in before his mother. The stench of singed hair lingered.

"I will not have you dripping all over the floor either," his mother said as she blocked his path inside. "Take off your clothes and then go inside to try to warm up by the hearth."

When he walked inside, Julien noticed that someone had covered the windows. Lirienne practically threw the blanket at him. After catching it and wrapping himself in it, he noticed that the others shivered by the hearth. He could feel his face heat as he realized that Máire sat down next to the hearth, warming her hands. She looked radiant.

He and the others jumped when his mother slammed the door closed behind her. She then mumbled to herself before handing off the wet clothes to the servant.

"You better not have made yourself sick with your carousing all night," she warned before sitting down at Julien's side. "I am too old to play nursemaid. Once you dry off, go to sleep. So much for my early morning," she grumbled as she patted Julien's shoulder, kissed his cheek, and then marched upstairs.

Rome

The sound of soft knocks disrupted his playtime.

"What is it? I am a little busy at the moment," the pope answered while placing a hand over the mouth of one of the women. He shushed the other as she giggled under the blankets.

"Holy Father, your presence is urgently requested in the courtyard," his clerk replied.

"On whose request," Pope Leo grumbled.

"Your Holiness, Michael Tolomei is requesting your permission to disembark," the clerk replied.

"So soon? I would not expect them to be ready. I shall like to see them."

"Michael anticipated your decision. The cavalry is in parade formation."

"Splendid," the pope said. "I shall appear momentarily." He sighed as he looked over the beauties in his bed. "I am most sorrowful that I must depart your company. The Lord's work is never done." He sat up and found his purse, before passing them coins as they began to dress.

He pushed aside a curtain and then pulled aside a gilded portrait of the Madonna and Child, revealing the small escape door that led to the secret exit of the Lateran palace.

"Thank you both for a most relaxing evening," he purred, allowing them out. He returned to his table and began washing himself.

Pope Leo wandered out to the courtyard and stared at the grand array of horsemen, clad in the leather armor popular within the empire, yet displaying his standards and emblems. They gleamed within the moonlight. Each man and horse remained still and silent with purpose and fortitude, and he beamed. Their right hands rested around their sheathed swords. The soldiers stared straight ahead.

A call echoed through the night, and Pope Leo could fathom Michael's voice.

"Draw blades!" he called out.

His noble warriors drew their blades in perfect unison and then saluted the pope. The song of the unsheathed swords sent a shiver down Pope Leo's back.

He raised his hand and made the sign of the cross.

"Brave warriors of Christ," he intoned. "Your valor, nobility, and faith will see you all through adversity to triumph. Pray every day and night for redemption, and it shall be yours. May He bless you and keep you."

He then made the sign of the cross once again.

"Sheath blades!" Michael ordered.

Pope Leo smiled as the sound echoed around the courtyard. He walked over to Michael and then looked up at him.

"You have prepared your men well," he said to Michael in a quieter tone. "I was hesitant to give you command of this cavalry so soon, but I am glad I had a change of heart and allowed you an earlier command."

"Thank you Holy Father." Michael smiled down at him. The general's green eyes seemed to glimmer.

"The rest will move out in the next few days," the pope resolved.

"We will sweep the approaches to Aachen in advance of your forces. This will guarantee a safe journey," Michael promised.

"I look forward to the day when we meet again," the pope said.

"I as well, your Holiness."

Pope Leo retreated to the position in front of the cavalry. "Know that the Father, Son, and Holy Spirit will look favorably on your services. May this army of light eradicate the darkness that surrounds our lands. May God grant each of these soldiers long life, and if they should fall, grant them peace in Heaven."

Michael held up his fist and shouted, "To victory and glory!"

Each soldier mimicked his movements. "To victory and glory!" they yelled before everyone dropped their arms simultaneously.

Michael then spurred his horse to the left, and the troop formation began to wheel to the left.

The cavalry commander held out his arm and yelled, "Forward!"

A strange discomfort surrounded Pope Leo as he watched them leave. All of the men's movements met in time with all the others. It seemed almost unnatural. Even the horses trotted in unison.

Nevertheless, the pope shook his worries away, wondering whether his servants could find more evening companions for him.

chapter twelve

Aachen

hen Talia walked into the great hall, all eyes followed her. The emperor's own seamstress had made her a gown of imported purple silk with golden threads interspersed in the silk, which made her dress gleam. Rosamund had then rinsed Talia's gold curls with henna, and they became like copper. Then, her maid had entwined golden thread in her hair. Her hair, clothes, and jewels all sparkled. She outshone every woman there. No others allowed their hair free.

She could see that most of the men sat at the long tables, grabbing pieces of wild deer, boar, hare, and... bear. Talia noticed that a few of the emperor's daughters danced and flirted with young men, while the emperor himself danced with Gundrada. Talia then became aware of several mortal men walking towards her, offering her their names.

"Such a pleasure to meet you all," she trilled as she passed them by, but they followed in her wake. She walked around the circle of dancers as they all joined hands. She then caught sight of the emperor and lowered her eyes in a demure fashion, and then he looked away.

Talia began walking again, studying the dancers. She raised her eyes, and the emperor's blue eyes focused on her for a moment, before distraction seemed to bring him back to the dance.

With the emperor's attention now fixed on her, Talia decided to flaunt her femininity by tossing her hair over her shoulder. She watched as the emperor become distracted with her movements. He seemed so distracted by Talia that the emperor stepped on another woman's foot! Always the gentleman, the emperor apologized for his clumsiness. Now she knew she had the emperor's eye, and the pleasure she felt at achieving the first stage of her plan made her giggle a little.

His eyes met hers again, and this time he smiled at her, before rejoining the dance, continuing until the song ended. While in wait for the next step, Talia picked up two cups of wine. She then saw Emperor Charles' eyes drifted towards her again. He then excused himself from his family and the other dancers. It was time.

She moved towards him and then extended the extra cup of wine.

"Thank you." The emperor took the wine and began to drink it before lowering the cup. "My apologies, but my memory fails me and I don't remember your name." His blue eyes sparkled with a mischievous light.

Talia began to drop to her knees, playing the part of a demure woman.

"Oh, this is a feast, stop that." The emperor pulled her up and managed to look a little embarrassed.

"To answer your question, Imperial Majesty, I'm Lady Talia of Époisses." Talia beamed at the emperor.

"Of course, now I recall. You're one of my guests," he replied.

"Yes, I've been here for almost a fortnight. I must say that I have found my visit here to be most enjoyable. Your family and the court are so hospitable and kind. It has been a bright spot in my life after my poor husband's death." She blinked back her false tears and offered him a brave smile. Talia hoped her smile reflected in her eyes.

The emperor then patted her hand.

"Imperial Majesty, please tell me about the hunt," she urged.

"Oh," he began with a little shrug. "I killed the deer and bear that we feast on now." His eyes grew distant, and she could tell he was about to tell a tale worthy perhaps of a bard. At least she hoped so.

"You see, I found a deer, a most awe-inspiring, eight point, large buck. So, I moved upwind, Talia. I willed my heart to become steady and quiet. I focused on a point on the buck's chest. Then, I witnessed a large brown bear stalking the same buck."

The emperor began to gesture as if he hunted a deer in his palace.

Talia smiled, hoping that he would continue. She hated to admit her love of good stories.

"The buck froze in place. I realized that by good fortune, and my angle, that I could hit them both. I pulled back," he explained while demonstrating, "and I let the arrow fly." His spoke the last few words with throaty whisper.

"And then?" Talia prodded as she touched his arm.

"Then I watched it move through the chest of the buck. The buck collapsed, and then the bear roared as the arrow landed in his chest. He let out this mighty roar and fell. I ran to the bear and shot it again in the chest, because I wanted to keep its head and skin as a trophy. Then the glorious bear warrior died."

Talia began clapping her hands, while others joined her.

The emperor faced her again, and his pale features reddened.

She batted her eyes and cooed, "Imperial Majesty, what a hunter you are. Perseus himself would find trouble in felling two creatures such as those with one shot."

The emperor chuckled. "Lady Talia, it was not one, but two shots."

"Of course, but that last was a mercy to the bear," she explained.

Talia saw him look up as the musicians started another round of dances. "Another dance begins," he observed. "Please join me."

"I'd love to," she purred before taking his arm. The dance brought them in closer contact with one another, enabling her to catch the emperor in her eyes and further influence him.

As they circled and twirled with other dancers, she lost track of time and herself during the fury of the dance.

After the music ended, the emperor retrieved wine for both of them. They then sat down across from each other at a long table.

Talia could vaguely remember the days of her grandfather's reign. Did Godomer of Burgundy sit with his social inferiors as Emperor Charles did? Perhaps not.

Simpleton. Commoner.

"It's most regretful that with all of this great company, we cannot steal away and speak in private. There is too much distraction in these walls," Charles murmured over the din of the music and the chattering.

"So, the emperor is imprisoned within his own home?" Talia asked as she smiled at him again.

The emperor laughed at that quip and slapped his leg. "I am a servant of my people and my family," he stated. "So, tell me about Lady Talia." His eyes became sharp. "I understand that you have a large number of your own land holdings in Burgundy."

"Alas, my poor husband had no male family members with whom to leave his property after his passing. It is quite difficult for a lady to survive on her own in these treacherous times, Imperial Majesty. A lady needs a husband or sons to protect her," explained Talia with a soft lilt.

"Yes, of course. There is only one lady I know of who rules her family's lands." The emperor's blue eyes studied her for a moment, as if judging her intelligence and motives.

"I have been most fortunate in my dealings, Imperial Majesty," Talia replied, though he still appeared to be examining her closely.

"Of course." The emperor smiled at her before continuing. "That is why we desire you to visit Aachen and my other homes often, so that we may all engage in business."

Talia returned his smile and then bowed her head for a moment. "That would please me, Imperial Majesty."

"Call me Charles," he said, before scratching his beard as if indecisive.

Of course, she had put that thought in his mind. Calling Emperor Charles by the full title of Imperial Majesty had grown too wearisome.

"As you wish, Charles," she uttered, while batting her eyes at him.

Then she realized that his secretary was approaching them.

The emperor sighed. "Ercanbald returns. Once the festivities have concluded, you and I can speak further."

"I would be quite delighted with that," Talia agreed.

"Imperial Majesty," the secretary whispered in his ear, though she had little trouble hearing him despite the noise, thanks to her gifts as a Lamia. "Your cousin requests time to speak with you."

The emperor rolled his eyes.

"Matters of state never seem to end," Charles explained to Talia as he arose from the bench.

"I understand all too well," Talia replied. She then stood up and moved in closer.

"We'll continue this conversation at another time," Charles murmured before he leaned in and kissed her. She returned his embrace and pecked at his lips. He then turned and walked away.

"Yes, we will," Talia whispered.

Vézelay

"From all accounts, the horde has attacked these villages," Dreu explained as he pointed out four towns. "We expect these villages to be attacked tonight, and perhaps these tomorrow." The garrison commander then looked over at Marcus and Julien, as if expecting them to say something else.

"Perhaps we can estimate where the hordes come from," Marcus chimed in. "They seem to be centering their attacks. Perhaps you can point out an origin point, Inspector General?" Marcus backed away from the map and allowed Julien to study the towns and small villages.

Julien looked a little green, but he managed to squint at the map.

"Saulieu, perhaps," Julien murmured. "It seems likely they would find a place to congregate before and after the attacks."

"I think you should travel to Saulieu," Marcus suggested to Julien. "Look around for caves, graves, and any other place that offers a safe location." He then motioned for Edward to come in closer. "Do you have anything they can use today?" he asked Edward.

"I can offer some incendiaries," Edward said. "They could assist in the battle."

Marcus nodded, and Edward began to empty his belt of incendiaries.

"It will only take a few hours to reach Saulieu. A bit longer if we travel at night," Julien observed.

"Why not travel during the day, Inspector General?" Dreu asked. "We would go faster, since the horses will be able to see their feet."

"We can do that," Marcus answered. "In order to accommodate our sleeping schedule, we will need to be able to sleep in complete darkness. We can travel in carts alongside you, though we would need long boxes to sleep in, even if the carts are covered."

"I'm certain that I can find some long, wooden boxes," Julien answered. "However, I'm not sure whether I can locate enough for the entire party."

"Then some of us will remain in Vézelay," Marcus suggested.

Outside the Ruins of Aventicum

The forests and grasslands between Rome and Aachen seemed endless. The two hundred horses appeared pleased for the extra torchlight during the new moon throughout their trek from the stony rubble of Rome through the ancient lands and forests of Gaul. The ruins of the old Roman city of Aventicum, established after the defeat of the Helvetti and their subsequent Romanization, lie not far from where they trod.

Then Mandubratius recalled the source of Marcus' honorarium, 'Helvetticus'. Marcus had fought with Julius Caesar in the Battle of Bibracte against the Helvetti. Mandubratius remembered that after he had first met Marcus, he had heard the gossip from the Gauls about Marcus' exploits on that particular campaign.

No Helvetti awaited them this time. Now, Mandubratius wished only to flush out the Strigoi, not the Gauls.

Soon, several of his staff joined him in the middle of the formation. Many remained silent, though he didn't feel like talking much either.

"Have you encountered the Strigoi before, Consul?" an unfamiliar Lamia officer asked, breaking the silence, as he made eye contact.

"'General', in front of the new converts," Mandubratius corrected in Greek.

"My apologies. I just did not want to address you incorrectly."

Mandubratius shrugged his shoulders and then returned to speaking in Latin. "No, I have not, but I know someone who has... Legate Patroclus."

The young officer bobbed his head, and then his features grew worried. "Did he survive... General?"

"Yes," Mandubratius admitted. "However, the interaction did affect him."

A call to the east silenced them all.

"Strigoi!"

"We will discover the effects soon enough," he reasoned aloud before shouting, "Left of the line, wheel right!" Mandubratius ordered commands to his men, hoping that this would assist the right side of the cavalry. The horses wheeled towards the Strigoi. He drew his blade, expecting a Strigoi to materialize in front of him.

He then heard cries, screaming, and mad laughter.

The horses began whinnying and started bucking riders. Mandubratius managed to manipulate his horse into remaining calm.

Riders fell, and torches dropped to the ground, starting fires.

While the smoke obfuscated his line of sight, he could still hear the sound of bowstrings being loosed, swords being drawn, and grunts. Through gaps in the smoke, he could see many riderless horses running, with fear in their eyes towards the west, and many of their riders he could observe lay writhing on the ground.

He could count only three Strigoi heads on the bloody field through the smoke. Then Mandubratius spotted a gangly figure in the distance, which had caught his attention. As he urged his horse forward, he witnessed more Strigoi running away. He aimed for the middle of the Strigoi and whispered a soft prayer to whatever Gods watched this battle that the corrupted blood-drinkers would not turn their orange eyes upon him.

Mandubratius managed to coax his horse into a full gallop, and soon he could strike the Strigoi from behind. Before Mandubratius could reach the blood-drinker, the Strigoi looked back at him for a moment, and in that instant, he felt a pinch in his head as he neared the monster. His horse began to panic and tumbled forward, crushing the Strigoi beneath him.

Mandubratius leapt to his feet, beheaded the trampled Strigoi, and looked for others, though he felt an urge to remain here, as his head ached. So, he sat in the grass as his lame horse, nudged his shoulder. From his vantage point, he could make out the remainder of the Strigoi running into the distance.

"In a minute," he mumbled in his native tongue as the horse continued to nudge him. "You can leave in a minute."

He did not feel like himself. His eyes now began to burn, as if someone had stuck a hot poker through his eye. Mandubratius closed his eyes, and time passed. The pain soon faded.

Mandubratius later opened his eyes, rose, and surveyed the damage around him. Most of the men appeared to be alive, though many seemed to be injured or fearful. A quarter of the horses had left their riders for safe fields. He glanced back at his horse before releasing it from his manipulation. It then wandered away.

"Set up camp," he ordered the soldiers that seemed to have their wits about them. He shook his head a little, as he considered what to do next.

"General, do you need a litter?" asked the same young officer who had approached him before.

"No, I think I need blood… human blood," he clarified, hoping his voice sounded stronger than he felt.

Mandubratius sat down again. "Please send half of the men that can walk into the nearest village. I smell mortals in the east…" Mandubratius could hear himself drawl. "Manipulate them into believing demons have been sighted near their village, and then bring them here for their safety."

"Yes, sir!" The officer saluted him and then motioned to some of the other soldiers.

Mandubratius lowered his head and closed his eyes, trying to regain his other senses. He had had no nightmares or eerie commands to hurt himself, but he did not feel like himself. He decided just to be silent for a while, until the mortals arrived.

Outside of Saulieu

Julien glanced back at the small party of gendarme and soldiers following him. The blood-drinkers had decided to explore the area around the caves for the next few nights, while Julien and his group of mortals had attacked, in daylight, the beasts in the caves.

Their successful daytime attack against the Strigoi had left him feeling somewhat uncomfortable and unsettled, yet no frightening visions haunted him, other than the ones of the dying Strigoi. The few Strigoi that had managed to survive Edward's incendiaries ran into the sun, bursting into vibrant flames.

How horrid a way to die,

Part of him felt a strange pity for the senseless beasts as they screamed and flailed in pain. He had ordered his men to behead as many as they could in order to end their suffering. Most of the men remained silent, grim, as they dispatched the Strigoi. Even Dreu seemed despondent. Perhaps a bit of light conversation would help them both recover from this malaise.

With his mind made, Julien urged his horse towards Dreu. Perhaps the garrison commander would have some advice about the intriguing question of Máire that went beyond the noncommittal remarks of Máire's family. They did not seem concerned with her emotional state, though neither, it seemed, did Máire.

"Are you married, Dreu?" he asked, upon maneuvering his horse to stand next to the commander.

Dreu seemed stunned by the question. "No, I am not, my lord," he answered, though like Julien before, Dreu's eyes remained transfixed on the men's brutal business.

Julien smirked. "I'm the third son, Dreu. It's highly unlikely I'll ever have a title, so you are elevating me beyond my status." Julien rotated his head to gaze at the commander. After a few moments, Dreu faced him. With the two men having made eye contact, Julien asked, "Are you seeking to marry?"

Dreu blushed for a moment. "I'll have you know that my friendship with your sister is nothing but that, a friendship. She is a true lady, and I would never seek to sully her."

"You have had eyes for my sister for a long time, Dreu. I'd sooner see her with you before seeing her with another friend of my brother. In fact, if you wish to court her, you should." Julien turned his head to regard the men, who seemed to be finished with their gruesome work. Many stood or sat about, staring at the carnage they had wrought.

Julien then regarded Dreu once more and continued the conversation where he left off in an effort to distract himself from the smoking, mutilated bodies of the Strigoi. "God knows she's been patiently waiting for it."

"Reginald would not be so pleased to hear that," Dreu murmured.

"Reginald could probably care less, at this point," Julien reasoned aloud with a shrug. He then changed the subject back to Máire. "Can I rely on your utmost confidence?"

"Yes, of course sir," Dreu answered.

"I know you are familiar with wooing. Would it surprise you to know that I have not had to woo any woman before? That is... not a lady of quality. They may approach me, but then they find out I'm poor, and so they excuse themselves," Julien admitted with a chuckle.

"I will say nothing," Dreu replied, though Julien could see him smile.

"There is this woman, you see," Julien explained. "She is exquisite to look upon, and she seems to know more than one would expect from just looking at her."

Dreu smiled again. "Intelligence can be very attractive. Beauty and brains are an enviable combination, Julien... at least that's my humble opinion."

"Well, this woman is unwed and is quite aloof, in fact. I mean, she seems to enjoy my company, but I am not used to being in the position of the hunter. Then again, she does not seem to care about taking time and diligence to attract a husband," Julien continued.

"So, what have you told Máire?" Dreu asked. Julien felt no surprise that Dreu knew of whom he spoke. "She is all of those things, and she is quite lovely. Even Remi thinks she is as lovely as the moon and stars."

Julien frowned for a moment, as Remi sounded like a better poet.

"Have you told her how beautiful she is? How she makes you feel around her? How she brightens your day?" Julien shook his head. "You haven't, have you?" Dreu asked as he met Julien's eyes.

"No, I have not," Julien confirmed.

"You may wish to tell her these things... otherwise, she may not be aware of your affections for her," Dreu stated. "I have the feeling that she is aware of little besides the battles we fight."

"… aware of my affections," Julien mumbled. He felt rather silly at this moment, since Dreu's advice would seem sensible to even a dullard.

"Yes, you need to talk to her, lavish her with gifts, write poetry, and give her flowers. Women love that… at least your sister says she likes it. I believe my poetry is horrible, but Lirienne says it comes from the heart, therefore it's precious."

"This is sound and good advice, Dreu. Thank you. Do you have any suggestions on subjects of poetry?"

"Speak of her intelligence," Dreu suggested. "I have a feeling that plenty of men tell her she's beautiful."

Regensburg

Seosaimhín could sense that a great many of her adopted children felt pain. Something within her demanded that she should call her children. She then turned towards her companions and murmured, "Send for all to return home."

She could almost hear the whispers on the wind as the Strigoi moved their lips, giving silent voice to her and Nagirrom's commands. She then returned to her quarters to continue her studies on the Strigoi. Innards lay scattered about, and blood pooled under the bodies of the dead.

Seosaimhín kneeled next to one of the dead blood-drinkers, and then she traced a finger over his head.

"Reveal all to us," she urged aloud.

Vézelay

The chirruping sounds of the crickets became a sharp distraction as the sun drifted towards the west and the night sky overwhelmed all Julien's senses. Soon he would arrive at home, but first he needed to see to the men's necessities.

As soon as the men stopped at the garrison, and Dreu came forward to salute him, and he asked, "My lord, where are–"

"On their way here, Dreu," Julien interjected, feeling a strange combination of restlessness and exhaustion. "I will return tomorrow morning. See to the men and to the horses. Dismissed."

Julien motioned for the guards to follow their commander. He then reined Rune towards the house and urged the horse into a laconic trot. The trot grew faster as Rune caught sight of the barn and began to wicker, as if knowing that the barn meant food and rest.

Julien pulled Rune to a halt, and soon he heard the running footfalls of the stable boy, who took Rune's reins. Julien dismounted and headed for the house. He then opened the door, ignoring the protocol of waiting for Ehren to meet him.

His mother's voice echoed from the room to his left. The great hearth brightened and warmed the hall, and his mother and sister sat side by side, wide-eyed. He could also see Patroclus' back from where he stood."Then what happened?" his mother inquired. Lirienne took a sip of tea and then waved at Julien as if distracted.

"They buried her alive in the Campus Sceleratus," Patroclus replied to a question Julien had not heard, "with a few days of water and bread. Such was the punishment for Vestal Virgins who ignored their vow of chastity."

Ehren cleared her throat. Embarrassed, Julien gave her his cloak.

"How horribly cruel," Lirienne stated.

"And utterly fascinating," Julien's mother trilled. Julien knew that she loved tales of corruption, romance, and sadness. "Do you know much of the cult of Isis, Patroclus?" she asked. "Oh Julien, I was hoping you would be back tonight. Welcome home."

Patroclus turned and asked, "My lord, how did our side fare?"

"That small group of Strigoi are gone, now," Julien answered. "We succeeded, and none of us fell." He could feel himself smile a little.

"Thank the Gods... I mean God," Patroclus said, seemingly cautious around Ehren, who soon left for the kitchen.

"Yes, thank them indeed," his mother agreed, as she embraced Julien and kissed his cheek. "You look worried. Come and sit with us. Patroclus tells the most engaging tales... almost as good as that yarn Marcus and Máire tell about the sorrowful Deirdre."

"Where is Máire?" Julien asked.

"She said something about the grove," his mother replied. She stuck her finger in her mouth and then proceeded to clean dirt off his face... a most humiliating process, only further mortifying him when he saw the Legate and his sister snickering.

"Mother," he complained while dodging her hand, feeling as though he were a child again.

"Fine then, look a dirty mess." His mother smiled at him and then backed off, holding up her hands.

He said nothing else as he turned away to go out the back door. The night was now deep and dark, although the thin crescent of the waxing moon and a few lit torches by the back gate gave some illumination.

Julien traipsed toward the grove, whispering a composed poem. "Sophia's exquisite student, illuminate all knowledge..."

No, that sounds like the bleating of a morose fool.

Then again, that particular title suited him. He should wait. Perhaps she would leap into his arms, cover him with kisses, and promise him her eternal love. He rolled his eyes at that thought.

When Julien reached the altar, no one stood there, and yet a small candle flickered at its center and a cupful of what appeared to be red wine and a handful of seeds lay beside the candle.

The sound of laughter and splashing water caught his attention as it resonated among the sounds of animals.

Julien walked in the direction of the sound, and when he got close, he could see a form in the stream. He chanced moving in closer, wondering whether he moved past the known world and into a mist-filled, mythical one. He watched a Goddess shake out her hair and blink her eyes, and this majestic form became Máire. As she arose from her seat in the water, a small amount of moonlight played off the droplets of water resting on luminescent skin.

Julien's poem dried up on his lips, and he could think of nothing more than his body tensing, demanding that he take her.

Julien noticed her eyes dart over him, and upon seeing him, she flipped a strand of hair over her shoulder. Did she puff out her chest? Her breasts seemed perfect. He then realized he stared at her and could not seem to stop. Time seemed to slow and then speed up.

She smiled and then motioned him closer with a finger. She seemed to point towards a tree, but he could not comprehend anything anymore. No, she wanted him to join her.

While Julien kicked off his shoes and clothes, she still beckoned to him. He could stand no more of it, and so he ran towards her. Then a peripheral stone seemed to come out of nowhere, and he tripped and fell into icy water that chilled him to the very bone. He gasped for breath, but he inhaled water. The chill infiltrated the core of his being, allowing him to forget the pain in his knees from landing on stone. As water cascaded over his back, he wondered whether he would find his feet again before succumbing to the cold blackness of the stream.

A pair of strong arms encircled him, and Julien felt himself come out of the water. Skin caressed him, and he finally understood that Máire cradled him in her arms, clutching him, as one would carry a child.

He caught his breath and looked up at her, though her eyes focused elsewhere. He looked on as Máire shook out her hair again.

Before Julien could think of anything to say, or thank her, he found himself lying on the grass. He watched her snag a blanket out of the arm of a tree. She then started to dry him off. She pulled him up into a sitting position so he could cough. The blanket then went around his shoulders.

Máire stepped back, took another blanket, and ran it over his hair. She then began to rub his arms and legs with the blanket. He could feel his teeth chatter together.

"Silly mortal," she chided softly in Latin, before lapsing into words he could not decipher. "What made you jump into the stream, Julien?" Máire asked, returning to Latin. She then sat down next to him.

Julien regained some control of his teeth and answered, "You beckoned me to join you in the stream."

She chuckled softly and smiled. "I was pointing to the blankets hung in the trees. I had hoped you would toss them to me so I could dry off. Why did you think I would ask you to join me?"

He hiccupped a little and stared into her eyes. "Because I thought you wanted me," he admitted.

"Oh," she uttered in a soft, breathless sigh, "is that what you wish from me?" He watched her stare into the distance for a moment before regarding him again.

"Yes…" he stuttered. "I mean, no… I mean, I think I love you." He leaned closer in order to run a finger over her lips.

"You think you do…" He felt her exhale. She then pulled away from his touch. "That is so very sweet of you, Julien, yet I am afraid that I cannot return that love. You see… I am cursed."

"Cursed?" he asked, though he remembered Marcus' story.

"Cursed to never love again," she replied. "Did Arwin ignore the favor I asked of him? I wished him to explain this to you." She sat down in front of him. "I cannot feel much of any emotion or passion, these nights. An ancient Druidess cursed me for killing her son. I killed her, but hatred and curses can survive death." She then looked away.

"How do you know you cannot love?" He slid his hands over her cheekbones and turned her face with care back towards him. "I will help you find love. I know I can. Until I saw you, I only loved one other, and I could never have her. If I can find love for you… I know I can help you find love."

"You are so kind," she whispered. "Alas, there are some things that cannot be undone."

"With patience, anything can be changed," he argued as he pulled her face closer. "You are so beautiful. When I saw you in the stream, I forgot everything I had planned to say to win you over. You rendered me speechless." He kissed her and felt pleasure as she moved closer to him. Her body trembled as she slid onto his lap. He pulled the blanket around them both, before forgetting himself again in her embrace.

He felt her mouth hover across his cheek and down his neck. A moment of sheer pain melted into delirious pleasure as he felt her teeth rasp his skin. A soft suction followed a gentle lick.

Julien leaned onto his back as she continued to tend to his throat. His body strained to feel more of her, and so he rolled her onto her back. His earlier pain from his near death experience had dissipated, as he kissed her lips and teased at her slick entrance with his free hand.

He watched her mouth turn at the corners before she rolled him back over. She stretched over him and then slid down around him. The poetry in his mind as he had beheld Máire before paled as their bodies fused in the eternal search for pleasure, satisfaction, and union.

Thought ceased as he slid a hand over a breast. His other hand caressed a hip and then her backside. Julien smiled at the idea of an extra hand, though that probably would be too much to ask for. Her eyes opened again, and he found himself lost in them as she moved in perfect symmetry with him. She leaned forward a bit, and her hair tickled him. As he heard their shared breath grow shallow, Julien closed his eyes and gave in to his increasing desire to explode. He uttered a soft cry as he heard her moan. She tightened her embrace as he shuddered. He kissed her lips and tasted salty vitae. He wanted to remain within her, but his exhausted body disagreed. She pulled back from him and stood up. She then walked toward the stream. A few moments later, he heard water splashing. Julien closed his eyes and decided to gather his strength.

chapter thirteen

"Gods, if that was passionless coitus without love..." Julien mumbled in an awed, half-whisper, though he forgot the rest of what he wanted to say. He sat up a bit, resting on his elbows, but he could not see his lover.

"Máire?" he called out, before rising to his feet, "where are you?" He could not see her in the grove or hear her splashing in the stream.

"How could you leave me after that?" he asked the winds. Julien then grabbed his clothes and dressed before racing into the house.

"Where is she?" he demanded, after finally finding his mother.

"Oh dear," his mother murmured as she held up a lamp. "She turned you down?"

His heart faltered for a moment. "Mother, what are you talking about?" Julien asked.

"Well, it was painfully obvious to all that you wanted her physically. I assume from your demeanor that she was not interested. Of course, you know many women are still attracted to you–"

"No, no," he repeated, cutting her off. "She did... I mean, she is interested. She said yes."

"Oh excellent," his mother cheered. "Arwin owes me ten sou! Oh, do not look so embarrassed, my darling. I have confidence in your charms," his mother cooed before giggling.

"You bet Arwin that I'd be successful and..." Julien stared at his mother in shock. "Have you seen her?" he asked.

"Máire?" His mother played with the edge of her sleeve. "I am not sure, though I think I heard someone ride out. Perhaps that was her."

He grabbed his mother's shoulders in order to get her attention. "Which direction did she go? She left afterwards, without a word. How could she say nothing?"

"I cannot tell these things," she answered. "It sounded like she went to the east."

"Saulieu," he muttered.

"Then perhaps you should hurry," she suggested, before leaning in to kiss his brow.

"Yes," he answered. "Sleep well."

"Why are you so upset that you are riding to go find Marcus?" Máire voiced in the midst of the silent argument in her head. "This is what the mortal Maél Muire would have done!" Her voice echoed, along with owls and other nighttime hunters, in the densely packed forest.

Her horse flicked his ears back at her words. For a moment, she remembered how often her favored horse, Biast, would do the same thing. Horses always listened, but their simple advice could make one long never to hear animals' voices again.

"I have not even taken flight," she commented to the horse. His ears pivoted, but he remained silent. "I left, fully expecting Julien to figure out where I went and catch up. If he does, it is all well and good, but I cannot love him. I cannot love."

She leaned forward and patted the bay's neck. "I feel something for him, but that is confusing as well," she murmured to the horse.

She also felt something for Arwin, Claudius, and even Edward, yet the feelings tripled for Marcus and Julien, but they could not be love.

Soon, Calais slowed to a sedate trot, as if sensing her decision to allow Julien to find her. Then again, something within her wanted to sob on Marcus' shoulder. Ignoring her desire to seek comfort with Marcus, Máire pulled Calais to a stop and mulled over her options… she could remain and speak to Julien, or she could send Calais home and find Marcus. Undecided, Máire pulled her feet out of the stirrups and stretched her legs. Perhaps now she could think.

"Calais, he is a very nice mortal. I enjoy his wit and his intelligence. He has adapted well to my idiosyncrasies, and Julien even gets along with my friends and associates. He seems not to mind that I am she who controls her destiny, and he does not seek to control my thoughts. I like him… probably too much for his own good."

Seemingly in response, Calais whinnied and stomped a hoof.

Within moments, Máire detected the scent and the hoof beats of a mortal rider traveling up the road.

Her horse turned his ears toward the sound and then shuffled his feet, as if waiting for her decision.

"I think he and I need to talk," she said before dismounting. "Stay nearby," she requested.

In answer, Calais whinnied as he nodded his large head.

The elder gray gelding foamed sweat. Julien slowed down to a walk in order to allow the horse a moment to catch his breath. Julien then heard a loud neigh to the west, and then he turned to see Calais. The other horse picked up his head from the grass, for a moment, before returning to graze. A shadowed figure sat nearby, beneath the trees. He nudged Zerbino towards the figure. Julien then dismounted and started walking through the pebbles and muddy dirt towards the silent individual. As he got closer, he saw Máire staring back at him. Anger welled up inside him. He gasped for breath, in an attempt to calm down.

"Why did you leave without saying a word?" he asked, though his voice choked because of his rage. He tried to control his voice.

She tipped her head to regard him. He could finally see her features. "I was… am… confused about how I feel. I always experience a strange puzzlement when I encounter someone who makes me have some feelings. I suppose in the past, these sensations might have been love. However, now I am bewildered." She paused, apparently waiting for him to take a seat across from her. He opened his mouth to say a few words, but she held up a hand and continued.

"I have been unable to love for almost 250 years. Can you possibly imagine how that would damage a person's perceptions? I am perpetually moody. I cannot predict how I will feel about someone at any particular moment." Máire closed her mouth and then looked at Julien, seemingly expecting him to converse with her.

"You sound like most women I know," he commented as he scooted towards the tree Máire sat under. He then leaned his back against it and continued, "except for the part about the 250 years, of course."

Julien saw a wrinkle crease her forehead, as if Máire tried to conceal her thoughts. She seemed to give in and then giggled, shaking her head. She snorted and then covered her mouth, in an apparent attempt to hide her glee. He could now fathom why Marcus, Claudius, and Arwin referred to her as 'endearing piglet' behind her back.

"I am going to tell your mother and sister that you find them moody," she warned as she shook her head. She soon stopped laughing and explained, "I do have feelings for you, Julien, yet it is not love. If you were to ask me to describe these feelings, I could not. All I ask is that you accept me for the temperamental woman I am. If you do indeed love me, I will do my best to give you some modicum of warmth."

He frowned at her remarks. "It pains me to hear you say those words. I cannot fathom being without love for so long. I might have ended my life." He stared into her eyes for a moment and then took one of her hands. Despite how active her hands seemed to be in battle, now they felt soft, though a little chilled. He stroked a finger over her palm and cooed, "I can tell you with conviction, Máire, that I love you."

She smiled a little. "You do not know me very well. Are you certain of this?"

"I am sure that what I believed to be love before was just a taste of what it was meant to be." Julien sighed, pressed her palm to his cheek, and then closed his eyes. "I would be lying if I did not admit this, but I obsess over you when you are not near. I reflect on your courage, your strength, and your beauty as well. Not many women I know of could do what you do, and I cannot help but respect and admire your spiritual skills. When you are near, I am amazed that I can hear anyone else speak. When I am close to you, I can smell lavender, roses, lilies, and honey. When I beheld you earlier in the stream, I first believed I had crossed a magical barrier to witness a Goddess of water. I felt compelled to worship you at your altar." He tugged her closer, wanting her again.

"What do you wish from a relationship with a woman?" she asked. Her face was inches from his.

"What do you mean?" He could not think anymore.

"Do you want children?" she asked.

He pulled her into his lap. "Perhaps," he answered.

"I believe you want someone to grow old with you, Julien. I cannot give anyone children, and I do not age. You should be with a mortal. I cannot possibly be what you need or want," she argued. "However, you must have very strong feelings for me, since you decided to chase after me. I cannot deny you what you so strongly wish."

Máire grew silent, before she leaned against his chest. Julien held onto her with his left hand while he stroked her hair with his right hand. He then noticed Máire look up and sniff the air.

"What is it?" he asked, as he pulled his hand from her hair.

He could see strong fear in her eyes. She then mouthed the word 'Strigoi'. She then disappeared from his sight. He glanced at the forest around him, but he could not see any danger.

Julien stood up, drew his sword, and started to find her, when a sharp thunderclap of pain moved through his body. A series of voices echoed in his ears, and then the forest seemed to melt away. Colors swirled, and the voices became a mocking cacophony. The dead victims of the Strigoi appeared as mold-encrusted figures, encircling him, smelling of pungent rot. The jowls on their victims elongated and their nails became claws as they transformed into hideous monsters. One moved closer and grabbed him by the throat. Julien felt pain as its sharp claws raked over his neck. It pushed him against a tree, and then the grotesque being shoved a hand into his abdomen. The agony made him fall forward, into the monster.

Julien's hands moved to his eyes, and a horrible, keening voice told him that freeing himself from sight would prevent more pain.

He felt himself fall to the ground, but soon the voices subsided enough, so that he could hear footfalls on the ground.

"Julien!" Máire shouted, though her voice seemed but a whisper amongst the cacophony. Then a pair of arms reached around him. He screamed, fearful a claw would plunge into his heart. Instead of feeling claws rending his flesh, he felt his hands being pulled away from his face.

"Oh, Gods," he heard Máire whisper. He opened his eyes and tried to see her, but only pain and a myriad of dark, pulsating colors in random swirls greeted him. He then felt cold hands wipe away slick wetness from his face.

"You have been affected by the madness of the Strigoi, and one of them fed from you."

His pain started to fade, and he began to feel giddy. Voices still spoke in his mind, yet he sought out Máire's words.

"You will die soon," she explained, though tears seemed to mar her voice, "unless I do something, and there is only one thing I can do. I can make you a Deargh Du, my child-in-darkness. Do you understand me? I must hear it from you."

There was a pause. Julien could not fathom her meaning.

"Do you want to live, or do you want me to let you pass?"

He could now feel her lips on his left ear. He soon felt a strange, new moisture fall onto his face. Everything else surrounding him seemed like a miasma of confusion, as his perceptions seemed to begin slipping away. Where he lay, who held him, who she held... he knew not the answers to these questions. However, her one question to him rang clear... did he want to live or die. There could be only one answer.

"Live," Julien cried out, hoping she could hear him. "I want to live."

He felt fingers slide and then push his neck to the side. Then, a moment of fresh pain wracked his body, and soon he felt whatever strength remained within wither away. Then, upon the brink of complete oblivion, a miniscule, yet blissful burning pleasure arced through his body, but it seemed to fade too quickly. Vague and quick images passed through his mind, bringing him a few paces back from the brink. Now, as his mind's eye peered beyond the edge to see what gifts oblivion would bestow, he could only sense his heart slow. Then time seemed to stop.

He sensed something pull away from him, and then he felt something wet press against his lips.

"Drink, please," he heard through the whooshing and whirling around the mouth of the abyss. Somehow, her pleading pulled him away from the edge, and he could feel a renewed connection between his mind and his body.

Feeling and control returned to his mouth. He then obeyed the instructions he heard and began to lick at a strange, salty, warm wetness. Soon, perplexing strength and clarity overwhelmed him, returning to him his memories and his perceptions.

Julien latched onto Máire's wrist, desiring to consume more of that substance, as the slightly nauseating and repulsive taste had become sweet, honey-laced ambrosia. Blood... he drank her blood, yet the realization did nothing to cease his consumption of this most vivacious libation. Herbs, mysterious spices, and distant traces of frankincense and myrrh infused Máire's blood. Soon the pain disappeared, turning into rapturous pleasure. A chill then settled through his body, making him feel alive.

Oh, never end... do not let this pleasure ever end!

He pushed all other thoughts aside as he continued to suck at her blood. A glimmering and vivid glow grew within, almost as if it were a physical presence. A warning in his mind soon told him of danger, and then he felt a hand start to push him away, but he ignored the warning and fought away the hand. He wanted, needed, more of that elixir.

A sudden, unknown force contracted within him, and then he found himself against a tree, about ten feet away from a shadowy Máire. He sensed her move closer. As she came near, the pain from the mortal realm disappeared in a blink, only to be replaced by a strange, new agony, which overwhelmed him. Julien closed his eyes, trying to shut out the pain, but he could feel his jaw and his head begin to throb. Soon the pain became too great, and he could perceive no more.

"Wake up, my lovely."

Something prodded Julien's left shoulder. He turned his head and opened his eyes, but he had to hold up his right hand to shield his face as a brilliant sun made him wince a bit.

A dark stranger with brilliant, blue eyes smiled down at him, crouched down, and then offered his hand.

"You look confused, young man," said the dark stranger.

Julien looked around and found himself in the middle of a mass of motionless bodies clad in a myriad of strange clothes. Among them, Julien could see naked men and women, clad only in blue paint, men in strange, green or gray helms holding odd clubs, and he even noticed a few Franks lay about, next to people of richer skin tones with feathers in their headdresses. He then found himself pulled up. Though his head spun a bit, Julien felt more or less himself.

"Where are we?" he asked the stranger. "Who are you?" he added.

"Where we are has many names. 'Tír na Nóg' is one, while 'the Otherworld' is another. Personally, I like to call it 'the sylvan path between the two roads'. You are in a place outside of your world and outside of your time. I am a guide on this road, and I help younglings find their way. My name is Adhamdh, and I am Morrigan's first son, the eldest Deargh Du. I spent well over a millennia on your world, but then the

Great Queen called me home. I am here to pull those who quest to their feet, dust them off, and tell them to prepare to meet with Morrigan. Of course, I have some curiosity about my growing family."

Adhamdh turned to look at the horizon as a raven landed on his shoulder, cackling. He then regarded Julien once more. "Be truthful. You will find Her answers more satisfying," Adhamdh stated.

Julien watched a black mist fall around the blood-drinker and the raven, and then the mists melted, but Julien now found himself alone.

He took an uneasy step and nearly tripped over a man clad in metal. Then, a cacophonous sound echoed throughout the field of bodies, and he turned to face the source of the sound. He witnessed an unkindness of ravens mesh together, forming a darkness that covered the sun. Screams echoed forth from their beaks as the ravens flew straight towards him. Julien flinched, fearing for his life, when the ravens stopped and just hovered a few feet away from Julien. Then their forms began to meld together in an expanding sphere of growing darkness. Soon, a figure walked from the darkness, which dissipated, along with most of the ravens, though a few flew about.

Julien's legs nearly buckled as the figure stepped closer. She wore only blue paint, covering her body in woven and interlaced designs of exquisite beauty, a leather belt incorporating the same style of design as her body paint, and a strange cloak that seemed to be made of feathers. In her hands she held a spear as tall as one and a half men and an oblong shield as tall as she stood. From her, he could hear the ethereal music of metal hitting against metal combined with blood-curdling screams. Her hair seemed indescribable. Sometimes it appeared to be the darkest of reds, and yet, sometimes it appeared to be the color of a raven's wing. Her black within black eyes met, his and he could not turn away.

"You are confused," the figure stated. "You will know me as 'Morrigan', though I have many other names, but 'Morrigan' will suffice for you."

Julien broke Her gaze and then stared at the desolate field of bodies. The ravens had congregated on the bodies and were now picking at bloodied wounds.

"M... Morrigan? I am Julien, though somehow, I suppose you knew that," he stammered. She said nothing... She seemed to wait with timeless patience, but for what was She waiting? Finally, it dawned on Julien that She waited for him to answer Her question... was he confused. "Yes, I am," he answered, though he still felt lost in his own thoughts.

"Were you expecting this instead?"

Julien turned around as the landscape changed. The ground became the purest white marble Julien had ever seen, and mists rose up to obscure the horizons. He looked back at his hostess, who appeared now in a gown of white with silver embroidery. A halo flashed above Her head, bright light surrounded Her, and a pair of white wings unfolded behind Her.

"Is this not what Christians believe in? That when one dies, you go to heaven?" She turned and regarded the mists. "One can hear the singing of angels for eternity."

Julien could hear a chorus of Kyrie Eleison echo through the limitless, marbled expanse. Still, this place seemed empty and bereft of warmth. He returned his gaze to Morrigan and said, "This is what the Church tells us, but it is not what I believe."

"So, what do you believe, young mortal?" the angelic Goddess asked.

"I suppose that my belief is an older one," he admitted, daring to stare into Her eyes again. "I know that what the Church tells us about death is mostly a lie, or at least, that is my suspicion. However, I would like to understand the truth."

Morrigan's face turned up in a bemused grin. "You are wise."

The white marble seemed to turn dark and became a stone floor. Then walls grew out of the floor and became solid stone. Brightly colored tapestries unfolded and rolled down the walls. Swords and strange armaments began to slide over the empty spots. He had never witnessed such things before.

Julien turned back to Morrigan and noticed that Her gown of white had disappeared. Morrigan now wore unfamiliar, courtly attire. She walked to a table and a pair of chairs. A strange board rested on the top, along with two rows of small, wooden figures.

The Goddess motioned for Julien to take a seat. "Please sit. Join me in a game," She requested.

Julien sat down and watched Her sit across from him. "What is this game called?" he asked, though some elements, like the board, seemed familiar.

"It is not surprising you have not seen this game. It will not be known in this form for some time. It is called 'Chess', but you will forget that when you leave this place. Shall we play, Julien?" She ran a graceful finger over the top of one of the game pieces.

Julien studied the board and wondered how he could ever hope to play this unknown game without guidance.

"White moves first," Morrigan instructed him.

He placed a cautious finger over one of the smaller figures. He closed his eyes, and then a sudden knowledge overwhelmed him. He recognized pawns, rooks, bishops, knights, and the king and queen. Their movements then burned into his memory. Now that he understood the mechanics of the game, Julien picked up a pawn and placed it in another square.

Morrigan smiled and then moved one of Her pieces.

Julien moved again, wondering whether he understood the dynamics of the game or merely moved due to a strange compulsion.

Morrigan leaned forward, moved a bishop, and took one of his men. After Her move, Julien watched Morrigan flick a curled strand of hair over Her shoulder.

"I do love this game, sometimes more so than Fidchell," She explained with a smile. "You must ask Marcus to teach you Fidchell, one of these nights," She added. "This chessboard is very much like the world as you know it. You have elements of

good and evil, both vying for control of the board."

After he moved a rook, She studied the game board and then took another one of his pieces with Her next move. "Sometimes, evil diminishes good."

Julien leaned forward and took one of Hers with his next move.

"Well played," She congratulated. "Sometimes, however, good diminishes evil. If the game continues in this manner, either good or evil will win. That would be unbalanced."

He watched Her move again and then asked, "What do you mean unbalanced? Wait... first, what happens when the game ends?"

"It ceases to exist," She replied.

"Can the game be stopped?" Julien asked, shocked at the seriousness of Her answer.

"No," She replied, "but the game can be balanced."

"How is that accomplished?"

His hostess smirked and then waved the question away like a bothersome fly. Suddenly, he heard the sound of stone hitting wood, and then Julien stared down at the board. In between the black and white game pieces were gray ones, interspersed between his men and Hers.

"You have added pieces, and they are all gray. What purpose do they serve, Morrigan?"

"Let us continue playing and you will see," She answered, before leaning forward and taking one of Julien's knights. He watched a gray piece move on its own accord and then knock out one of Hers.

Julien reached over and took one of Her bishops, and then he watched as another gray piece maneuvered and knocked out one of his pieces.

"I see... the gray pieces equalize the colors on the board, but what happens when there are no black or white pieces?" Julien asked as he stared back at Morrigan.

"That does not happen. As you can see, some of the gray pieces turn white while others turn black."

"So, even though the pieces on the board are in constant flux, balance is maintained," Julien ascertained aloud.

He watched Morrigan beam at him.

"The gray pieces are the Deargh Du," he added.

"Yes, the gray pieces are my Deargh Du, and sometimes others," She answered.

"And with the renewal of the white and black pieces, the game continues."

"Yes," She replied.

"But that seems unbalanced, in a way... the game must end at some time," Julien observed as he looked at Her again, albeit a little wary. He began to wonder whether he now asked too many questions.

"Sadly, yes," She answered. "This game at some point beyond time will end.

However, Julien, like all things, it will begin anew."

A tapestry on the wall then caught his eye. Julien arose from his chair and walked over to the tapestry. His eyes became drawn to a spear and a waving pennant, which seemed caught in a mythic breeze. He then felt everything change around him again. The new, fresh breeze gently played with his hair. He then felt a hand on his shoulder. He turned his head and saw that Morrigan stood next to him. Her face gave a soft, beautiful glow.

He returned gaze to these new surroundings. Soon, Julien could hear the sounds of metal hitting metal. He then observed two groups of men and cavalry, one side clad in blue and the other in red, stare at each other across a muddy field hemmed in by thick forest on both sides. Both forces wielded armaments, but the blue soldiers wore nothing but metal. Even their huge horses wore armor. The red soldiers, however, wore metal armor of a different design and hue, though some wore leather or linked metal armor. Some of the red soldiers also bore large bows as tall as men. Julien's jaw dropped a bit at their size.

"Isn't war exhilarating?" Morrigan lilted. "Men of two different sides coming together to decide which side is right and which side is dead. Of course the players have different reasons, and the tools of death always change, but the hatred, the violence, and the taking of life always remains the same. This is one of my favorite battles... Agincourt, I believe. On this side of the field are nearly six thousand brave souls who believe their king has rights to this throne, and their king is among them."

Morrigan then pointed to the soldiers in blue. "This army of around thirty thousand soldiers is tired of their enemies' incessant demands for tribute and believes that the king of their enemy has no rights to their throne." She turned back to him and asked, "Julien, where is the balance in this battle?"

"There appears to be no balance," he answered. "The red soldiers are severely outnumbered." He watched as many of the red soldiers launched a volley of arrows through the air that could not possibly reach their targets at that distance, but he managed to push away those distractions. "The blue soldiers' knights will be on them at any moment, my la... great queen."

She nodded before asking, "So, you base your observation on the number of soldiers and their shiny equipment?"

Julien took another look at the muddy field and the forests on both sides. The arrows seemed to shimmer in motionless flight. Time paused, and it gave him a chance to study the metallic warriors in blue. "Those knights seem so disorganized, and that mud must slow their advance. How can they possibly see through that metal covering their faces? In addition, the soldiers on foot behind them seem to be too densely packed. Perhaps fortune favors the red army, today."

Time caught up, and he watched the arrows begin to hit the blue soldiers. Most bounced off their armor, but a few penetrated holes in the face and struck the horses in vulnerable areas. The cavalry could not out flank the archers, and many knights' horses became impaled on spikes the archers had driven into the ground to protect them. The charge halted, and many panicked horses charged the lines of soldiers in formation behind them, as the rain of arrows continued. Armored men at arms then began to trudge through the mud towards the red army, even pressing them back a bit, but as more of their men fell, the sounds of battle turned to panic. More arrows continued dropping from the sky in a deadly swarm. He watched the group of armor-clad soldiers in blue begin to slip and fall into wet bogs, many drowning in their own helms.

"Nature maintained the balance here. However, what you do not see, Julien is that it is not entirely nature that serves the balance. You see, a Deargh Du convinced the commander of the blue army, Charles d'Albret, that this tactic would be successful. If the Deargh Du did not intervene, d'Albret would have put a smaller force forward and sent out groups to flank Henry's army, and they would be celebrating a victory by now instead of fleeing."

Time seemed to move faster, now. Soldiers in blue littered the muddied field, and then a mist blew over the battlefield. The mist soon parted. Julien found himself in the field littered with bodies upon which the ravens fed. He turned back to regard Morrigan. She was back in Her cloak and blue paint. He also noticed the bodies of several of the blue clad soldiers from the battle he had just witnessed.

"This is where those who upset the balance go when they die," he reasoned aloud as he stared into her midnight-colored eyes.

"Yes. They are judged here," Morrigan answered as she leaned against her spear. "Some I punish, some I set free after they have learned something, but a few deserve oblivion. You, Julien... you will not be lying down amongst these bodies. You are not being judged."

"Then why am I here?" he asked.

"You have been chosen by a Deargh Du to walk the path of the Deargh Du. This is not a path for everyone. In fact, I was hesitant to bring you this far on your journey. The Deargh Du maintain the balance. Without balance, the world will end. With balance, it continues. My Deargh Du serve the balance with direct intervention, as you witnessed on the chessboard, and sometimes with a whisper, as you beheld at the field of Agincourt. Those who we have to kill or are killed by our action in our fight to maintain the balance come here. The judgment is not mine alone, but the judgment of many."

"Why did you show all of this to me?" Julien asked. "Would it not have been easier to tell it to me?"

"Because, once you start down the path, you cannot turn back," Morrigan answered. She then motioned to several roads before them. "You must decide whether you wish to maintain the balance by sending those who have upset it here." Morrigan waved her hand from her left to her right, and then the corpses disappeared. The endless white expanse of marble returned, and she became an angel again. "Or, you may come here." She waved her arms in a flourish again, and everything turned black.

"Or, this is the third option. This place is misleading. It is not really so bleak.

It is, after all, what you choose to make out of it. For instance, imagine you are on a grassy knoll during the summer. Envision butterflies dotting the landscape, birds singing, fae joining you in a dance. Now, close your eyes and imagine what you want to experience."

Julien closed his eyes and then heard to soft songs of the birds on the wind. He opened his eyes and the grass seemed endless. Morrigan had changed as well. Now she wore a simple cloak and a long linen dress. Little creatures even began fluttering about, twirling around his body as if they wanted him to dance.

"In this place, you chose your existence. It is not your reality... it is the Otherworld, or part of it," Morrigan explained. "It is not the Christian heaven or hell, but I think it is perfection itself. It will exist if you chose it. However, there is still the path of the Deargh Du." She turned back to regard him. "Do you wish to continue in the life beyond to serve this noble purpose? You will have my eternal appreciation."

"So, my choices are heaven, this Otherworld, or I can become a Deargh Du and help you maintain the balance," he reiterated.

"Yes. What do you choose?"

"I would like to be a Deargh Du," Julien answered.

"Why do you wish to be Deargh Du?" Morrigan asked, while placing a hand on his arm. A strange energy bounded from Her body to his.

"Because," Julien stammered, stumbling with words for a moment. "My life to this point has had no real purpose. I desire to be part of something greater than what I am. In addition, I am not ready to rest. Both Heaven and the Otherworld seem to be where one goes when they are finished with life. I am not finished."

She embraced Julien, holding his body with her left arm while holding his face against Her hair with her left. Julien sniffed Her hair, inhaling Her beautiful magic. She then kissed his cheek.

"You have passed my test. You shall become Deargh Du. Take heed in what Marcus and Máire tell you. They have great wisdom, even though they make wrong decisions sometimes, yet..." she said before pulling away and then staring into his eyes. "There is something else I feel you must know."

"Yes, Morrigan, what is it?"

He watched the Goddess' face as Her smile faded.

"Be gentle with Máire."

"But I am gentle with her," he answered, "as gentle as I know how to be."

"She feels that she is cursed, and because of that, she feels that she cannot love. She, in fact, has rejected most emotions. She is quite miserable now, and has been for over a century. Try to convince her that she can feel and love. You see, there is no curse. Máire's doubts are within herself. She cannot be told that there is no curse, because she will not believe it. However, she can be shown that she can love. It will not be easy, Julien, but assist her in finding love."

"I will, my Goddess," he answered.

Morrigan looked away and said, "I suppose now is the time." She laughed, and he could hear something of the Deargh Du in that laugh. "Time," Morrigan repeated, "as if that has bearing in this place outside of time." She turned back to him. "You must return from whence you came and begin your journey as a Deargh Du. Remember to listen to the words and advice of those traveling with you on the path of the Deargh Du, especially your mother-in-darkness and Marcus."

Julien could feel a weight settle around him. He soon found himself laying down and then stretching out on the warm grass. He yawned and closed his eyes. "Thank you," he whispered with his last ounce of depleting strength.

A warm kiss settled on his cheek.

"You are welcome, my child."

Julien remained unconscious through the physical transformation, but at least his body began to heal. Máire looked at the sky for a moment before closing her eyes. Her instincts warned her that they would never reach Vézelay in time, whether she traveled by horse or with flight.

Then she remembered that during the chase and ensuing battle with the Strigoi, she had found a small, well-made shack, which could be a suitable place to spend the day. She whistled for Calais, and he trotted towards her like a frisky colt.

"Just the supplies, my friend," she whispered, before taking saddlebags and patting Calais' neck. The gelding returned to munching on the soft, green grasses on the muddied ground.

Máire placed the saddlebag over her shoulder, and then she picked up Julien. His blood seeped onto her clothing from his partly healed abdominal wound and from his eye sockets, which now held budding, new eyes. His lips parted in sleep, and she noticed new teeth growing.

A few minutes later, she placed him within the small safety tent. The hunters had left several stinky blankets in the cabin. She found nails and attached these to the walls.

Máire then lay down next to Julien and placed one of the less fragrant blankets over him. She slid down next to him and wrapped herself around him, hoping he would not wake up and try to leave during the day. She yawned and then closed her eyes.

chapter fourteen

The sounds of Julien drifting in and out of consciousness woke her. Máire stroked her left hand over his soft, brown hair. She then bit into her right wrist again and placed it at his lips. His eyes opened, now completely re-grown, and she watched them glow green. He began to suckle cautiously upon her wrist.

"I am sorry for waking you," she explained. "I believe you need this, though." Máire slid her left hand under his neck and helped him sit up. She felt the delirious pull of blood from her body and closed her eyes.

"What happened?" His words cut through her dreamlike state and pulled her into reality.

Máire opened her eyes and stared down at him. Julien's blue eyes had returned, and he no longer fed from her. He ran his right index finger over his lips and then stuck the finger into his mouth.

She lowered his head and neck and lay down next to him. "You do not remember?" she asked.

"I remember some things," he admitted in a throaty whisper, "yet so many things seem disjointed and random. I remember an unkindness of ravens and a woman of such strength."

"A Strigoi attacked us. I managed to kill it, but not before it sent you its madness. We have both seen the unfortunate effects of that madness on mortals, so I believed–"

"You believed I was going to die," he ascertained, interrupting her.

"Yes," Máire answered.

"Then, why am I not dead?" he asked.

She blinked back a few tears, but they managed to escape nonetheless. "I saved you, but I had to change you."

"How? How did you save me?" His hand slid over hers.

"I took your blood and gave you some of mine," she explained. "I asked you whether you wanted to live, and you said 'yes'. The only way I could save your life was by making you like me."

"Like you," he whispered.

"Yes. You are Deargh Du now, Julien."

"I remember now a most beautiful dream," he purred. "The Goddess formed Herself from the flock of ravens. She and I spoke about the balance, and She offered me a choice to pick a path. This is the journey I wish to take. I wanted a purpose in life, and She seemed pleased."

Máire sniffed as more tears began to fall. "I failed you. I should have explained the journey more and what becoming a Deargh Du means."

She felt fingers wipe at her tears. She then found herself staring into his eyes. "Do not worry yourself, Máire. This is what I want. I am glad that I can continue to live. Now, I have purpose." He pulled her closer for a gentle kiss.

She returned the soft kiss before moving away. "I can sense night is here. Can you sit on your own?"

She watched him try to control his newly formed body.

"No I cannot," he whispered. He seemed confused.

She sat up. "I will feed and then you will feed." She stared at him, vaguely remembering her first night. Julien seemed so content and quiet. "Please stay here."

"I can barely move," he groaned, while giving her a listless smile. "The Great Queen told me to listen to you and Marcus. I will not leave."

She scooted out of the tent and rose to her feet. She then walked to the door and whistled to the horses. They soon trotted over to her.

"I am sorry that I did not take proper care of your needs," she murmured, horrified that she forgotten that they would have had to deal with the annoyance of their tack all day. She unsaddled them, removed their bridles, and began to gorge herself.

Máire wandered back into the shack and pushed away the tent. She sat down behind Julien, helped him sit up, and placed her arm in front of him. She tried to remember whether she and Marcus had done the same. Her own faded memories of her transformation paled next to her memories of the past evening.

"I am sure Morrigan told you much about what it means to be Deargh Du, but there are certain physical things I will teach you now." She smiled as his teeth pierced her offered wrist.

"You know we are beings of the night, and you know we are immortal, to a point. We feed on mortals as well as other blood-drinkers. We can kill mortals during feeding, but it is most important that we only do so when necessary in moments when they threaten our safety. We cannot kill off our food supply... besides, unjustified murder is unbalanced. We also feed on animals, yet we cannot feed on them entirely... to do so makes our humanity fade." She pulled her wrist away from Julien and continued her teaching. "Usually, our first night after the transformation is a night of insanity, yet I see no signs of madness in you. There are a variety of physical and mental changes during the transformation."

"Did you say physical changes?" Julien asked.

"Yes. Your bone structure, musculature, eyes, teeth… everything changes… even your height. I grew two inches taller when I changed," Máire explained.

He turned his head to look backwards at her. "How does that happen?"

"The Deargh Du have much in common with the Fae, and they are the most beautiful beings in the world. So, when a mortal transforms to Deargh Du, his or her body becomes perfect and beautiful in every way. This is one of the many gifts from the Goddess."

"How different do I look?" he asked.

She smiled. "You are most breathtaking, even more handsome than before. Even your injuries have healed."

"Injuries?" he asked.

Máire did not want to trouble Julien with an explanation of how close to death he had come last night, so she decided to speak in general terms. "Any injuries, scars, broken bones, or other ailments you have suffered through are now gone."

"Amazing! May I see what I look like?" Julien requested with a smile.

She opened her pack and pulled out her sword. "Hold this, and I will take you outside. There is still fading light, and the moon gives us some illumination as well. In addition, you and I can create some brightness of our own."

She picked him up and carried him out into a clearing.

"This is night time? It seems so bright," Julien said.

"One of Morrigan's gifts. Now witness another," she intoned before creating illumination around herself.

Julien seemed astounded by the bright light emanating from her, but he soon focused on his reflection in silence. After a moment of studying his face, he met her eyes again.

"I… you were right. I am handsome."

"You were a beautiful mortal to begin with, in body, mind, and spirit," she told him. She then watched him drop her sword.

"I must rest," he whispered.

She lifted him over her shoulder, grabbed her sword, and carried them back inside. After tossing aside the sword in the tent, Máire set Julien on the floor and placed blankets over him.

Julien's eyes fluttered open for a moment. "Do you love me, Máire?"

She swallowed a lump in her throat and whispered, "You are my son-in-darkness," before kissing his brow. She then slid down next to him and wrapped an arm around him.

Outside Saulieu

"How much further until we reach Vézelay?" asked Claudius.

"You and Máire can be quite annoying with these constant inquiries," Marcus grumbled to Claudius.

"Just be glad you're flying over the woods instead of traveling on horseback like those travelers–" Claudius cut short his words upon sniffing the air. "Well, it appears that a rather large group of Lamia is traversing the Empire on horseback."

"Not just any group," Marcus muttered. He levitated to get a better look at the cavalry. "They wear the uniform of the papal army, and of course my closest friend and ally leads them. Stay here, Claudius... I wish to speak to their commander."

His lieutenant uttered a dry chuckle. "Say hello to that Lamia bastard for me."

"I plan on doing as little greeting as possible," Marcus answered. "Be prepared to intervene if necessary, but keep yourselves hidden." Marcus then landed with stealth into a copse of trees, before walking out towards the cavalry. He wondered as to the wisdom of his decision.

Upon making eye contact with Mandubratius, he waved his arm at the Lamia.

The Lamia motioned his cavalry to stop before trotting over to where Marcus stood. Both horse and rider came to an abrupt stop.

"You aren't a very good rider," Marcus commented.

"I haven't had the need to ride a horse in centuries," Mandubratius replied. "Ah, what we must do to keep our masks in place."

Marcus frowned. "Indeed. Why are you here with such a large force?"

"Ah, straight to business. So many decades to catch up on, and you journey straight to our current predicament. Very well, my friend... to business. His Holiness has sent me to act as his Emissary with Charles, fight this darkness that we know as the Strigoi but they believe to be demons, and protect Christendom," Mandubratius answered with a ready smile.

Marcus rubbed his forehead. "I see. Is the pope aware that his army is marching through the empire in a manner that resembles a conquering army?"

"Conquering?" Mandubratius chuckled. "We're acting as the spiritual protectors of Emperor Charles and his people. We are on our way to Aachen to give him that announcement. Besides, we are but a vanguard... a paltry thousand mounted men at arms could hardly be considered a conquering army."

Marcus muttered under his breath before asking, "So, we are still to aid each other in fighting the Strigoi, while you seek to place a wedge between the emperor and the pope?"

"Of course we'll assist our comrades. This is just to keep the mortals busy with one another. After all, if they weren't worried about each other, they might very well notice some of our very odd habits. Besides, the emperor forgets who placed the crown on his head. Pope Leo will join us in Aachen with a force of ten thousand," Mandubratius purred. "So, have you seen any Strigoi?" he asked, changing the subject. The Lamia cocked his head to the side as if seeking out intruders.

"We have killed about forty," Marcus answered. "How many have you killed?"

"Six."

"Excuse me, sixty?" Marcus felt a smile tug at his face.

"No, only six," Mandubratius confirmed, appearing a little annoyed.

"Well, I'm certain you will find more soon," Marcus replied, as he tried to keep from laughing. He then glanced at the army of Lamia in the distance. "So, of this force of one thousand supposedly mounted cavalry, may I ask why there are men on foot who are clad in riding gear?"

"During our last encounter with the Strigoi, some of the horses ran away in a fit of madness," Mandubratius answered. "I see, despite their efforts to hide, that your party of Celtic warriors seems quite small now. Perhaps it is time to increase numbers."

"What you're trying to suggest in your usual polite manner is that I should send for reinforcements?"

"Well put, General," Mandubratius answered.

Marcus motioned for Mandubratius to come closer. These were Lamia, and at this distance, nothing said between them could be considered private. Mandubratius dismounted his horse and then approached him.

"Oh, what now, Marcus?" Mandubratius whispered, apparently having fun with the clandestine nature of their conversation.

"I find it hard to believe, no wait a minute..." Marcus trailed off for a moment. "I do find it easy to believe that you'd feel fearful enough to ask for more warriors. The Deargh Du, Sugnwr Gwaed, and Ekimmu Cruitne here killed forty Strigoi, and your grand force of one thousand killed only six. Yes, I can see why more of the Celtic lines are necessary to protect you. Without us, you and your recruits would be dead," he murmured in Mandubratius' ear.

"Are you quite finished raving about the prowess of the Celtic lines?" Mandubratius asked in a hushed voice.

"Yes."

"Well then, are you going to call for reinforcements or not?" the Lamia queried.

"I will consider it."

"And I will consider that an affirmation," Mandubratius replied. He then grabbed the reins of his horse and slid a foot into the stirrup, before hopping up onto his chestnut horse.

"If Eire had any value, you would have saved a thousand gold pieces if you had just said 'yes'," Mandubratius pointed out.

"If you engage in open combat against the armies of the emperor, he may request my intervention, and if he does, I will intervene," Marcus informed him.

"When we meet again, let us hope it is not on the field of battle," the Lamia added, "although, I wonder how that would turn out... you and I on opposite sides on the field of battle. Ah... seems like old times." Mandubratius chuckled and then nudged his horse towards the cavalry.

Marcus grunted and headed back to the forest, entertaining himself with the thought of beheading his old enemy, but he dashed those thoughts away. Their small party could not handle all of the Strigoi. However, Mandubratius was right... it was time to call for reinforcements, and so Marcus needed to send Claudius to Bath and to Ard Macha to get them.

Vézelay

Patroclus watched Lady Heloise pace about after dinner. Her son had disappeared, chasing after Máire last night. He walked over to Mac Alpin and suggested, "They should have returned by this time. Perhaps we should go search for them."

He watched the elder blood-drinker close his eyes in thought. "Yes," Mac Alpin answered. "I would hate to think that they were attacked by the Strigoi. Let us leave straightaway and hope the two of them are in some lover's nest after losing track of time. Lady Heloise?" Mac Alpin called and then headed in her direction.

"Gracious hostess, we feel most apprehensive–" Patroclus began.

Mac Alpin chuckled a bit. "Excuse the Legate. He still speaks as if he were addressing Amata. We are going hunting for your son and Máire."

Patroclus watched the woman's eyes light up in appreciation.

"Thank you. Is there anything you need for this journey?" she asked.

"Nothing, dear lady, except the direction your son took."

"East," Lady Heloise answered. "We thought she may wish to join the others."

"We head towards Saulieu, then," Patroclus said, while giving a slight bow to the Lady of Vézelay.

As Arwin started to hedge towards the door, the servants began to scatter in order to allow them out.

"How shall we communicate?" Patroclus asked.

"I will fly, you run. Wave me down every five miles, and I will keep my eyes on you," Mac Alpin stated. "We will go east towards Saulieu."

"I wish I could fly. I must confess my jealousy," Patroclus admitted.

Mac Alpin barked a loud laugh. "There are some definite advantages to flying, Roman, but if a Strigoi attacks you, you collapse. If they attack me, I have a long way to fall back to the earth!"

Patroclus smirked. "We will meet in five miles, then." He started running, hearing the whoosh of air as the Ekimmu Cruitne took off in flight behind him.

"Anything so far?" the Legate asked Arwin as he caught up to him on the road. They were perhaps ten miles away from Vézelay. The Ekimmu Cruitne was sniffing the air with his eyes shut, as if concentrating on the varying scents of the forest.

"Perhaps. Follow me," Mac Alpin called as he ran into the woods. About five hundred feet from the road, Mac Alpin halted, and kneeled down, and began fishing something out of the green leaves of a bush.

"Máire tends to wear much of her jewelry," he explained, before handing a bracelet to Patroclus. "This is not hers, though." He sniffed the air again before looking at the tracks on the ground. Mac Alpin then took a few paces to the west.

"Someone lay here, doubled over in pain, Patroclus. And look... thick, dried blood, and what are these?" Patroclus watched as Mac Alpin knelt to the ground and picked something from the dirt. Though ants covered it, the Legate could see that Arwin held an eye... with bright blue coloration. The Ekimmu Cruitne stood and said, "This appears to have been a Strigoi attack. Someone, probably Máire, picked up the wounded, Julien, I presume, and carried him towards the west." Mac Alpin picked up the other eye and with care placed them both in a leather pouch on his belt. He then drew his sword.

"Why do you draw your sword?" Patroclus asked, feeling a tinge of nervousness.

"Where there is one Strigoi, several may hide."

"Yes," Patroclus nodded, before drawing his own blade. He followed after the Ekimmu Cruitne, dodging tree roots and rocks.

His guide stopped again, sniffed the air, and then sheathed his sword.

"What now? Why did you put away your sword?" Patroclus asked in a nervous whisper.

"I smell two horses," Mac Alpin whispered back. "Horses are not fond of the Strigoi. In fact, we have seen horses affected by the Strigoi." He chuckled. "Two horses together suggest that our associates are safe and together, though I can only imagine in what condition we will find Julien."

"Do not take this as an insult, but I believe I will hold onto my sword," the Legate advised.

"Very well," Mac Alpin whispered back as he motioned to the west. "You may lead us."

Patroclus walked through the sylvan path and soon heard Arwin inhale and then exhale, apparently taking in the scents of the forest. He looked back at his guide and caught a strange look pass over the Ekimmu Cruitne's features.

"Something is different," Mac Alpin stated in a rather enigmatic fashion.

"What is different?" Patroclus asked.

"I cannot put my finger on it," Mac Alpin answered. "Let us continue."

They trudged forward, and then they both noticed two horses grazing on soft grasses next to a small hunting cottage. Their saddles and bridles hung from pegs set into one of the walls of the shack.

Mac Alpin knocked on the door and pushed it open.

Patroclus peered through the opening and noticed that Máire reclined on the floor next to Julien, who sat in the only chair in the small cottage.

"Lady Heloise has grown worried, as have we," Patroclus admitted. He then noticed the Ekimmu Cruitne studying the inspector general.

Arwin grinned. "Julien, you look different."

"What are you talking about?" a groggy Julien asked as he looked up at Mac Alpin.

The Ekimmu Cruitne studied Julien for a moment. "Did Máire cut your hair?" he asked, seemingly in jest. Patroclus could even tell that something seemed different about Julien.

As the inspector general stood up, he seemed taller.

Mac Alpin pointed at Máire. "Banbh Ceanúil did you–"

"Yes," Máire answered, cutting him off.

"To him?" Mac Alpin asked as he nodded towards Julien.

"Yes," she said.

"Indeed?" Mac Alpin queried again, this time with a broad smile.

"Yes, Arwin, I did," Máire answered.

Mac Alpin chuckled heartedly.

"A Strigoi attacked me," Julien stated. "I would have died from the madness. Máire offered a chance for survival. She saved me the only way she could."

"Máire, you selected a child-in-darkness well," Mac Alpin praised.

"I am not a child," Julien retorted with a pout.

Patroclus chuckled. "How old do you think we are, Julien?"

"Hmmmmm." Julien looked them over and then said, "Máire looks to be mid-twenties, and you are thirty-five, Patroclus…" He stared at Mac Alpin for a moment. "… and Arwin, you must be around forty-five, are you not?"

Patroclus tried not to laugh.

"Then am I wrong?" Julien queried.

Máire grinned. "You have forgotten already," she chided him in a gentle fashion. "Two hundred and sixty one," she said while pointing to herself. "The Legate is about seven hundred, I believe."

"I am nine hundred and thirty years old," Mac Alpin added.

Patroclus watched Julien open and close his mouth in abject surprise.

"You are all ancient," Julien murmured.

"Yes, you heard this before from Marcus and me," Máire admonished in a playful tone.

"I know, but I sort of forgot." Julien rubbed his forehead. "What does that make me?"

"A youngling son," stated Mac Alpin, "Máire's child-in-darkness."

"I can see your point about my age, yet I have an issue with the words 'son' and 'child'." Patroclus noticed Julien blush.

"Why?" Máire and Arwin asked in unison.

"The terms seem somewhat incestuous," Julien muttered.

Mac Alpin chuckled. "It's just a description." He turned back to Máire. "What have you taught the lad?"

"Only the basics," she replied. "He has been too weak to do anything rigorous."

"Until now," Julien added.

"Well, we have five hours until dawn," Mac Alpin observed. "If we did not have horses, we could make it home and give him a lesson or two about blood-drinkers before the sun comes up."

"We do not need to worry about the horses. I can tell them to go home. Deargh Du have some ability to understand animals, though the gift generally increases with Druidic training."

"Teach me that," Julien pleaded with a grin.

"I wish to see this as well," Patroclus commented, since he had never heard of such a gift before.

"Wait a moment. Do we not need to wait, for the transformation to end? Isn't that right?" Mac Alpin asked, seemingly unsure of his conclusion.

"Well, he seems to have required a shorter period of mental transformation due to the Strigoi attack. I believe Julien is ready."

"Then, let us pack. We can send the horses on their way to Vézelay and show this youngling how to fly," Mac Alpin reasoned aloud.

Patroclus clucked his tongue. "If only some of us could be so lucky."

Mac Alpin chuckled. "Lad, as a Lamia, you have a silver tongue worth envying."

"True, true," Patroclus agreed with a smile. "I can talk more than your share of women into joining my bed."

"Will you two do your share of packing or not?" Máire asked with a smirk and more than mild annoyance.

Julien found himself staring at Calais and Zerbino. The horses stared back at him as if bemused with this lesson of his.

"Just tell them as you would tell anyone else," Máire instructed. She stood a few feet away from him, next to the Legate and Mac Alpin.

"Zerbino and Calais, I wish for you to return to your barn in Vézelay," he requested.

Calais turned around, stared at Julien for a moment, and then swatted his tail from side to side, which succeeded in whacking Julien in the face.

"Calais does not believe you have given him enough treats," Máire explained with a chuckle. He watched the Deargh Du cross her arms over her chest.

"Perhaps it would be best for me to watch you do this," Julien suggested.

"No, you tell him yourself." He heard a soft and throaty chuckle emanate from her throat.

"Well what language did you speak in?" he asked.

"It does not matter… they understand, no matter what language you speak in. Animals do not always understand by words, but they do converse with each other in signals and age old behaviors."

"Calais and Zerbino, if you go home now, I will give you extra treats… carrots, apples, or whatever else you two wish," Julien offered, hoping a bribe would sweeten the deal.

He watched the horses regard one another for a moment. They then stared back at him for a moment before turning and walking leisurely down the road to Vézelay.

"Well done, Julien," Máire congratulated as she patted his shoulder. "They should arrive an hour or two after dawn. Now, we have a flying lesson. Mac Alpin, how did we teach Edward again?" she asked as she turned back to regard the Ekimmu Cruitne.

"I remember." He watched Arwin and Máire nod to each other as the horses did earlier. They then wrapped a hand around each of his arms.

"Until we meet again, Patroclus. Do try to keep up," Máire goaded.

"Are you ready for this?" Arwin asked Julien with a smile. Without further preamble, they flew up into the sky. Julien felt his breath come out in short gasps.

"Now," Máire called out, and then they released him.

The first moment of the drop seemed to last forever. Julien began to plummet towards the ground. Wind rushed through his hair as he experienced the exhilaration of the fall, and his clothing billowed around him. As the ground rushed towards him, Julien assumed he would feel a growing fear, but he realized that he felt lighter than the air slashing at him. His descent began to slow. After a few moments, he discovered he could will himself to slow his descent and then stop completely. He spun around and found himself upside down. He then noticed a tree in the distance, and before he could contemplate traveling to the tree, Julien found himself touching its branches and leaves.

Arwin and Máire appeared at his side.

"I see you are finding flying to be an entertaining as well as a useful tool," Máire observed.

"It is truly wonderful," Julien acknowledged.

"Now, can you tell me where our Lamia companion is?" Máire asked.

"I can see the road," Julien stated, as he stared to the east. "There he is." Patroclus' figure moved with determined speed towards their shared target.

"He is very quick," Julien added.

"Well, let us see which of us can reach him first," Mac Alpin suggested.

"Will we be able to overtake him?" Julien inquired.

"Yes. Even though the Lamia are quick runners, we are more nimble, and we can fly. We do not have to deal with the terrain that they do." She then regarded Julien and asked, "Are you ready?"

"Three, two, one," Arwin counted off, "go."

The three of them took off towards Patroclus.

Patroclus could not help but feel some amount of envy. The blood-drinkers of the Celtic lines seemed to display such strong bonds of loyalty. Then again, he only knew a few, and those were to be respected.

He reflected on the lack of respect he felt for the current leaders of his own kind. Any show of respect for the other lines would be studied with great deliberation. Would he be able to trust any of these beings? Certainly, he could trust Marcus, perhaps even Claudius. Neither man could turn his back on Rome.

Máire had raged at Amata's treatment of him in Bath... a move that surprised him, but then Hibernians took the notion of hospitality to strange levels. Time would only tell as to the trustworthiness of Máire and the others.

Patroclus pushed himself to run faster as he smelled three immortals moving closer. Despite his assumption that it could be his associates, it could also be the Strigoi.

He turned to his right and noticed Máire and Mac Alpin running alongside. A split second later, he heard a sound of pain and a heavy thud.

Patroclus stopped and then chuckled at the sight before him. Julien had overshot a perfect landing and had flown into a tree. They walked over to look at the new blood-drinker's predicament.

Julien smiled up at them. "Did I win?"

"Not only did you not win, you managed to hit a tree," Máire teased her new son. "You need more practice landing."

"Agreed," Julien acknowledged. "Arwin, give me a hand." The Frank lifted an arm, and Mac Alpin pulled him to his feet. "Thank you. Can we try again?" he asked, looking rather like an eager child learning to walk.

"An excellent suggestion," Mac Alpin stated. "Legate, perhaps you would like to fly the rest of the way?"

"Only if you do not drop me," he warned.

"I promise nothing," Máire taunted as she winked at him. She then wrapped an arm around Patroclus, while Mac Alpin slid another arm about his back. Before Patroclus could take a calming breath to steady his nerves, he could feel the wind at his feet. He closed his eyes, reveling in the motion upward.

Julien opened the door and shooed away the exhausted servants. As he entered the hall, he heard the sound of a crackling fire in the hearth. His mother turned to face him and arose from her seat. She rushed over to him, and for a moment, she seemed older. His mother stared up at Julien and then tilted her head askew, much like a confused child.

"Something is different," she murmured.

"Yes," he answered as he regarded his traveling companions. "Could you please excuse us?"

"Lady Heloise," the three of them bowed their heads before turning and then walking towards the basement.

"What happened?" his mother asked, after they had left. She tugged him towards the hearth. "You are like ice."

"I almost died," Julien admitted.

"How?" she whispered.

"A Strigoi attacked me last night. Máire killed it, but not before he took over my mind. I started tearing at my eyes and throat. She had asked whether I wanted to live and said that she could help me, but it would change me forever." He stared into the flames in the hearth. "I told her that I wanted to live, and so she made me like her." Julien stared back into his mother's eyes.

"You are Deargh Du?"

"Yes. I passed the tests of Morrigan, though I cannot remember much of our discussion," he admitted.

He felt his mother's warm hands rest on his cheeks. She then turned him to look down at him. "Is this what you want, Julien?"

"Yes, mother, it is."

He found himself in her comforting embrace. "I am so very pleased for you. Oh, the things you will learn and see... the lives you will lead. I envy you, in so many ways. No wonder you seem so... tall."

"I am sure you could become Deargh Du," he said as he smiled down at her.

His mother laughed gently. "I am too old to live many centuries in this body. Besides, how would you feel having your mother leaning over your shoulder for eternity?"

"It is strange to consider that I will continue in this form for a long time."

"I am sure you will get used to it," she stated. "Have you fed?"

Julien raised a brow. "Truth be known, I am a little hungry."

She raised her wrist to his lips. "Then feed from me."

Though he felt awkward at the prospect of drinking blood from the very woman who gave him birth, Julien took her hand, with some reluctance, and bit into her wrist, taking a few sips. After he finished feeding, she smiled and closed her eyes a moment.

"Thank you," Julien said before he kissed her wrist. Though Máire had not yet taught him how to heal, he held his hand over his mother's wound and willed it to close. With some effort, the bleeding stopped, and new skin began to form. He stopped and then looked at his mother.

"You are my son, and I will help you in any way necessary," she answered softly.

"I almost forgot... the horses will arrive in a few hours. I will explain it later. Apparently, Deargh Du can make requests of animals. Tell the stable hands to give them some apples or treats, if you have time."

"Yes, yes... the sun rises soon. Go to sleep."

She nudged Julien towards the basement and said, "Sleep well."

"I will," he replied. He began to walk down the steps, wishing his bed waited for him. Perhaps he would move it into the basement tomorrow night.

Marcus stepped through the open gate and tromped towards the main house. His earlier good mood had faded. He had sent Claudius flying towards home and then to Ard Macha with a report and a letter for Sáerlaith.

As he approached the house, a strange scent drifted with the night breezes, and soon Marcus sensed Máire walk towards him.

"What did you do?" he accused her. He could already tell by her pensive glance that something had changed here… something drastic.

"Why am I to blame?"

He took her arm. "I smell you, and I smell someone that smells like you, but different. You did something." He stopped walking.

The front door opened and Julien leaned out. One sight of him answered all of Marcus' questions. He then met Máire's eyes.

"How could you do that?" Marcus asked, though he tried to keep his voice calm. "You thought it would be alright to force our lives as outcasts on another, who would be just as isolated as we have been?" He exhaled and tried to calm himself.

Máire's eyes lit in a moment of rage. "You and I have a family worth much more than most of those who call Ard Macha home!"

Marcus dropped her arm and shook his head. "I am sorry, Banbh Ceanúil. What happened?"

Máire's eyes became as calm as green grass in a gentle breeze, once again.

"I was on my way to find you," she admitted, speaking in Gaelic. "He followed me, after we… had spent some time together."

He muttered under his breath before adding, "I can guess why Julien followed you. If I could have headaches these nights, you would be the primary source of them, Maél Muire! What will we do with another one of us who the others will consider to be blight on Morrigan's name? If you have not forgotten, until this crisis with the Strigoi, we both were banished from Eire upon pain of death, unless mitigating circumstances warranted our trespass, which they did."

She looked saddened and distraught. "I… I have not forgotten. My aunt died in Bath away from Eire… Sitara died away from Eire… Berti's son with Sitara died…" Máire began to cry. "I have not forgotten."

Marcus knew she had many reasons against bringing another Deargh Du of their cursed line into existence, and yet, that is what she did.

"Please, tell me why you did it, Máire? Was it about me? Did you want to upset me?"

"I didn't do it to upset you."

"I know, I know," he murmured. "I know you better than that." Despite Marcus' fury, he knew he needed to keep Máire calm. She could be as volatile as one of Edward's concoctions, at times. "Just tell me what happened. Why did you do this?" He could sense Julien joining them.

"A Strigoi arrived and started to kill him," she explained. "I saved him the only way I could. When you had transformed me, you could not have said that you didn't wish to protect me, and last night, I had to protect him."

"Banbh Ceanúil, there is a difference between why I transformed you and why you transformed Julien." He met Máire's eyes.

Máire shrugged. "I don't see that much of a difference. I asked you for protection and to preserve my life, and he asked me for the same." She turned towards Julien. "Please wait for us inside," she instructed his grandson-in-darkness in Latin.

"Are you certain?" Julien stared at both of them.

"Yes," Marcus replied. He watched the youngling mull the request over for a moment. Then, Julien turned back towards the house and entered the building.

"He will be doomed to spend his nights with us and our friends. He will have very few Deargh Du allies," Marcus mumbled in Gaelic. "Julien and you don't love one another. Rather, he loves you, but you have feelings for no one." He half-growled his last sentence.

Máire sighed. "Do all Deargh Du experience romantic love with their children-in-darkness and their fathers- and mothers-in-darkness? Sáerlaith's children are all female, and yet she prefers the company of men. I know many other similar cases."

Marcus shrugged. "It's not simply romantic love, Máire. You have to love your children unconditionally, and with some, that can be… difficult."

He watched her lips purse.

"You are upset that I cannot return your feelings," she muttered, looking a little angry at his comments.

"Yes," he admitted. "That, and you cannot even offer feelings freely. He will need your love and support."

"Julien told me he wanted to survive, and Morrigan allowed him to return to this realm. Who are we to judge Her decision?" She shrugged. "I will support him if he needs me."

"Yes, he will need your support." Marcus felt as if he repeated himself. "Let's go inside. I need wine, mead… something."

He walked into the house and through the great hall towards the tables and hearth. Máire left his side to find refreshments, he presumed.

He then sat down and sensed Julien approach him.

"Are you upset at the turn of these events?" Julien asked in Latin.

Marcus sighed and stared into the fire, aware that Máire returned with bloodmead. She poured their drinks.

"I am... concerned," Marcus stated. "First, until the Strigoi presented themselves, neither Máire nor I could set foot upon Eire, or we would have been executed."

"Executed?" Julien asked, astonishment evident in his voice. "Why?"

Máire answered before Marcus could. "It was my fault... I accept all blame."

"For what?"

"On Sáerlaith's orders, Marcus and I secretly executed a few Deargh Du who had wished to return to our bigoted, isolationist ways. However, I failed to kill our last target, and she convinced the council to exile us from our home, from my only home."

"Isn't your exile over because of the Strigoi?" Julien asked.

Marcus jumped back into the conversation before Máire could speak. "I suspect we would not be welcomed back, and it remains to be seen whether the Deargh Du forces Claudius is mobilizing will even follow my orders."

Julien seemed worried by the admission. "Are you... are we... will we be in any danger when the Deargh Du arrive from Ard Macha?"

"The warriors of the Deargh Du, those who fought against the Lamia, anyway, seem to still respect Marcus. It is the druid class that seems to mistrust us, hate us. They are the ones who now control most of the larger council, save Sáerlaith and the Council of Five. Sáerlaith has had to make many sacrifices," Máire explained.

"As have we all," Marcus added.

Julien seemed somewhat placated by the news that at least the warriors would likely get along with the group. Still, the youngling needed to know more about why there existed a schism between factions amongst the Deargh Du.

"So, because I became Deargh Du through you, Máire, I would be ostracized?" asked Julien.

Máire leaned forward and answered, "Partly, but their strongest reason for mistrust or hostility towards you is the fact that you are Frankish."

"What does my lineage have to do with any of this?" Julien asked. His face grew dark.

Máire patted his arm. "Sit and drink, and we will explain things."

The youngling sat next to her and then finished his drink in one swift motion. Julien lowered the cup, and his face grew calm.

"The Deargh Du have long held mistrust of people from other nations," Máire began. Marcus watched her smooth Julien's hair in a calming gesture. "The Deargh Du especially mistrust those people of nations that have schemed in the domination of other, weaker countries, whether those people have an active role in that domination or not. The Deargh Du have been isolated for many centuries."

"Julien, I am a Roman, a hated enemy by many long-lived Deargh Du who have lived through Rome's rise and fall," Marcus added. "When I first arrived in Eire by accident, I massacred a village and many druid novices at a local grove." Julien's eyes opened in shock. Clearly, he had not anticipated that Marcus could have committed such brutality, but Marcus knew Loch Garmon only scratched the surface.

"Morrigan punished me by forcing me to become Deargh Du, which is usually a rare gift given only to a chosen few, as punishment. She wanted me to take my own life, but I survived. Over time, I earned Her forgiveness."

"Your transformation into a Deargh Du was your punishment? But how could such a beautiful gift be seen as punishment?" Julien inquired, though Marcus could still see unease behind his eyes.

"I did not know what I was, but I knew I had become something different. Food would not sustain me, and I had to figure out the hard way that I needed blood to survive. Worst of all, I could no longer feel the sun's embrace. Morrigan, in the guise of a raven, would taunt me day and night to end my life under the sun. I ignored her and survived in the grove on putrid snakes." Marcus felt himself shudder at the memory. "So, since I was not made aware of these gifts, I saw my transformation, at least originally, as punishment."

"In fact, after being granted my freedom, I did not meet another Deargh Du for almost six hundred years," Marcus added. "I still do not see too many of them. Only a few seem to enjoy my company. This isolation is not easy for me or for Máire. Even though she is Hibernian and was a most worthy candidate for transformation, she is my child-in-darkness, and for that, she is ridiculed and held in contempt. We have heard many refer to her as 'The Roman bastard's slut'." Marcus noticed a bemused smile on Máire's face. His earlier anger began to fade into mist.

"As if I would be any happier with those doddering fools, Marcus," she stated. She then stretched a hand across the table, and their fingers entwined. To Julien, she said, "I am very appreciative of the gifts I have received. I chose my position with Marcus. No one else would be my father-in-darkness."

"Julien, if we had had a choice, it may have been better for you if Claudius had called forth The Hunter or if Mac Alpin transformed you into an Ekimmu Cruitne. They are respected in their lines… well, for the most part, and they do not have to deal with the racism that Máire and I, and now you, must endure."

"I only had one choice, Marcus." The Frank's blue eyes settled on Máire.

"That choice was not to die. If that means being an outcast with you and Máire for eternity, then so be it. You two are doomed to my brutish company as well." He chuckled and then rose from the table.

Máire stood and took his arm. "They will doubt you are a Deargh Du," she stated.

"Morrigan confirmed it," he answered, appearing confused.

Marcus stood and walked over to their side of the table. "There is an important secret I must tell you. No one other than you, me, and Máire, and a few who know this truth, can know this." He leaned in to whisper in Julien's ear. "All of the Deargh Du stem from one son of Morrigan, save three, now. You see, I am the second brood of Morrigan."

"That means—" Julien began before being cut off.

"It means that Máire is second generation, and you are third," Marcus added, interrupting him. "Her Gifts are stronger at the trunk than the leaves. You, my grandson, are closer to the trunk of the Goddess than most Deargh Du who are currently alive. If the other Deargh Du discover that we have a closer link to Morrigan, they would probably hunt us down and kill us. So, we pretend to be lesser Deargh Du, although, sometimes, there is an occasional possession by Morrigan," he admitted. "That leads to events which are difficult to explain away."

Máire cleared her throat a bit. "The last time the Goddess possessed my limbs, I wiped out a small army of Lamia, and I came close to killing Mandubratius."

"Who is Mandubratius?" Julien asked.

Máire grinned for a moment. "You know him as 'Michael Tolomei'."

"Yes, I believe he wishes to bring forth a war between the pope and Emperor Charles," Marcus stated. "We are not quite sure why he wishes this, though it is probably one of his many games. He probably loves the chaos and finds it entertaining. Sooner or later, I think he'll realize that this game doesn't work well when Strigoi are involved. He cannot manipulate them like mortals." Marcus gave a bit of a shrug. "I spoke with Mandubratius last night. He led a thousand-man cavalry to prepare the way for the pope, who wishes to meet with the emperor, along with an army of ten thousand soldiers."

"I suppose he manipulated the Holy Father and told him that demons overwhelmed the villages in the empire and that war was the best option," Julien reasoned aloud.

Máire grinned. "You already understand the machinations of the Lamia well. Who can fathom why they do these things. Sometimes, I believe Mandubratius plays at these games because he would find eternity quite dull without these distractions to keep his mind occupied."

Marcus chuckled softly. "I know chroí. Goddess, protect us all when

Mandubratius finds a night without games. Who knows what he would do for entertainment then."

After a few moments of reflection, Marcus heard a knock at the door. Julien got up from his chair and then walked to the front door. Marcus followed behind him. After Julien opened the door, Marcus saw one of the garrison guards standing outside.

"My lord, a message arrived from Auxerre," said the guard as he handed a letter to Julien and then departed.

"This is from Philippe, the new garrison commander in Auxerre," Julien stated after skimming the note. "He says the pope's army passed them on the way to Aachen."

"Let us tell the others to prepare. Arwin and I will go to Aachen. Claudius is on his way to Briton in order to gather the Ekimmu Cruitne and Sugnwr Gwaed. Then, he will go to Eire to meet with Sáerlaith to rally more forces," Marcus said.

"But Aachen is important to me, personally," Julien pointed out. "I should go with you to see Emperor Charles," he stated after closing the door. The blood-drinkers walked into the main room with the large hearth. The others lingered in front of the fire. Amata, Lady Heloise, and Lirienne worked on repairing torn blankets.

"What about the emperor?" Lirienne asked.

"The papal forces are moving towards Aachen," Máire clarified. "Marcus and Arwin are going to tell the emperor." Mac Alpin headed for the basement to begin packing. Amata handed a blanket to Lady Heloise and followed him.

"And I am going with them," Julien added.

"You are in no shape to travel, Julien," Marcus countered.

"What do you mean? I feel fine," Julien argued.

"You have not been properly trained on using any of your new skills or gifts," Marcus explained. "You and Máire shall stay here. She will teach you what you need to know."

Julien sighed. "I suppose you are right. Please give Emperor Charles my apologies for not joining you and Arwin.

chapter fifteen

áire's left arm moved around Julien's back. She then gave him a twist of a smile.

"I have never done this before, so please try to be patient with me. I am attempting to remember my own training, but the memories have faded with the passage of time," she said as they walked towards the grove. A few candles burned brightly upon the altar.

"How can I not be patient with you?" Julien murmured. He hoped the excitement of learning new skills would surpass the building desire to meld with her again, though his longing waned as he smelled and then witnessed his mother and sister sitting in the grass.

"Please sit and contemplate the altar," Máire instructed as she walked him to the northern corner in front of the altar. She sat directly behind him, while his sister and mother stood at the opposite corners. He could hear them drop to their knees.

"You are becoming one with the surroundings and with the balance. The Gods and Goddesses connect us with nature and each other. We are all one, then... all part of the glorious cycle. Close your eyes and consider this cycle and the balance."

Julien did as ordered, trying to think of nothing. Unfortunately, this practice magnified every single sound in the immediate surroundings. However, after a few minutes had passed, Julien's thoughts seemed to clear for a few precious moments.

"Open your eyes and examine the altar," Máire whispered. "Study how the moonlight reflects off the stone. Now, close your eyes again and imagine a silken cloth of black blotting the light reflecting from the altar. Imagine a permanent, inky blackness surrounding the altar. Feel this curtain emanate from within."

He wondered whether anything had happened during Máire's moments of silence.

"Extend your own shadow over and around the altar," she added. "Now, open your eyes, Julien."

Julien opened his eyes and saw that blackness veiled the candles.

"I cannot see the altar... the night seems to have swallowed it," his mother commented.

"Well done, Julien." Máire's voice seemed to indicate that she smiled at him. "Can you feel the curtain of blackness?"

"Yes," he admitted, as the weighty presence seemed inescapable.

"Excellent. Now, draw it down around yourself," Máire requested.

Julien closed his eyes to silence his thoughts. He then sensed the black curtain start to move. Soon, the darkness enclosed him.

He could hear his sister and mother begin panic a little.

"Shhhh," Máire said. "Julien is still here with us. Now, blot out the entire grove."

He concentrated on spreading the darkness, and he felt all grow silent. The crickets and birds stopped their chattering, and even Lirienne and his mother remained silent.

"Very good," Máire praised. Her voice soothed his worries. "Now, let the darkness dissolve and melt away." He watched as the moonlight returned, the altar resumed glowing with bright candlelight, and the night creatures began to speak again.

"I am very impressed," Máire commended. "Drawing down the darkness is an easy skill, but for centuries, many of our kind have forgotten its usefulness. Do not neglect this skill, for it gives us a great advantage. Now, our next lesson is glamoury," she stated. "The eyes are said to be windows to the beauty within. The beauty of the soul is a thousand times brighter than the mere surface. We Deargh Du are blessed, in that we have the beauty of the fae, but there is also a strong inner beauty that we can project to mortals and immortals."

Máire paused for a moment and then continued her instruction. "Glamoury is this process, and it allows us to make mortals believe that an event within the confines of our reality is but a strange fantasy or dream. This can influence a decision or make someone forget their strongest beliefs. This lesson is harder than the last. Julien, go to the village and use the beauty inside to convince one of your vassals to join us."

She stood up and dusted herself off. "Ladies, let's go inside and work on those blankets. We will wait for you," she said to Julien. "Do not disappoint."

He watched Máire smile again. He could feel the force of her glamoury for a few moments, before she released him from the intoxicating sensation. Máire turned away and began to follow his mother and Lirienne inside their home.

"Two hours," Lirienne pouted with a sigh while turning over the hourglass. "My little brother has no consideration for those who are sleepy." She then yawned.

Máire inhaled and exhaled in a great sigh. "He is nearby, Lirienne." Lady Heloise poured them all another cup of wine. "In fact, he will arrive in a few minutes."

Within a few minutes, the door opened, and she watched Julien walk in with a young woman following behind him. A single glance at the girl revealed that Julien did not hold her in his thrall.

"Very good, Julien," she applauded. "Next time you do this, try using glamoury." She raised a brow at him.

"I think this lesson does not require our participation," Lady Heloise reasoned aloud before tugging on Lirienne's arm.

Julien gave an annoyed huff. "Whatever do you mean?"

"This young lady is somewhat convincing, but her eyes belie that she is not in a trance. In fact, her eyes follow me now," Máire stated. She looked over the women, a prostitute, she presumed, and asked, "Did he pay you?"

"Sorry, my lord," the prostitute apologized with a smile. "I am not the actress I hoped I could be." Then to Máire, she said, "Yes, my lady, he paid me."

"I will demonstrate this lesson now." Máire turned back to regard the young woman and smiled.

The prostitute inhaled an unsteady breath and then lowered her gaze.

Máire moved in closer and gently raised her chin. "I could never harm you, chroí." She felt the woman's fear fade. She then walked around the prostitute.

"Sing a song for us," Máire bade the young woman.

Without a moment of hesitation, a soft voice sang of beautiful, sun-filled days of love.

"This is a most important skill," Máire said. "You must learn this." She then waved a finger at Julien. "You may stop now," Máire instructed the prostitute. The young blonde then stopped singing.

"Are blood-drinkers susceptible to this talent?"

"Sometimes," she answered.

"What about other Deargh Du?" he queried.

"Some," Máire replied. "I would not suggest trying it. Many consider it rude. Now, try it with her again."

Máire backed away, releasing her control of the lovely prostitute. She watched Julien concentrate, and finally she felt a weak thrust of glamoury.

"Much improved." Máire then took a knife and handed it to him. "Now, scratch her, and if she does not react, you can learn how to harness your strength in healing."

His brief moment of concentration faded as he took the knife from her. The woman screamed.

Máire grasped at the strains of glamoury and caught the young woman's hands. "That was nothing more than a bad dream," she told her as she nudged Julien. "Julien, this requires concentration. Your life depends on this working if you have to feed. If you cannot heal her wound and convince her that this was nothing more than a strange fancy, she will report you."

"I understand," he said.

"No, I do not think you do. I have had to hunt down those before who chose not to hide through healings and glamoury. Can you handle this life?" Máire asked, while attempting to control her irritation.

"Yes, I can do this!" he said to her.

"Then do it," Máire answered. She released the control of mortal and watched him take over.

Julien spent some time making sure that the prostitute became lost in his glamoury. Máire watched him move in, closer. He could tell that he hungered. Julien tossed the knife aside and began to feed from the prostitute. After a few moments, he licked the wounds and then backed away.

"Now, you have a wound," she stated, wishing she could have more patience. Marcus never seemed to be short-tempered with her during the learning process. "Place your hand over the wound and watch the wound close in your mind."

She watched Julien focus, and the wound healed itself. He took a few steps back, allowing Máire to examine the wound. "I healed my mother earlier after feeding from her. This is an easy skill for me.

"Excellent," Máire said as she smiled at him. "Now, convince this woman that this experience was just a wild dream from an overactive imagination and that none of this ever happened."

Máire listened to Julien instruct the prostitute, but she could not understand much of his conversation, as the language of the Franks still confounded her. As he spoke, Máire could sense that the strength of his glamoury increased.

Julien stopped, and then his blue eyes settled back on Máire. "I should release her now."

"No. We should take her to the middle of the village," Máire countered. "It would make your words to her more convincing."

"Why am I here? Did my services not meet satisfaction, my lord?" the prostitute asked as she looked around the dark village. "Did I drink too much?"

"You did fine. Go home now and sleep well," Julien stated. The woman nodded and then began walking to town. Julien turned back to Máire and smiled. "It would seem that I was successful."

"Do not gloat just yet, Julien. Tomorrow night, I will check on her to see whether she remembers the encounter as reality or just a dream. Do you have any questions?"

"A few," he admitted. She felt his hand grasp hers, and then she met his eyes.

"If we are on a ship for many days, what do we do?" Julien asked.

"Unless we travel with a group that cannot fly, that hardly ever happens. However, when we travel with others who cannot fly, we feed off the rats, livestock, and sailors if our needs warrant it. Once, we all slept in the ocean. If you go deep enough, you can survive the sun. You would secure yourself to rocks with seaweed or ropes. The first time I did that, I was frightened, but the fear passes. I first felt like I was drowning, but then I realized that was silly as we do not need to breathe air to live. Then I experienced the chill and pressure of the deep, but I managed to overcome those sensations as well."

"What if we are in the country and need to sleep?" Julien asked.

"We can bring tents, or we can hide in caves or holes in the ground if there is nothing else to shield us from the sun." She felt his fingers trace over her hand gently. "Sometimes, when we travel with mortals, we can use wagons that have hidden compartments. Marcus has a few of those carts in Bath. I have even heard rumors of some blood-drinkers using bags to hide in during the day, though I prefer to have a tent handy."

"Which blood-drinkers are the best in battle?" he asked.

"I must admit a bias in that I believe my line to have excellent warriors," Máire answered. "Then again, we have some disadvantages. It is the individual person that can be successful or fail in battle. Some would say as a line, the Ekimmu Cruitne are the best warriors, though it depends on the battle conditions." She sighed and then felt a little annoyed. "The Lamia are quite skilled in battle, but they are confined in their patterns. There are exceptions, as much as I hate to admit it. For example, Mandubratius... I mean Michael Tolomei, is very strong." She sighed again, hating it when that deceiver entered her thoughts.

"I can sense the sun rises soon," Julien warned.

"Yes, we should go home," she acknowledged.

Aachen

Talia looked up from her meal to look over the emperor's informal quarters. These chambers appeared to be almost as lavish as the great hall. Earlier, before this private dinner, she had believed his tastes would be simple. Then again, someone else could have decorated these rooms.

Talia pushed the food around her plate as the emperor talked about an elephant that a Caliph had sent to him from Baghdad.

"I should take you to see Abul-Abbas, Talia, although I must warn you that he can be smelly. I do believe he takes after me, sometimes."

"How big is he?" she inquired. Talia could not deny that she had a strange desire to see this beast.

"He's the largest beast I've ever seen, and he is quite docile," the emperor replied. "He also eats more food than I believed possible. Part of me wonders whether the Caliph sent Abul as a joke to see if I could manage to keep him fed." He tore off a piece of bread and sopped up some meat.

"Speaking of food, aren't you hungry?" he asked.

Talia leaned towards him and smiled. She hoped he would notice her breasts pushing forward. "Charles, I have to keep my figure, or else I'll never find another husband."

"So you're still unwed," the emperor observed as he raised a brow and smirked.

Talia covered her mouth and giggled. "For the moment," she murmured, in what she hoped to be a seductive manner.

"What a coincidence, so am I." The emperor rested his chin against his right hand. A few magnificent rings sparkled in the lamp light.

"Really? Are you not married?" Talia tilted her head a little, allowing herself to look concerned. "How is that?"

"Honestly, I've had four wives. Luitgard died last year." His countenance became somber. "She died of a wasting illness. However, I must admit I still love Hildegard the most of out all of my wives," he explained. The memory seemed to bring a whimsical smile to his face.

"I had no idea you had so many wives," Talia whispered. "Have you considered marrying a fifth?" She leaned further forward and began to unfold his mind. The emperor's eyes gleamed, revealing his interest. Then a throat cleared, interrupting her manipulation. Charles pulled away.

"Imperial Majesty, a visitor awaits you in the great hall," Ercanbald informed him.

"Hmmmm?" The emperor still smiled at Talia.

"A visitor awaits you in the great hall," Ercanbald repeated.

Talia tried to reign in her fury. Why did she wait so long to seduce him? She lowered her eyes, pretending to ignore the discussion.

"Who is it and what do they want?"

"It's Marcus of Bath, Imperial Majesty."

"Just him?"

"Yes Imperial Majesty."

Talia kept her eyes on her food as she considered the name 'Marcus of Bath'. She knew Marcus and his band operated out of Bath and that the

Deargh Du and the other Celtic lines wandered about the Empire looking for the Strigoi. Could this 'Marcus of Bath' be the same Marcus? She shuddered at the thought of that, yet she did have an urge to look at him, to see whether it was Marcus, the Roman Deargh Du, and see whether he appeared as beautiful as she remembered. Marcus did have the eyes of an angel... a very warlike one, at the very least.

"Oh, very well, Ercanbald." The emperor stood and looked down at her. She risked looking up into his blue eyes.

"I'll be right back, Talia. This should only take a minute. Let my servants know if you need anything." He patted her hand and walked out of the room. The wooden door closed behind him.

Talia stood up and followed the sound of the emperor's heartbeat through the hall. She could sense the presence of another blood-drinker, but then she realized that he could sense her as well. Still, she may as well spy on their conversation.

Talia peeked out from around a column and observed the back of Marcus' head. Not much had changed. He still had the bearing of a soldier of the Roman Republic and the beauty of the fae. She then saw the emperor greet his guest.

"Imperial Majesty, I have just arrived from Saulieu," Marcus began. "During my travels back to Vézelay to meet with the inspector general, I witnessed the papal emissary leading a cavalry force of one thousand soldiers towards Aachen."

The emperor began to pace the hall and rub his chin. "How is it that my scouts have not said anything about this papal army marching towards Aachen?" he asked while turning towards Marcus.

"Imperial Majesty," Marcus inquired, "have you received any reports between here and Rome?"

The emperor motioned towards Ercanbald, who walked up to the emperor. "Have we received any reports in the last few days regarding Rome?"

The secretary shook his head. "None. It is most unusual," he noted.

"Perhaps your scouts have been captured and possibly killed, Imperial Majesty," Marcus added.

The emperor's ears began to turn red. He turned away from Ercanbald and Marcus. His face appeared to be twisted into rage.

The emperor seemed to take a moment to calm himself, and his face grew more placid. He then turned back to his guest and subordinate. "Roust the garrison," he ordered. "Send out messengers to all the corners of the Empire and inform them that they are to return to Aachen. Tell Charles and the rest of my sons to join us here."

The emperor became silent for a moment before asking, "Where is the inspector general?"

"He is ill, Imperial Majesty. Lady Heloise insisted on taking care of him."

Talia noticed a smile light the emperor's face for a brief moment.

"Am I to assume that you will return to Vézelay, Marcus, and start the hunt again against these murderers plaguing this empire?" Emperor Charles asked.

"Yes, Imperial Majesty." Talia noticed the Deargh Du lower his head in a bow.

"Excellent. Then, can you and your associates escort a few of my scouts to confirm these sightings of the papal army?"

"Of course," Marcus answered.

"Then you, your associates, and my scouts will set forth tomorrow night." The emperor then faced his secretary. "Ercanbald, please make those arrangements." Then to Marcus he asked, "Tell me, how is the inspector general handling his new duties? I do also hope Lady Heloise is well."

Talia turned away and returned to the dining room, as their conversation would likely yield no more delicious fruit. She sat down at the table, wondering whether Charles would return to her. Soon, however, she could hear and smell him as he neared the room.

The door opened and then closed. She looked up and smiled, though the emperor's features remained tinged with scarlet.

"I'm sorry, Talia," he began, "but I'm going to have to cut our dinner short."

Talia stood up again. "I understand, Imperial Majesty." She tugged at the ties for her dress, and it fell to the floor.

"Perhaps you don't have to leave so quickly," she murmured. Perhaps sex would prove the most useful tool in manipulating this Frank.

As he stared at her, his earlier rage diminished, and he seemed somewhat stunned. His surprise produced a ready smile. "Perhaps my departure can be delayed for few minutes."

She strode towards Charles, embraced him, and began to undress him. "We may need a full hour," Talia murmured.

Regensburg

"They will arrive soon," she assured them.

The Strigoi stared up at her as Seosaimhín paced the grove. The sacred symbols on the trees bound them as a sacred family. The fire in the center glowed, and tiny fire fairies drifted in and out of their realm.

"The Soulless Ones and their friends will soon arrive in greater numbers, yet we have winged Lord Nagirrom to aid us during these times." Seosaimhín walked around the fire, finding pleasure in the warmth. She then tossed sacred herbs into the fire, and the fragrant smoke intensified.

"Nagirrom calls for you all," she intoned. "You can all call to Him as well. Let's call for Him now." The sound of flapping wings excited her.

"Time to grow and increase our strength by numbers. Time for your brains to expand," Seosaimhín cried out with a chuckle. Her work on the Strigoi had already yielded some success. Their intelligence increased, though the process took time. The newly turned Strigoi, created from those others who have benefited from Seosaimhín's new techniques, revealed an incredible acumen. Perhaps they could wield new talents and skills sooner than anticipated. Her army would be massive soon, and all would die in Nagirrom's name.

Outside Saulieu

Mandubratius sat down to read through Talia's missive. She rambled about Marcus and a group of his associates tattling on him to the emperor. She then moved on to bragging about the latest gifts the former Frankish king had bestowed upon her. They had slept together a scant week ago, and already, according to Talia, he seemed to defer to her in all matters.

"I'll believe that when I see it for myself, Talia," Mandubratius mumbled to himself. Talia tended to exaggerate her influence over mortals. Mandubratius folded up the letter and fanned himself for a moment. The nights had grown shorter and warmer.

"Sir."

Mandubratius waved away the salute from the soldier, who had just entered his tent. "What is it?" He had expected this, though Mandubratius had not been able to concentrate on this game of late.

"The pope has arrived, but the emperor's men have intercepted him and are speaking to him."

Mandubratius nodded. "I think I will go meet them as well."

He rose from his seat and left his tent, ignoring the offers of a horse. He walked away from camp and the ceaseless drills of his cavalry. As he strode into the night, Mandubratius considered his growing regret of this rather large force of young Lamia. He and the elder Lamia found it hard to control them. Drastic measures might be needed to maintain order.

When he found himself out of the sight of the camp, Mandubratius ran to the south. Miles passed as the stars lit a green path through the trees. The smell of mortal blood and sound of their heartbeats grew as he neared the meeting place.

He scanned the skies for blood-drinkers. Marcus and his associates probably hid or had delivered a message to the emperor and allowed him to handle this on his own.

Mandubratius neared the small camp and turned an ear to the men on horses. He watched the emperor and the pope dismiss their staff and then walk to the sheltering arms of a tree. A series of torches burned.

Mandubratius leaned in closer to see them and then narrowed his eyes. Both men appeared solemn. The torchlight in the distance made their faces strange and monstrous.

He pushed aside those odd thoughts and concentrated on their conversation.

He heard a sigh from the Holy Father. "Our church has suffered many losses, my son," the High Priest began.

Emperor Charles' face tightened. He quelled what seemed to be a growing rage. "Holy Father, the Church, and Her henchmen have massacred the families of victims. There is no proof that a demon walks the earth, killing priests and our people." The emperor turned towards the pope. "My soldiers, gendarme, and some mercenaries have managed to kill forty of these murderers. These are very human murderers. You've been played for a fool, Leo. One of the mercenaries told me today that you have sent a snake towards Aachen. He found their nest, and my scouts verified their position. We have managed to avoid them through these mercenaries' help."

The emperor's gaze wandered to the trees again. "They informed me that this person is your emissary, Tolomei."

"Now you are trying to provoke an attack. I just want to protect my flock," the pope challenged.

"Your flock needs you for spiritual guidance," replied the emperor, as he regarded the pope once again. "My soldiers, my family, and I can protect the people of this empire that you gave me."

"I see little, if any, protection," Leo hissed. "I am going to place a papal garrison at every cathedral for protection, and I will leave a sizable contingent in Aachen."

"Very well," Emperor Charles stated as he turned away again. "Then I shall increase the garrison in each of those villages to protect your protectors. After all, we are the only ones who have killed these murderers. We have demonstrated our mettle."

The pope inhaled and appeared to dispel his ire. He then lowered his gaze to the ground for a moment.

"I have been informed that my cavalry has encountered a few of these demons, or murderers, as you call them."

"I rode by your cavalry. I heard that they number almost nine hundred, though half of them do not have horses. This cavalry of yours suffered greatly at the hands of the enemy, did it not?"

The emperor turned back towards the pope. "I hear these murderers are hard to kill, Leo. Let the warriors in your flock deal with this menace. The next time you come to Aachen, you are welcome to stay in my palace."

The Holy Father gave the emperor a smug smile. "If you ever desire to return to Rome, you are certainly welcome to stay at the Lateran Palace."

"Very well, then." Emperor Charles motioned to his soldiers. "Pray for me when you return to Rome."

Pope Leo said nothing.

The party of Franks left, heading in the direction of Aachen.

Mandubratius then approached Leo as the emperor and his guards disappeared over the horizon.

"I will take you to our camp, Holy Father. The emperor has lost all of his humility, has he not?" He kneeled and then kissed the extended ring.

"Indeed," the pope murmured. "Stand up, old friend. Let's go to this camp. I need to pray for guidance."

Vézelay

"Lady Heloise, wake up please," Alais pleaded as she patted her lady's shoulder.

Heloise grumbled. Julien was right about sleeping odd hours. As soon as she found the pleasant escape of sleep, Alais had arrived and persisted with waking her.

"Yes, what is it?" Heloise tried to keep her voice pleasant. However, the sound of people talking brought her further from sleep. Heloise, now alert, sat up in bed.

Alais grabbed her robe and handed it to her. Her servant seemed quite nervous and ill at ease. Her youthful features appeared hardened. "It's your son, my lady," the younger woman said.

"Julien? At this hour?" Heloise considered going back to sleep, but then why would he send Alais to wake her? "What does he need?"

"Pardon me, my lady, but it is your first born, Reginald, who has requested your presence. He has brought many people with him," explained Alais in a clipped tone. "He was most–"

"He was demanding," Heloise supplied.

Alais nodded her head.

"That is Reginald," Heloise surmised aloud with a sigh. "He decided that he was the man of the house after his father had died. Please, tell him I will meet him in the great hall."

Alais nodded her head and then left the room.

Heloise got out of bed and started to rummage through her clean dresses. She started to quickly dress. A few moments later, she patted down her hair, but she decided that she had no time to don a veil.

Loud and angry stomps echoed through the rooms, and then her eldest flung her door open.

"There is not time to wait for decency, mother!" Reginald yelled. His voice echoed in the room as he walked in, though despite his manner, he blushed as she finished dressing.

Heloise sighed and met his eyes. Reginald favored his father a great deal, with his light brown hair and dark eyes. Once, he had been considered the most handsome of her boys, but Julien, as a Deargh Du stunned her with his beauty.

"Oh, come now, Reginald... you were never embarrassed when I fed you as a baby." She sat down to pull on her shoes. "From your reaction, one would think that you were Oedipus himself facing Jocasta."

"Who on earth is Oedipus? We do not have time for these stories, mother." Reginald yanked her hand and started to pull her out of the room.

"Alright, what is so urgent, and why are all those people outside yelling? Why are you not in Divio?" Heloise asked, taking odd steps because of her missing shoe.

"We were attacked," Reginald said.

Heloise felt her body chill.

"The Str... the demons that I have heard about?"

"No, mother, the papal army," Reginald answered. He stopped tugging her along and turned to face her. He always had been rather demanding.

"The pope? What is he doing in Divio?" Heloise asked.

"The pope was not there himself," Reginald answered. "He sent an army to carry out his orders."

"What are these orders?" Heloise bit her lip.

"The orders to cleanse those who are related to the victims of the demons," Reginald hissed, as fury flamed his eyes.

"Cleanse? How?" Heloise demanded.

"As in execution, mother. I managed to–"

Heloise held up her hand. "Before you continue, I need to retrieve your brother and his friends."

"Julien is here... with his friends? What friends? I was not aware he had any."

"Yes," Heloise confirmed as she motioned Alais, who stood nearby, over. "Please wake Julien and his associates. Tell them that Reginald and I will join them shortly."

Alais nodded and then scurried down the stairs.

"I will meet with you directly, after I get my other shoe," Heloise stated as she nodded to Reginald.

"Mother, why are you and these people sleeping during the day?" Reginald asked.

Heloise tried to think of an appropriate answer as she hopped back to her room, but she took too long for her impatient first born.

"This is not related to the spells you conduct at night, is it?" Reginald demanded. "Are these so called friends fellow witches?"

Heloise stopped and turned back towards him. "Reginald, I know not of what you speak."

"Mother, please do not play the simpleton. I know about your circle of women, and I have done my best to keep others from discussing it. If I had not learned about it, others may have turned against you and your friends and informed the church." He took her arm. "You could have been excommunicated or worse."

"My son, you take great risks on my behalf," Heloise replied in an attempt to quell his high spirits and placate him, at least until she could put on her other shoe.

"Indeed, and I have been passed over for promotions in the emperor's army because of the whispers I could not silence," Reginald added. "Aldabert and I both worked to hide proof of these matters."

To her reckoning, Aldabert had never seemed all that bothered with her eccentricities. "I am truly sorry," Heloise offered.

She watched her son suddenly swipe at his eyes.

"It does not matter now. Divio, which I have sworn to protect, is in the in the hands of the enemy. I have lost my wife and my two sons. Our people need food and water."

Heloise, stunned by this grave news, gave in to her tears and cried into her hands. She then reached out to embrace Reginald.

How could little Jakelin, Ledger, and the beautiful Flor be gone?

Reginald held up his hands and avoided the attempted embrace. "I am not ready to grieve yet. Work must be done."

At that moment, Alais raced to the foot of the staircase. "My lady," she called, "your son and his friends await you."

"Thank you." Heloise wiped her eyes and tried to stop crying. "Come," she bade, as Heloise took Reginald's arm and lead him downstairs toward the cellar.

"Why are we going to the basement?" Reginald asked. Heloise heard a suspicious tone in his voice. Her eldest son then moved ahead of her. Heloise glanced down to the entrance to the basement and noticed the blood-drinkers standing in their traveling garb.

"Brother," Julien began. "It is very good to see you again."

"Why is everyone here in the cellar?" Reginald asked, repeating his question. "Have you joined in our mother's heretical practices of witchcraft?"

"These are not witches," Julien responded heatedly, "nor am I. We have been charged by the emperor to seek out and destroy the murderous bands of killers stalking the empire. Whatever gave you the crazy notion that we were witches?"

Heloise sighed. Julien and Reginald never got along, even before Flor and Reginald married. The two of them would snip at each other like wary wolves. Aldabert had managed to get them to stop arguing. However, when their brother died, their disagreements grew louder. She hoped Julien would not give too much away when he discovered that his first love had died.

"You and your friends are just now waking!" Reginald yelled back. "You sleep here in the basement, not in a proper room. I know about our mother's secret society of witches."

"We have been tracking these bands of killers for days," Julien replied. "They only attack at night, so in order to face them without dropping dead of exhaustion, we have begun to sleep during the day. Have you ever noticed how bright this house is during the day? Have you ever tried sleeping during the day?"

"No," Reginald admitted grudgingly. "I imagine I would not be able to sleep. What about mother's coven?"

Heloise sighed. Reginald would never be able to understand. "I am not a witch, Reginald. We are witnesses of the Divine Mother. We gather in a holy circle to sing our praises upwards to the mother in order to give to her son."

"But I hear you and these women do this naked!" Reginald challenged. He looked horrified.

"The removal of our clothing lays us bare to the Holy Mother's love. It is a symbolic expression of our oneness with one another," Heloise rationalized aloud.

"I see," Reginald murmured, though he still managed to look suspicious. "Then these guests are not witches."

"That is correct," Julien replied.

"Then who are they?" Reginald looked over the blood-drinkers as if he were still suspicious.

"They are comrades in arms," Julien explained. "We all met in Aachen. This is Edward, Patroclus, Amata, and Máire. Three others in our party are going to Aachen and Briton. As I said earlier, we are on a mission for Emperor

Charles."

"Perhaps now you should turn your attention to the papal army invading our lands," Reginald grumbled. "Who are these murderers?"

"Men, not demons," Julien answered. "They don fearsome masks of Satan's image to strike fear in the hearts of Christians."

"How do you know of this?" Reginald asked. "Do you have any prisoners?"

"We have encountered these murderers in Briton," Máire answered. "We interrogated them there, but none lasted long after questioning. Soon after, they all commit suicide."

Heloise watched Reginald stare at Máire for a moment before returning attention to Julien.

"So, you have not captured any in the empire?" he asked Julien.

"We killed forty," Amata answered, "but we have not captured any."

"You see, they are most vicious during our forays against them. They force our hand in their deaths," Máire added.

Reginald sighed. "I am not speaking to these women. Julien, are you a man, or do they have your tongue?"

Heloise watched Julien's eyes glow in fury. "These women, you so easily dismiss, are warriors and leaders in their own lands."

"Women warriors?" Reginald laughed. "Women leaders?"

Máire drew her blade. Reginald stopped laughing as his eyes gazed upon the steel tip at his throat. Reginald then finally looked at Máire.

"Hmmm... now, can women wield swords?" Máire hissed.

"And you two are leaders as well as warriors?" Reginald asked.

Heloise wandered down towards Julien and took his arm.

Máire pulled away her sword and sheathed it. "I am chieftain of my clan in Eire. That is a position of leadership, one that is earned by deeds and by reputation and not birth," Máire answered. "Lady Amata is the matriarch of a family of thousands."

Reginald turned to address the Legate and Edward. "And who are you two?"

"I am–" Patroclus began.

"He is one of my advisors," Amata interjected.

"And you?" Reginald asked as he stared at Edward.

"I am the village fool of Bath," Edward replied. "I am kept about as comic relief from the stresses of battle. It is a very high distinction in our clan."

Heloise watched as Patroclus and Julien chuckle a little and Máire smiled. She vaguely remembered something in legends from the lands to the north that fools were considered very wise.

Reginald looked Edward up and down. "Yes, he does indeed look like a fool to me."

"Edward does a wonderful impression of Emperor Charles," Máire said with a smirk.

Heloise watched her elder son frown.

"Another time, perhaps, chieftain." Reginald stared at Julien for a moment. "Flor is dead," he murmured. "And so are Jakelin and Ledger. Only Clotilda and I survived the attack from the papal army."

Julien's eyes became downcast and sorrowful for a second, but then he seemed to allowed sympathy to mask his features. Heloise prayed that Reginald would not see Julien's earlier emotions. Julien and Flor loved each other, but they could never be together. Flor's father would not have considered such a match to a third-born son.

"I am very sorry for your loss," Julien said.

"Thank you. Are there more in your band?" Reginald asked Julien. "These few warriors seem to be too small of a number to affect any real defense."

Heloise closed her eyes for a moment in grateful relief.

"Yes, but they are in Aachen now, and Claudius is going to Briton to bring forth more warriors who can deal with these murderers," Julien replied.

"I hope for their sakes that they avoid the papal army," Reginald scoffed. "So, His Holiness lies about what this enemy truly is. Either way, we have little time for these pointless pleasantries and your fool's inane jokes. I need your assistance outside with these vassals, Julien. They are whining about food and water, and most cannot even lift a sword. If they had risen and followed my orders, we could have convinced the army to retreat... but no, they ran like rabbits."

"There is an old Roman saying that a mob is no more an army than a pile of building materials is a house," Patroclus offered.

"What?" Reginald turned towards the Legate and marched over to him, attempting to look imposing and frightening. "I am having a private conversation with my brother! You have no right to listen or interject."

Patroclus' posture changed. "Sir," he said. "I have been a military officer for too many years to have to put up with this attitude of yours. Are you challenging me to a contest?" Heloise saw that the Legate's jaw was set in a thin line. The Legate's eyes seemed to radiate fire.

Reginald waved him off as if impatient with the conversation. "I have too many concerns to deal with this." He then crossed his arms over his chest and stared at Julien.

Julien gave Reginald the same obstinate stare that Heloise always witnessed when the two of them started a disagreement.

"So, will you help me outside, little brother?" Reginald asked in a manner that revealed it was not a true request but an order.

"No, I will not," Julien answered.

"You defy me? I am the oldest brother. You must do what I say," Reginald demanded.

"I am under orders from the emperor himself to follow the ways of these murdering bands of evil-doers, and that means we sleep during the day and come out after sunset. It is only by this methodology that we have killed as many of these murderers that we have!" Julien yelled back.

"That is the worst excuse I have heard from you!" Reginald thundered back. Reginald then grabbed Julien's shoulder, and Heloise watched him prepare to throw a punch.

"Papa? Papa?" Clotilda ran down the steps with the exuberance of a typical five year old.

Reginald scooped up his daughter before pointing a finger at Julien. "I shall deal with you yet," he promised.

"Papa, was that Uncle Julien? I want to see him," Tildy demanded.

"No, that was someone else," Reginald replied, before the door slammed shut.

"We have a few more hours until sunrise," Amata commented. "Perhaps we should use this time wisely and get some sleep. Lady Heloise, you look very tired. Why do you not remain here with us?"

Heloise shook her head. "I need to get dressed and help look after my son's vassals. Sleep well."

She noticed Máire sitting on Julien's bed and patting the other side, waiting for him to join her. Hopefully, Máire would offer Julien some compassion, comfort, and sympathy.

As Heloise walked upstairs, she could hear strains of their conversation.

"It is good that rudeness does not run deep in your family," Edward stated.

"My elder brother is horrible," she heard Julien say. "Sometimes, I think he and I are not related at all."

Heloise covered her mouth and walked outside to hear her eldest son send Alais' father, Allowin, with a message to the garrison.

chapter sixteen

fter Reginald had paced about in front of one of the tables, he looked out the window and noticed one of the garrison guards moving up the path to the house. Reginald stormed out of the house and confronted the man.

"Stop dawdling… do you know what force is coming to bear down on us all?" Reginald demanded, incredulous. "Where is Dreu?"

"My apologies, my lord," the soldier greeted. "I managed to escape the garrison through the secret passage, though our commander could not escape. I am Remi, the second in command. The papal army has us surrounded."

Reginald grumbled under his breath, trying to ignore his mother and sister as they handed out clothing to the dirty and threadbare vassals. He then heard the cellar door open and close. His younger brother and his friends soon joined him.

"Finally," he groaned, "Julien and his friends have come out to play." He watched as the red-haired woman came up to the soldier.

Why does that woman not cover her hair? It is blasphemous.

"Remi, please provide us with a report," she requested.

She says 'please' as if she made a request and not an order… What kind of leader can she be?

Reginald watched Remi blush a little as he turned to face her. "Yes, my lady," Remi acknowledged.

Reginald took an unsteady breath. "You take orders from her too?" His tone made the soldier stand at attention.

"Please ignore him, Remi. What is your report?" one of the men in Julien's company stated… not the pretty blonde fool, but the other blonde one.

Reginald started to pace again, remembering the blade at his throat from before and the woman's deadly glare.

"Five hundred men claiming to serve the pope are on a mission to cleanse evil from the land. They are demanding the surrender of the garrison and control of the town," Remi stated.

"How many men are under Dreu's command?" the soldier asked. Reginald could not bother with the names of underlings, especially Julien's underlings.

"We have but fifty," Remi answered.

"How much time do we have to comply?" Reginald heard his brother ask.

"Two hours," said Remi before lowering his head.

"How did you get out of the garrison?" the other woman asked.

"We have a secret entrance. We have used it before as an escape tunnel. I was able to escape, but I was lucky, my lady," Remi replied.

"We need to evacuate the garrison and the village," the red-haired woman muttered.

"Impossible," Reginald argued. "We tried that very tactic in Divio, and most of my vassals, as well as my wife and my two sons, were cut down."

She cleared her throat and met his eyes. "Calm yourself, my lord. Hysterics will not assist us in surviving this night. You can grieve for your family and your people after tonight." She turned and looked over to Julien. "Let us consider what needs to be done. We must kill the guards at the hidden entrance, and then release Dreu and the rest of the guards. Then, Reginald should lead his people into the forest. Edward will create a grand diversion, one that doesn't involve setting houses afire, and we will escape with Dreu and the rest of the garrison into the forest."

"Absolutely not," Reginald stated. "Julien will lead our people out of Vézelay. I am the soldier... I will deal with the papal army." He stared down at the woman. "Stop telling me my place. Remi will aid Julien in leading our people out of Vézelay. I will lead this party of guards against the remaining army."

Máire shrugged. "As you wish."

Máire looked over at Patroclus and Edward. Julien and Amata left with Julien's mother and sister, leading the villagers of Vézelay and Divio to the forest to escape. She had no idea what Reginald had planned. She and the others decided to leave him to his own devices with the few soldiers that remained from Divio.

"We can go kill them outright," Patroclus began. "That will allow the garrison to escape."

Máire shook her head. "No, I don't want to kill them if we don't need too."

"But they've been killing villagers indiscriminately," Patroclus challenged.

"I do not wish to add to the death and misery this situation has caused," she argued. "Besides, I think we can render them insensate without needlessly killing them. You know how to manipulate them, right?" she inquired as she met Patroclus' eyes.

"Of course, but how will we carry out this attack?" Patroclus asked.

"It's simple," she began. "Edward, here, will mount a distraction. I will fly in through the top of the fortress. When the time is right, Patroclus, you will render the remaining soldiers unconscious without too much damage."

"Again, how am I to do that?"

"You're the soldier, figure it out," she answered with a shrug.

"Máire, my skills are in killing an enemy, not knocking him out." She looked at him and reflected a moment of glamoury to him.

Patroclus sighed and then swiped at his hair. "I will try my best."

"What kind of distraction would you like?" Edward asked.

Máire realized that this would probably be a big mistake, since Edward loved setting off his incendiary devices. However, they did need a large distraction.

"The details do not matter... just make it noisy enough to cause mass chaos and draw the army away from the garrison," she answered.

Edward smiled, revealing his teeth. "I believe I can manage that."

"Good." Máire heard herself squeak a little. "How much time do you need?"

"Were I mortal, I would need an hour, but given my current capabilities, I would say I require ten minutes to deploy the necessary devices and detonate them," Edward advised.

"Excellent!" She attempted to rid herself of all of her worries. She then turned her attention back to the Legate.

"In eleven minutes, you will see me open the door, Patroclus. The moment I open the door, I expect the path to be clear."

"Understood," he replied.

"Very good. The hourglass turns... now."

She flew towards the top of the fort. She could see Edward racing around to the south of the fort and begin setting out his devices. Patroclus moved in closer toward the two guards standing at the hidden entrance. Máire cloaked herself in darkness and began to consider how best to convince the garrison to leave the fort in the time allotted.

Dreu tried to calm down and keep his anger from rising. He still could not believe that papal soldiers had surrounded his garrison and were holding the village and the noble family as prisoner.

Why would the Church do such a thing?

Dreu forced himself to stop thinking about the motives of the Church. He had deployed his men along the perimeter of the walls. They could hold out for a little while, unless the papal forces decided to burn them out. It would be easy for them to let a flaming arrow set the entire fort ablaze.

After pacing along one of the walls for a few minutes, Dreu called over a young soldier and asked, "Has Remi signaled from the house yet?"

"No sir, no signal," the soldier replied. He then asked, "Sir? What should we do when the papal army attacks?"

Dreu stared at him. He and Remi would need to train this one further, if they lived beyond this night.

"We shall defend ourselves," Dreu replied. "Dismissed."

The soldier nodded and then returned to his post.

Dreu's stomach growled. Their interrupted and abandoned dinner would probably be cold by now. He considered ordering the men to find rations of bread and wine, when a woman stepped from the darkness, as if she wore shadow. Dreu almost shrieked. He swallowed his fear and surprise as the form became familiar.

"Máire? How did you...? What are you doing here?" he stammered.

"I snuck in here from the outside," she answered, as if such a thing would be normal and obvious. "I'm here to help you all escape," she added.

"Escape to where? We are surrounded," he stated, forgetting she probably already knew that fact.

"That will be remedied soon enough," she explained. "I'm sure you have many questions, but I need you to gather your men near the secret entrance as quickly as possible. Keep them silent."

"And then–"

"...and then the very earth will shake, and most of those men surrounding you will run off. The few who remain by the secret entrance will become incapacitated. We will all leave, then, and you will help guide the villagers to safety," she answered, before looking around. "It is a good thing that there are no torches lit. The papal army will not see your men leave their posts. Make sure they do it quietly."

"But how... ?" he began to ask.

"You have less than six minutes. Hurry."

Máire seemed to ooze back into the shadows.

Dreu felt an impulse to reach out for her, but her warning made him rush towards the perimeter.

Patroclus wondered how he would manage not to kill mortals. Thousands of options, better than this plan, came to mind. They could easily fight off the army. After all, the army would not have given them any such consideration. Why should he obey Máire's request?

As if in answer to his concerns, Patroclus feared if he killed the guards, then she would not forgive him, but why would that even bother him?

Crazy Deargh Du.

He could respect them in some ways, such as Marcus, whose battle plans made sense. Máire's battle plans, however, made little sense.

He looked over at the two soldiers guarding the secret entrance and considered how to make them unconscious. He decided that he could manipulate them into hitting each other over the head, and that would make them both unconscious. He then waited for the right moment.

Loud waves of explosion and wind interrupted his concentration. Multiple blasts flashed from the south, and flames rose into the air as structures and trees began to burn.

Edward and his firepots.

At this point, he only had about thirty seconds to take out the guards. He watched the majority of the soldiers run towards the south, as the officers barked orders at the lower ranks. The two soldiers guarding the back entrance remained.

Patroclus pulled away from his hiding place and started to walk towards them. He aimed his gaze at them. As soon as they looked at him, they became trapped within his influence. Then, in the middle of the mind-bending, he realized another soldier raced towards them wielding a drawn sword.

"Who are you and what are you doing here?" the soldier demanded.

The surprise shocked Patroclus, and his manipulation wavered. Now freed, the other two soldiers drew their blades.

Patroclus smiled at the third soldier… he had no other choice. "It appears that I am to be your doom." He drew his sword and sliced the throat of third soldier. He then focused on the first two again.

"Stop!" he shouted. The soldiers stopped moving, but they looked confused. "Drop your swords," Patroclus ordered.

The one to his left complied, while the other resisted his request.

"I have no time for this," he hissed. Patroclus stepped towards them and quickly slammed the pommel of his sword into face of soldier to right. At the same time, he slammed his left fist into soldier to his left. They both fell to the ground.

At that moment, the secret entrance opened, and Máire poked her head out.

"Patroclus?"

"It's clear."

"Get your men moving towards the forest," she yelled down the passage. "Edward?" Máire asked as she looked about.

Edward ran towards them. "I'm here."

"Nice distraction. Please escort these men to the tree line."

Edward nodded and then motioned for the garrison to follow him.

Máire walked over to Patroclus. She seemed to notice the two unconscious guards as well as the third one. Patroclus watched her eyes trace the long trail of blood exiting the dead soldier's wound. He then witnessed a boiling anger grow in Máire.

"I thought I told you not to kill any mortals," she uttered, though with much silence.

"This one broke my concentration. I had to defend myself," he answered in a low voice.

"You could have rendered him unconscious without killing him," she stated.

"You weren't here."

Her face turned dark for a moment, but then she seemed to realize that the papal forces might hear her. "We will speak of this later. Let's go." she said.

And so, we shall.

As they raced into woods, he wondered when she would begin to nag him about the death of this pitiful soldier.

"Am I the only one who–"

A series of explosions broke Reginald's train of thought, as the earth shook beneath him. Then he noticed something that appeared to be a man flying through the night skies, but he decided that the blasts must have brought on a hallucination.

As fires raged around him, he could see the soldiers of the garrison running towards the forest. The figure that Reginald had convinced himself did not exist landed behind the soldiers and started leading them into the forest. Some of Julien's other associates followed the garrison guards with a disconcerting ease. Reginald started running for the forest, as he continued to hear the mass confusion of the papal forces.

He caught up to his little brother and pulled Julien aside, away from Lirienne, his mother, and that dark-haired woman with the strange eyes, away from their prying ears.

"I witnessed people flying," he hissed at his brother, now realizing that he had not hallucinated what he saw. "Only birds, angels, and demons can do that, and I do not see any wings on your friends."

"You saw nothing," Julien answered. His brother seemed to illuminate light as he spoke. A strange smile appeared on Julien's face, and he could swear that he witnessed his brother's eyes glow.

Alarmed, Reginald grabbed a small, blessed cross from his pocket and pressed it to Julien's forehead. "This is our mother's doing. She called down these demons, did she not?" he demanded.

Julien grabbed him and began shaking him. "Our mother is not evil," Julien countered and then pushed him aside with seemingly no effort,

Reginald found himself on the ground. He then stared at his brother in shock, wondering from where he had found this strength of his.

Julien crouched down, and in a calm voice said, "Forgive me, brother. You are overwrought with the death of Flor and my nephews, as am I. Join our journey to Aachen. There are too many papal soldiers remaining now to return to Divio or Vézelay." Julien then stood up.

"You are not my brother. He disappeared long ago, and I don't know what you are," Reginald spat at Julien. He rose to his feet and threw a punch at Julien.

His brother, or whatever appeared in Julien's form, ducked away and then grabbed his fist.

"I am returning home, and I'm taking Clotilda with me," Reginald gasped as he struggled with Julien. He then uttered a yelp as Julien squeezed his hand. A radiating pain moved through his arm.

Julien looked over to his associates. "He will alert them to our presence if he goes back," he whispered.

A heavy hand clasped over, his mouth and Reginald could feel himself being lifted. Julien's friends gagged him and bound him. He could not fight his way out of their trusses.

He could see then Julien talking to the red haired woman, who patted his arm. "You'll be able to do this right one night, but now we need you to go to Aachen and see whether emperor can send troops and tell the Holy… man to pull back his army."

"It will take me little time," Julien replied.

"Be careful. The Strigoi can attack quickly." She sounded worried to Reginald. "Do not forget to eat when necessary. Remember who are…"

"Time is of the essence. Farewell." Julien turned and ran into the dark forests.

The dark-haired woman joined Máire. "So, what will we do with our trussed friend? We can't carry him forever. Let me handle him," she said. Reginald felt a chill run up his spine. "After all, this is my field of expertise."

The other woman laughed. Reginald pictured himself being penetrated, humiliated, killed, and then defiled by these spawn of Satan.

"I bow to your skills of manipulation, Amata. Thank you," she said to the brunette.

He could not hear the rest of their conversation, as Reginald had begun fighting his bindings again.

The dark haired woman stepped away and then stopped at his side.

"Hello again," she teased with a smile. "I am Amata." Reginald tried to look away, but her eyes fixated on his, and he found that he could not look away. "You know, people see the strangest things during a fire. Once, I believed that I witnessed a feat of magic. It was stunning and I had faith that what I saw was real. Then, my father pointed out how the magician's fast-moving fingers dazzled the eye while his other fingers worked their 'magic' unobserved. His trick seemed so obvious, after knowing how he did it. Sometimes what we see is not reality, Reginald."

Those eyes... that voice... how could he ignore them? Reginald soon realized that her words began to make sense. He would survive... these women were not hell spawn... he did not see a man fly... all would be well with the world if he just learned to respect others.

Heloise sat down on a soft bed of leaf litter under a large oak and ran a hand over the dirt and leaves. She scattered the leaves and dirt over her cloak as she stretched out to camouflage herself. Máire and the other blood-drinkers had taught everyone tricks to keep themselves hidden during the day, in case the papal army caught up to them.

These beds would not be comfortable, but she thought this slight discomfort beat being found. Heloise closed her eyes, thinking of her old friend in Aachen.

The sound of her eldest yelling made her squeeze her eyes shut her in hopes of ignoring Reginald.

"Get ready to move. We're leaving soon," he bellowed.

As Heloise pulled aside the blanket, she resisted urge to sneeze. She turned her head to her right and noticed many of the garrison soldiers and the vassals looking confused.

"I said get up! I'm the Lord of Divio, and we must leave now!" Reginald persisted in his orders. He grew louder as he seemed to become more annoyed.

"But the rescuers said to sleep during the day and that we'd travel at night," she heard Alais state.

"Where are these so-called rescuers? They are at your homes, raiding your pantries," Reginald informed them.

Heloise stood up.

"Or perhaps they're stealing your personal crops," Reginald added. "You don't know exactly where they are and what they are doing."

"Reginald, stop this," she hissed in an angered whisper. "Do you wish to bring death to us all?"

"I'm trying to lead us!"

She tried to shush him. "Keep your voice down." Then she gestured to everyone else. "Get back under your cover," she advised.

"What do you think you're doing, mother? These are my vassals. I decide what we should do." Reginald's voice carried, causing her temper to flare. She hoped her granddaughter would not hear her next words.

"Insolent, irresponsible child! Don't you think you're too old to be taken over my knee?" she uttered in a snarl.

"Mother–"

"If we sleep at night, the murderous papal army will catch us and kill us in our sleep. The people and the garrison soldiers know this, and that is why they travel at night, as are we. Also, our friends who rescued us have not left us. They are hiding in the dirt as we are. Your shouting will draw our enemy to us, so stop dominating your betters, and get back in your hole, my son!"

Reginald's appearance grew dark. His eyes betrayed that he was beyond angry, but he kept his mouth shut. He continued to glare at her, as everyone else finished spreading leaves over themselves. She returned to her own bed.

"Don't think this is over between us, mother," Reginald hissed at her back.

Heloise ignored him and then tucked herself in.

Where did I go wrong with Reginald?

The scent of mortals caught in the Legate's nose. The sounds of shod hooves on the hard ground echoed in his ears. Patroclus leaned forward in the tree and stared at the long lances, spears, and banners of the papal army in the distance.

A man in a green cloak motioned them forward as he pointed at the ground towards the tracks.

Patroclus leapt out of the tree and raced towards the traveling party. He dodged his way around the mortals and towards the front. He then found Máire and took her arm.

"We must talk," he whispered. "Come with me. Bring whoever you need to assist in making a decision."

She motioned for Amata, Dreu, Edward, and Lady Heloise to join them. He then noticed Reginald following them all.

"We have trouble," he informed Máire.

"The army is catching up," she stated.

"Yes, they are following us. There are about twenty mounted soldiers and a ranger scout. They should be here in about half an hour."

"The woods are thick enough to set up an ambush," Máire observed. "An ambush could convince these soldiers to back off and perhaps discourage others from following."

"Edward, are we lucky enough to have any more of your noisy firepots?"

Máire asked as she turned to face Edward.

"You should know by now that I'm always prepared," Edward answered. Despite eccentricities, Patroclus found Edward's creations to be most useful in any battle.

"It was indeed quite foolish of me," Máire said with a grin. "Edward, could you climb in the trees and wait until they walk underneath you? I'm sure you know what to do when the time is right."

Edward nodded his head and then took a few steps back.

"Amata, Patroclus, I want you to be on either side of the cavalry. I will take out the scout. I will signal when it is time for the attack."

"Excuse me," Reginald interrupted.

The Legate admired how Máire ignored the whelp's attempt to dominate the situation. "My lord, you, Dreu, and your mother will need to lead your people in case of a problem. They trust you, and they need your strength," Máire replied. "Please." She seemed to study Reginald for a moment. Perhaps she reasoned whether Reginald could stand to witness a little glamoury. While it was not as effective as the Lamia's gifts of persuasion, he appreciated the beauty of glamoury.

The Frank's eyes wavered for a moment. He turned away, and then the co-consul met Reginald's eyes.

"I understand," Reginald murmured. "Come," he intoned as he motioned for the two mortals to follow him.

"Thank you," Máire said before nodding to Amata.

"Will you whistle?" Amata queried.

"No," Máire answered, "but rest assured, you will know when it is time to attack. Now go and get into position."

Máire watched the party of mortals travel into the distance ahead. She stared at the starlit skies for a moment, trying to think of the best way to kill the ranger and yet keep the soldiers in one place. She expected the horses to shy and bolt amid the explosions, which would both help and hinder her plans.

She then sensed the army drawing near, as well as Amata and the Legate moving to the sides of the path. Máire decided to crouch and cloak herself in darkness.

The scout moved closer. His scent made her desire blood, yet there would be precious little time for that slow death.

As Máire drew her sword, she heard voices calling for the scout. She watched as he turned to face the oncoming army. She knew this needed to be done now.

Máire grabbed the scout by his chin and sliced his throat. She then spied the commander approaching her, calling for the scout. She reached for a small knife and prepared to throw it.

The commander stopped and then surveyed his surroundings..

Máire dropped darkness on the commander and then threw her knife at his face. Then a sudden explosion echoed around her, deafening the scream from the commander and making her feel a little dizzy.

The initial explosion caught one or two soldiers off guard. They collapsed face down in the dirty path. Horses neighed in fear and tossed their riders aside.

Amata and the Legate joined her in killing whoever tried to pass them. Edward leapt from the tree, taking out a few more, including the ranger.

Máire took the ranger's bow and quiver and began shooting at a few of the soldiers racing away on horseback.

Patroclus managed to pull one of the papal soldiers from his horse, kill him, and leapt onto his horse. He charged towards the retreating soldiers.

Edward lobbed another grenade towards the retreating forces, and more soldiers fell from their horses and became trampled.

Máire whistled to the three other blood-drinkers. She listened as horses whinnied and wounded soldiers moaned.

"They're not all dead," Amata pointed out as she swiped away some blood from her face and licked her hand.

Máire shrugged. "I think it is prudent, Amata, to allow some of them to survive so they can warn the others to stay out of the woods. They will not want to chase after us without their tracker. Let's rejoin the mortals." She then raced towards the party of refugees in the distance.

Ard Macha

Aisling knocked on Conlan's door.

"Enter, Aisling," her father-in-darkness called out.

She then stepped into Conlan's dark quarters. Her father-in-darkness had given up much of his possessions in order to purify himself. The silver trappings of wealth in the Deargh Du stronghold no longer graced his now humble dwelling, though a series of mixing bowls lay at Conlan's feet. While the scent of Sponnc wafted through the room, only a few smoking leaves remained in the small hearth. Aisling inhaled the mixture and closed her eyes.

"What did our Queen say?" Aisling inquired while sitting down across from Conlan.

"Her words to me were strange and mysterious," Conlan answered, before scratching his moustache. His dark eyes grew green in the candlelight.

"I have always found calling to Her difficult," Aisling admitted. Morrigan's words and tests confused her to no end.

"As do many of us," Conlan added with a bemused smile. "Her words are a puzzle or a riddle to solve. She wants us to better ourselves. She told me to maintain the balance and that she charged me with that sacred duty. I asked Her about that monstrosity of Rome, but then Her eyes became as midnight and she would say nothing about him. She is a Goddess of fury and blood, and sometimes matters are sealed from our ears... matters, we are not meant to understand in this realm."

"Do you think She regrets him?" Aisling pondered aloud while staring at the bowls. She had not crossed Marcus often during his brief stay in Ard Macha, but that spawn of his... Máire. Oh, Aisling knew Máire well.

Conlan raised a brow in contemplation. "He is a test, Aisling, a test from the Phantom Queen. We have fallen from our path and have failed Her test. It is up to our faction to put our line on the right track in order to maintain the balance."

Aisling nodded her head. "We will become pure again, old friend. Oh yes, I did have something to tell you. The thousand volunteers of the Cothromaigh have left to fight the Strigoi abroad. They travel to Briton in order to meet with the bastard races."

"Good," Conlan answered. "Then, the supporters of Sáerlaith and that Roman bastard are gone. Sáerlaith and her Council are now alone."

Aisling pushed her long hair behind her ears and asked, "What about the arch druid?"

Conlan chuckled, revealing merriment in his eyes. "He is an old wolf with no teeth, Aisling. He's in the library, of course, with his nose in scrolls, trying to find answers to the riddle that plagues that strange bitch, Máire. You two have a history together, do you not? Anyway, I think Érémon is there as well. We must take care of the arch druid. I can do it myself... I must do it myself. Ruarí stands in the way of purity and balance."

"I can get Érémon to leave. Besides he has no strength... he's just a youngling. And where is Caoimhín?"

"He will join the travelers in the Field of the Judged in the Otherworld. That fool follows Sáerlaith."

Conlan arose and pulled out a sword. "Come. The time is right for this sacrifice."

The arch druid remained silent in his prayers, barely acknowledging the youngling who put away the scrolls and left him on his own. He relished the silence of these last few nights for his searches, though their research on 'curses' had yielded nothing of use.

Ruarí then sensed a new breeze in the eternal winds that drifted through his home. Whispered warnings drifted to his ears about changing elements and reactionaries... those who wished a return to their earlier ideals and isolationism. Part of him wished to seek safety and shelter in Morrigan's caves in Connacht with Sáerlaith and the others destined to maintain the balance. He knew the warnings, which echoed through the stronghold, that these reactionaries would kill whoever prevented them from completing their coup.

Ruarí inhaled and exhaled, allowing himself to part the mists. His bond with Morrigan had grown by leaps these last few nights, and so he no longer needed the Sponnc to give him mental clarity in order to pass through the gates.

Morrigan approached him, as Her midnight-colored cloak trailed behind Her. Its feathers whispered with every movement. Her body remained glorious and radiant, and he felt he needed to cover his eyes from Her blinding beauty.

"Ruarí, old trusted servant and grandchild of Adhamdh, reveal your beautiful eyes to me," Morrigan pleaded.

He lowered his arm so She could see his eyes. "Phantom Queen," he murmured as he kneeled and lowered his eyes.

"Ruarí." Morrigan's warmed hands took his and brought him out of his crouched position. "Stand, please." He looked into Her eyes and found himself transfixed in them, for a moment. He then found his mind and rose.

Morrigan took his arm and began walking with him towards a great table.

He fell silent, unsure of what to say at this moment. Motion above him caught his eye, and so he looked up, and he saw that the skies above turned dark, signaling a storm.

"You know they will rise against you."

He felt a moment of shock to hear Her speak again. He faced Morrigan as they approached the table.

"Yes, Great Queen, I know. However, I know this is a test for us all."

"There is a rift within the Deargh Du... one that was not unexpected."

"But why allow this to happen?" Ruarí asked.

Morrigan beamed at him. "The heart of the Deargh Du is unbalanced. In order to achieve balance, there must be chaos and strife. Only through destruction can creation and rebirth occur. I love my children, both the blood-drinkers and those strange mortals, but this is how it has to be, Ruarí." She squeezed his hand. "Please sit."

Ruarí sat down. "I understand," he said. "I accept my role, whatever it is to be, Phantom Queen."

Morrigan placed Her hands on his shoulders. "Dear child, it is only part of your journey that is ending. There is still a long road ahead for you. However, this road will lead you into my realm."

"Thank you, my Queen."

Morrigan leaned forward and kissed his brow. He felt dizzy as Her lips lingered on his forehead. Morrigan pulled away and sat down. He then heard footsteps and turned towards the noise. Adhamdh joined them. His hair had grown, but his eyes remained the same.

"Hello, youngling," Adhamdh greeted with a smirk.

"Youngling indeed!" Ruarí teased as he returned a smile. "I thought you were still exploring the mortal realms," he said.

"Sometimes I do," Adhamdh acknowledged. "However, this world is outside of time. This is not such a bad existence, Ruarí. As fascinating as the world you exist in is, this place calls to me."

Morrigan moved to embrace Adhamdh. "Thank you for joining us, my son."

Adhamdh sat down across from Ruarí, and then Morrigan joined Her first son.

"Ruari, I know you have doubts, even though you would not speak of them," Adhamdh began. "The Deargh Du need to grow. They need to learn, and yet, so many fear it. They must form partnerships with other races. However..." he explained before pausing. Adhamdh then leaned his elbows on the table. His eyes focused on his own, and Ruarí found himself unable to let his eyes wander. "... there is such a schism in the Deargh Du that we must have one side distance itself from the other. Therefore, the other side will have to learn new things and accept that the mortal world changes, one way or another. They cannot be eddies in the river. Either they can learn again on their own, or they will deal with the consequences. The Deargh Du who are committed to embracing the balance will be reformed and will remain in the mortal world to act as a balance." As soon as his words faded, Adhamdh turned towards his mother-in-darkness.

"The cost is high," Morrigan stated, while Her dark eyes grew concerned. "Many of my brood will be lost. However, it is the only way to gain unity and balance. Unfortunately, you are one who must be lost to the world, at least in your present form."

Ruarí sensed movement around his corporeal self. A Deargh Du approached his body in the mortal realm. "I am not alone," he whispered as he felt a moment of tenuous fear.

"It is time, Ruarí," Morrigan whispered. "Take a deep breath."

As he watched, Morrigan and Adhamdh faded away. "I have never had any doubts," he called out to Her, hoping his voice did not waver.

Ruarí materialized into his body and sensed Conlan behind him. He opened his eyes and turned to face him, wishing to die with his honor. The Phantom Queen and Her glories awaited him.

"So, you decided to kill me yourself?" Ruarí inquired as he smiled. His voice revealed only calm determination.

"It is what must be done," Conlan replied.

"Indeed, that is true," he answered, before whispering, "Morrigan, grant your servant passage to your realm." A sharp pain passed through his body but then faded.

Ruari felt himself begin to fall, and yet he felt his weight fall away from him. He drifted towards the newfound, sundrenched glory of the Otherworld and Morrigan's home.

"Welcome, dear great-grandchild," She whispered in his ear.

chapteR seventeen

áerlaith steeled herself to remain calm as she read a message from Conlan that his sycophant, Aisling, had just delivered to her. Conlan wanted Aisling to escort her to the council meeting chambers. Aisling waited while Sáerlaith read the note.

Though the term "sycophant" had come to mind, Aisling seemed to be the real power behind Conlan. Sure, Conlan thought his daughter-in-darkness obeyed his every whim, but Sáerlaith knew Aisling had used her share of Sáerlaith's former wealth to pay tributes and bribes all around Eire. Sometime soon, she knew Aisling would usurp her father-in-darkness, and then she would become a true threat.

"I hope this note brings good news," Aisling stated as soon as Sáerlaith had raised her head, though she had finished the note many seconds ago. Aisling's voice dripped with excessive sweetness and courtesy. Even her manner seemed prim and polite.

"I am well, thank you," Sáerlaith responded. "It seems that I am needed in the council chambers and that you are to escort me."

"Indeed. Oh, I do hope you have forgiven me for that nasty business I had to put you and your friends through all those years ago. It was business, not personal. Anyway, I would like to believe that enough time has flowed, like water under a bridge, so that we might become friends. Would you like to become friends with me?"

Something seemed amiss, as the normally cool and distant Aisling spoke to her with an uncommon graciousness. Even her senses warned her of potential calamities, but she could not avoid the inevitable.

"I would desire that above all things, Aisling," Sáerlaith lied as she rose to embrace her new 'friend'. Aisling wrapped her in a great hug and then kissed her. Sáerlaith struggled to keep her true feelings hidden, lest Aisling suspect any duplicity, but as long as Sáerlaith could pass herself off as Aisling's friend, perhaps she would survive the anticipated leadership change in the isolationist faction.

"Well," Aisling said after releasing herself from their embrace, "shall we retire to the council chambers? No doubt Conlan is there waiting for us."

Sáerlaith panicked. She knew she needed some kind of protection, but she could not be seen decking herself out in armaments. She needed to be alone for a moment so she could conceal something, but that meant she needed for Aisling to leave. Sáerlaith snuck a quick glance around her office, looking for an excuse to delay, when she spotted a letter she was writing to Aoife of the

Ekimmu Cruitne.

"Forgive me, Aisling, but I must finish this letter… it is council business and must be done."

"Very well. I shall wait in the hall for you." The woman then left her office. Aisling seemed most accommodating… too accommodating. She had a plan, and she would soon execute that plan.

For that reason, Sáerlaith fastened a sword, a gladius, which Marcus had sent as a gift for her a few years ago, to her belt and then she concealed it as best as she could with her clothes. She then calmly walked out into the hall and the proceeded with Aisling to the council chamber.

Sáerlaith opened the door to the dark chamber and noticed that only one candle flickered in the shadows. The lone candle glowed above a table in the front of the room. Sáerlaith stepped into the room in order to get a better view of the table and a strangely shaped object obscured by shadow caught her eye. She inhaled sharply, realizing that Ruarí's head rested on the table. Her emotions wavered between shock, sadness, and anger. She then heard others gather behind her.

"What is the meaning of this atrocity?" she growled, before uttering a wordless cry as her hot tears began to fall. "Who has murdered our Arch Druid?" She rested her hand on the pommel of her concealed sword.

"I did." Conlan's voice rang in her ear. Contentment and joy laced his words.

Sáerlaith swallowed her tears. "Guards, take him into custody," she ordered as she turned to face Ruarí's killer, yet no one stepped in to take him. "I said, guards, take Conlan into custody!"

Conlan started to laugh. "Sáerlaith, you will find that no one here will follow your orders."

"Conlan, what have you done?" She stared into the faces of those she thought were her friends.

"The great council has unanimously removed you from office, my friend," Aisling stated.

Sáerlaith had completely miscalculated the situation. Aisling did not bribe people to follow her… she bribed them to follow her father-in-darkness.

Sáerlaith watched as Aisling took a few steps closer. Other traitors fanned out to either side of Conlan to cut off any means of escape.

"This council does not have that authority. Only the Council of Five does!" Sáerlaith snapped, hoping to remind everyone of his or her duties.

"Not anymore," Conlan murmured. "You see, we dissolved the Council of Five with the consent of the leading members, and the Great Council has wisely selected me to lead the Deargh Du. We are returning to our roots, Sáerlaith, to our days of purity. Besides, the Cothromaigh is not here to protect you."

She knew by the look in Conlan's eyes that he had probably killed the Council of Five. She felt a great deal of pity for Fianait, Ruarí, Etain, and Nuadin, but then she remembered that she had sent Nuadin to one of the local chieftains to assist in healing the aged warrior's sore joints. Perhaps she could get to him, but she needed to get out of here first.

"Conlan, why did you kill the arch druid? He was our greatest connection to the Phantom Queen," she whispered.

"Because he deviated from Morrigan's plan and led us astray, Sáerlaith," Conlan ranted. "We know he was the reason behind the consensus for your bad decisions. He allowed foreigners to ally themselves with us. He permitted the Lamia to come here and did not protect our borders. You both tolerate that monstrosity of Rome and his minion atrocity!"

"The majority of those were my decisions, and the rest we all agreed to," she challenged, though she felt her words sounded meek.

Conlan began to laugh. "You are little better than a cumal to him."

She felt her anger rise at being labeled a slave.

Conlan continued. "You have never had any real power. Ruarí was the true authority."

"And what do you intend to do, Conlan? Will you kill whoever does not meet your standards of purity?" Sáerlaith channeled her rage into confidence. If she wanted to live, she needed to act soon.

"You..." Conlan spat after he stopped laughing. "You, I will leave to bask in the rising sun so your ashes may be carried by the morning breeze." He turned towards the guards and ordered, "Subdue her!"

Sáerlaith drew her blade from concealment, lobbed off one guard's head, and then wounded another.

"Seize the traitor who bears foreign weapons!" Conlan yelled.

Sáerlaith watched as the oncoming group of Deargh Du tried to rush her, but she managed to fight her way past them with a strength she did not remember. Arms, legs, and heads lie severed in her wake.

She escaped into the hallway and dropped darkness on herself as more armed guards approached. She then flew through the stronghold, hoping some friends would arrive soon, when a hand grabbed her and pulled her into the library. At first, she thought she had been captured, but then she saw Fianait, who bolted the door. Others stood in the room with them.

"Shhhh," Caoimhín whispered.

Three of the other members of the Council of Five smiled at her, though little mirth shown from their distraught visages. Seamus and three other mortal attendants bowed to her. Sáerlaith then noticed Ruarí's headless form. Upon seeing the corpse, she tried in vain to blink back her tears. "I will miss him," she whispered.

"As will all of us," Caoimhín offered. "However, he has joined Our Lady now, and we must survive this night."

Seamus presented her with a change of clothing. "My lady, I am sorry that the clothing is not very pretty, but it was all I could muster." Her seneschal's face reddened in what she thought was either anger or embarrassment.

"Seamus, this will suit me fine," she answered before touching his shoulder with her right hand. She then started to change out of her linen finery and into her coarse traveling gear. The other surviving members of the Council of Five appeared to be ready.

She nodded after she finished dressing.

Fianait, the youngest member of the Council of Five grinned and said, "Very few Deargh Du know this," Fianait began, "but the hallways we walk every night are not the only passageways in this complex." She pulled down a sword arm on a statue, and then a hidden passage opened. "Let's go."

Sáerlaith motioned for the attendants and the other council members to move ahead of her. "Hold the hands of the mortals," she whispered. "We cannot afford to use torches." She then pulled the secret door shut and locked the bar in place.

"This will buy us some time," she again whispered.

They began to race through the corridor. Soon, they arrived at an intersection.

"Which way, High Councilor?" Caoimhín queried her.

Sáerlaith closed her eyes and prayed for guidance. While she supervised the creation and concealment of these emergency tunnels, she could not remember them well.

"Right," she answered, hoping that direction came from either her memories or from Morrigan Herself.

They continued their escape. Soon the passage began to descend, and they heard running water.

"Follow me," Sáerlaith advised as she started following a path that seemed appropriate. At the next intersection, they kept going straight.

The smell of water flooded her nostrils, and the sound of a rushing river could not be ignored anymore. After a few more paces, she felt cold wetness inundate her shoes. Etain caught her arm as they reached the last chilly step. Her water–drenched feet made her shiver.

"Careful. It is slippery here," Etain whispered.

The wet and cool passage they had followed led to a ledge in the cavern. A fast running stream stretched in front of her.

"Blackwater," she whispered, as it was the name of the river that fed this stream. "Let us ensure that the mortals survive our wet journey," Sáerlaith instructed the other Deargh Du. Then in prayer, she pleaded, "Please guide us to our destination."

Sáerlaith dove into the water with Seamus, and soon she heard the others join her.

They all started to swim with the current, with the Deargh Du helping the mortals. "Hold your breath," she advised her servant before preparing to swim under a low ceiling. He nodded after taking a deep breath, and then both of them dove below the ceiling. She tried not to dwell on how disconcerting Seamus must find it to be submerged in this cold, dark water. Even Sáerlaith, who did not need to breathe, found her fear growing.

With loud intakes of breath, both mortal and blood-drinker sucked in air upon resurfacing on the other side. Then the sound of wind ahead caught her ears, as they neared the point where the stream joined the river. Within moments, the night sky with all of its bright stars greeted them.

They soon climbed out of the river onto a small beach. Sáerlaith stared into the darkness in the direction of their old home.

"I'm sorry we had to leave our home. Let's bypass Ard Ghlais and head east towards Briton. We must make sure we are not followed. Nuadin will meet us there, I hope."

As Nuadin reached the gates, a series of strange sensations approached him from the Stronghold. He turned away, deciding not to ignore his immediate aversion to his home. Something must be wrong, terribly wrong.

His inclination to take flight changed as darkness surrounded him. Nuadin thought to unsheathe his sword, but a heavy weight landed on him, and then all turned dark.

He awoke and found himself naked on a cold floor.

"Take him, he's awake."

Nuadin moaned as nameless Deargh Du forced him to his knees. Its blurred face cleared and became Conlan.

"The powers have changed here and become pure. You are no longer councilor. In fact, we have yet to decide whether you are to live. It's up to you," Conlan stated.

Regensburg

The last stragglers from Briton had arrived. The blessed children swarmed the old Ekimmu's headquarters, and they all needed a new home.

Seosaimhín studied her family and smiled. "We shall leave for now and fly with the birds to find a new place for us all. Transform any mortals that come here, and destroy any blood-drinkers."

One of the Strigoi grunted.

"We must work on your speaking skills. Yes, they've improved, but we must make you better… later."

She then took to the air.

Coast of Briton, Kingdom of Sussex

Claudius landed at the well-lit beach. Instead of the gentle whispers of the sea, loud music and other sounds of celebration greeted him upon his arrival. He wondered what feast he had missed, since Imbolc passed many nights ago. Many blood-drinkers caroused about, singing and frolicking… some on the beach, some in the sea, and some in the air.

Claudius saw an Ekimmu Cruitne he did not recognize and decided to find out why they were celebrating. He walked over and then tugged at her elbow. The blood-drinker faced him with a cherubic grin plastered on her face.

"What happened here?" Claudius asked. "Who's in command?"

The blood-drinker pointed in the direction of a large tent, before belching into her hand. She moved back into the crowd of revelers.

Claudius walked into the tent and placed himself near the circle of who he recognized as being the primary officers. Claudius wondered whether they still used the Roman tactics that he and the others had utilized. Out of deference to their lineage and the need for some hierarchy, they called the lead officers 'general'. However, some still used the term 'Chieftain'. He began to listen to the conversation. Thankfully, he recognized some of the officers' names and faces, but many of them he could not remember or had never met.

"These monasteries are the latest target of the Vikings," a lower level officer explained as she pointed to a mark on the map.

"I wonder what their plan is. When will they strike next?" an Ekimmu Cruitne named Fyfa murmured.

The conversation gave Claudius the distinct impression that the high officers ignored him, though a few of the lower ranking officers stared at him but said nothing.

"Has any thought been given to the enemy that just left the shores to the South?" Claudius asked, deciding that he could no longer wait.

Maddog glanced at him. "Oh… Claudius," he wheezed. "You smell of fish brine. You've arrived a week late to participate in the battle, which is in line with your usual tardiness."

Claudius sucked in a growing rage. Maddog was younger than Máire and Edward, so he had hoped for some respect.

"And how long did you fight these Strigoi?" asked Claudius.

"A few hours, once we arrived," Angus, another blood-drinker Claudius recognized, stated as he met Claudius' stare.

Claudius uttered a humorless chuckle. "Let me guess... you had two thousand warriors pitted against one hundred Strigoi, you lost five hundred in a matter of hours, and then the enemy headed back out to sea while most of you were insensate... correct?"

Fyfa uttered a frustrated noise. "Yes... that sounds about right," she admitted.

"And how many of them did you kill?" Claudius asked.

"Twelve," Angus replied, dejection clear in his voice.

"And here you sit, worried about a group of mortals who attack monasteries for gold, when your warriors are celebrating as if this were a magnificent victory," Claudius roared, "when clearly, you were soundly defeated."

"This from a blood-drinker who prefers the company of foreigners, shirks his duties when they become dull, and who lectures us when he wasn't here during the battle!" Maddog huffed.

Claudius slammed his fist against the table. "I've been fighting the Strigoi for almost a month, and my party of less than a dozen Sugnwr Gwaed, Ekimmu Cruitne, Deargh Du and Lamia..." he uttered another mirthless laugh, "... yes, Lamia... have managed to kill forty in that time with minimal losses."

"You've cobbled together a band of these lines, including the Lamia?" inquired a young Sugnwr Gwaed he didn't recognize, who tried to hide his own disbelief.

"Yes. The Strigoi have sent most of the continental lines into hiding. The Lamia who have been most threatened by their expansion, have established a peace treaty and an alliance with the Deargh Du." Claudius shrugged as he heard the sounds of shock and surprised.

Claudius decided it was time for more surprise. They would all argue over alliances with the Lamia, but perhaps it would be easier to lie a little. What did he have to lose? He did not have any love for the council of the Sugnwr Gwaed or the Ekimmu Cruitne.

"Arwin MacAlpin and I agreed to the terms of the alliance for our respective councils," Claudius added.

"How dare you step over the decisions of the councils," Fyfa growled, while her eyes glowed silvery-blue.

The gathered officers made further noises of outrage and threats against himself and Arwin. Maddog and Angus then managed to silence the others in the tent.

"Don't you both think you were overstepping your authority when you made that pledge on our behalf?" Angus uttered in a half-growl. His eyes revealed his fury.

Claudius took a deep, though unnecessary, breath. "First, our acceptance was unofficial, but we did send letters to both councils advising them of the situation and requesting ratification to this alliance. Since we have received no replies to our communication, we assumed we had approval. Then we traveled to the Empire, where we ascertained how large of a threat the Strigoi posed. Our visit made all of us aware of the need for greater participation by our lines. That is why I'm here, to ask both of you to send a thousand of your warriors each with me to fight the Strigoi. Since you four sit on the Council, you should have no trouble explaining why you sent a thousand to the continent."

The tent grew silent for a moment, but an eruption of shouting ended the peace.

"The Deargh Du have dispatched a thousand warriors, and the Lamia co-consuls have dispatched several thousand of their forces. That means more than half of the Lamia will fight the Strigoi. I urge you to mobilize your troops and to stand alongside the Deargh Du and the Lamia, united against the Strigoi scourge," Claudius yelled at the generals.

Angus hushed the others. "Now, Claudius, the Strigoi have left and pose no more threat to us. We must turn our attention to the east."

"No... no... no... no... NO!" He felt utter frustration at their shortsightedness. "Don't you see what this was? This was a probing action by the Strigoi, which means they will be back and in far greater numbers."

"But the Vikings—" Fyfa began.

"—did not wipe out a fourth of your forces just seven nights ago!" Claudius interjected. "The Vikings have raided our coasts for quite some time, and they shall likely continue, until the balance of power changes with the mortals. However, the Strigoi represent an imminent threat."

He could hear more muttering in various languages.

Angus leaned forward in his seat. "We do not believe the Strigoi are a significant threat." Despite the Ekimmu Cruitne's words, Claudius could hear hesitation in his voice, and he witnessed worry in Angus' eyes. Did Claudius even smell fear from the blood-drinker?

He decided to pursue an alternate approach. He cleared his throat and lowered his voice. "What you really mean to tell me is that you Sugnwr Gwaed and Ekimmu Cruitne do not understand the Strigoi, and because you don't understand the Strigoi, you fear them. That is why you deny they are a threat. You refuse to look south across the water, for fear they will look back at you. That is the way a coward sees the world. Are the Ekimmu Cruitne and Sugnwr Gwaed cowards?" Claudius inquired before shaking his head.

Another eruption of voices swelled in the tents, and from the sounds about him, this discussion had attracted the attention of the warriors, who now gathered around the tent.

"No, I don't believe so. I know many brave blood-drinkers in those lines. I think it's the leaders who are cowards!" Claudius shouted for the crowd's benefit as he smiled what he hoped to be a vicious, predatory grin at the officers in the tent.

He heard the drawing of swords, but he kept his hands away from his blade. The blustering from officers continued.

"Are you challenging us?" Maddog hissed.

Claudius concentrated on calming his voice and body. "I'm not challenging your authority. I'm merely pointing out that the Ekimmu Cruitne and Sugnwr Gwaed have an opportunity to contribute warriors to an alliance united against the Strigoi... an alliance that has had many successes so far. When we defeat them on the continent, they will never return to Briton. Then, you would be able to focus all your concerns on the Northmen. All I need are a thousand warriors from you," indicating the lead councilor for the Sugnwr Gwaed with his head, "and a thousand warriors from you," indicating the lead councilor of the Ekimmu Cruitne. "Now, I've said my peace. Discuss my proposal if you so desire it. I'm going to join in the drinking and the singing. I feel like celebrating. Let me know when you have made a decision."

Claudius turned on his heel and left the tent. Cheers greeted him, and someone handed him flagon of mead. Then he felt a touch, and he turned to see a beautiful, black-haired warrior. She smiled at him before motioning for him to follow her. However, it seemed as if Maddog had other plans for him, as Claudius could sense his approach.

Claudius excused the woman warrior and then turned to face Maddog. The other blood-drinker's eyes became golden, revealing his hatred.

"The majority of the officers of both the Ekimmu Cruitne and Sugnwr Gwaed have agreed to release one thousand warriors each to your cause," Maddog relayed.

Claudius lowered his flagon and prepared himself to thank Maddog. However, Maddog began to tremble with rage, but he continued talking.

"Know this, Claudius. There will be consequences because of your actions and your words."

"I understand," Claudius answered. "Who will command the warriors?"

Maddog inhaled and then replied, "Claudius Metrius Sertorius and Arwin Mac Alpin will be in command." Maddog's words, though delivered in anger, seemed rote... memorized.

Claudius nodded his head. "And what of the alliance, Maddog?"

"It is in our best interests to ratify the alliance, and we will do so when we meet with our respective councils. We nominate you and Arwin as our ambassadors to the alliance."

"Thank you," he said, while trying not to smirk or sneer at Maddog.

"Do not thank me," Maddog countered. "I wished for you to be beheaded here and now. However, that was not the consensus of the officers." Maddog spat on the ground and then turned away. He took slow steps back towards the tent, but before he entered, Maddog looked back and whispered, "Consequences, Claudius, grave consequences."

Claudius closed his eyes and then raised the flagon to his mouth. He had an army, but at what personal cost? His political reputation was not anything to brag about, so when compared against the Strigoi threat, his reputation amongst cowards seemed quite low on the great scale of priorities.

Regensburg

Seosaimhín flew above the treetops, unsure what would work for the blessed children. A cave would do nicely, but she could see none. Perhaps the time had come to change direction, but then a stone caught her eye. Trees surrounded the stone… how strange. She found a circular clearing around the trees and decided to land in order to examine this find further.

She landed in a patch of vines and leaves and then tramped over towards the stone. Seosaimhín pushed away the brush and then realized that a small altar rested beneath the leaf litter and dead forest debris. She tossed aside more branches and dead vines as the ancient symbols grew clear.

"The writing of the ancients," she purred. Seosaimhín then ran a finger over the indentations. She swore she had witnessed these markings before as a mortal Druid.

Seosaimhín turned east and tried to walk through the debris, but it became too much trouble. She then levitated towards a center point and landed in front of a large bush. She began to pull away the branches and found the stone marking the eastern point of grove.

More script marked this rock. She found herself singing in joy at the find.

Seosaimhín turned to her right side and found another companion stone. She flew towards it and began to clean it.

Within a short time, she had exposed the scribbling on all of the marker stones, and then her song reached its zenith.

She kicked through the rubbish and found the altar again. She then jumped on top of it. The energy of the earth moved through her.

"This is where I shall teach my blessed children!" she called to the winds.

Coast of Briton, Kingdom of Sussex

Claudius awoke to hear snoring in his ear. He pushed over the snorer and stood up, before rubbing his eyes. He tried to remember what it was that he needed to do first this night.

He found a bowl of cold water, ducked his hands in the icy water, and splashed his face. Now, he could remember his duties.

Claudius stepped out of the tent and found a sleepy-looking mortal bugler eating porridge. He whistled to the bugler, catching his attention.

"Call for assembly," Claudius ordered.

The bugler nodded and then rose from his seat. His tuneless song made Claudius wince and then cover his ears in pain.

He heard moans of agony from the sensitive Sugnwr Gwaed. Their complaints would wake the Ekimmu Cruitne.

The hung-over warriors gathered in staggered lines.

The officers joined the menagerie and kicked people into place, but they fell silent when they looked at him.

He studied the field of two thousand warriors. Most still looked half-asleep. Perhaps it would be best to give them a short introduction to their new duties.

"Many of you know me, but for those of you who don't I am Claudius Metrius Sertorius of the Wild Hunt. Your officers chose me to lead you into battle against the Strigoi in the Empire. My associates and I have had success fighting them, but with the combined might of the Sugnwr Gwaed, the Ekimmu Cruitne, the Deargh Du, and even the Lamia, we shall prevail. I will call a regimental briefing for all officers in half an hour to discuss the details of our mission. You are dismissed."

He then marched back to the command tent. All of the senior officers from the last night had left, though he could not say he found that surprising or undesirable. Claudius righted one of the chairs, which had been overturned at someone's unhappy exit, and then sat in it. Soon after getting comfortable, he sensed a blood-drinker approaching him.

He turned his head and watched as a tall, blonde warrior pulled back the tent flap. She smirked at Claudius as she entered. "Maddog and Fyfa wanted to slice your head off because of your insults last night," Blodwyn informed him, though he could see mirth in her eyes.

"I had to wake them out of their stupor, somehow. It's been awhile, Blodwyn. How are you?" He stood up, approached her, and kissed her. She had been the first Sugnwr Gwaed to approve of his leadership after his first meeting with the Ouphe.

"I've been better, and I've been worse," she answered. "I'm still recovering from the earlier celebrations. You certainly did wake them. You did well to walk away when you did, Claudius. Things have changed again... things are always changing here."

Claudius sat back down and motioned for her to sit as well. "So, has everyone left but you, Blodwyn?"

She lowered herself into the chair next to him. "Not everybody. Cathair Mac Domhnaill from the Ekimmu Cruitne is staying behind as well. The rest of the senior officers left with the remainder of the army, which won't be joining us in the Empire."

"Where is Cathair?" He did not remember this blood-drinker.

"So, you're the one who told off Maddog," an unfamiliar Ekimmu Cruitne greeted as he strolled into tent. "Well done. I heard you weren't even drunk when you said it."

Claudius stood and clasped arms with Cathair. "I wasn't in the mood to deal with either council's excuses," Claudius answered. "So, what did you think of the controversy last night?" he asked. "Take a seat." He motioned for Cathair to take another chair.

"Sounds like a lot of your line don't exactly care for you. What did you do?" Cathair asked as he sat down.

"I suppose there are too many politics in my line… who is worthy of the hunt, and so forth." Claudius sighed for a moment. "I got tired of it, and before I left, I had called many of my peers weak. Oh, I did also kill the current leader's brother-in-darkness in a matter of honor. He spoke ill of my family… rather my friends."

"Hmmmm, no wonder you have more friends in other lines than your own," Cathair replied. "Well, can't say I exactly agree with what goes on in council chambers. I prefer to use a sword to solve my problems."

"Well, you have two thousand and two friends with you now," Blodwyn commented.

"Two thousand and two?" asked Claudius.

Blodwyn smiled and clarified, "Yes. Cathair and I have been ordered to interpret and relay your commands to each of our armies."

"You can't be serious… so I don't speak the languages well enough? Am I to lead by your consent?" Claudius grumbled.

"No, that's what the rest of the senior officers ordered us to do, but that seems like cack to me… too many generals controlling the legion, utter chaos," Cathair stated.

"Of course, appearances must be kept for now, so we'll travel with you and fight with you, but as far as the men are concerned, you're the leader. I'm not planning to change that status," Blodwyn added.

"You've heard my opinion," Cathair stated.

"Then I thank you both for your trust and confidence in my abilities," Claudius answered.

Blodwyn's eyes sparkled. "Anyone who puts a man like Maddog in his place and walks away smiling deserves my support and conviction. Besides, you and your friends saved me during that Ouphe attack. I do not forget such things."

Claudius then noticed Cathair sniff the air. "They are arriving," he said.

"So, what is the plan?" Blodwyn whispered as someone raised the tent flap.

"Wait outside, please," he instructed the junior officers. "We are not quite done yet." They looked at their commanders and then left.

He motioned for the other senior officers to lean closer. He then whispered, "Once we are done here, I am going to leave both of you to travel to London with the troops and prepare to make sail."

Cathair's brows rose, revealing surprise. "You're not joining us?"

"I'll meet you there, but I have to fly to Bath first to get word to the Deargh Du to meet us on the Frankish coast. On the way there, I want you to drill our warriors in combat for half the night. They look sloppy, and they will need to become a fighting force again before meeting the Strigoi," Claudius answered.

Blodwyn and Cathair both nodded.

"Then I hope these Deargh Du won't need training as well," Blodwyn teased with a grin. "What am I saying... Marcus trains them, correct?"

Claudius chuckled. "I'll call the others back to begin the briefing," he said. He then backed away and stood up. "Alright," he yelled, "come back in and gather by the map!"

Regensburg

"Come, my blessed children, and join us in the circle of power," she called to the Strigoi, who milled about in groups towards Seosaimhín.

"This will be your home, our home, for now. I will teach you to master your abilities. Our home is sacred. We shall restore it to its former glory, beginning tonight. Remove the branches, vines, and leaves."

They stared at her, blankness in their eyes.

"I will show you," Seosaimhín offered as she picked up a few branches and then led them into the woods. She dropped the branches there and began to return to the grove.

A few Strigoi began to copy her motions, and soon, all of the Strigoi carried debris into the woods.

"Excellent, my blessed children."

Searoburh

Claudius found himself thirsty and in need of sustenance. He could smell a town in the distance. Perhaps it would be Searoburh, at least, that was what the new locals called the village that he and Marcus still referred to as Sorviodunum.

Claudius landed in a back alley and headed towards the market. Torches lit the paths, and so he ducked into the shadows. He moved through the gloom, searching for someone who could offer him some sustenance.

He glanced over at one of the shoppers and noticed a man, who coughed loudly towards his family. Claudius shifted his gaze, figuring they would need their blood.

He then caught sight of a female traveling at a healthy pace. However, the sound of a babbling baby changed his mind.

Soon a few children raced by him, but he was not that hungry… besides, children's blood tasted weak.

Another woman caught his eye, and he watched her totter as if inebriated. She giggled as she tossed dark hair over her shoulder.

"Hello my donor," he whispered to himself.

As Claudius crept towards her, he planned to take her hand. In anticipation of the pounce and the taste of her vitae, he licked his lips.

Then the woman turned to the side as a voice rang out. "Hilda! There you are! Come look at this shop. Such marvelous treasures!"

Hilda giggled again. "Alright, Eadburga."

Claudius watched her take more unsteady steps towards a dark and fragrant shop.

He turned to start his hunt again, but the scent of her still teased him.

"The hunt continues," he murmured.

He stepped out of shadow and followed her into the shop.

The smell of incense overwhelmed all the other smells, making Claudius coughed a little. He waved away the onslaught of smoke and sneezed, surprising himself by his reaction.

He the walked through the shop, trying to find Hilda, but the shimmering lamps, pungent whale oil, wood, stone, and strange minerals distracted him.

The shopkeeper had displayed dubious relics of unknown saints, animal bones, and some strange musical instruments.

Claudius lingered for a moment, thinking over the challenges they would set for Máire, making her fly around the world retrieving trinkets and baubles. Marcus had said no more, but how long after the end of the Strigoi threat would it take for Máire to get bored of inactivity? Maél Morrigan's attention span could be termed 'miniscule'.

He smiled as a trinket caught his eye. Claudius picked it up and then turned to find the shop owner. He then witnessed a reflection of himself in a highly polished, bronze mirror that gleamed like silver.

Claudius dropped the toy on a display stand and then moved in closer to look over the design. He ran a finger over a five-pointed star on the mirror. "Aphrodite," he whispered.

A throat cleared behind him, and then a face joined him in the mirror. He had not even realized that a mortal had approached him.

"Beautiful, isn't it?"

Claudius could find no words. He just nodded.

"This mirror is very special." The shopkeeper's eyes sparked a strange, blue fire. "It is a replica of a mirror forged by Hephaestus himself as a gift to Aphrodite. Sadly, soon after this copy was made, they say barbarians spirited away the original after the sacking of Athens."

Claudius found his tongue. "It's so beautiful." Blast, he would never get a decent price for this now. Nonetheless, he tried to regain a shred of shrewdness. "So it's a copy, you say."

"Indeed. Alexandros, the foremost craftsman, at the time, copied the actual mirror in exacting detail. The finest artists and scholars of the time could not tell the difference when looking at the two side by side. Only when they looked deep into their reflection could they distinguish the original from the copy," the shopkeeper answered.

"Why was that?"

"Ah, an excellent question. You see, this copy is not imbued with the magic of the original."

"Magical properties, you say?" Claudius found his curiosity piqued. Even though most merchants of such rarities often boasted of magical elements, most were fraudulent, intended for the unsuspecting mark. However, Claudius knew some magic existed in the world... he was Sugnwr Gwaed, after all.

The shopkeeper nodded his head. "Yes. Legend has it that it always displays the true beauty of the observer... the inner beauty, if you will. Since Aphrodite's inner beauty and exterior beauty were high, she spent all day and night staring into it. The other Gods had to pull her away from it. Hera took it from her and gave it to a poor widow, who then remarried and had beautiful children. They became a powerful family in Athens. It stayed with the family until Athens was attacked again."

"You know much about the history of this mirror," Claudius commented. He tried to ascertain whether this was just a tale intended to elevate the mirror's value, though why bother spinning a yarn about an object not for sale.

"I know the full story of every item in my shop," the shopkeeper explained as he gestured to his wares.

Claudius smirked. "So, where is the original?"

The man rubbed his beard and chuckled. "Rumor has it that it is in Constantinople. It would not be beyond the imagination to believe the

Basileus Irene has it. After all, if she were to lay eyes on it, she and it would not be easily separated."

Claudius shrugged his shoulders, hoping to clear visions of this mirror out of his head. "Well, I must go. I have a long journey still."

As he turned away, the shopkeeper moved quickly to intercept him. Claudius tried to ignore the stranger's frenzied steps as he tried to keep up with him.

"Did I mention that the original's magical properties may help those who seek to find their own beauty inside? Even the ugliest people are truly beautiful inside. They say Hephaestus himself became beautiful in this mirror," the shopkeeper called out.

Claudius stopped and considered that statement for a moment. He then looked back at the mirror, and something within called to him.

"How much for the copy?" he asked the shop owner.

The mortal rubbed his hands together and revealed a pleased smile. "One hundred silver."

"All I have to spare is eighty," Claudius answered, lying about the amount of money he carried.

The shopkeeper chuckled. "No... your travel clothing is well mended. You are not poor. Ninety."

Claudius shook his head, ignoring the desire to press his wishes on this stranger. "Fine. Ninety it is then."

The shopkeeper plucked the mirror from the wall and began to wrap it. "Would you like it delivered?"

"No. I am on my way to Bath. I will take it with me," Claudius answered as he passed the money over to the shopkeeper.

"A beautiful town. This mirror will be very happy there. It will be happy wherever there are smiles." The mortal then passed over the mirror to Claudius.

"Thank you." Claudius opened his large traveling bag, placed the mirror inside, and then hoisted the sack over his shoulder. As he pulled the door open, Claudius realized that he had forgotten about Hilda and his stomach. Figuring he could find another from whom he could feed, he stepped onto the threshold.

Then the shopkeeper called out, "Have a safe journey, my friend. Oh Claudius, tell Maél Muire, Marcus, and even that shifty Mac Alpin that Berti misses them."

Claudius stopped in his tracks and turned towards the interior of the shop. Emptiness and a lack of pungent scents greeted him. Only dust and cobwebs covered the shelves. The shopkeeper had disappeared along with his wares.

Claudius backed away from shop and into the dirt paths. He released the door and returned to the sky… his meal forgotten.

Sáerlaith felt exhausted, but she continued flying, ignoring the pain in her shoulder from holding onto Seamus. He had tucked his head into her shoulder as they took off, and he whimpered every once in awhile in fear. Somehow, however, concentrating on Seamus' fear relieved her from considering her own.

Sáerlaith looked over at Etain. The other Deargh Du had begun straggling behind halfway across the sea between their home and Brycgstow.

"I need to feed… I need to rest," Etain complained.

"I know," she called back. "I know. Feed yourself with the knowledge that we must reach safety. They are coming after us, Etain. Resting is not an option for us, now. We will reach Bath and Marcus' protection soon."

Sáerlaith hated lying. While she sensed no Deargh Du behind them, she felt in her heart that they were being chased.

She soon witnessed lights in the distance, and then the shadow of Bath appeared. As they came closer, she could see tents set around the beautiful home.

Her body tensed as she sensed a Deargh Du approach. Sáerlaith placed a hand on her sword.

What if our enemies have arrived before us? No… these are the thousand warriors waiting to go to Francia and the Empire.

It made no sense to expect these to be enemy Deargh Du, but she could not help but feel fear. Then she recognized the Deargh Du who approached. It was Maon.

"Sáerlaith?" he asked. His eyes reflected confusion.

Sáerlaith nodded her head.

"We'll land at the house, Caoimhín. Assemble the… what is left… just get all of the leaders together, please."

"Right away," Caoimhín acknowledged before flying towards the house, still carrying a mortal.

"Sáerlaith, what is wrong?" Maon asked as he flew to her side and wrapped an arm around Seamus. "I will carry your Seneschal."

"I appreciate your wish to assist me, Maon, but I have grave news and new orders for you and the other sentries," Sáerlaith answered. "There has been a coup. I fear that we are all who have escaped. They may be pursuing us. I need you to patrol the air and ground entrances, Maon. "

Maon's mouth opened in shock.

"Challenge any blood-drinker you see. A perceived friend may be an enemy, especially if they're Deargh Du. Is that understood?"

"Yes, Councilor," Maon responded as he bowed his head in respect.

Sáerlaith shook her head. "I am no Councilor, Maon. There is no Council left."

Claudius flew into Bath and witnessed the flickering lights of torches surrounding his home. Claudius felt relief, as they could leave for the Empire in a night or two. He would follow with the Ekimmu Cruitne and whatever Sugnwr Gwaed wished to take a boat journey.

As he mulled over the options, a figure dropped from the clouds and challenged him.

"Sugnwr Gwaed, state your name and your business here," the sentry shouted.

Claudius blinked at the sentry, who seemed familiar. "I'm Claudius Metrius Sertorius, and I live here."

The Deargh Du lowered his spear.

"My apologies," the unfamiliar Deargh Du said. "I will signal to the others so they don't fire on you when you reach the camp."

Claudius nodded. This experience seemed most unfriendly. The Deargh Du raised a hand and allowed it to glow. Then two flashes of light from the ground blinded him for a moment.

"It's safe for you to approach the encampment now," the Deargh Du said. "Please stay in a straight line from here to the gate where they will confirm your identity."

"Why are there extra security precautions?" Claudius asked.

The sentry's eyes grew sad. "Much has happened. The answers lie below. Go now."

Claudius flew towards the gate. He thought over what may have happened. Had the Ouphe returned? Did the Strigoi come here? He continued his thinking upon landing at the gate. Two, armed Deargh Du looked at each other. One nodded and then they both sheathed their blades in unison.

"Maon?" Claudius asked after recognizing one of the Deargh Du.

"Right this way, Lieutenant, they're expecting you," Maon said as he pushed open the gate.

"Who are they, Maon?" he asked as he walked through the gate.

Maon stepped through the gate after him and closed it. Maon's face remained grim.

"I have no words to express..." Maon shook his head. "Just follow me."

They marched towards the main house and through the doors. Claudius could not see of the servants anywhere... just warriors. It seemed almost as if he were in a Roman encampment. He heard no music and smelled no mead. Some Deargh Du removed decorations from the walls and packed them away without a word.

Maon approached a door and knocked. "Sáerlaith, Caoimhín, Claudius has arrived."

"Sáerlaith is here?" he whispered.

"No one told you?" Maon asked as he turned back towards him.

"Told me what?"

The door opened and Sáerlaith walked towards him. She appeared haggard and smelled of grime and saltwater. Her eyes told a mournful story.

"Ard Macha's gates are closed to us. Our brothers and sisters-in-darkness tried to kill us." Sáerlaith's eyes lowered for a moment. "We are all who have escaped."

chapter eighteen

Outside of Verviers

andubratius kicked his way through the younglings, cursing himself in silence for creating this mess. The pope would return from a tour of the holy sites in the region and find monsters in this cavalry.

"Fedele!" he called for the highest-ranking member of his staff to survive the Strigoi attacks. He then motioned for the Lamia to follow him into his tent. As he sat down, Mandubratius heard another fight erupt. How he wished he could simply make these ignorant Lamia disappear.

"Sir," Fedele acknowledged as he approached the desk. "How may I be of service?"

Mandubratius stared at the young Lamia for a moment before asking, "Have you noticed a lack of discipline amongst the new men?"

"They are acting with little restraint, sir. They are certainly not as polished as they were weeks ago. Perhaps–"

Mandubratius raised his right index finger. He glanced around the tent, suspecting ears everywhere could hear him. "Fedele, would you care to join me on a jaunt on horseback? We should get a better view of the camp." His riding skills had improved somewhat.

"Won't the Strigoi find us?"

"We won't be going that far," Mandubratius explained before rising.

"Alright," Fedele acknowledged with a nod.

"Excellent." Mandubratius crossed to the tent's exit and whistled before calling out, "Saddle our horses." He heard names called and his orders repeated.

Another youngling walked over with two horses. Mandubratius jumped up and settled himself on his horse, while Fedele mounted the other. He nudged his horse forward, and Fedele followed him.

After a few miles of traveling, he turned back toward camp and stared at it. Fedele stopped, awaiting orders. Mandubratius dismounted his horse and dropped the reins. The horse started to graze.

"What do you see, Fedele?" he asked while indicating the camp.

"I see soldiers, going about their business, but there is a lot of fighting. I also see the bodies of mortals strewn about. What do you see, Consul?"

"I see a personal embarrassment, Fedele." As Mandubratius turned his head to regard Fedele, he could see shock in the other Lamia's eyes. "Yes, my embarrassing mistake." He then uttered a humorless laugh.

"I believe..." Mandubratius continued before pausing for a moment. "I believed that in a night, I could have grown a legendary army of Lamia that would destroy all traces of the Strigoi. They were going to be a cornerstone... a return to what we once were, Fedele. However, my failure was underestimating the effects of our gifts." He shrugged a little.

"If I had the time and men, we could have spent months training them, Fedele. However, I believed that since they had discipline, it would work without extensive training." Mandubratius then returned his gaze to the camp again. "It did not."

"What will we do with them, Sir?" Fedele asked.

Mandubratius chuckled and then shook his head for a moment. "That, Fedele, is what I've been pondering the last few nights. Do you wish to know what I've concluded?"

"Of course." The stoic, young Lamia looked very serious.

"They have to be eliminated, Fedele. All of the new younglings."

Fedele nodded a little.

Mandubratius then noticed a few more fights start in the camp. "'How', is the real question, Fedele, how do we kill them?"

"They outnumber us by a high margin," Fedele began. "We would not be effective trying to kill them ourselves in combat."

"Correct."

"The Strigoi haven't attacked recently. We can't rely on them to kill these new younglings," Fedele added as Mandubratius began to pace a bit.

"Agreed," Mandubratius answered.

"Therefore, it seems our best option is to send them on a mission somewhere where we know they'll be annihilated." Fedele turned to face him. His dark eyes now revealed a reddish cast.

Mandubratius nodded. He had already considered where to send them.

"The Moorish blood-drinkers would make quick work of them," Fedele stated.

"Too far," Mandubratius replied.

"Hmmm... that leaves out the Algul to the east then."

"Indeed," Mandubratius agreed.

"That leaves the north."

Mandubratius nodded.

"You could send them to Eire," Fedele suggested with a chuckle.

"Too far," Mandubratius countered. "I was thinking of Dubris, off the coast of Briton, where a large army of Sugnwr Gwaed, Ekimmu Cruitne, and

Deargh Du will be leaving to join Marcus and his party."

"You intend to send an army of Lamia to the coast of Briton to attack our allies?" Fedele looked a little worried.

"It would eliminate these younglings, who are not up to our standards," Mandubratius explained.

"How do you intend to prevent this attack from turning the Celtic lines against us?" Fedele asked.

"That's not really my concern, Fedele. It's a worry for Marcus. After all, he must maintain the balance in Eire, Briton, and here. However, I will send a note to explain things, and I'll put it in a beautiful bag. The Celts love pretty things. I know I do." Mandubratius then grabbed his horse's reins.

"When will they be departing?" Fedele queried.

"As soon as we get to camp, we'll tell them that the demons have attacked Briton and that Leo is requesting their immediate intervention," Mandubratius replied while climbing back onto his horse.

"Excellent plan, co-consul," Fedele commented before grabbing his mount's reins and settling on his horse.

"Please don't take this in the wrong manner, Fedele, but had any other elder Lamia survived, I would talk to them just as I spoke with you. This is no special privilege. However, you came to the same conclusions as I, faster than many of them would have. Now, let's get back to camp." He gave the horse a squeeze, and they took off in a slow gallop.

Outside of London

The torches in the distance lit a bright and distant path to the ancient fortress. Claudius wished to say something to break the silence, yet he remained quiet, as did all the Deargh Du in their flight. Some, no, most of the Deargh Du had not even traveled outside of Eire. As they flew, they scanned the landscape without saying a word.

As they approached their meeting point, Claudius could sense sentries in the sky and on the ground.. The Ekimmu Cruitne would have been aware of their presence long before their arrival. The warriors of the Sugnwr Gwaed and the Ekimmu Cruitne waited below in parade formation. Upon seeing the officers leading both armies, Claudius mused over how no Deargh Du had volunteered to act as their temporary military commander.

Claudius then turned his eyes towards Sáerlaith, who frowned at the vast skies, and suggested, "We should be more precise in our descent."

She nodded but said nothing. Her eyes seemed empty and her face slack.

"Do as you see fit," Caoimhín whispered.

Claudius signaled to the Deargh Du behind him, and then his commands echoed in a near silent whisper. They then moved into formation within a few breaths. He felt a great deal of pride in them for their perseverance. He could see Blodwyn and Cathair approach the front of their respective forces as they remained in formation.

The Deargh Du landed precisely between the other two races of blood-drinkers. Claudius then approached Cathair and Blodwyn and embraced them both.

"What has befallen the Deargh Du to look so stern?" Blodwyn whispered.

Claudius looked over at Sáerlaith again. Her eyes remained focused on distant skies.

"We'll discuss that later," he whispered. He then cleared his throat. "Now let's make camp for the day. We'll move out to the ships at dusk."

Cathair and Blodwyn nodded.

"Most impressive by the way," Claudius commented.

Cathair chuckled. "They sobered up well enough."

Claudius smiled and added, "I figured that traveling might help. I'll dismiss them." He then marched away from the three groups of blood-drinkers to stand before all three armies. He turned to face them and shouted, "Set up camp! Dismissed!"

Warriors dispersed and began setting up tents.

A few minutes later, he walked into the officers' tent with Blodwyn and Cathair. Claudius beckoned for Sáerlaith and Caoimhín to follow.

Blodwyn and Cathair's staff joined them after gathering chairs for their superior officers. Claudius took a chair and offered it to Sáerlaith, but she shook her head. He then moved it to a spot by the map and settled down. Cathair took a chair but remained standing.

Claudius then turned towards the head of the Council of Five. "I now have been told to say that on the behalf of the Ekimmu Cruitne and Sugnwr Gwaed councils, we're so pleased and honored to have the assistance of the Deargh Du in this alliance against the Strigoi."

"I am no longer the head of the council," Sáerlaith corrected. "There is no council." Her voice constricted with held back tears. She then turned away from the conversation looking angry.

"Please forgive our ire," Caoimhín stated to Cathair and Blodwyn. "The Deargh Du have split into those who wish to follow and serve the balance and those who wish to purify themselves of outside influence, to the point of eradicating anything not of our own culture."

Cathair's face grew gray.

"How many are left?" Blodwyn asked.

"Will any others join us?" another officer asked.

"This is all of us," Sáerlaith stated, "those who fled the massacre at Ard Macha, those who came from Bath, and the few in the Empire."

"So, what is our plan," Cathair asked.

Claudius sighed. "I have been given leave by the Deargh Du to represent them in tactical matters until we reach Marcus. Our plan remains the same. We leave for the boats and sail for the Frankish Empire."

"Are there no plans to take back Ard Macha?" Blodwyn asked as he looked from Claudius to Sáerlaith.

Sáerlaith looked back at Blodwyn and Claudius, who witnessed her haunted stare. "I fear..." Sáerlaith closed her eyes and continued, "I fear that we shall not see our home for many years." She rested her hands on a chair. Claudius could not fathom the depths of their loss... her loss.

Just then, the tent flap rose, and an Ekimmu Cruitne, one of the junior officers, walked inside and approached the officers.

"Sir," he said to Claudius, "There is a scout with an urgent message from the coast near Dubris."

"Send for the scout to join us," Claudius ordered.

The officer left the tent and soon returned with a wet and smelly Sugnwr Gwaed.

The Sugnwr Gwaed lowered her cloak and warned, "Sir, the Lamia are attacking Dubris."

"What?" Claudius almost started laughing at the crazy notion that their allies the Lamia would choose this time to invade Bri... the Kingdom of Wessex. "Are you sure? How are they dressed?"

"It is most odd," the scout continued. "We witnessed them land on a ship and exit on horseback. They wear an unfamiliar uniform, but one of us believed them to be wearing the uniform of the pope. They seem to act like mortals, sir. It was very confusing. They are demanding the surrender of Dubris, and they have already killed several farmers."

"Did you see Mandubratius or any other Lamia you or someone else might have recognized?" Claudius inquired. These could not be their Lamia allies.

Could there be other Lamia?

"No one saw anyone they recognized. Sir... they were riding the horses... not feeding from them."

Claudius steadied himself against his chair. "That is most... perplexing."

"What should we do?" Cathair asked.

"Is the alliance over?" Blodwyn added.

"Do we continue to the empire?" another officer queried.

Claudius continued to hear the chatter of the Ekimmu Cruitne and Sugnwr

Gwaed, while the Deargh Du remained stoically silent. Before emotions ran to high, Claudius waved his hand to quiet the voices.

"It is clear we must intervene. A Lamia army is attacking the mortal civilian populace within our borders," he stated. "However, before attacking, we shall seek their surrender. If they are hostile, we will respond in kind. Further, if the opportunity presents itself, we need to find out who they are and why they are attacking Briton."

"That means taking prisoners," Blodwyn surmised aloud.

"Yes," he answered. "Once this sad affair is concluded, we have the sea to traverse and an army of Strigoi to defeat. Whether we add the Lamia to that list of foes remains to be seen. Let us not rush into confrontation before we know why those of their blood are attacking," he continued. "For all we know, this could be some independent army not associated with Mandubratius. More information is needed. Agreed?"

Most who were present nodded, and a few grumbled a surly assent.

"Excellent, then we'll leave for Dubris as soon as we pack the camp."

As the lower ranking officers began to carry out chairs, Claudius walked over to Sáerlaith. "I apologize that we must cut short your rest, but we need the Deargh Du."

Sáerlaith's haggard eyes met his. "The Deargh Du will endure, and we will join our brothers and sisters in this battle." She then left the tent.

Other warriors moved into the tent and prepared to pack supplies. One warrior met his eyes, questioning in silence Claudius' presence in the tent. Claudius decided to step out of the tent, and he watched as the warriors began to disassemble the camp. He felt a strange thrill at watching the armies prepare for their journey under his command.

Dubris

Horatio watched with horror as his friend, Renatus, and two others walked into the small town's church and yanked out two priests, taking them into their custody.

He closed his eyes for a moment as he contemplated the horrors over the last few weeks. Horatio had received a field promotion in the Angelic ranks a scant two weeks ago, but he felt great remorse at the perceived duties of Angels. Renatus had claimed that Horatio's remorse could be Satan's temptation to let sinners go without being punished.

The three soldiers bound the two skinny priests and began to drag them towards the ring of cavalry. When they arrived, Renatus began to question the priests.

"Where are the demons and those touched by the demons? Where are they hiding?" Renatus demanded.

"I... I... don't know what you are talking about! There are no demons in Dubris!" the older priest sputtered.

"You lie to protect those who are impure?" Renatus shouted.

Horatio wondered whether he could be in hell at this moment... a hell where old friends became monsters.

The priest fell to his knees and then raised his hands in prayer. "I do not lie. I swear by the love of Jesus Christ, there are no demons here."

Renatus turned to a sergeant. "Flay him, and the other, until they either speak the truth or Satan takes them."

The major's words echoed through the town. "Bring me more of the unclean. I must interrogate them and discover where they are hiding their demon brethren."

Horatio then heard a woman scream and begin to whimper.

"This child was caught trying to flee the village," another soldier reported as he dragged a small boy by his hair towards the major.

Horatio watched the child's eyes turn fearful at the scene, staring open-mouthed as the priests began screaming in fear and in pain.

The major pointed at the child and yelled, "You see! This child is possessed by a demon! There is no doubt. The demons have infested this village."

He could hear agreements from the others, but Horatio lowered his eyes, for he could not agree. Why were his fellow angels punishing this village? Of course, everyone else appeared convinced of the people's wickedness, but Horatio could not condone their actions.

He felt fearful of speaking out. He had already tried his best, in the camp in the empire, somehow, to escape most of the fights. If he had said anything, they would have pulled him from Amadeo and torn him apart. Yet, his anger rose with the cries of fear from the village.

Horatio then sensed a presence, and he noticed the others were looking around as well. Even the priests' screams subsided and became a whimper, as the soldiers had ceased their torturing.

"Call the men from the perimeter, have them form in battle array," the major shouted, before leaping back onto his horse. Then a steady whistle blew.

Horatio joined the other young officers and then took the reins of his horse. He patted Amadeo's shoulder. He knew something approached... something not mortal, so he unsheathed his sword and waited for orders.

"Hold your weapons!" the major ordered.

Then Horatio saw a small group of a half dozen strangely attired men and women approach them on foot. They appeared to be armed but held no weapons. They looked serious, but they displayed no other emotion.

"Who are you? Friend or foe?" the major shouted.

A dark-haired soldier stopped a few feet in front of them and stared at the major with dark, somber eyes.

"I am Claudius," said the stranger… perhaps their leader. "We are here to discover what gives you the right to attack Dubris."

"The devil stalks Anglo-Saxon Kingdoms," answered the major. "We are here to eradicate Satan's presence."

"Why are the Lamia concerned about Satan's presence here?" Claudius asked. He stretched out a hand to the major's horse. The horse whickered, but then he stuck out his nose to sniff at Claudius. Horatio noticed a small trace of a grin on the stranger's face.

"Lamia? What are Lamia? Are they the devil's servants?" the major shouted at Claudius, ignoring his mount's sudden interest in the man.

Horatio watched as the warriors in the distance whispered to one another. The man, who had introduced himself as 'Claudius', backed away towards the others, though he kept his eyes on the major.

"You do not serve Mandubratius and Amata, co-consuls of the Lamia?" Claudius asked, though his tone suggested he knew the answer. Claudius then stopped, though he still stood ahead of the other men and women. He then seemed to survey the cavalry forces against him.

"We serve His Holiness, Pope Leo III, The Holy Church in Rome, and the will of God. We are part of His Angelic forces here on earth. Now, I ask this question again… are you friend or foe?"

Claudius returned his gaze to the major. "If you cease this ill-conceived hostility towards these poor mortals return to your boats, and return to Rome, we will be friends, but if you resume this attack or take hostile action against us, we will be enemies." Menace crept into Claudius' voice, causing Horatio to shudder a little.

Despite his trepidation, Horatio locked eyes with the enemy soldier, and saw that a grim determination had entered the other soldier's eyes. Horatio then lowered his eyes, feeling a great deal of shame for his part.

Were Angels supposed to doubt their deeds?

"I do not believe you," the major challenged. "I believe that Satan himself has led you here to deceive us and turn us away from our God-given duty. We shall purify this village, but before we do, you will be purified." Then to his men, he yelled, "On my command, charge these demons!"

Mounted soldiers formed into a three-line formation, while those without horses stood in formation behind. Upon seeing the major lower his right hand, the horses and men began to trot towards the small gathering of men and women. After a few strides, the horses moved into a gallop.

Horatio had joined the third line by the left flank. He advanced Amadeo at a slow jog, lagging behind his line. No one seemed to notice him, as the other soldiers appeared to be focused on running down horseless foot soldiers.

No honor will come from this one-sided battle.

As quickly he had ordered the charge, the major shouted, "Halt!"

The horses ahead seemed agitated as Horatio caught up with them. He wondered why they had stopped. He then glanced towards their targets and then became astonished upon seeing no one. Their targets disappeared into the darkness.

Then a thick fog seemed to surround them, and he could hear thunder in the distance. He turned Amadeo to look to the rear, and Horatio realized that darkness surrounded them.

The major rode around the front of the cavalry shouting, "Hold your position. Steady! Await my orders!" His voice squeaked with what sounded like fear.

Horatio then heard many of his fellow soldiers begin to pray.

Indistinct figures then appeared from the mist on all sides. His senses reeled as they had earlier when the enemy first approached them. The enemy completely surrounded the cavalry.

He could see them clearly, now. They had not drawn their blades, though some held spears, but they too were lowered.

The enemy soldiers stopped, and then Horatio heard a voice, which sounded like Claudius.

"You have one last chance to withdraw. Do you accept?"

The major's posture remained fearful, though the men looked to him.

"What are your orders, sir?" Renatus called out, but the major said nothing.

"Formation, prepare to charge to the east," Renatus ordered. "Wedge formation!"

As the cavalry moved into formation, Horatio made sure his horse remained on the left flank at the back corner of the formation.

He could still see Renatus and the major from his vantage point. As Renatus glanced back at the major, the higher-ranking officer looked pleased. Then the major nodded.

"Attack!" Renatus yelled, ordering the charge. Shouts echoed through the field as officers guided their soldiers in keeping formation. Horatio led Amadeo towards the assault, though he still kept back.

The enemy warriors did not move, as if they were not going to defend themselves. Then the situation changed, as the enemy combatants disappeared once again.

Then screams from the cavalry deafened him. Horatio looked from the left to right side and observed the carnage as the enemy warriors attacked both mounted and unmounted cavalry with both thrown and thrust spears. Many soldiers fell from their horses.

Then he heard what sounded like a voice coming from above. Horatio tilted his head up to gaze at the night sky. He could see that some of the enemy warriors actually flying overhead, as if they were walking on an unseen platform above, hurling spears at the cavalry.

Some of his fellow soldiers remained mounted on their horses, but more and more fell. The flying warriors soon landed with a whoosh and began beheading every single papal soldier.

Horatio remained frozen, watching his friends die. Why did he not fight? Why did cowardice overwhelm him now? He knew the cavalry had performed evil deeds, but should he not fight alongside them now? Within moments, the enemy had beheaded everyone else. The victors of the strange battle then turned to face him, though he wondered why he still lived... they could have easily killed him. He then noticed that all of the horses remained still, and not one of the warriors cheered.

Horatio then dismounted Amadeo before dropping his scabbard, removing his helm, and kneeling on the ground. He said, "I surrender," before staring at the grass.

Unfamiliar words echoed. He could hear three men's voices and a woman's voice chattering to one another other. Horatio inhaled, about to ask what they intended to do with him, when a hard blow to his head turned his world dark.

Sáerlaith and the other officers stood off to the side of the remains of the Lamia soldiers. She kept silent, as she could find nothing to say. After all, they had lost their home. She had tried to call to the Goddess to ask for guidance, but no answers had come to her. How could she continue to guide the Deargh Du without Her assistance? Every time she tried, silence greeted her... silence and darkness.

Claudius and others spoke to her, but she did not listen to them. She then noticed that Claudius had stopped talking and watched her with a polite, yet expectant, look on his face. She realized that he had asked a question and awaited her answer. A tiny flame of embarrassment touched her.

"I... I... I'm sorry, I was distracted. Please explain further." She primed her ears.

"I understand," he said. "The prisoner is still unconscious."

She walked around the collapsed soldier. "Do you have any means of waking him?"

Claudius traded looks with Cathair.

"Would you..."

Cathair lowered his eyes. "We should restrain him, if you wish for me to do it."

Sáerlaith watched Claudius nod. She remembered stories of Ekimmu Cruitne bringing pleasure, and at times extreme pain. They loved the rush of giving pleasure, but in general, they seldom utilized torture. She wondered whether that talent came from the Ekimmu.

"Restrain him," Claudius ordered the guards, "and move him into a kneeling position."

"You realize the chains won't hold him," Blodwyn stated.

"Yes," Claudius answered, "but he probably doesn't know that."

The guards put the soldier on his knees, and then Cathair placed a hand on the young man's shoulder.

Sáerlaith watched, intrigued. Soon, the Lamia opened his red eyes and then emitted a sharp gasp of pain.

Cathair raised his hands and then backed away from Horatio.

The soldier uttered a soft cry and then asked, "Why aren't I dead?"

The others looked at one another.

"You still live because it serves us now," Sáerlaith explained. "If you no longer serve us, you will die as your friends did."

"How do I serve you?" the soldier asked in a squeaky voice.

She looked at Claudius and begged him to answer, though her thoughts faded like mist.

"I wish to ask you questions about why you're here," Claudius stated. "If I remove these restraints, do you promise to remain in my custody and submit to my questions?"

She studied Claudius, thinking that he offered too much kindness to this Lamia. However, this was his home, and he was in charge, so Sáerlaith held her tongue.

"I swear," the soldier whispered.

Claudius nodded. "Remove the restraints," he told the guards. After they removed the chains, the soldier lowered his head for a moment.

Claudius offered him a hand and helped the Lamia get to his feet. He then looked at the other blood-drinkers gathering around the circle. "If you have other duties, return to them."

His calm command still carried a mild threat, and it made the other warriors scurry in various directions.

"Follow me," Claudius said to the soldier. He motioned for Sáerlaith, Caoimhín, Blodwyn, and Cathair to join them in the tent.

She sat down in one of the chairs, while the others seated themselves. Sáerlaith raised her brows as Claudius motioned for the Lamia to sit down with them. The young soldier took a stool, revealing his own surprise.

"You seat our enemy in our presence?" she whispered to Claudius in Gaelic.

"Our enemy has surrendered, pledged to answer our questions, and swears he will not attempt to flee. If you disagree with my tactics, please wait to discuss it with me alone later," Claudius replied, before turning back to their captive.

"I'm Claudius Metrius Sertorius of the Hunt," Claudius began. "To my right is Sáerlaith of the Deargh Du line. The gentleman on her right is Caoimhín, who is also Deargh Du. Next to him is Blodwyn, who is of my line, the Sugnwr Gwaed, and the warrior next to you is Cathair Mac Domhnaill of the Ekimmu Cruitne. Please tell us your name."

The soldier's blue eyes lowered for a moment, but then he politely made eye contact with Claudius. "I'm Horatio di Reate of the Angelic Army of Pope Leo III. Are you of other Angelic orders?" The soldier's eyes studied everyone's in the tent. "I am afraid I'm an uneducated man, when it comes to information about our kind. They told us so little."

"Angelic order?" Sáerlaith blurted out in Latin.

"Yes... 'Deargh Du', 'Sugnwr Gwaed', and 'Ekimmu Cruitne'... these are names I haven't heard before. You fly and fight like angels. I assumed that those names were like... archangel," he said. Horatio seemed to be blushing. "I am probably wrong and have insulted you all in some way," Horatio offered.

Claudius turned to Sáerlaith and muttered in Gaelic, "He doesn't know what he is." His words belied incredulity.

"Is that your Angelic language?" Horatio asked as he looked up. "May I join your order? I will humble myself in Jesus' name if I am given the opportunity to prove my faith. I do not deserve this honor, but I will do my best to serve the Angels of God."

Sáerlaith watched Horatio lower himself to his knees again.

Claudius turned back to Horatio and suggested, "Perhaps Horatio and I need to go on a walk," he said.

Claudius gestured for Horatio to rise. "Please get up. There is no need to kneel." The adoration present in this soldier's eyes for the 'Angels' surrounding him made Claudius feel a little uncomfortable, so Claudius tried to think of how to best approach this matter. He knew part of him wanted to laugh at this amusing development.

When Claudius started walking, Horatio followed him. After several paces, Claudius turned his head to look at the other blood-drinkers, and they still looked to be in shock.

The two blood-drinkers headed into the darkness towards the field where the horses that grazed. He noticed one look up and stare at Horatio for a moment.

"Have you fed recently?" he asked Horatio.

"I don't eat food anymore," Horatio replied, looking confused.

"Of course," Claudius answered. "I assumed that. I know you have desires for other sustenance. I have them too. You and I know what it means to feed. I thought it best that you have something during this chat."

Horatio met his stare. "Thank you, but no, sir. I was told we could only feast after a victory."

Claudius smiled for a moment. "The army has changed little since my day. I am familiar with the methods of starving soldiers in order to encourage a victory." He walked towards the horse that watched them with limpid eyes. "He is your horse, yes?"

"Yes he is. Amadeo is his name," Horatio answered.

Then to the horse, Claudius whispered, "May he take from you?" as he stretched a hand towards Amadeo.

Claudius could hear an affirmation, though with a stipulation.

"He agrees. Do be gentle, Horatio. Amadeo said the last time hurt him, though he knows you didn't mean to cause him pain. He likes your company, Horatio."

"How did you…" Horatio asked, though Claudius just stared at him while patting Amadeo's shoulder.

"A gift from my patron," Claudius explained. "Now feed."

Claudius stroked Amadeo's neck once more with his right hand before whispering, "thank you" in the horse's ear. He then watched Horatio extend his canines and feed from Amadeo's neck.

Once Horatio finished, Claudius healed the wound and then began to walk. The other horses looked at him as he moved through the field. He then heard Horatio thank Amadeo before falling in step with him.

"How old are you, Horatio?" he asked.

"Eighteen," the youngling answered.

"How old do you think I am?" Claudius inquired.

"I imagine you are ageless, sir. May I ask if you came into being as I did? How did you become an angel?"

Claudius shook his head and met the Horatio's gaze. "Horatio, I'm not an angel… I don't even serve the Christian God. My patron is Cernunnos, God of the Wild and Lord of the Hunt. He transformed me over eight hundred years ago, when I had marched over this land with two Roman legions. I was but thirty two when I became Sugnwr Gwaed, the British line of blood-drinkers."

Horatio backed away, as if horrified. "What you're saying makes no sense," Horatio whispered.

Claudius stopped walking and turned to face Horatio, "I'm sorry. I know it is difficult to understand, but you and I are not mortals or angels. We are blood-drinkers, created by deities as a blessing, or sometimes a curse. The Deargh Du and Ekimmu Cruitne have the blood of a Goddess in their veins, whereas Hera cursed the progenitor of your line. We are not angels, but we can serve our Deities for the greater good of this world and the world beyond." He paused and then asked, "Do you remember the name of the person who changed you... transformed you?"

Horatio continued backing away. "No, no."

"He or she fed from you and then you fed from them, did you not?" Claudius smiled for a moment, as Horatio still looked as though he were in shock. "You weren't born this way."

Horatio shook his head and continued taking careful steps away from Claudius, though the two men kept eye contact.

Claudius decided to close the distance between them. As he began walking, he asked, "Would you like to know why I spared you?"

Horatio stopped backing away. Claudius stopped walking and remained silent, letting the youngling Lamia think over the question.

"Yes... I would."

"Shame," Claudius explained. "You were ashamed of what the other so-called angels were doing, but it wasn't just the shame. I felt that you understood you were something beyond mortal, yet not Angelic. You weren't blinded, as the others had been."

Horatio lowered his eyes again.

"So tell me, what were you ashamed of? Why didn't you take joy in the suffering of those whom you believed to be possessed by demons?" he asked.

Horatio's eyes looked up and examined him for a moment. "I saw their actions against those innocents as atrocities. Angels do not inflict atrocities against innocents, mortal man does. It sickened me to see my friends believing that God had ordained their actions, that they should wield such brutality in His name. They were not angels." Horatio paused as clarity wavered in his eyes. "I am not an angel either... I see that now. It is confirmed." Horatio then dropped to his knees and began to sob.

Claudius felt pity for him. He then sat down cross-legged across from Horatio. "I can't imagine what your transformation must have been like," he offered.

Horatio hiccupped and then stopped crying. He then swiped at his reddened face, trying to wipe away his tears.

"No one else seemed to have a problem with it," Horatio muttered before sitting down on the ground.

Claudius rested his palms against the grass. "I will help you understand what you are, Horatio. I believe that with my guidance, you will be able to decide who you are." He then stood up.

"I'd like that," Horatio agreed.

Claudius pulled Horatio to his feet. He could sense the sunrise. He chuckled as they began to walk back towards the tents. "In addition to informing you of your nature, I'm supposed to be interrogating you. What can you tell me about your orders?" Claudius asked as he looked at Horatio again. "Why were you sent here?"

"An Emissary of the pope, General Michael Tolomei, said that the pope wished for us to come here and destroy the demons that had settled in these kingdoms," Horatio answered.

Claudius stopped mid-step. "Michael Tolomei?"

"Yes," Horatio replied. "Is there something wrong?"

Claudius stared at the encampment.

"It's just that this discovery brings a strange new twist to our alliance against the Strigoi," Claudius explained before he resumed walking.

"Strigoi?" Horatio looked confused.

"Yes, the so-called demons are another line of blood-drinkers, like you and me," Claudius answered.

Horatio seemed to accept his answer. When they arrived at his command tent, Claudius held up the tent flap and motioned for the Lamia to enter the tent. After he entered, he could see that the other officers in the tent all looked a little upset. He also saw that a beautiful bejeweled scroll case rested on top of the desk.

"What's this?" Claudius asked as he picked up the scroll case.

"Look inside," Cathair prodded.

Claudius opened the case and removed a scroll. He unrolled it and then read the script. He felt some surprise at seeing the Gaelic.

"What does it say?" Horatio asked.

Claudius turned to Horatio and placed the scroll on the folding desk. "It would seem that you and your friends were lambs sent to be sacrificed on the altar of our alliance."

Horatio could hear them railing back and forth to each other in what sounded like the bleating of goats, at times. However, some of their words seemed drenched in beautiful sounds.

Horatio felt some shame in having forgotten their names, but he hoped it would not be an imposition to ask again later. He lowered his gaze as the other warrior watched him with a steady eye. Horatio winced at the memories of pain, so he tried to concentrate on other matters.

He turned to study the others who remained in the shelter of the tent. The dark lady and her silver-haired companion continued their loud conversation with Claudius and the others. Their appearance made him feel quite simple and plain. The beautiful words continued, gaining in pitch and volume.

"Sir," Horatio addressed Claudius.

Claudius' golden eyes regarded him for a moment then turned dark.

Horatio leaned closer to Claudius in order to whisper in his ear, fearful of what the others might hear.

"Are you talking about me? I'll offer no resistance if I must be killed."

He watched Claudius smile for a moment before he suggested, "Perhaps it would be appropriate for our guest if we spoke in Latin." Horatio could sense an order within the quiet and polite request.

The others shared a look with one another and then nodded.

Horatio could tell that Claudius held some sort of rank, yet Horatio considered that he would not be the highest-ranking officer among these ang... blood-drinkers.

The male warrior cleared his throat. "As I was saying, as much as I hate to admit it, and as much as I'd love to torture that Lamia bastard, until we speak with Mandubratius, we should not see the Lamia as hostile. After all, I suppose he may have seen his younglings as a threat to the alliance."

Horatio felt his bile rise in his throat. He already knew he hated Michael Tolomei. Therefore, this Mandubratius and the rest of the Lamia were not to be trusted.

"After sending us to our deaths, you feel he should suffer no consequences? You have every right to break this alliance and hunt him down," Horatio rallied back.

A deafening silence surrounded him, and Horatio wondered whether he should be afraid, but his rage kept him from feeling any other emotion. The other blood-drinkers' eyes revealed a strange mixture of emotions, ranging from ire to a highly nuanced fear.

The dark and beautiful lady's eyes turned away from her friend, the man with the moon-colored hair, and regarded him.

"Youngling," she addressed him. "No one here is suggesting that the Lamia go without consequences for sponsoring mortals that they convinced were serving their God and sending them to slaughter. It was very wrong of them to hide your true nature from you and the other soldiers. That is a travesty." Her eyes now burned a brilliant green, but then they returned to a somber brown. "The Lamia will be punished... soon," then her voice turned husky and gentle, "just not tonight."

"Why wait?" Horatio asked. "Let's sail now and attack them. You have thousands. How many do they have?"

The dark lady's eyes grew green again, and Horatio felt a moment of fear. He could not remember a time when a lady frightened him as this one did.

"Young Lamia, you lack an understanding of how potent and precarious the enemy that stands against all of us is," she stated.

"I don't understand how any being could stand against you," Horatio stated in a near whisper. "You fly!"

Horatio sensed quick movement and became aware that Claudius had moved from one side of him to the other in a manner that nearly made him jump in surprise.

"The Strigoi do not attack with steel, muscle, or wood. Their weapons are unseen and even more deadly."

Something in Claudius' voice chilled Horatio's blood and disturbed him, while his eyes burned golden and revealed an unfamiliar ferocity. Then Claudius began to back away.

"What kind of weapon could kill and yet not be seen?" Horatio asked, fearful of the answer.

Claudius moved in closer, a few inches away from Horatio's face.

"They corrupt the mind with horrible images and the nightmares of madmen," Claudius intoned. "They squeeze the mortal mind in ways you don't want to comprehend and offer only a gruesome and horrific death. Most of the blood-drinkers leave a mortal alive... why kill when your quarry can live to feed you again? Not so with the Strigoi. Also, the Strigoi can force blood-drinkers to experience a prolonged nightmare. I hope you never have to suffer that."

Claudius took and step back and lowered his eyes. "My encounter has left a scar in my mind that will never heal. Yes," he said as he lifted his eyes and examined the others. His voice and face grew hard, "I am afraid of the Strigoi. Yes, most of us here, perhaps all of us, are afraid of the Strigoi. We need an alliance with the Lamia. Only when we are united can we stand a chance against this foe."

Claudius' features softened again. "Now do you understand, Horatio?"

The blood-drinker sat down and appeared tired. Two of the officers appeared to be in shock, but the beautiful ones did not appear to be surprised at all.

Eyes turned towards him as Horatio tried to find words.

"I understand," Horatio stated, hoping they did not expect him to say more.

The silver-haired man looked up to the ceiling of the tent for a moment and then announced, "The sun rises quickly, as we all know. We should go to sleep soon?" The man's posture and tone indicated that he asked a question.

Claudius inclined his head, in a half-nod. The others began to leave the tent in silence, though some blood-drinkers remained. Many of them stared at the tent flap after the others had left.

"I'm sorry for expressing my experiences in such a fashion," Claudius began. "I needed to convince everyone how dangerous the Strigoi truly are. No one else has been touched by their madness in this group." Claudius sighed. "I was sincere when I said I hoped you would never undergo their touch. No one deserves such an experience."

Horatio turned to study the tent flap. The entire incident sounded worse than his transformation into a Lamia. He found nothing to say.

"Do you have a place to stay?" Claudius asked.

Horatio sensed the sun nearing the edge of the horizon. He then shook his head. He heard Claudius chuckle.

"Don't worry. There are a few extra cots here. You're staying with me... I insist." Claudius then started to pull off his boots as the others, both men and women began to undress as well.

"I'm to stay in the command tent?" Horatio asked.

"Well, I am the commander, for now, and I offered to help you find yourself. The best way for you to do that is to tag along with the rest of us, though we are not of your line. There are spare blankets in the bag," Claudius answered.

Horatio grabbed some blankets, walked over to one of the cots, sat down, and began to pull off his boots and armor.

Claudius yawned and lay back in his cot. "It's going to be a long night tomorrow. Go to sleep." His new friend closed his eyes.

"I think I had a long night tonight, sir."

Claudius opened his eyes and stared at Horatio with a ready grin. "Yes, but tomorrow night will worse. The Ekimmu Cruitne hate crossing water. It's their geis... I'll tell you what that means when I'm not so sleepy. Get to sleep, soldier."

Horatio sensed an order in his words. He then closed his eyes and drifted into sleep.

chapter nineteen

Near the Isle of Testerep

aoimhín wandered back into the captain's quarters after speaking with the captain on deck. The smell of illness faded as they neared land, but he felt quite ready to escape the ship.

Claudius and the others, excepting Cathair and his staff, examined the map on the captain's table. Caoimhín assumed Cathair remained with the rest of his line in the lower bowels of the ship. Healing did little to help the Ekimmu Cruitne on board, although Sáerlaith remained down below, doing what she could to help them, as it seemed to keep her mind off the problems in Ard Macha.

"The Captain says we will land at Oostende soon," Caoimhín informed Claudius.

Claudius looked up and grinned. "So, how long do you think a Deargh Du can keep a mortal oblivious in their glamoury?"

Caoimhín chuckled. "I'm not sure to be honest," he admitted. "I suppose we'll find out."

"A few hours do you think?" Claudius asked, now looking serious.

"I believe we can accomplish that, if we are fed," Fianait answered, before lowering her head. "Sorry, I hope I did not interrupt."

Caoimhín shook his head. "I have not attempted such a feat for that long, so I believe your experience is as important as anyone else's." Actually, he felt a little grateful that one of the Council members had stepped in to assist.

"Good," Claudius acknowledged as he met both of their gazes. "Then you will be the distraction. Find any mortal near the port and make sure they don't notice our arrival. Perhaps others can bring down the darkness to shield us."

"We'll make sure to cover any escape routes in case someone is frightened," he said, meeting Fianait's eyes. She nodded back.

"Good. I think we can all agree that stealth is required. We don't want to look like an invasion force," Claudius added.

"A sound plan," Blodwyn murmured. "I will be quite glad when this sea voyage is complete."

Claudius chuckled. "One night I shall tell you a true sea voyage tale. This is a mere jaunt with just two nights of travel."

Blodwyn laughed. "I just mean that I'll be very happy when the Ekimmu Cruitne are back on solid ground."

Caoimhín started laughing outright. "I'm sure the thousand Ekimmu

Cruitne on all of these ships agree with your words and sentiment," he joked, before pushing his hair behind his ears.

Claudius snorted and then shook his head. "Horatio, bring that other map of the empire over to the table, please."

The Lamia placed a large map on top of the table.

"Alright," Claudius began as he tapped a point with his right index finger. "Here is Testerep, and there is the tiny port of Oostende. When we disembark, we'll go into the village of Oostende and into this forested area to camp. We will keep as silent as possible. From there, we can travel on to Aachen or go south towards Burgundy. It shouldn't take us too long either way."

Caoimhín watched the others nod their heads. He did so as well. Then he heard the captain command to drop anchor.

"Let's commence. Relay my orders to the other ships," Claudius stated. "Let no trace of our landing be left."

Aachen

Charles wrapped an arm around Talia's waist, pulling her closer to him. She smiled as she contemplated how this manipulation had been going easier than expected.

"You're very amorous tonight," she cooed. "I am sure such sustainability is only known in legend."

Charles chuckled and smiled. He then leaned back in bed and turned his eyes in her direction. "And you, I have never known a woman to take such abuse without begging me to stop."

"You excite me, Imperial Majesty." Talia began to kiss him again. She tugged at his lips, impatient for more attention. She worried at times that Charles would become distracted with his duties and toss her aside like his other mistresses and concubines. "Your very presence makes me moist," she whispered.

She heard him chuckle again. "Talia, please," he said with a smile, revealing the radiance of the sun. "Talia, I believe we are past the honoraries. Call me Charles." His eyes then grew distant and somber.

"What is troubling you, Charles?"

He examined her for a moment, as if trying to decide whether he could trust her or not. Then he revealed, "I feel as if the pope is challenging my authority to govern the empire. Part of me wonders whether he has already selected someone to take over the government."

Talia tried to hide her surprise at his candor. She did not even manipulate him now. She mused for a moment whether he were dense or foolish. She kept silent, deciding to let him reveal more.

The emperor stretched his arms overhead. He then sat up a bit and studied her again. "Well, Leo did not say that I was not fit to rule my own empire, but he vehemently accused me of improperly dealing with the murders plaguing our home. He claims that the attacks were made by the devil. He, in his infinite wisdom, has decided to intervene in what he is convinced is an ecumenical matter."

She continued staring at him and said nothing, hoping he would feel comfortable enough to babble more. He then began muttering to himself, and she felt inclined to say something.

"So, what is the pope doing?" Talia inquired as she ran a fingertip over his hand. He had some of the strongest hands she had ever encountered, for a mortal.

"Pope Leo and his forces are some distance from Aachen, although he has also sent his armies to enforce his rule in my empire. The most disturbing thing is that I have heard rumors that he is ordering the execution of those related to the afflicted. It's quite shameful."

"Afflicted?"

"Yes, Talia, those poor people driven mad during the attacks on the churches."

She allowed her face to reveal horror. She sat up and rotated her body so she could face him.

The emperor rolled on his left side and faced her. He began to play with a gilded tendril of her hair, and soon, his eyes revealed lust.

"What will you do?" Talia asked, though she found herself distracted, growing aroused as he stroked her hair.

"I will do as I have already done," he purred. "I will disagree with the Holy Father and wait for my sons to arrive. Then we'll send him home." Charles then pulled her towards him.

Talia grinned, feeling her hunger begin to rise. She shoved Charles onto his back and straddled him.

"Imperial Majesty!" called a familiar voice from outside the room.

"Damn your secretary," Talia hissed.

The emperor made a frustrated noise. "What is it now, Ercanbald?" he called out.

"Julien de Divio has arrived with desperate news from Vézelay."

"Mmmmmm," Charles muttered. "I needed to speak with him anyway. I'm glad he recovered quickly. I will be there soon, Ercanbald!"

He turned back to her. "My apologies, Talia, but sometimes duties must come first."

"I understand," Talia stated as she pushed back her hair. She could try to manipulate him back into bed… he had not yet sated her, but that might seem suspicious. So instead, she smiled at the emperor and watched him dress.

"Come, join me if you wish," the emperor offered with a smile. "I have an announcement to make, and I would like for you to be there."

Talia returned his smile and answered, "Of course, Imperial Majesty." She wondered what this announcement might be. *Perhaps he will propose to her. He did say this was important, after all.* "I will join you as soon as possible." She must bathe and dress… with haste.

"Julien!" Emperor Charles greeted as he embraced the inspector general. "Don't bow. Tell me, what is going on in Vézelay? Marcus already informed me about the murders in the empire. How is your family?"

Julien felt a little shock at the familiar greeting. *Then again, his mother and the emperor knew each other.*

"Imperial Majesty, the town of Divio has been overrun with papal forces. They killed anyone who had a shred of contact with the victims, including my sister-in-law and my nephews. The survivors traveled with my brother, Reginald, to Vézelay. Then the papal forces attacked Vézelay. The garrison and the mercenaries helped all of us escape. They are on their way here, Imperial Majesty, for your protection."

A strange smell caught Julien's attention. He turned and noticed a golden-haired woman watching him and the emperor.

Charles nodded. "They will have my protection, Julien, I promise you. If they need a safe place outside the walls of the city, take them to Prüm Abbey." He then paused for a moment. "I also have an announcement to make." The emperor raised his hands and addressed the crowd.

At that moment, Julien glanced around the small gathering. He then noticed that the blonde woman beamed a radiant smile as she moved towards the emperor. Julien could sense that she was another blood-drinker. She smelled very much like Amata, *so she must be a Lamia.* He tried to hide his shock.

"This young man saved my life and serves this empire with distinction. For your actions and courage, I grant you lands. You are now Julien de Divio, Count of Auxerre. Thank you again." The emperor turned back towards the blonde woman, who looked quite annoyed, but then her beaming false smile reappeared. *Julien wondered about her presence here.*

"Thank you, Imperial Majesty," Julien said while he bowed, though his thoughts focused on discovering whom this stranger could be and what she wanted.

Julien began to leave the main hall, considering why he had been given Auxerre, not that he would ever complain about receiving a gift, but his confusion regarding his gift and the strange Lamia multiplied.

Then he heard Ercanbald's voice say, "Inspector General?" He stopped walking and then turned back to face the secretary.

"Emperor Charles asks that you wait for him in his private meeting quarters. He wishes to sign the papers of title." Ercanbald then waved over a guard. "Please escort the inspector general to the emperor's meeting room," he said to the guard.

"If you follow me, my lord," the guard intoned before leaving.

Julien walked behind him for several paces down a hallway, before the guard motioned for him to go into a quiet chamber, which held a desk and two chairs. Julien sat down in one of the chairs and closed his eyes for a moment, trying to contemplate the events of the last few moments and the mysterious Lamia in court. He then heard the guard step out and close the door. After several minutes, the door opened again, and Julien opened his eyes and jumped to his feet.

There she stood, looking quite regal, the woman he had seen at court. Her hair seemed somewhat copper tinged, but golden threads gleamed within her strands of hair. Her blue eyes studied him.

"Am I in the wrong place? I was informed to wait here," he said. Her stare made him quite nervous. He felt an intrusion in his head, and so he focused on shutting his thoughts away. Perhaps he should distract her.

"I was told to wait here for Emperor Charles," he said. "I believed you were he, for a few moments, but I can see that you are not."

She beamed radiance and laughed. "I am not sure if you mean to flatter or insult me, my lord, but I am neither emperor nor a man."

"Perhaps it is your bearing," Julien admitted. "I must say you present a very patrician and dignified manner. Perhaps you have ruled over people before?" He wondered whether discovering that about her would lead to her identity.

"Such sentiments from a man... I had heard that you were a strange one, Inspector General." The Lamia chuckled again. She seemed to skip into the chamber. "I am Lady Talia of Époisses, and you are Julien de Divio, Count of Auxerre. I believe we are neighbors."

"Of course," he said. "It has been quite some time since I last visited Époisses. It is a beautiful village. How is Lord Guilbert?"

"He is dead," she stated. The Lamia then dismissed the guards by merely looking into their eyes. They closed the door when the left.

"There now, no more prying eyes, Inspector General." Talia's eyes moved over him again. "I understand that you are acquainted with an old friend."

Julien felt some confusion, but he kept up his mental guards. It seemed Talia wished to distract him as well.

"My, you do have good mental facilities," Talia purred. "You display much fortitude to avoid my rather rude endeavors to know you better." She smiled as he felt her attempts to examine his mind begin to fade. "Do not worry, sweet youngling, for your secret is safe. Did Ma-Michael sponsor you himself?"

Julien stared at her hair for a moment as he tried to find a good answer. "It was not him directly," he explained. "The Strigoi attacked, and I was rendered helpless. Michael wounded my assailant and Laudalino sponsored me. They said I have some importance, but I am clueless to what importance they meant. Michael bade me continue my life as if nothing had happened, with the expectation that I would gather information about the Empire's responses to the Strigoi and His Holiness."

Will she accept my lie as fact?

Talia moved in closer to him. Her angry eyes flashed red brilliance. "But you gave vital information about the movements of the papal forces to the emperor."

He stared at this Lamia, trying to control his fury and keep his thoughts secure. "I was merely attempting to maintain appearances. They attacked my homes. People would be suspicious of my affiliations if I had not given truthful reports."

Lady Talia backed away. Her eyes then grew clear and blue again as her face lit in another false grin. "That is a reasonable explanation. I apologize for misjudging you."

"Not at all," Julien replied, thankful she accepted his lie. He bowed his head a little, remembering the displays of respect Patroclus would make in deference to Amata or his mother.

"Can I rely on you to do a favor for me?" Talia asked.

"Of course my lady," Julien answered.

"I am most..." Talia's face became forlorn. "I miss my friend, and I have not been able to keep up with current events. If you were to see Mandubratius, would you learn of his plans and tell him that I have useful information for him about the emperor and his forces? The emperor is in my control, now."

"'Mandubratius'? Oh yes... Michael's real name." He could remember that now.

Talia placed a hand on his arm. "Since you are one of us, I supposed it would not hurt to tell you these things," she purred. "I manipulate the emperor, and he manipulates the Holy Fool."

"Yes, it is quite amusing that he poses as the papal emissary," Julien stated, seeing Talia's weakness. She appeared to be lonely, and she gave too much away.

Talia laughed. "I have no idea why he took that title, yet he could be doing this for his own amusement. Mandubratius enjoys a good game."

Julien then heard a new heartbeat at the door, and so he turned his face towards the door, anticipating who the new arrival might be.

"Imperial Majesty," he greeted, just as Lady Talia echoed the same sentiments. Julien watched the emperor's face light.

"What a pleasant surprise to find you here, Lady Talia," said the emperor.

"I was just speaking with my neighbor, Julien," Talia said, with a voice of honey. "My lord," she addressed as she turned towards Julien, as her eyes glittered like rare gems. "Please feel free to call upon me when your duties allow." Talia then turned on her heel and walked out of the room.

Julien still wondered about her motives, but perhaps Marcus and Máire should know of this strange Lamia. He then realized that the emperor motioned for him to sit, so he lowered himself in his chair again.

"You seemed surprised at the reward," Emperor Charles began. "The former Lord and Lady of Auxerre died a few days ago of a strange cough. I know your family is well thought of in Burgundy, so I felt it best to pass it on to a man who deserves much more than he has received... one who surprises me with his ceaseless service to me and to my family."

Julien tried to think over a proper response. "I have no idea what to say," he admitted. "Thank you, Imperial Majesty... but that woman here earlier, she worries me."

"Mmmmm, she's a fun distraction and little more." The emperor's eyes revealed his true feelings. "Returning to the subject of your work as my lead gendarme, I am most impressed with you. Here." The emperor then handed over papers and the signet ring of Auxerre.

"I have sent a messenger to Auxerre informing them of my decision, but I also informed them that you would be delayed in joining them. If they have any problems, your mother can assist them, I am sure. The papal army will also be departing soon, Julien, once my sons and their armies arrive." The emperor's smile grew as he finished his statement.

"How is your mother?" the emperor asked. "You must tell her that she should visit Aachen. I miss hearing her laughter."

Julien found that statement odd.

"She says you always tell the best hunting stories, and she wishes you would visit Vézelay," Julien replied, hoping he did not overstep boundaries.

"That is an excellent suggestion," the emperor agreed. "I am sorry that we do not have time for a proper chat, but we both have our duties." He then rose from his seat. Julien stood as well, and they embraced.

"I wish you success and a good journey. Be careful," the emperor advised as he patted Julien's back before starting for the door. Julien held the door open for him.

"Thank you, Imperial Majesty, I will do my best to assist you and your empire," Julien replied.

Outside of Metz

Mac Alpin closed his eyes for a moment, enjoying the feel of wind against his face. After a few nights with the Imperial Army, he had been thrilled to escape in order to return to Vézelay.

"No more stops," he said to Marcus. "I know you have an innate urge to help mortals, but I am sure they can handle the papal forces."

"I know," Marcus muttered. "I realize I slowed our departure, but I wanted to direct some of the units of the Imperial Army towards those villages with small garrisons."

Mac Alpin then grunted as he witnessed flickering torch lights in the distance.

"Another camp," he muttered while pointing towards the western group of lights.

"Definitely not friends," Marcus replied. "It looks like they're settling in for the night."

"Mmmmm, they haven't adjusted their tactics yet," Arwin added.

"It just proves all the more that they aren't here to fight demons. They are here to punish the emperor and his subjects. Do you smell any other camps?"

Arwin stopped flying and levitated. He sniffed and then found something. He then spun around a little to face Marcus.

"There is something faint to the south… military, I think, as they smell of incense and leather," he said, as he began to fly towards the south again.

"No," Marcus interjected. "I think you need your nose examined. They look Imperial to me. Let's keep going. Sunup is in a few hours, and we should get much closer to Vézelay."

Mac Alpin stopped and inhaled again. A familiar scent lingered from the north. He rotated his body again and began to move to the north.

"What is it?" his friend whispered.

"I smell Deargh Du," Arwin replied. "It's Julien. He's coming from the direction of Aachen."

"Then let's allow him to catch up."

Mac Alpin stopped and then nodded. He then stared down at a road below. "So, what do you think is down there?" he asked Marcus.

"I would guess that is a checkpoint," Marcus indicated while examining his nails.

"Yes. It appears the guard is taking a piss break. Let's give him a drink,"

Mac Alpin suggested as he raised his flask of mead and looked at Marcus, who raised a brow and looked back over at him.

"I don't think your arm is that steady," Marcus stated. "Besides, why waste good mead? We need to move on quickly as soon as Julien arrives."

"It's as steady as it's ever been. What will you wager?" he asked Marcus.

"Nothing. Don't waste your rations," Marcus warned.

"What are you two doing?" Julien asked them just as he arrived at their spot in the sky.

"We were just waiting for you," Marcus answered.

"I was going to prove that my arm is steady as it's always been," Arwin added. "Besides, it would have been a great joke. Were you in Aachen?"

"I had to leave Vézelay for Aachen. The papal army arrived in Divio. As far as I know, Máire, Edward, and the others are leading the mortals in this direction," Julien replied.

"We should start flying to the south again. Move on you two," Marcus urged.

"You are little better than a slave driver, Marcus," Mac Alpin taunted.

"Best hurry, or I will find a whip," Marcus replied.

They started flying again.

"Oh yes, I received a reward from the emperor. I'm now the Count of Auxerre, for some reason," Julien stated. The youngling looked quite pleased with this announcement. "Even though I'm not sure how I'll be able to be a Count and a Gendarme at the same time."

"The way you're going, you'll be the emperor soon," Mac Alpin teased with a chuckle, "and I'll still be sharing a house in Bath with two Roman soldiers, a son-in-darkness who wants to burn everything in sight, and that frustrating piglet."

"You sound a little upset," Marcus observed aloud, interrupting his thoughts. "Why don't you drink some of that mead that I didn't let you waste?"

"Roman know-it-all," Arwin grumbled. He slowed down and then opened his flask. As he took a few swallows of the sweet mead, Arwin came to a stop. The two other blood-drinkers also stopped.

Arwin kept himself from closing the stopper, as that would be impolite, and passed it over to Marcus with a grunt.

"Thank you." Marcus raised the flask and began to drink. He then finished and held it out for Julien.

"I don't think that I have a taste for mead."

"Then drink more and you'll develop one," Marcus chided.

Julien took it and began to drink. He made a bit of a face as he held out the flask to Arwin, who then reached for his flask of mead.

Soon, Arwin detected another familiar scent, and an idea came to him. He closed his eyes and sensed the wind currents. He opened his eyes and judged the distance. Mac Alpin then levitated a little toward the south until he floated in the right position. Upon saying the word 'oops', his flask slipped from his grasp.

Edward managed to sort his way through the usual smells. Bad rations, oiled leather, and the stale and pungent odor of unwashed bodies often turned his stomach a little. Yet, when Edward turned to his left, the somewhat cleaner smell of livestock made his stomach untwist. A farm would be a suitable place to rest during the day.

He sniffed again and recognized the smell of Ekimmu Cruitne and Deargh Du in the distance. He looked up into the skies, and then a metal flask hit him in the head.

"By Morrigan's strength!" he shouted in exasperation. He then rubbed at his temple, trying to soothe the pain, though minor, from the impact.

"Arwin, I recognize your ill-timed sense of humor and this metal flask!" Edward yelled into the sky.

"I swear, it's not my fault," Arwin called out to Edward.

Julien and Marcus landed nearby, and then Mac Alpin landed a few feet away. Arwin looked concerned, though Julien looked somewhat annoyed. Ill-contained humor lit Marcus' eyes.

"This is not the time for fun and games!" Edward shouted as he tossed the flask to Mac Alpin.

"I dropped it, and by luck you were there," Mac Alpin said with a shrug. "What are you doing here this time of morning?" He still sounded jovial.

"I am helping escort the survivors of the papal army," Edward answered. "Where have you three been? Drinking and carousing as usual?"

"Marcus and I went to Aachen. The emperor sent us to show his forces where the papal army hid their camps, and then we sent some legions to reinforce the garrisons in some of their villages." Arwin looked the dented flask and sighed.

"I spoke to the emperor about attacks on Divio and Vézelay," Julien added. "We all met a few minutes ago."

Edward grunted.

"How many mortals and where are they?" Marcus asked.

"One hundred and twenty mortals, and they're directly south of us."

"Is there a plan?" Mac Alpin asked.

"There is a farm a short distance from here," Edward began. "We would be within a few miles from a papal contingent, but we could stay there if we make sure the mortals remained quiet."

Marcus nodded. "That would be better than digging holes again. Are you done pouting?" he asked Arwin.

"Yes, for now," the other Ekimmu Cruitne stated as he shoved the container into a traveling sack.

They then began to follow Edward towards the mortals.

Reginald chuckled as Clotilda's feet hit him on the chest as she sat on his shoulders. He grabbed her feet and said, "Stop it, Tildy."

She patted the top of his head, but then she turned as wolves howled.

"Papa, the wolves won't hurt us, right?" He could hear concern and a little fear in her voice.

"No, my sweet, the wolves will stay far away from us. We have torches and armed men... and women." He tried to keep his voice light. The idea of armed women in their party bothered him, not to mention that their clothing and manners seemed inappropriate for Clotilda to witness.

An owl hooted, and Clotilda stirred again.

"An owl, papa." He watched her point to the east. "I want to see it!"

"Sorry, Tildy, but we have to stay with our party."

"If you're scared, you can give me your sword, and I'll protect you like the Fire Queen."

"Fire Queen?"

"The pretty lady with hair of fire," Tildy informed him. "I want to wield a sword like she does."

Over my dead body.

"But Tildy," Reginald began to explain, "most women aren't warriors. Most women stay at the hearth and take care of their husbands and children. Wouldn't you rather do that?"

"Can't I do both?" He could almost hear a bit of a pout in her words.

He tried to think of a reply, when the sounds of shouts and alarms interrupted him. He ran towards the main ground and wordlessly passed Clotilda to his mother.

As Reginald ran past most of the villagers, his hand rested on his sword. Soon, however, the sounds of panic became rejoicing and cheering.

"Part," he ordered to the garrison as he moved through the soldiers. He then saw that his brother and two strangers had arrived, and then they began speaking with Edward and the other mercenaries.

"Julien," Reginald said, feeling relief at his youngest brother's arrival. "I didn't expect you so soon. Where are the horses?"

"Reginald," his brother answered with a grin, "the horses went lame after a hard ride. We walked the last two miles."

"You went all the way to Aachen and came back so soon?" he asked after he pulled Julien aside. "Who are these people, and why is everyone welcoming them?"

"Brother, calm yourself. All is well." Julien patted his shoulder. "I did manage to see Emperor Charles. He can spare no soldiers, but he has given us leave to fortify ourselves in Prüm Abbey. He is sending word to the abbot."

"I see." Reginald bit his tongue. The emperor seemed far too concerned with his own protection to do right by his vassals, but Reginald managed to push aside his anger and ask, "Who are your friends, brother?" They certainly seemed popular."

"I will introduce you. They are... Máire's family. These men assisted the garrison in fighting the murderers that moved through the forests near Vézelay. That is why they are welcomed back."

Reginald felt a moment of sadness, perhaps even jealousy. "If that is so, I wish they had been in Divio."

Julien nodded. "I am sorry we were not there to help." His brother's face grew sorrowful. "I–" Julien interrupted himself as the two mercenaries turned to face Julien. His brother then gestured to him and said, "This is my older brother Reginald. This is Arwin Mac Alpin and Marcus of Bath."

Reginald nodded to both of them. "Thank you both so much for coming to assist us. I... and my vassals are so very grateful."

The bearded one nodded back to him.

"The honor is to serve," the clean-shaven one answered. Marcus offered a stiff head bob before inclining his head to speak with some of the other mercenaries.

"Perhaps we should continue our journey to Prüm Abbey," Reginald said. "We're not far from there now, are we?"

He noticed Máire move towards Marcus, and they embraced. Then they began speaking rapidly in some language Reginald did not understand. The one called Mac Alpin joined in their conversation. What sort of a name was Mac Alpin anyway? He hated being left out of the conversation and felt they were most rude to do this.

Reginald cleared his throat. "May I be included in this conversation?" he asked. He tried to not sound upset, but he could hear a growing edge to his voice.

Marcus turned back to him. His blue eyes reflected a strange and sparkling green. "I apologize, Reginald, but we were discussing personal matters, and our Latin is not always so good."

"I understand," Reginald said, feeling himself calm a little, "and I apologize for my abruptness, but I wish to begin traveling again. If we leave now, we can reach Prüm by nightfall."

"We need to rest," Marcus informed him. "There's a farm a few miles from here. We can seek shelter there and start again this next night."

Reginald felt his features turn incredulous. "We're fleeing to a secure place provided by Emperor Charles, and you want us to sleep for twelve hours and start out on our journey then?"

"Yes," the mercenary replied.

"What possible reason do you have for wanting to put our lives in jeopardy this way?" Reginald demanded.

Marcus looked back at Mac Alpin, who shrugged.

Marcus' eyes moved back to him. "We're exhausted. We haven't slept in two days."

Reginald noticed all of the other mercenaries looking at him as if he were a strange fool.

"You're all tired?"

"Yes," they all answered.

"What kind of lazy mercenaries are you?" Reginald asked. "Fine, then. I shall lead my people to Prüm without your protection. You can all sleep in the barn, but don't expect me to be welcoming if you decide to grace the abbey with your presence."

"Pogue mahone," muttered Mac Alpin, and his strange words revealed what seemed to be a fierce and growing ire.

"What did you say?" Reginald hissed.

"He bid you a fair journey," Marcus answered without a second of hesitation, as if he expected something would be said.

Mac Alpin grumbled something and turned away.

Liar.

"Well then," Reginald drawled as he looked over at the other mercenaries, "pogue mahone to you all." He turned on his heel and walked away.

Julien caught up to him. "Reginald, why are you wishing to split from us?"

Reginald felt his bile rise as he turned to face his little brother. "You consider them 'us'? What has come over you, brother? I would have thought you and I would be splitting from them!"

Julien's eyes lowered for a moment. "Máire saved my life, and they now treat me like family."

"But I am your family," Reginald argued. "Our mother, our sister, and my daughter are your family. Why can't you stay with us?" he asked as he stared into Julien's eyes.

Julien returned his stare and answered, "I have to stay with them."

Reginald's fury rose, although he tried to control it. "Do as you will." He then began walking away.

"We will join you in Prüm," Julien offered. Reginald could hear that his brother continued following him. "I am just fearful because you will not have our protection during your march."

"I don't need your protection," Reginald stated, as if tossing the words over his shoulder.

Julien stopped following him. Reginald felt a little disappointment that Julien displayed the typical behavior of a third son. He thought his brother had grown beyond his self-centeredness.

As he walked towards his mother, he noticed all sorts of questions in her eyes.

"We are traveling to Prüm Abbey," he informed her. He then turned to walk towards the garrison soldiers. "Get everyone up! We need to start moving."

"Where are Máire, Amata, Edward, and Patroclus?" his mother asked while appearing to look around them.

"They are all resting somewhere with your other son," he answered. The party began moving towards the north again.

"That's right, mother," Reginald uttered. "Julien didn't even bother to greet you."

"But the mercenaries–" Lirienne commented.

"We don't need them," Reginald interjected. "Dreu and his men will protect us. Plus, you have my sword to defend you."

His mother looked angry. "If that is what you think…" she stated as she urged the horse to move on, "… I hope you are right, for all of our sakes."

Reginald continued walking, comforted by the fact that he was right.

chapter twenty

ulien held his tongue as he fumed at the memory of the conversation. It had happened only a half hour before their arrival at the empty farmhouse. Perhaps the landowners had deserted it during the Strigoi attacks and decided to move to a village or town for safety.

Everyone appeared to be weary as they climbed into the root cellar. Several large bowls of clean water had been set out, and all of the blood-drinkers washed their faces, hands, and feet with the cold water. They then grabbed blankets, muttered wishes of restful sleep to each other, and nearly collapsed in exhaustion.

Julien edged his way closer to Marcus, who still remained at the bowls, cleaning his hands, face, neck, and feet in a most fastidious manner. Julien felt some impatience with Marcus, as the elder Deargh Du began looking over his nails. He had more important things on his mind than Marcus' bathing ritual, though he tried to keep from revealing his annoyance in his voice.

"Why did you allow Reginald to leave?" he whispered.

"Julien, do we need to discuss this now? Can't this wait until sunset?" Marcus whispered in reply while staring at Julien.

"No, this cannot wait," Julien insisted.

"Very well." Marcus finished grooming himself and then grumbled something while running a hand over a small amount of beard on his chin.

As Julien awaited the answer, he felt hostility grow within himself.

Marcus stepped away from the bowls and answered, "Well, Reginald is a leader of the people of Divio. He felt this course was best for them, and I am in no position to judge him."

"His people include my mother, sister, and niece!" As Julien's voice grew in volume, the others grumbled their dissatisfaction.

Marcus sighed and then leaned back against a wall with his hands cushioning his head. "Julien, the sun was arriving, and there was no way that we could have done anything. Besides, the Strigoi will not attack them during the day."

"I'm not worried about the Strigoi… I'm worried about the papal army. They drove us from Vézelay! They are still out there." He motioned wildly as he spoke. "Don't you think that the papal army will try to seek revenge after what happened there?"

Marcus sat down on one blanket on the floor and then covered himself with another. "It's possible that they may be captured," he intoned. "However, I

---

think no harm will come to them. You should go to sleep," Marcus advised as he closed his eyes.

"You don't know that." Julien tried to remain calm.

A voice, which sounded like a cranky Edward, broke through the silence. "Shut up and go to sleep."

Marcus opened his eyes and stared up at Julien, who remained standing. "What would you have me do, Julien? Would you have me gather the force of the seven of us here in this root cellar and begin searching for your brother in the savage sun?" Marcus snapped. "If you wish to begin such a foolhardy mission, you may do so, but I doubt any of us will join you. In fact, I doubt you would live long."

Julien grew silent, wishing that the sun could fade away early, just this once.

"If they are captured, they won't go far," Marcus added in a gentler tone. "They will have civilians with them, and civilians move slowly. We will ambush the papal forces tomorrow night, and rescue your people, if need be." The elder Deargh Du then closed his eyes again.

"What about Divio?"

Marcus' eyes remained shut. "I suggest you pray that the men responsible for the massacre at Divio are nowhere near your family, because at this moment, there is nothing we can do. For that, I am sorry."

He could tell Marcus meant it, but he could now see evidence of the callous Roman general within. He said nothing else, as Marcus' face seemed to relax.

"Either go to sleep, or I'll hit you with the hilt of my sword, and then you'll pass out. I'm exhausted, Julien. You're as wearying as Máire can be sometimes. Questions, questions, questions… you and she demand answers to so many questions," he mumbled.

Julien set a blanket up where he had kneeled. He then pulled off his boots and pulled up another blanket.

"I hope you're right," Julien said.

He half expected an answer, but he only heard snores from Marcus, now.

Heloise berated herself for relying on the blood-drinkers protection too much, but then Clotilda's half-snores interrupted her worries about this journey. She glanced down at her granddaughter as she slept in her arms. At the same time, Lirienne led Zerbino on the small path.

Her daughter turned towards her and offered a flask. Heloise smiled and shook her head. If she had not been so worried, this would have been a beautiful ride.

The gleaming radiance of the sun made Heloise blink. Her eyes watered at the strength of the morning sun. She had adjusted herself to Julien's hours, and now the daylight seemed harsh.

The columns of garrison soldiers and civilians followed her eldest, who seemed to exude confidence, though she knew it was but an act. Her eldest had often needed to put on a show of confidence after his father died.

Reginald never displayed the leadership of his father or Julien. Then again, her youngest earned every scrap of leadership through hard work, though Reginald served the emperor as a high-ranking soldier from the beginning. Such privilege made him arrogant.

After the latest interchange between Julien and Reginald, her concern and apprehension had increased. Julien would never yield to Reginald, and Reginald would never acknowledge his brother's good sense. Heloise pondered what it would be like had the two brothers switched places.

Suddenly, the columns stopped, and Heloise raised her head to see what had happened.

Scores of soldiers wearing the uniform of the papal regiments surrounded them with raised swords and drawn bows. Most of the arrows and swords pointed towards the garrison soldiers, but a few lingered on unarmed vassals. Heloise wrapped her arms around Clotilda, praying to whoever could hear her thoughts that Reginald would handle this sensibly.

"Surrender now," a voice called out from the milling soldiers.

"By whose authority?" Reginald asked as he turned to face the east.

"By the order of His Holiness, Pope Leo III."

Heloise could see that Reginald's expression boded trouble.

"I do not recognize anyone's authority in the empire, other than Emperor Charles and his family," Reginald responded.

Heloise dismounted Zerbino while holding onto Clotilda. She then started walking towards Reginald, in the hopes that seeing his daughter would remind him that he needed to proceed carefully. They had vassals to protect, after all.

"The pope has supreme authority to quash those possessed by demons," one of the officers in the papal forces stated.

"There are no demons here," Reginald replied. "The sun has risen, and we are on a pleasant stroll through the woods."

The officer frowned at Reginald's words before demanding, "Surrender, or you will be purged."

Clotilda became very heavy in her arms, yet the child still slept.

Reginald seemed to study the soldiers surrounding their party. "If we surrender, I request that the civilians be allowed to leave without further molestation from your soldiers."

"It is not an issue as to whether you will surrender. It will be unconditional, or else you will all die," the officer replied.

"But the civilians–"

"They must remain so that our priests can judge whether they have been tainted by the demons," the officer stated.

"But–"

"There is no more discussion, you will surrender now and submit yourself and your vassals to the priests' judgment," the officer ordered. Heloise could see his eyes wander over all of them.

She could tell Reginald's fury by the color marking his face. Julien would have realized the hopelessness of the situation and made plans for an escape. Then again, Julien would not have left without an escort. They would all suffer for Reginald's folly.

Heloise could almost feel the archers prepare to let loose their arrows, and Clotilda seemed to grow heavier by the second. She studied her son's features and knew he would resist. She knew she would have to stand and surrender for him, risking her life, and perhaps Clotilda's as well, to do so. She firmed her grasp of Clotilda in her right arm and began to sprint toward Reginald, waving her left hand.

"We surrender, do not fire. We surrender," she called out.

Out of her side vision, she could see the archers train on her, and in front of her, she saw Reginald's eyes bore into her.

She then reached the highest-ranking officer and then knelt in front of him. "Please don't slaughter us for my son's arrogance," she begged.

"Mother, do not interfere," she heard Reginald reply.

"Who are you and what authority do you have over these people?" the officer asked her.

"I'm Lady Heloise of Vézelay," she answered. "These people are my vassals and family."

"Some of these people are my vassals," Reginald uttered, sounding perturbed with her interruption.

"Silence," she hissed at him. She then returned her stare to the officer and allowed her eyes to plead with him.

"Very well," the officer said. "I accept your surrender. Have your vassals and your son throw down their weapons."

Heloise turned her eyes to Dreu, who nodded.

"Do as he requests," he told the soldiers.

She then realized that she had not heard Reginald drop his blade. Heloise strained to get to her feet, and then she turned towards Reginald, locking eyes with him. "You will surrender," she uttered in a low tone. She allowed her voice to reveal a certain amount of force.

"I will not."

"You would sacrifice us?" she asked in Frankish. After Heloise shifted Clotilda onto her hip, her granddaughter awoke with a grumble. "You would sacrifice your daughter?"

"They will kill us all anyways," Reginald replied with a dark stare. "I would rather die fighting than on my knees."

Heloise took a few steps closer. "You must trust me, Reginald. They will find us tonight and free us. No one will be killed if we honor the terms of this surrender."

"You wish to trust that... mercenary?"

"Trust me," Heloise demanded. "Throw down your weapon," she urged through clenched teeth. "If you had trusted me and Julien before, we would not be in this predicament."

She witnessed a battle in Reginald's eyes.

"Papa, I want to go home," Clotilda whined. Her granddaughter's plaintive voice made her wish to cry again.

Reginald looked as if he might burst into tears. He then reached for his scabbard, removed it, and then tossed the scabbard and his father's sword to the ground. A few knives landed near the sword.

"I surrender," Reginald said to the officer.

The officer nodded and then motioned another soldier forth.

"Take these people to our camp and confiscate their weapons."

The swordsmen sheathed their blades and arrows returned to their quivers.

The officer of the papal forces walked over to Heloise and inclined his head in a small bow.

"Your vassals are very lucky to have such a selfless leader," he commented.

She nodded back to him.

"Move this way, please," a lower ranking soldier ordered as he motioned her forward.

"I hope you are right, mother," Reginald whispered in Frankish.

This felt right.

Prüm Abbey

Mac Alpin and Edward remained above, smelling for Julien's family's party, while Julien sat on a rock with Máire, who began carving a piece of wood. Her eyes remained steady and calm, though a thin thread of excitement surrounded her. He then turned to the east as the Legate ran towards them.

Patroclus inhaled and exhaled. "The monks say they host no pilgrims or travelers tonight. However, a large party of soldiers from the pope demanded provisions during the day."

"Provisions for how many?" Marcus asked.

"Three hundred, sir."

"Is there anything else we need to know, Patroclus?" Marcus asked.

"Yes, general. One of the monks confided that a soldier mentioned something about purging civilian captives," Patroclus replied.

Julien threw a fist at Marcus' shoulder. The elder Deargh Du simply stood there and took the hit. "I knew you should have never let Reginald leave. You should have talked him into staying. This is your fault."

Máire grabbed his arm and turned him to face her. "Julien, now is not the time," she said. He could see her eyes regard Marcus, and a silent accusation lay within her green eyes.

Marcus observed her for a moment before he turned towards the other blood-drinkers and asked, "Were there any other wagon or cart tracks?"

"Yes, there were four cart tracks and a dozen riders that departed from the east entrance," Mac Alpin answered. "They continued southwest."

Marcus' eye became a strange silver color for a moment. "I promise we will rescue them, Julien. Arwin, please head southwest with Edward and find the encampment. We will follow. I'm trusting that you can send Edward back to us with details. We'll then join you and attack with stealth. We'll disarm the papal soldiers and dispatch them."

"All of them?" Julien felt a small icicle of guilt in his heart.

Marcus stared back at him, appraisal in his eyes. "Yes, is there a problem with that?"

Julien wondered why he felt some surprise at Marcus' inability to accept dissenting positions.

"It's just… some soldiers are following orders." He found his own opinions on the matter too vague.

Marcus uttered a sigh, revealing some impatience. "Would you be so forgiving were you to find your niece crucified?"

The horror of that question left Julien silent.

"Don't you think any soldiers left alive would want to retaliate? I seriously doubt we can free the civilians silently. We'll have to kill the papal soldiers," Marcus added.

Julien didn't want to admit that it made sense, so he lowered his face and studied his boots for a moment before glancing back at Marcus.

"So, are there any other dissenting opinions?" Marcus asked as he looked over the six other blood-drinkers. "Fine, then. Edward and Arwin, move out. We'll be a mile behind you. Patroclus, Amata, can you two keep up?"

"You would do well to keep up with us, general." Amata's tone revealed something of a desire to return to lightheartedness. The Lamia then turned and began to run.

"Let's go," Marcus said as he took to the air.

Outside of Prüm Abbey

Everyone slept, exhausted from the march, as Reginald played with the soupy remnants of dinner's gruel. A few pieces of unidentifiable meat lay amongst the lumpy sludge.

Nobody had spoken to him since their capture. Even his mother avoided him. Now he wished he had listened to Julien.

They sat on the ground or milled about within the papal army's camp, surrounded by soldiers.

His mother wandered about, touching shoulders and whispering Frankish words of encouragement, begging the vassals not to flee and that their rescuers would arrive soon. He would have done this as well, but he knew that these simple farmers could guess at the truth... that he feared for his life and his family. He hoped that soon his courage would return and that he could provide some good judgment.

Just then, the call of nature interrupted his contemplation of the past day's events, and so Reginald waved over a guard.

"I need to–" he began to say as he motioned to the latrine.

"Of course. I will call for an escort." The guard whistled and motioned over to another soldier.

"That's really not–" he began as the soldier motioned for him to go to the latrine. Reginald sighed and began walking. The soldier followed him and then stopped to give him a little privacy.

A few minutes later, he stepped out of the latrine and looked for the guard. Reginald then found the silent guard laying in the grass a few feet away with a telltale slit across his throat.

He had not heard a sound, and he wondered whether bandits had attacked or a murderous band of killers had found them.

Reginald took a few cautious steps towards the camp. Other bodies lay scattered over the ground, and yet his daughter slept next to his sister. No guards remained standing. He felt the urge to run towards camp.

"Hello brother," he heard Julien say.

Reginald turned around to face Julien. He noticed the mercenaries cleaning their blades against uniforms of the papal army.

"Where did you come from?" Reginald asked.

"The abbey," Julien answered. His shoulders moved in a slight shrug.

"We couldn't find you, but the monks said that they had to give food to the papal army, so we followed the cart tracks." Julien then motioned towards the carts in the distance.

Reginald stared at the field of the fallen and asked, "Are they all dead?" He then watched his brother's eyes move towards Marcus.

"Yes, all are dead," the mercenary answered in a grim and somewhat reluctant tone.

Nobody appeared to be rejoicing, boasting, or gloating, but that might be the nature of these soldiers.

The sight of a tonsured head made him inhale and feel all the more discomfort.

"The holy men as well?" he asked as he looked at Julien.

"Yes, those as well," Marcus answered.

"Why kill the servants of God?" he whispered, feeling dread.

Marcus turned back towards him. The calm and business-like manner became menacing. Reginald felt a great deal of fear as a raging darkness seemed to surround this soldier.

"Those innocent priests and monks were going to condemn your vassals to death, as they have many innocent people," the mercenary hissed at him.

"But… they treated us with generosity and kindness," Reginald replied, wondering why he continued with such foolishness. He then saw Julien lower his head and back away.

"They lulled you into submission, my lord, so you'd be easy to kill tomorrow," the monstrous soldier informed him in a strange growl.

"You don't know that," Reginald insisted. "Everything was fine until you traipsed in here with your… band of men and women. Then you all massacred these soldiers and holy men."

"We've given you your lives back, yet all you do is complain," Marcus pointed out as he stepped closer. His eyes burned a strange color in the moonlight. "Perhaps the world would be better without your heartbeat." Bloody menace shone in his eyes.

Julien placed a hand on Marcus' arm. "Please don't do this," he murmured. Marcus turned towards Julien, and then Julien lowered his hand.

"My brother is an arrogant fool, but he is my only surviving brother," Julien stated.

"I will cease being a threat when your brother apologizes and thanks us for saving his life, the lives of his family, and the lives of his vassals. Otherwise, the earth will receive an offering." The threat chilled Reginald's body and soul.

Marcus' eyes glared at him, and then a strange radiance surrounded the mercenary.

Reginald went to his knees.

"I apologize for my insults," Reginald began, feeling an odd compulsion to continue, "and I thank you for the services you have performed in our rescue. I further wish to acknowledge that it was my poor judgment that led us to this point. Please have mercy on me for the sake of my daughter."

Reginald found himself gasping for breath after pleading. As Marcus stared down at him, Reginald witnessed a coolness return to those strange eyes.

The other man nodded his head in response, before saying, "Julien, help your brother to his feet, and tell him that his apology is acceptable. Wake your family so we can start for Prüm Abbey." The soldier then turned away and began barking orders to his subordinates in a strange tongue.

Julien pulled Reginald to his feet and whispered, "You don't realize how close you came to death."

"Yes, I believe I do," Reginald replied. "Thank you for intervening."

"You can thank me by respecting my opinion, Reginald. I'm not just the third son. The emperor gave me two titles, Inspector General and Count of Auxerre. I have more experience than you in some things." His brother's face turned up in a nervous half-smile. "However, I will grant you know much more about assisting and leading your vassals. Now, let's wake up mother."

Prüm Abbey

Marcus heaved a sigh of relief as they walked into the abbey's cloister. The process of leading mortals slowly through the forested paths and avoiding small groups of bandits allowed him too much time to consider all that had happened since sunset.

A pudgy and rather cheerful balding man with large dark eyes brushed his way past his robed monks. The Abbot Sigibert smiled at them without reservation and appeared to be surprised at their arrival. He seemed to study their larger party again and then stepped in closer. The sharp-eyed mortal spied the stolen goods, and his eyes darted to the carts every few seconds.

"My, that was a quick journey to find your friends. Thanks be to God and His saints that you rescued them... Marcus, was it?" The abbot turned back to smile and nod at Julien and his family. "Lady Heloise, such a pleasure." The abbot embraced her and kissed her cheeks. He then pulled back and turned his eyes back to Marcus. "I hope it was not a difficult feat."

Marcus shook his head. "None whatsoever, Abbot Sigibert. By the by, I remember hearing from one of your staff that some of your goods were taken from you recently."

"Taken?" the abbot asked, beaming.

"We discovered five carts of provisions and a great deal of wine. We assumed the army took these items from you, and we are returning them." Marcus motioned to his left as many people moved forward with the horse-drawn carts in tow.

The abbot's smile widened and his eyes grew large. He then rubbed his hands together. "Bless you. Where should I send the priests?"

"Priests?" Marcus heard confusion in his voice.

"Oh yes, for those poor souls who lost possession of their ill-gotten goods." The abbot frowned and his words grew quiet and angry. "Stupid fools. We give so much to the Holy Father, why must he tell his soldiers to take our essentials?"

The abbot stopped speaking and seemed to force a smile on his face. "Forgive my rudeness. Food and shelter are available in the cloister, but Marcus, please tell me where to find those soldiers?"

Marcus nodded and said. "Three miles to the southwest."

The abbot motioned for three robed figures to join them. He said something to them in Frankish, and then the priests left. The abbot turned towards him again. "I sent some of our priests to find our friends. Do you expect others will inquire about our friends to the southwest?"

Marcus considered the question. Until the troops arrived, they might as well stay close to Aachen.

"It's possible. We could stay and serve you as your protection in exchange for lodgings and provisions for ourselves and for our friends and their vassals."

As Abbot Sigibert appeared to be considering his offer, Marcus could sense Julien move closer.

"My family will provide a substantial donation to this abbey, in addition to the protection we offer," Julien added.

Sigibert smiled again. "That would be a most generous and suitable gift, Inspector General." The abbot then returned his gaze to Marcus. "You are all welcome to stay with us as long as you wish." His eyes then drifted towards Julien and his mother.

"Would you like to visit Aldabert?" the abbot asked. His tone became less gregarious, and his eyes reflected gentleness.

"Perhaps later," Lady Heloise answered, though she paled for a moment. "We must take care of the living now." Her lips turned up in a wan smile.

The abbot patted her hand. "You visit Aldabert whenever you wish. Please, tend to your flock, my lady."

"Thank you," Julien said. He then took his mother's arm and began to lead her towards the mortals.

The abbot stepped closer to Marcus, and the mortal's eyes became conspiratorial. "How did you kill all of those soldiers with only four men?"

Marcus smiled at the Abbot and answered, "Why, with God's grace, Abbot Sigibert. That, and we had the assistance of Vézelay's garrison soldiers." He could sense the abbot wanted a grand tale of battle and victory, yet the Abbot would never accept that Amata and Máire would have had a part in that victory.

"Indeed," the abbot answered. "I would like to hear about this one night. Now, excuse me... I must see to the needs of my other guests, but you must tell me about it soon." The abbot then walked away.

Marcus heard the gates close, and then he felt the burdens of command begin to ease.

Máire returned to the business of setting up her bedroll, amid coughing over the strong smell of incense. The sconces lit the catacombs with a strange smoky light. Marcus had talked Abbot Sigibert into allowing them to stay in the catacombs during the day. Máire found satisfaction in the silence of the dead, but she felt annoyance with Julien and Marcus for acting like childish boys refusing to speak to one another.

She looked on as Amata and Patroclus set up their bedding on stone benches. It seemed to be a most painful bed, but perhaps Lamia preferred stone beds. She then watched Mac Alpin yank his tunic overhead and begin washing himself with holy water.

"That's holy water," she heard Julien state.

"What's so holy about it?" Mac Alpin asked as he shook out his hair. "It looks and feels like ordinary water to me."

"It's been blessed," Julien added. He still looked to be in shock.

Arwin stepped away from the basin and asked, "Will it protect us from the Strigoi?"

"No, but it doesn't seem right to use it for washing," Julien argued.

Marcus reached into the basin and splashed himself with the water. "So, you're saying you're not sure what it's for either."

"I..." She watched Julien's face twitch a little. "I just know the priests say to respect it, and they only seem to use it for anointing and blessings."

"So, it's like sacred oil, then." She witnessed Arwin and Marcus exchange looks and then realized that this game would continue.

"No, it's water..." Julien appeared frustrated.

"You seem quite confused. Arwin and I have the excuse of being heathens. Is this not the doctrine you were taught as a child?" Marcus asked. Máire could see merriment in his eyes.

"Aldabert knew the intricacies of holy water, but I do not," Julien answered.

"Enough is enough," she interjected, interrupting the fun. "Julien's probably as much of a heathen as any of us."

"You wish for us to stop teasing the lad?" Arwin asked with a chuckle. "Why would we stop? This is the most fun I've had in weeks. After all, Máire, you and Edward are hardly entertaining these nights."

"Edward and I learned not to leap into old blood-drinker's games," Máire grumbled.

"But you have to admit that he deserves some ill-treatment," Marcus hissed at her in Gaelic. "It's mild now, but it will get worse if he doesn't apologize soon." He and Mac Alpin then turned away and headed towards their bedrolls.

"Why do I have a feeling that was an insult," Julien snapped at her in Latin.

"He wishes for an apology that he deserves," she hissed back at him.

"Why should I have to apologize? Things were going quite well until Marcus allowed Reginald and my family to leave."

"You struck Marcus and argued with him when a decision had been made," she rallied at Julien. "You have shown him no respect, and agree with him or not, he deserves your respect."

"Why should I offer him respect when he's acting like a barbaric mercenary now?" Julien yelled back at her. "I have a title and lands, now. I am both Inspector General and Count of Auxerre!"

Máire grabbed Julien's collar and began to drag him down into a dark passage. He had pushed her too far. She then shoved him against a wall and slapped a hand over his mouth.

His eyes revealed fright.

"I'm going to tell you and remind you of a few things, Inspector General," she whispered. "You have apparently forgotten much in the last few nights. I'm certain Morrigan told you to obey Marcus and I, did She not? However, I will give you more to consider. Marcus commanded the Tenth Legion under Julius Caesar and fought against the Gauls and Britons. When Morrigan trapped him in a grove and forced him to choose between continued torture and a quick death, he took the torture." She took a quick breath before continuing.

"When given an opportunity to redeem himself, Marcus completed every task and earned Her respect. He united the Celtic blood-drinker lines against the Lamia forces, and then defeated their army." She tightened her grip over her son-in-darkness' mouth as her voice grew in volume.

"He is my father-in-darkness, and your disrespect to him reflects poorly on me. He is your grandfather-in-darkness. Marcus saved me from the horrific possibility of becoming Lamia. Most recently, he saved the lives of your family and vassals. Do you not think he deserves respect for this? Apologize!" Máire then released him.

Julien lowered his gaze and stared at her boots. "I suppose you are right."

She lost her temper and punched Julien in the stomach.

"You suppose?!"

Julien grimaced, holding his stomach. "You're right." He uttered a half-groan. "I will apologize. Please forgive me."

"Thank you, I forgive you," she nodded. "I hope Marcus will accept your apology." She knew Marcus would, but she decided that Julien needed more of a nudge.

Máire then watched as he left the hallway. She was following him when she noticed Amata watching her from where she lay.

"Next time, berate your child when we are not all trying to sleep," Amata growled. "I need my rest, after this past night's activities, and I do not see myself as horrific!"

"You are not, yet would you say the same for your brother-in-darkness?" Máire asked. She sighed upon witnessing Amata's burning eyes. Lamia must take their rests seriously, or perhaps her assessment of Mandubratius stung. "My apologies for interrupting your rest, Amata," she added.

Amata closed her eyes and shrugged.

After Máire arrived in the main chamber, she witnessed Julien shining Marcus' boots.

Marcus smiled at her. "I will have clean boots for a few nights," he informed her in Gaelic. "Thank you, Banbh Ceanúil."

"Mmmmm," she said in Gaelic as she moved her bedroll next to Marcus. "Perhaps you should suggest he polish my boots as well." She then yanked off one boot and made a face at the stench from her feet. "I wish that water really made things smell holy."

"I will see to that if he needs further punishment. However, he has had a lot of stress to go through in the last few nights. Be somewhat merciful with your son, Banbh Ceanúil. After all, you still try my patience, at times."

Marcus winked at her as he played with a plaited strand of her hair.

She smiled back down at him. "I will be kind tonight." She then lay down, wrapped herself up, and closed her eyes.

chapter twenty-one

Aachen

Talia wandered around the mortals as they pulled large hunks of boar, venison, various fowl, and lamb from the tables. She scanned the palace for other blood-drinkers again. She hoped Julien had visited Mandubratius with her message, though her trust in the new Lamia waned as the passage of time lengthened.

Talia could see the members of the Imperial family whispering amongst themselves. Her influence over Charles also seemed to fade into obscurity. How could Mandubratius continue his manipulation of mortals for so long? Perhaps such talents and powers increased with age.

She closed her eyes, imagining herself at her grandfather's home during his feasts. Talia then bumped into a young mortal girl and accepted the muttered apology with a wave of her hand.

Where could Charles be?

The dim-witted Ercanbald had informed her that Charles could not be disturbed. She tried to manipulate the secretary, but he never seemed affected by her tricks. Perhaps Ercanbald had been manipulated so many times already that he knew how to avoid those traps.

Her senses soon reeled as another blood-drinker came into the great hall. Had Julien returned? Did Mandubratius arrive to assist her?

The music stopped, and then Emperor Charles walked through the revelers, guiding a blood-drinker whose beauty and grace left the mortals stunned and speechless. She gleamed like a living alabaster statue. Her gentle features revealed a ceaseless confidence.

"Shite," Talia whispered.

Another Deargh Du in Aachen? She must be a Deargh Du.

Talia studied the woman and wondered whether this was Marcus' mother-in-darkness. They displayed the same nauseating radiance and ageless air. Talia wrinkled her nose at Charles, though he seemed to ignore her as he continued to smile at his friends and family.

"Damn your glamoury," Talia murmured under her breath. She began nudging her way closer to the aisle. Then the Deargh Du made eye contact with her and even winked at her.

The emperor reached his simple throne and then motioned for another chair to be brought forth for his guest. A guard raced up towards them carrying a seat. Somehow, the entire exchange occurred in silence. Everyone continued to stare at the Deargh Du.

Emperor Charles then cleared his throat and then announced, "Please allow me to introduce Lady Sáerlaith Ní Adhamdh, my most honored guest."

The Deargh Du smiled at the mortals, but then her radiance seemed to decrease. The emperor then motioned to the musicians, and music and the dancing began anew.

Charles turned away from the merriment, focusing his entire attention on this Sáerlaith. He smiled and became animated, as if he tried to impress the Deargh Du. He paid attention to each answer Sáerlaith uttered, and he even placed a hand over hers.

No wonder Talia had lost influence. Marcus must have sent this one to take her place! The emperor would not stand a chance against glamoury such as this, but Talia still felt she could bring him back. She walked over to his throne to try to regain her place at Charles' side.

Talia pasted a bright smile on her face and held her head high. People moved out of her path, and soon she felt the secretary's eyes on her. She turned her eyes back to Charles, ignoring the rest of the court.

"Hello Charles," she purred, allowing her eyes to gleam seductive promises.

"Talia," Charles answered, though his attention remained on the Deargh Du.

She felt anger rise. How could he just ignore her? "Would you care to dance with me?" she asked him.

Then she noticed Sáerlaith nod to Charles, as if the emperor needed Sáerlaith's permission to dance with her.

The audacity of that Deargh Du wench!

Charles turned to Talia and answered, "Of course." He then offered one last smile to Sáerlaith before taking Talia's hand in his. The master allowed the dog a chance to play. The dancing paused for a moment, as the two of them took positions, and then began again.

Talia tried to keep her annoyance to herself, though she could tell that Charles kept checking on Sáerlaith.

"So, Charles, have you been thinking over what we spoke about the last time we were together?" Talia queried, while keeping her voice sweet and sunny.

Charles' eyes revealed confusion. "I'm sorry, Talia, but what did we discuss? I'm embarrassed to say that I don't remember."

Talia shut her mouth, refusing to give voice to her rage. That damned Deargh Du had removed Charles' memories, somehow. However, she managed to keep her eyes cheery and her face congenial.

"Charles," she began to explain, hoping to keep herself calm, "I know you're just playing games with me. We were talking about marriage."

Charles' eyes, which had been gazing upon Sáerlaith up to this point, settled on her. She had all of his attention now, but his smile faded, and his eyes turned dark, revealing suspicion. He continued dancing with her. Before their dance had begun, Talia had resisted using her charms, but perhaps now he needed reinforcement. She steeled herself and allowed her manipulative charm to grow in strength. Then Charles' features softened.

"Marriage? Why would we be speaking about marriage?" he asked.

She stared at the emperor, flabbergasted. "Because I would be an excellent Empress," Talia explained. "I have political connections, I'm well educated, beautiful, and I will bear many strong sons."

The emperor stopped mid-step, broke their embrace, and stared at her. She realized the game might be over if she did not use all of her manipulative skills to win Charles over again. "Don't you think I'd be a good empress?" Talia asked as she concentrated on manipulating him.

"Lady Talia," Charles politely countered, "you do indeed possess many fine qualities, and I'm pleased to consider you a close friend. However, despite your stance that you have sufficient political connections, my people have no idea who you are. The future Empress must have the love of my family and my vassals, from the lowliest servant to my dearest friends and children."

Talia noticed that the dancing had ceased and that all eyes watched the scene. She could hear whispers about the gall of this peasant to try to capture the emperor. Some replied that she was little more than an unknown bottom-dweller, trying to become something beyond her place.

"I'm truly sorry," Charles stated before bowing to her. "Thank you for the dance." The emperor then walked back to his chair. The Deargh Du stood as he approached, and the people at feast smiled and lowered their faces in respect as the emperor walked to his seat.

If she were not so focused on keeping up her appearances, she would run, screaming, through the halls to the outside. Instead, Talia weaved through the crowds as they parted, though mocking eyes taunted her as she fled.

Sáerlaith watched the scene with the Lamia and prepared for a massive, emotional explosion. The Lamia appeared furious, but said nothing more as she left the hall. Sáerlaith had to wonder why a Lamia would try to infiltrate high society in such a strange manner. Yes, they liked strong leaders and royalty, but they tended to skulk in the background. Not to mention, this one performed terribly. Sáerlaith found the entire situation nearly laughable.

The emperor motioned for her to sit down, and so she did. Sáerlaith smiled as she contemplated why a Lamia would act in this manner. What was there to gain? Perhaps she gave too much credit to this Lamia, and it was nothing more than what it appeared.

She leaned in closer to Emperor Charles and asked, "Who was that young lady?"

Charles smirked, as his right brow rose a bit.

"I was being polite," she whispered with a chuckle.

"Indeed," Charles agreed. His eyes twinkled and then became the color of the seas, or at least the color she remembered from the past. He then leaned back a little and answered, "That was Lady Talia of Époisses, one of my more demanding mistresses. She had the erroneous perception that she was Empress material." His amusement then faded. "She's a jackal with dreams of being a lioness."

"I believe you are correct. She seems quite antagonistic towards me, as if I were a challenger for your attentions."

The emperor smiled again. "Are you not?" he inquired as he winked at her.

Such arrogance! Did all mortal men here in Francia behave in such a manner?

Sáerlaith frowned and then stated, "It was not my idea to be paraded about in front of your vassals as your latest conquest, when that is certainly not the case."

The emperor's smile grew pained, and shock became apparent in his eyes, though he said nothing.

Sáerlaith tried using a smile. "Did my comment surprise you, Imperial Majesty?" He appeared to be attempting to compose himself.

He uttered a strange squeak. "As a matter of fact, it did. You are only the second woman who has rejected the notion of becoming an empress since I became emperor."

Sáerlaith chuckled at that. "Oh, and who is my competitor?"

The emperor uttered a dry laugh. "Her name is Máire of Ulster."

"Ah, that explains it," Sáerlaith stated.

"You know her?" The emperor asked.

"Oh yes. She is family. I've been trying to find her... and Marcus."

"They are at Prüm Abbey," the emperor replied.

"I must see them." She felt her mask fall away as she tried to control her voice. She realized that leaving still required decorum, so she motioned for the emperor to lean in closer.

"I am so sorry for my rudeness, but I must leave and find them as soon as possible," she informed him.

"Will we see you again?" he asked.

"If you wish it, of course," Sáerlaith answered. "Now, how shall I exit?"

"Take my hand," the emperor said as he rose. "I will escort you out personally."

She placed her hand in his and then smiled to the guests, who moved aside, creating an aisle for them. She heard the vassals whisper amongst themselves in their native language as the emperor led her towards the side door.

She could sense the Secretary follow them. As they approached the exterior of the palace, the emperor stopped and then turned toward his servant.

"Lady Sáerlaith requires horses and an escort to Prüm Abbey," Emperor Charles stated.

She placed a gentle hand on his shoulder and countered, "Thank you, but I have a carriage and an armed escort waiting for me."

"Very well, to reach the abbey, head south on the old Roman road," Charles informed her.

Emperor Charles embraced Sáerlaith as she leaned in and kissed him. "Thank you for the lovely evening, Imperial Majesty. We will meet again soon." She returned his smile as he released her. She then heard the doors and the gates open.

She proceeded to walk through the dark paths towards the city's torch lights. Soon, familiar smells greeted her nose, and then Sáerlaith reached Claudius and Caoimhín.

"Prüm Abbey!" she shouted while pointing to the south with a flourish of her hand.

They took to the air… all three thousand blood-drinkers.

Outside of Verviers

While the camp girl's legs remained wrapped around his waist, Mandubratius saw that her eyes darted about. He presumed she might be as bored as he felt.

The idea of killing her squirmed within his brain, but would it be worth the trouble? He had already fed on her, but her blood left much to be desired.

Mandubratius stared down at the camp girl. She looked utterly miserable. Perhaps it would be mercy to kill her.

Just then, his senses reeled as he sensed another blood-drinker approach. He pulled himself away from the camp girl and kicked her off the blankets. He then picked up his sword and found himself face to face with Talia.

"I almost killed you," he warned. "You should know better than to enter unannounced."

Mandubratius looked back at the camp girl as she lay unconscious on the floor. The slight tang of her blood flavored the air.

He heard Talia sigh, and so he prepared himself for a long story.

"I need your help," she pleaded.

He expected her to say more, and so he waited for a moment, though she remained silent, as if waiting for a reply. He took the time to find his tunic. Mandubratius studied Talia further. Except for the grime and her messy hair, she looked stunning. He then sniffed her and detected trace scents of cooked meats, perfumes, and perspiration.

"Was there a feast I missed, or perhaps an orgy? I would be so hurt if someone neglected to invite me." He smiled at Talia.

"I came here to ask for your assistance, not to be mocked."

He decided mocking her would teach her a valuable lesson. "What help do you need from me, other than to unfasten your dress? Anyone here would be willing to help you with that."

"I'm serious!"

"So am I." He stretched his arms overhead and watched Talia throw a cup to the ground.

"I take it that things didn't go as you expected," he ascertained aloud, trying not to laugh at her rage.

"I want to be the Empress!" Talia yelled through tear-soaked eyes.

He moved in closer, disturbed by the volume of her voice. She sounded like a pouting child, at least, more so than usual. "Say that louder so His Holiness can hear you."

Talia responded by taking bowls, cups, and a flask. She began to throw his belongings against the tent floor and the walls.

"I'm not going to speak to you until you calm down," he demanded.

Talia grabbed a boot and it threw it in his direction. The instant the boot left her hand, his smile disappeared.

Mandubratius deflected the boot, punched Talia, and then spun her around. Talia landed on top of the unconscious camp girl.

Mandubratius pulled on Talia's hair, yanking her head up. Her bloody and welted face increased his rage.

Her eyes then focused on him, and she looked frightened and angry.

"You know, I don't mind an occasional fit, Talia." He stared at her through lowered eyelids. "I generally find them quite entertaining, but I do take exception to having objects thrown at me. Now, will you behave so we can carry on a polite conversation, or am I going to have to knock you as senseless as this camp girl?" He kicked the mortal and heard a soft and wordless moan.

Talia's fear seemed to wane, and she appeared to swallow her anger. Mandubratius released Talia and allowed her to climb to her feet.

He then backed away before walking towards a set of chairs. He sat and then motioned for her to take the other chair. Talia now resembled a mad crone, with her disheveled hair.

She sat down and stared at him in silence.

Good… she understands that I will only tolerate so much.

"So, you wish to be Empress," Mandubratius reflected as he studied his nails, "married to Charles and so forth… Is this the big plan you've been working on?" He allowed sarcasm to lace his words. He could smell her rage, but she took a breath, and it started to pass.

"It didn't start that way, but yes, that is what it became."

"What have I taught you about the goals and methods of our kind, Talia?" He tried to keep an edge out of his voice.

"That is not my role, Mandubratius." Talia met his stare. "I'm choosing to ignore those lessons."

"You cannot choose which lessons to follow and which to ignore," he informed her.

"You do!" Talia's voice rose.

"In what way do I ignore the lessons?"

Talia appeared to consider her thoughts. "How about your attempt to acquire the Phallus Maximus?" She inhaled and then continued. "You had no subtlety… just overt aggression."

"Perhaps," he mused. "However, the higher one's rank within the Lamia, the greater the amount of latitude in interpretation of these lessons. You don't have the age, skill, or rank for a loose interpretation."

"You gave me leave to pursue my interests," Talia argued.

"As long as your interests served the Lamia," Mandubratius clarified as he rose from the chair and began to pace while studying the interior of his tent.

"Of course my plan would have served our kind, Mandubratius. Think of the influence over these lands we'd enjoy." Talia waved her hand about as she spoke. "Think how we could manipulate the emperor to conquer more lands. Think of the wealth!"

"Under different circumstances, your plan could have been successful," he answered.

Talia tilted her head and asked, "What do mean by that?"

Mandubratius could have sworn a massive headache would start at this point, but it had been centuries since he experienced one. "Let's assume you had convinced Emperor Charles to marry you, Talia, whether he loved you or not. You could not function as an Empress."

"Why not?" she demanded. He could see consternation and stubbornness growing in her eyes.

"Because you can't see the light of day!" he sputtered, wondering how that important facet of their lives had escaped her.

Talia shrugged, seemingly unconcerned by that explanation.

"Most of the emperor's vassals expect to see their Empress in the light of day. They would never see you and therefore never accept you! If he knew your true nature, he would divorce you at the very least... at worst you'd be burned, or whatever other bizarre ritual they'd use to rid the empire of a monster."

"If he loved me, he wouldn't divorce me," Talia argued. Her eyes now glowed red.

Mandubratius started to laugh at her infantile viewpoint. "You... don't know your intended very well, then," he sputtered between his chortles.

"I know Charles better than you think," Talia snapped. "I know he's worried about finding a leader for his people. I know he dislikes his sons, as they are either fools or sullen. I also know he wants a wife to take care of him."

Mandubratius sighed. "Enough. You're not getting the point." His lessons were wasted on her. He sat back down and stared at Talia. "If the Franks are outraged by your rudeness, he'll rid himself of you. If you believe me to be incorrect, he's done it before."

"How do you know that?" she asked with incredulity in her voice.

Mandubratius felt a prickle of rage. How could Talia ask such a thing?

"I am Lamia, and it is my nature to know these things," Mandubratius growled as he moved quickly towards her. "If you paid attention to my lessons, you would not be asking such ridiculous questions. I honestly do not know why I bother instructing you!" he hissed.

Talia tucked her face into her arms and cowered away from him.

"I should probably just take your life here and now," Mandubratius continued, as he jerked her chin towards him. Talia's eyes remained squeezed shut, and she winced as he squeezed her chin. "All this time between us has been wasted, and I do not wish to waste another moment on you."

"Please don't kill me," she pleaded, finally opening her eyes, and yet she studied his feet.

"Give me one reason why you don't deserve to be silenced forever."

"I possess information," she whimpered.

He smirked. "You believe that you have information that I do not already possess? I'll grant you that it's possible, but unlikely. Let's say you're correct, Talia... I'll spare your life," he offered as he grabbed his sword. "However, if I already know this information, I'll kill you, here and now. Then I will have all of these Lamia fuck your corpse."

Talia stopped sniveling and stared at him. A soft groan from the camp girl distracted him for a moment, but Talia turned and hit the young mortal woman on the back of the head. The camp girl then became silent.

"Marcus has returned," Talia stated. "He is at Prüm Abbey with the vassals and lords of Vézelay and Divio."

"That's in–"

"I'm not finished," Talia interjected.

He then motioned for her to continue.

"Marcus has recruited another Deargh Du to serve in the emperor's palace. She took my place at the emperor's side."

He felt intrigued. "Who is this Deargh Du?"

"She's an elder with the bearing of a queen," Talia began. "I forgot her name, though she has usurped my opportunity to be Empress."

He chuckled. "If this is who I believe it to be, Talia, becoming Empress is not on her agenda."

"What?" Talia asked with a confused expression.

"Sáerlaith doesn't engage in petty relationships with mortal sovereigns. She's the matron of the Deargh Du, their chieftain, but I must wonder why she would be here in Charles' court. This intelligence is most intriguing. Therefore, I will allow you to continue to live."

"I have more," Talia added, as she placed a hand on his arm.

"Then continue," he bade Talia as he smiled at her.

"A Lamia has sponsored the inspector general."

"Really? So Julien de Divio is Lamia?" he asked.

Talia nodded her head. "I know, because I spoke to him earlier and he knows about us. I assumed he was one of us."

"Hmmmm, most interesting… that bears investigating." He thought over matters for a moment. "Within which abbey were Marcus and the rest of his party residing?"

"Prüm Abbey," Talia replied.

"Excellent. That's not very far from here," Mandubratius reasoned aloud. "Perhaps we should visit them…" He stared at her and felt his desire grow. "However, I was not sated by this mere camp girl…"

Talia pushed him towards the blankets and then straddled him.

Prüm Abbey

Heloise decided to allow the monks to continue ministering to her vassals. They seemed to be in better spirits, since the abbey provided food and wine. Now, it seemed the whole experience could be seen as an exciting journey to many of them.

Reginald had left to go brood and nurse his wounds. Perhaps he loitered at Aldabert's grave. Lirienne watched over Clotilda, who had become cranky and tired over their adventures.

The idea of sleep seemed to be a good one, so she moved to a quiet corner with her mind on sleeping and sat on the ground.

Then a figure moved with a strange stealth into her field of view. She inhaled a little, fearful at the sudden apparition. Then the figure spoke with a familiar voice.

"Mother," Julien whispered as he tilted his head a little to study her.

She smiled at him. "You must tell me what it's like now... to be Deargh Du. Is it still all you wished it would be?"

"Strange," he answered as he sat down next to her. "I have upset Máire and Marcus," Julien admitted before closing his eyes, "though I hope our relationship will recover soon."

"I imagine that it is difficult to establish some common ground at times," Heloise reasoned aloud as she wrapped an arm around him. "They come from different places and times." She then felt him become tense. "What's wrong?"

Julien looked up at the sky. Heloise followed his gaze and then glanced up at the blinking stars. Nothing appeared to be out of the ordinary. Suddenly, a growing darkness snuffed out the starlight, and shadow fell. Her eyes adjusted, and then she saw a few nameless figures appear on the ground. The shadow then receded from the figures, and with the light from the torches she could see them.

Claudius crouched down next to Julien. A young man with a very sparse beard stood at Claudius' side and studied her and Julien with curious, dark eyes. She noticed a covered package attached to his back.

Julien then stared back at Claudius.

"You're Deargh Du now. I suppose that I should not be surprised. I thought you were Máire or Marcus," Claudius stated before he inhaled again. "Interesting."

"They're in the catacombs I think," Julien offered as he looked over at the stranger and sniffed. His eyes turned wary and sparkled green. "Who are you?" he asked the stranger.

"We can't go into details now, but he's one of us." Claudius then grabbed Julien's outstretched arm and pulled him up. "We need to go speak with Marcus now."

Julien looked at her and suggested, "You should probably come too." She noticed his eyes turn nervous at the prospect of dealing with two beings who probably found her son utterly confusing and vice versa.

"Of course," Heloise acknowledged as she held her arm out for Julien so he could help her from her seat. As she followed them thousands of figures seemed now seemed to appear from the shadows. Soon, the stars re-lit the skies.

Marcus inhaled and then closed his eyes. He could sense the approach of several blood-drinkers, but he preferred to hear Mac Alpin's account, as he had the better nose.

"I would suspect that you already know this, but it appears Claudius had some success. I smell three thousand warriors of the Celtic lines approaching and one Lamia," Arwin reported before studying his nails for a moment. "Do you suppose they accosted Mandubratius?"

Marcus smirked. "Doubtful. He'd have a larger escort join them." He then began to walk to the outside. He heard Mac Alpin follow him out of the catacombs.

As soon as Marcus reached the starry night, he felt a great deal of pride as he watched the warriors he, Arwin, and Claudius had trained establish a perimeter and then land in formation. He then nodded his appreciation to Caoimhín and Fianait.

Then he saw that Claudius and Julien approached from the cloister, yet another familiar scent grew, and he felt some surprise as Sáerlaith stepped past many of the Deargh Du warriors. He rushed to embrace and kiss her, but something about her eyes kept his feet in place. Something horrible had happened. He waited while she walked towards him.

"Lead me someplace we can speak in private," she stated, though she offered him no other greeting and seemed to be in no mood for idle conversation.

"This way," he murmured. Marcus turned and then flew into the catacombs towards a far recess in the lower levels. Sáerlaith followed him. He landed at the recess and then turned to face her.

"What is it you wish to tell me?" he asked after she landed close to him.

Sáerlaith dropped to her knees and began to wail sobs of mournful anguish into her open hands. Marcus attempted to think over what could have happened, yet nothing touched his blank mind. Now he began to feel distress at her cries.

Marcus dropped to his knees and reached out, but he hesitated. Before he could consider anything else to say, Sáerlaith grabbed him and embraced him. She sobbed on his shoulder.

After several moments of crying, Sáerlaith finally found her voice. "Our home has been taken by force… from within."

What did she mean? Could such a thing be possible? Disbelief, rage, and sadness flashed within.

"How could this be?" Marcus whispered.

"Conlan did it," Sáerlaith growled into his shoulder, "with the help of that bitch, Aisling. He waited until our warriors had left to join our allies, and then he struck. I knew I should have let you and Máire destroy what was left of Donal's allies, unbalanced or not! After Máire's failure killing Aisling, I should have killed her myself and then gone after Conlan. Oh, Morrigan warned me that there would be consequences, but I never imagined they would be so great."

"Who else was with Conlan?" Marcus felt his jaw clench in rage, wishing he had followed Sáerlaith's desires so many years ago. He felt guilty for his selfish feelings. He may have felt like a cutthroat, but it had been Her calling for him to kill those people… and now Sáerlaith and the rest of the Deargh Du must pay for his objections.

"The larger council… he said they chose to disband the Council of Five, and then they murdered Ruarí." Sáerlaith began to hiccup a little. "We escaped, the Council of Five… all but Ruarí and Nuadin, Morrigan help him now." She inhaled and then pulled away a little. "All the way to Briton, I looked over my shoulder, fearful that they would strike with sudden, overwhelming force."

"Why did they do such a thing against our Matron?" Marcus asked. Although he knew of the politics, he did not understand them.

Sáerlaith began to sob into her hands again, so he began to stroke her hair.

Sáerlaith sniffed again and continued. "Conlan and his followers could not feel Morrigan anymore. They felt that She had abandoned us or was testing us. I think that they believed they needed to purify the Deargh Du and become isolated again… at least that's the impression I had when we ran for our lives."

Guilt gnawed at Marcus. He knew that his place within the Deargh Du divided them and that his inaction to carry out the rest of those murders condemned him further.

"My ideas brought this about," he admitted to Sáerlaith, "and the fact that I did not kill Aisling and Conlan as you had asked."

Sáerlaith stopped crying and looked up at him with red-rimmed eyes. "You cannot blame yourself for their actions, Marcus. We cannot even blame Máire for not killing Aisling after you had decided to commit no further assignations. Those other Deargh Du… the purists… they are cowards, and they only attacked when those who would stand against them were gone."

"But if it wasn't for me–"

"–there would be no Deargh Du," Sáerlaith interjected. "The Lamia would have wiped us out. The only way we can endure and prevail is to stand with our allies."

He knew Sáerlaith spoke truth, but he still felt guilt and rage. Marcus nodded his head, though his rage still grew at the idea of those traitors moving against Morrigan.

"We will return to Ard Macha. We will then take it back in Morrigan's name!"

"No." The word reverberated through the catacombs. Its utterance revealed great pain. "No," Sáerlaith repeated in a softer voice.

"Why not?" He felt his rage grow even more. The desire for blood and death at Ard Macha warred within. "Why not?" More words seemed impossible.

"Our duty is here first," Sáerlaith answered. Her hand then moved to his shoulder. "You, of all of us, should understand duty."

He mused over that word for a moment... 'duty'. "I know," Marcus admitted. "However, when our duty here is complete, I'll return to Ard Macha and I'll cleanse those who have forsaken the Goddess!"

A tingle of limitless power shook him as he uttered his oath.

Sáerlaith walked out of the recess and felt a growing doubt. Why had she not encouraged Marcus? They should return to Eire and smite those who turned away from the balance.

Damn Strigoi. Damn purists.

She heard throats clear and the loud muttering became soft as she trailed out of the lower levels. Blood-drinkers moved aside from her to allow her access, and they even held their belongings so she would not trip on them. She realized that she and Marcus had kept the younger blood-drinkers from some much-needed rest.

The strong smell of Lamia drifted through the gentler scents belonging to the Celtic lines. Sáerlaith had witnessed Amata and the Legate earlier, then there would be the youngling, Horatio, yet she could smell two others. Then the fog cleared in Sáerlaith's head.

She studied faces and witnessed the Lamia female from Aachen. Another Lamia stood beside her, and Sáerlaith inhaled an uneasy breath as she studied him... dark haired, tall, green-eyed... that was how Máire and Marcus described 'him'.

The Lamia made eye contact with her as if he knew that she sought him out. His eyes filled with utter mischief, and she knew then that it was indeed 'him'.

He winked at her, at least it looked like a wink, before turning his head to speak to the Lamia from the emperor's feast.

Sáerlaith turned towards Marcus, whose eyes revealed surprise.

"What is he doing here?" Marcus whispered.

Sáerlaith offered a slight shrug and then inclined her head towards the female Lamia, who appeared to be afraid to look in any direction for fear of being scrutinized by the Celtic lines. Sáerlaith then watched Marcus return her shrug.

Soon, she witnessed Máire duck around Marcus and stare at the woman. A boiling rage changed Máire's calm features into a swelling hate.

Máire then yelled, "You!" The growl made others turn towards Máire and the Lamia. Máire then stepped towards the Lamia female, grabbed her throat, and shoved a blade towards her pale flesh.

The female Lamia gurgled as her eyes moved towards her companion. The tension in the room rose.

"Máire, hold your weapon," Marcus ordered as he stepped towards his daughter-in-darkness.

"She turned my uncle into a monster," Máire growled at Marcus.

Marcus said nothing else, though his eyes remained on Máire.

Máire then pulled the blade away, yet her face still revealed a churning rage.

"If I kill you this way, I become the monster you are, Teá. You are nothing to me." Máire stepped away and then sheathed her blade.

Before Sáerlaith could turn away from the ugly confrontation and consider, again, why the Lamia meddled this way in Charles' court, she sensed Mandubratius step beside her.

"Such a shame," he cooed before clucking his tongue. "I was rather hoping that Marcus would let them fight. If you ask me, there is nothing more entertaining than watching two sweaty women wearing sparse clothing trying to kill one another."

Sáerlaith avoided his eyes. "I do not believe I invited you to wrest control of my ears, Awvarwy."

"Oh…" he replied in that sweet and whispery voice, "so you wish to address me in the familiar. That must mean that you are warming up to me. Perhaps soon I may warm your bed."

Sáerlaith inhaled as he pressed into her head. She felt that coitus with him might serve to get him to shut up, yet she wondered where that ridiculous thought came from. She then reminded herself that he had manipulated many, and so she tried to think of how to reply to his rather disturbing offer. However, a strange fear of saying or doing something stupid paralyzed her.

Then the female Lamia flounced between them with burning eyes and challenged, "This is one man with whom you will not be sharing your bed!" She then grabbed his arm and attempted to pull Mandubratius away.

The co-consul of the Lamia turned towards his lover and smiled. "Not now sweetie, the adults have to talk. Go tend to our bed. I'll be there in a moment."

She released his arm and walked away with a perturbed frown over her lovely features.

"Now, that that's settled," Mandubratius purred, "what is to be done about the Strigoi? They are still walking the earth, and I say they are plotting a return."

"I know how to deal with the Strigoi," Claudius interjected. Sáerlaith felt a great deal of gratitude as Claudius interrupted the strained conversation.

Sáerlaith looked on as Máire joined the conversation. She studied Horatio for a moment, as did several of the others, and asked, "Who is your friend Claudius?"

"This is Horatio from Dover... my new initiate." An unusual defiance overwhelmed Claudius' eyes. She witnessed tension around her from the blood-drinkers who knew there was no way a Sugnwr Gwaed would serve as mentor to a Lamia.

"Did you say something about a solution to the Strigoi problem?" Marcus asked, in an apparent attempt to divert attention from Horatio.

"Yes," Claudius answered. He grinned and then turned Horatio around to reveal a strange and beautiful mirror. "This is a copy of Aphrodite's mirror that is in Constantinople with the Basileus Irene. It is supposed to bring out the inner beauty of the viewer. On my way to Bath, I stopped at a shop in Searoburh, and the merchant told me a tale of this mirror's sister. The original has magical properties that may help find their beauty. He said something about how Hephaestus himself became beautiful in this mirror. If a mirror helped a God, perhaps it could help the Strigoi."

Sáerlaith noticed Mandubratius cease smiling, and his face reflected nothing but seriousness. "I have seen a mirror like this in the Porphyra within one of Irene's palaces in Constantinople, yet I have never gazed into it. I know that she always has to have it near. Something about it seemed worrisome, so I avoided looking into it."

"Are you sure this mirror will stop the Strigoi, Claudius?" Marcus asked.

Claudius shrugged a little. "I do not know for certain, but they may attack in greater numbers, and without a defense, we would not be able to hold them off for very long."

"Then, we should obtain this mirror," suggested a young Deargh Du who stepped forth. Something seemed very familiar about him. Sáerlaith inhaled and then realized that this one must be... Máire's first child-in-darkness. He carried himself as a Frankish noble would, but he displayed the beauty of their line. His sea-colored eyes intrigued her.

"I wish to lead the mission to reclaim the mirror," he stated. She could sense a desire to prove himself to the others.

"What?!"

Sáerlaith jumped a little at Arwin Mac Alpin's loud exclamation.

"Youngling, this is a bit beyond your duties in the past. Have you ever even been to Constantinople?" Arwin asked, seeming to control his temper.

She noticed Máire stare into the youngling Deargh Du's eyes and smile.

"We appreciate your enthusiasm, Julien, but perhaps someone more experienced in these matters should lead us," she said. She then took his arm and began to lead him aside.

Julien started to say something, but Máire shook her head. "You can join us," she offered instead, "and we can all learn more about each other during this journey."

"But–" he began to protest, but Máire placed a finger on his lips.

"Please," she bade.

Sáerlaith watched Julien smile and say, "I will follow." She then heard a chuckle.

"The puppy has no desire to be alpha male now," she heard Mandubratius murmur.

The youngling's posture changed, and his eyes displayed amazement. He then pushed past Máire and drew his sword.

"You will rescind that insult and apologize, Tolomei!"

Mandubratius stopped chuckling and seemed to size up the Deargh Du. "Then I apologize, Inspector General," he offered.

"Tolomei? Oh yes, the game continues. His name is Awvarwy, but most know him as Mandubratius," Máire commented with a sneer.

"Only my friends may call me Awvarwy, and since there are few here, I expect only to answer to 'Mandubratius'," he stated. He then smiled in Sáerlaith's direction again. "I think I should lead this expedition," he added.

Marcus laughed outright at Mandubratius' statement. "If you insist, we… will both lead the mission."

Mandubratius nodded and said, "Very well, Marcus."

"When do we leave?" Patroclus asked.

"We cannot leave yet," Amata grumbled. "The current crisis that forced us into this abbey has not been resolved."

"Oh yes. The small matter of the papal invasion," Mandubratius mused aloud with a chuckled.

"By the Goddess," Arwin grumbled with a great deal of impatience in his eyes. "Yes, the papal invasion. Did you happen to have a strong or weak hand in this?"

"Oh, I was merely set up by events beyond my control. I was only there to observe," Mandubratius uttered in a purr.

She watched Claudius' eyes turn dark again. "Did you not order the invasion of Briton with your cavalry, composed of Lamia, who you told were Angels?"

"It had to be done. Did you not receive the letter with the explanation? Granted, I did mean for Marcus to read it."

An impatient glare grew in Marcus' eyes. "Tell us more lies, Mandubratius."

She caught a brief nod between Claudius and Marcus. Perhaps they planned to discuss what had happened in Briton later.

Mandubratius sighed. "The truth is so boring. Lying is much more entertaining. Besides, do you really want the truth? Do the affairs of the emperors and popes truly concern us? After all, the Deargh Du have been manipulators of mortal events in Eire for millennia, as have the Lamia. So, do not pretend that you are more in the right than I. Besides, the situation will work itself out at dusk."

Marcus stared at Mandubratius but said nothing, and yet Sáerlaith could gauge his rising irritation.

"You may not be aware of this, but the emperor has amassed a sizable army that he is hiding outside of Aachen. In some places, they hide in plain sight, a tiny bird told me at dawn. This army will come together and force the Pope to go home to Rome and take his forces with him, and I will help press the matter with His Holiness."

"A small bird you say?" Máire asked as she cocked her brow.

"Yes," Mandubratius drawled, "and he was delicious."

Máire made an annoyed sound and then strolled towards her bedding. Her child-in-darkness joined her.

"I suggest that in the late afternoon, we make preparations to leave the next evening, assuming all will go with this plan," Marcus added. "I'm going to find my bedroll." He then walked off. Claudius and Horatio followed him, as other blood-drinkers began settling in.

Sáerlaith realized Mandubratius studied her again.

"Now, I believe I was going to warm your bed," he murmured.

She watched the blonde Lamia swoop in and grab him.

"Oh no you're not," she hissed at her sponsor.

Mandubratius chuckled and then waved at Sáerlaith. "It appears that I'm spoken for this morning... perhaps another time, Sáerlaith."

She watched the female Lamia slap Mandubratius across the face, but then his smile grew. As the Lamia dragged Mandubratius away, Sáerlaith noticed him lean over and pinch Máire's backside while the oblivious female Lamia tugged his arm.

Máire looked up, and her face appeared to be a solid pink blush as if she had finished feeding. Julien then touched her shoulder and Máire studied him for a moment. She then smiled, and her blush faded.

Sáerlaith sat down on her bedding and rolled onto her side, feeling nothing but the cold surrounding her heart. She then decided to write a bit, feeling that through writing, she could make sense of her situation. She gathered some writing utensils and then sat down at a table.

Why have I not walked out into the sun?

I have lost our home to people I believed to be our brothers and sisters... people I lived with for centuries, if not longer. I did not see the betrayal in their eyes before that night and I heard no whispers of their treachery. Did I not wish to see the signs?

Surely, they were about, but part of me must have ignored them. I was blissfully ignorant of the horror that was to come, and because of that, I did nothing to prevent it.

I was negligent as leader of the Deargh Du.

I admit this fully. I make no excuses, and I blame no one else.

Since I am guilty, what is to be my punishment? Should it be my death? How many lives would I have saved if I paid attention to what was going on around me? Many, I suppose, though some would still be dead.

Ruarí would still be alive. I miss his wise counsel and his friendship, but I cannot change what happened, and now I must face the consequences of my inaction.

Is my death an appropriate punishment for this crime?

Perhaps it is, but Morrigan has not seen fit to take me.

Do I succumb to my guilt, taking matters into my own hands, and walk into the sun? Or do I let Her guide me through whatever penance She finds most deserving of my crime?

There can be only one answer.

I shall walk the path Morrigan sets for me.

If that path leads to the sun, that is where I shall walk, but for now I walk the night.

Sáerlaith glanced around the catacombs and began blowing air onto the ink of her new scroll. She leaned an elbow against the small table and rested her chin in her hand.

Sáerlaith hoped that sleep would bless her soon.

Continue the journey
with...

Curse of Venus
Morrigan's Brood Book IV

Coming in 2012

about the authors

Heather Poinsett Dunbar

Born in Houston, Texas, Heather began writing her first book at age eight. While her grammatical structure left much to be desired, she continued to hone her writing and storytelling skills. During a college internship in London, England, her curiosity about ancient cultures and mythology intensified. She backpacked through Europe, fell in love with Scotland, cried at the retelling of part of Ulster cycle, garnered ghost stories from the Beefeaters at the Tower, wandered the Roman ruins in Bath, and danced around the stones in Avebury.

After spending all her spare time studying these new interests in many libraries and on the road, she began working on her masters in Library and Information Science at the University of North Texas. She now resides in the Houston area with her husband and three cats. She loves exploring the local culture as well as the many Celtic festivals and events in Texas. She works in the Houston Public Library system and her favorite authors include Morgan Llewellyn, Neil Gaiman, Terry Pratchett, Evelyn Vaughn, Alison Weir, and Randy Lee Eickhoff.

Christopher Dunbar

Chris Dunbar was born in Greenport, Long Island, New York and then moved to Texas as soon as he could, at least that is the story he tells to native Texans, such as his wife. Chris keeps searching for ways to leave Houston, like moving to Auburn, Alabama, Dallas, and even San Antonio, but Houston just keeps reeling him back. Chris' day job is performing Business Continuity and Disaster Recovery, but his night job is coming up with creative ways to wound and maim the characters he and his wife Heather created. For fun, Chris enjoys the occasional novel and video game, but he also likes to delve into his Scottish ancestry and tool leather. When he can find the time, Chris pretends to play the Bodhran and the didgeridoo, much to the chagrin of his cats Lucius, Ophelia, and Clyde, not to mention his wife Heather. Chris is also an avid wearer of the kilt.

published and future works

Title	Synopsis	Release
Morrigan's Brood Morrigan's Brood Book I	Eire is invaded by a race of blood-drinkers seeking an artifact they believe will restore them to power. Yet the Deargh Du, the protectors of Eire, are not prepared to defend the island. Only with the help of a Roman general from an earlier time can they hope to rise up against the invaders.	Dec. 2009
Crone of War Morrigan's Brood Book II	The Lamia expeditionary force has gained a foothold in Eire and has formed an alliance with a powerful Irish chieftain and his malevolent mother. To reinforce them, a massive Lamia army, which is departing Rome, will soon give them enough power to conquer Eire and find their lost treasure. Will the Deargh Du and their new-found friends be able to protect Eire from the invaders, or will the Deargh Du's suspicion of other blood-drinkers allow their enemies to be victorious?	July 2010
Madness Short-Story	Following the events of 564 CE, madness strikes one of the Lamia's most important personages. Can the Lamia march on, or will this insanity cast them into civil war?	April, 2011
Reckoning Short-Story	Following the events of 564 CE, the Deargh Du must come to grips with change or see old strife resurface, which could tear the Deargh Du apart.	June, 2011
Dark Alliance Morrigan's Brood Book III	A new menace threatens the Balance within the Holy Roman Empire as vicious murders of both mortals and blood-drinkers spread throughout the empire like wildfire. Can a hastily formed alliance between archenemies thwart this new menace, or will festering hatred bring about the empire's doom?	Sept. 2011
Curse of Venus Morrigan's Brood Book IV	The Strigoi, the Cursed of Venus, have spread through the Holly Roman Empire and parts beyond like a plague. In response, Pope Leo III takes advantage of the scourge to settle an old score with the man he placed on the throne: Charlemagne. Will their bitter rivalry send the Empire further into chaos and destruction, or will their Deargh Du "angels" save them from themselves and from Venus' Cursed?	TBD 2012
Shards of Light Morrigan's Brood Book V	Many sets of eyes peer through the mist, watching events unfold as the dark alliance seeks out an ancient device that they hope will uncorrupt the menace that has nearly brought the Holy Roman Empire to its knees. However, not everyone beyond the mist is content merely to watch.	TBD 2012

Other Morrigan's Brood Series titles include <u>Odin's Chosen</u> (Book 6, in progress), an as yet un-named Book 7, and <u>Dynasties of Night</u> (Book 8, in progress).

Other works include <u>It's in the Cards</u> (a novella, in queue for publication) and <u>A Year and a Day</u> (novel, on hold).

www.ingramcontent.com/pod-product-compliance
Lightning Source LLC
Chambersburg PA
CBHW030918260626
47169CB00002B/299